THE ROSE DAWN
Stewart Edward White

FOREWORD

THE author has written this story mainly from personal experience and recollection. He has, however, used freely two books dealing with land boom days. These are T. S. Van Dyke's *Millionaires of a Day;* and T. R. Sanford's *The Bursting of a Boom.* From Van Dyke's really classic description the psychological sequence has been followed very closely; and from the Sanford book some of the auctioneer "patter" has been lifted bodily. This has been done with full appreciation and gratitude: and the author wishes here to record his indebtedness.

THE ROSE DAWN

CHAPTER I

I

COLONEL RICHARD PEYTON stepped to the edge of his veranda and looked up into the early morning through the branches of his over-arching live oak trees. He was very proud of those trees, for they were taller and more wide spread and branchy than any other live oaks in Arguello County; and that is saying a good deal. In fact so impressive were they that the Colonel had named the five or six acres they occupied *Cathedral Oaks*, thus placing them apart in all minds from the Rancho de la Corona del Monte, which was the Colonel's real property. Every morning thus the Colonel stepped early to his veranda's edge and looked up. And every morning something mysterious of the new day came down and met his spirit; whether it was a sound, as the low soft cooing of mourning doves; or a scent, as of something released by the dampness of fog or dew or the winter rains; or a sight, as of the slant of golden or sliver light, or a solemn belated owl, or the sailing of slow clouds down the wind. These things he absorbed, and they grew into his subconsciousness, and thus became part of him, so that at last he rose to a mild scorn of all who did not likewise arise betimes.

"By Godfrey, Allie!" he would cry to his plump, bright-eyed, alert little wife, as he strode around the breakfast table to kiss her ceremonially. "I cannot understand these slug-abeds! They miss the best of the day!"

And then he would seat himself across the table and beam about. The dining room thereupon resumed its natural size:

3

for as long as the Colonel was afoot it became much smaller
than even its actual and modest dimensions. The Colonel
was not over six feet, and he was slender; but he had presence.
Everything except the Cathedral Oaks and the Sierra del Sur
seemed rather undersized when he was around—and, they
only just fitted. As a matter of fact the ranch house, when
analyzed right down and stripped of its vines and its coco-
matting and its big pink seashells and its wonderful haircloth
mahogany and its doilies and stuffed birds and steel engravings
and traditions and such matters, would have turned out to be
merely a rather small one-storied board-and-batten structure
with a wide veranda running all the way around it, set comfortably amid the huge live oaks. It took a very clear-headed
man to do this analysis. I know of two only; and they made
their discovery with considerable surprise.

But this particular morning of one spring of the eighties
was an especial occasion. The Colonel did not, as was his usual
custom, take a look at his oaks and his green half moon of lawn
with its border of plumbago and geraniums and other bright
flowers, glance down the perspective of his avenue of palms
that led to the distant Camino Real, breathe deeply of the
sparkling morning air, and so return to his table. On this one
day were the most important matters afoot. It was Allie's
birthday, and on that anniversary the Rancho de la Corona del
Monte—hereafter, except on ceremonial occasions, let us call it,
like the rest of the country, Corona del Monte for short—turned
itself inside out and had the biggest barbecue picnic of the year.
So the Colonel put on his low-crowned, wide-brimmed Stetson
and took his way around the corner of the house.

The Colonel, as has been said, was tall and slender. Beneath
his Stetson his clean-shaven face with its hawknose and kindly
eyes looked remarkably young and vigorous. Yet on closer
inspection you could not have missed the network of fine quizzical lines that seamed his countenance; nor the delightful winter-
apple quality in the colour of his lean ruddy cheeks; nor the calm,
lofty dignified set of the mouth as in the portraits of Washington,
Franklin, and their compeers, which means not so much loftiness
of soul as lack of teeth. No, the Colonel was getting on. You

never would have suspected it from the movements of his long figure in its black frock coat. The Colonel never suspected it at all. No one had told him, not even life itself.

He moved around to the back of the house, humming some-thing quite tuneless under his breath. On his way he did a number of little things of which he was not fully aware. He plucked successively leaves of the bay, the camphor tree, and sweet geranium, rolled them in the palms of his hands and inhaled their aroma; he took off the cover of the *olla*—the earthen evaporation jar hanging from a tree—and inspected its supply of cool drinking water; he pulled up a number of weeds from the brilliant flower borders and concealed them carefully beneath the shrubbery; a flaming humming bird poised buzzing in front of his face—he held motionless until the little creature had darted away. None of these things could he have repeated to you. A modern psychologist would have told you they were products of his subliminal. Manuelo, ranch foreman, at present superintending the preparations for the barbecue, would have shrugged his shoulders and said:

"Eet is the *señor*. He ees like that."

Same thing.

But near the kitchen door the Colonel awakened from this sauntering, buzzing happy dreaming. In the course of his prog-ress hung the substitute of that day and place for the modern icebox—a framework covered with layers of burlap over which water constantly sprayed. The evaporation lowered the temper-ature. This contraption possessed, of course, a door; and the Colonel's hand reached for it, as his hand had reached for the fragrant herbages or the cover of the *olla*. And then the alarm bell of his mind rang violently. The Colonel withdrew his hand as from a red hot iron, and looked about him with a comi-cally guilty air. None too soon. Almost on the instant the back porch screen door opened behind him.

"Good morning, Sing Toy," said the Colonel.

"You wan' blekfus?" demanded Sing Toy.

"Presently. Pretty soon," said the Colonel, managing a dignified retreat. He did not hasten his steps; yet one psychic-ally endowed would have said he hastened. The expression of

the calm, bland white-clad Chinaman on the doorstep was as
blank as still water; yet the sensitive would have distinguished
accusation and reproof. Sing Toy had a queue, as did all the
Chinamen of those days. It was almost as expressive in some
ways as a dog's tail. The rest of Sing Toy remained as immovable
as a bronze Buddha, but the tip of his queue wriggled ever so
slightly, and in some subtle manner disapproval of all who
investigated his domain overcast the day.

Thus roused the Colonel stepped out more briskly. He
passed the large stables and their neatly whitewashed corral
fences with hardly more than a glance, opened two big swing
gates and proceeded with brisk steps between a double row of
small houses toward another group of live oaks beyond it and
atop a small, flat hill.

But he was not to be permitted to pass unchecked. A bevy
of very small brown children swooped down on him noisily,
came to a dead halt and an equally dead silence a few paces from
him and stared, round-eyed and expectant. They were very
handsome children, somewhat grimy, with sketchy garments
and bare feet. The Colonel thrust his hands behind the coat-
tails of his frock coat and contemplated them gravely. They
stared back without either embarrassment or impertinence.

"*Buenas dias. niños,*" observed the Colonel at last.

"*Buenas dias, Don Ricardo!*" returned the little group in
chorus.

From this point you are to consider the Colonel as speaking
in the soft and beautiful language of California, with a deepening and mellowing of his natural manner. The Colonel continued to survey them for some moments, his blue eyes twinkling, the fine network of lines deepening. The children stared
back.

"I will wish you good day," said the Colonel at last, moving
as though to pass.

The great soft Spanish eyes about him clouded with dismay,
the red full lips drooped at the corners, but the polite chorus
came bravely back:

"God be with you, *señor.*"

The Colonel laughed aloud, thrust his hand in his coat-tail

pocket, and brought it forth filled with little hard peppermint lozenges. These he distributed, one to each, receiving a succession of staid "*muchas gracias, señor.*" He continued his walk. The children, sucking ecstatically at the fiery sweet-meat, fell gravely in behind. Some lank black-and-tan hounds stretched at full length in the dust rapped vigorously with thick tails—thus raising a smudge—; arose and shook themselves—thus raising another; and trailed along, too.

Half way up the gentle slope that led to the second grove of live oaks the Colonel was met by a very lean, dark saturnine man with long, drooping moustaches and deep, vertical muscle-lines running across his countenance. He too wore the low-crowned Stetson with the addition of a woven, horsehair band. As to the rest of his costume, he affected the modern rather than the traditional, although he was evidently pure Spanish. That is to say, he wore a vest but no coat, and tucked his striped trousers into soft-legged, high-heeled boots. His shirt sleeves, however, were bound by very frilly pink elastic bands with huge rosettes; his waist was encircled by a leather belt studded with *conchas* of silver; at his heels clanked loose spurs of great size, inlaid with silver, jingling with little clappers at the rowels, strapped with broad carved leather, ornamented at the buttons with silver *conchas* fully two inches across. A picturesque enough figure to satisfy any small boy, even though he carried no traditional "gun," nor wore traditional *chaparejos*—"chaps." This was Manuelo, major domo, after the Colonel the most important figure on del Monte.

He swept his hat from his head; the Colonel raised his Stetson. Formal and stately greetings were exchanged according to the formulae in use among the Spanish. They fell in step and continued up the hill.

"All is in order, *señor?*" the Colonel asked.

"All is in order, *señor*," assured Manuelo. "It was a matter of anxiety that young Juan had not returned with the pepper sauce promised us by the Doña Paredis. There is no pepper sauce like that of the Doña Paredis."

"That is true, *señor*," observed the Colonel.

"But happily he has returned at dawn. Why inquire?

Here is the pepper sauce of the Doña Paredis delivered—
Bright eyes or bright wine, *señor;* who knows?"

"And to leave either at dawn," said the Colonel, "is both
penance and testimony of a soul devoted to duty in spite of all."

"Or a late remembrance that he must meet Manuelo," added
that worthy, a little grimly. "But here are matters for your
inspection, Don Ricardo."

Beneath the wide spreading branches of the live oak tree
had been built row after row of long board tables flanked by
benches. These were evidently of long past date, for their
lumber was browned and weather stained. But already they
were partly concealed by pyramids of fruit cunningly heaped,
by batteries of cutlery and tin plates and cups, by long loaves
of bread, by tin pans full of walnuts and almonds, by bottles
and glasses of condiments and jellies. A number of young girls
and older children were darting here and there with armfuls of
flowers which they arranged artfully still further to hide the
brown planks—brodea, the great white Matilija poppies, Mari-
posa lilies, branches of mountain lilac, and above all great quantities of glowing golden-orange California poppies, like morsels
of sunset entrapped. A very fat Californian woman sat on one
of the benches and directed these activities. She had smooth,
shining black hair, and a smooth, shining brown countenance,
and beautiful black eyes from which unexpectedly youth
peered.

"The tables are beautiful, *señora,*" said the Colonel.

"*Ay de mi,*" sighed the fat woman. "These children—they
know not the old arrangements of flowers. When I was a
young girl——"

"The *caballeros* gave you little time for flowers, *señora,* that
I'll wager. It must be so, for never have I seen the tables better
than to-day."

Señora Manuelo raised her fan from her lap to her face. The
change was startling. The lower grosser part of her countenance
was covered. Only were visible the slumberous youthful eyes,
the smooth brow, the shining black parted hair. Returned for
a magic moment was all the beauty of her youth. The Colonel
bowed in farewell, shaking his head slightly.

"No, never time for flowers, *señora;* for men are not blind."

Two of the tables at the end were covered with white table-cloths, and furnished out with china and glassware and silver. This was for the Colonel's personal guests as distinguished from the ranch retainers and those of his neighbours. Here two pretty girls were engaged, selecting from some wash tubs of roses. They were very pretty in a soft young rounded fashion, with the lustrous, dreamy eyes and shining hair of their race. Not yet had they begun to ape the complexities of the American toilette. Their rather full, curved young figures were clad in plain white starched muslin, and their hair was parted smoothly and confined in the back by high fan-shaped combs. Each had thrust one of the roses intended for the decorations over her left ear. I regret to say also that each had plastered on an inordinate quantity of white powder; but that was the custom. At the Colonel's approach with Manuelo they ceased their activities and stood side by side.

"The table is most beautiful," said the Colonel.

"*Si, señor,*" they bobbed together, breathlessly.

"You have plenty of roses?"

"*Si, señor.*"

"Do you enjoy yourselves at the *merienda?*"

"*Si, señor.*"

The Colonel surveyed them quizzically. They were very correct, very respectful, very much in earnest to do the right thing before the master of the Rancho. His hand sought his coat-tail pocket.

"Did you ever see anything like that before?" he demanded, holding up one of his peppermint lozenges.

They looked at each other, and their hands groped for each other seeking encouragement at so embarrassing a question.

"Señorita Ynez Calderon, and you, Señorita Dolores Ygnacio," said the Colonel, "you are a pair of solemn frauds. You treat me, *me,* as though I were the holy father and the blessed San Antonio and a total stranger, all in one. And last year," he turned to the saturnine Manuelo, "last year, mind you, they stood before me barefoot, in *camisa* only, and begged me for these!" Again he held up the peppermint.

The girls dissolved toward one another in horrified protest.

"Oh, Señor! Oh, Don Ricardo! Not last year! Many years ago! We are *doñas* grown these.five years!"

The Colonel bore down on them, bowed low, and bending forward in his most courtly fashion stopped their protests by thrusting between their lips one apiece of the celebrated peppermints. Then he bowed again gravely and turned away, leaving them giggling, their dignity all gone.

The two men now approached the heart and centre of all this activity. Behind three tables of a construction more substantial than those just visited was enclosed a large open space. Here several fires were burning. Over some of these fires kettles had been suspended. Others had been built under grills or grates, and were being plied with oak and willow fuel in order to establish beds of coals. The pits had been heated, and even now contained the bull's head, the huge joints, and the mutton of the main barbecue. All this was presided over by a very sleek, stout good-looking Californian, who was perspiring freely even thus early, and who wore a look of busyness, responsibility, and care evidently out of his usual character. He seemed to have two official assistants—young swarthy chaps: at least, two young men of the many present seemed to be doing something. One was whetting a finishing edge to a pile of long, thin butcher knives. The other was mixing something in a bowl. Of the rest a few squatted about on their heels, staring rather vacantly and in general at the preparations; a few more seemed engrossed in some sort of game about a blanket; but most were, though idle, very much interested in what was passing—especially girls. Two of them had guitars on which they strummed as a sort of sweet and plaintive undertone to their conversation. Every few moments they, or two or three of the others, or even all the group together, would catch a few bars of the lilt and sing it forth full voiced—a few bars only, so that it seemed almost as though a passing breeze had lifted and let fall melody. To one side, on rough trestles, rested two aromatic barrels. A single old one-eyed man sat on a camp stool by them. Two laughing youths, their hands on each other's shoulders, stood before him.

"Not one drop, José, most worthy José, when we tell you that our throats are dry from the telling of your praises? And see, we have ridden across the arroyo trail since last evening. It is a long ride, as you well know. Ours is not a case like all of these others. If Don Ricardo were to know of us he would instantly command us refreshments."

"He can easily know of it. Tell him yourself. Here he comes," growled José, with considerable relish.

The two youths took one glance of consternation over their shoulders and fairly ran right and left like scattered quail, pursued by delighted laughter from all those who had heard.

After a word with the grim old guardian of the wine, the Colonel passed to the open-air kitchen. The young men instantly arose to their feet, offered and received a stately greeting, and as instantly slid back into their strenuous occupations.

"How is the meat, Benito?" the Colonel asked the cook. "Does it meet with your approval? Will it be worthy of our guests and of your skill?"

Benito's smooth, brown moon-face took on an expression of ludicrously painful consideration.

"The beef, Don Ricardo," he replied, "is the best we have had since the year when the blessed Virgin sent the October rains. Especially is that true of the roasting beef; which is, of course, as it should be. But the mutton——" he turned half away in an eloquent movement, as though abandoning the whole question in despair.

"The mutton is as good as the beef," struck in Manuelo. "I myself gave orders for it to come from the hills on Los Quitos. I myself saw it both before and after killing. The mutton is good."

"It is undoubtedly as the Señor says," replied Benito politely, conveying quite the opposite opinion.

"We have good mutton at Los Quitos," said the Colonel, "and both Mariano and Manuelo should know how to select. What is the matter with this, Benito?"

"The mutton is good, I do not deny, Señor. It is in prime condition, it is tender. But the mutton of the Island is better. There is a flavour, very faint to be sure, but which one can distinguish—it would have been better to have brought the Island sheep, as always, instead of going afield to this Los Quitos——"

"Fortunately we have Benito with his knowledge of the old days to make up the difference," said the Colonel. "This rascal Benito," he addressed the saturnine Manuelo, "would be relieved of all trouble. He could make a delicious *carne* of a burro."

The Colonel's little convoy had by now succumbed to various temptations and had scattered. Only remained to him Manuelo and two solemn hounds. The former he dismissed. The latter accompanied him on his return journey.

At the edge of the live oak grove he stopped for a moment and looked abroad, removing his Stetson to allow the wandering breeze to play across his high, narrow forehead and to lift his rather long, silky white hair. Beyond the village of his retainers, beyond the wide low barns and sheds and the whitewashed corrals, beyond the green of the Cathedral Oaks, spread the broad acres of the Rancho. Hill after low hill they rolled, oak dotted like a park, green with the grasses of an abundant year or washed bravely with the brilliant colour of flower-masses as though a gigantic brush had been swept across the slopes. At last they climbed into foothills, and then into the milky slate of mountain ramparts against the sun. But the Colonel knew that they climbed those ramparts and descended part way the other side—thirty thousand of them, these acres. In the opposite direction, across the flat of the valley, across the King's Highway, across the waving of a broad tule marsh, was yet another low rim of hills, also oak-dotted like a park. And over their crest the Colonel could make out a flash which was the sea. Beneath the oaks it was safe to vision the cattle slowly gathering for shade—the Colonel's cattle: and he could only have guessed at the number of them. Up in those sagebrush hills shining gray, up in the chaparral of the rampart mountains, sheep were moving slowly like something molten that flows—the Colonel's sheep.

As the Colonel stood his eye rested on only two evidences of human occupation other than his own. Against the base of a hill five miles away—or ten—one could not tell, the air was so diamond clear—amid the green of trees gleamed white buildings. These were of the Rancho de las Flores belonging to the Colonel's friend and neighbour, Don Vincente Cazadero. At one time the Rancho de la Corona del Monte had also belonged to Don Vincente, indeed the two properties had been part of the same original grant, but there had been various perplexing matters of borrowings, and extravagance and mortgages and some disputed titles and squatters and a whole host of vexatious stinging little matters. It seemed on the whole simpler to get rid of them at a bite. The bite was Del Monte. Las Flores still comprised forty thousand acres; and Don Vincente and the Colonel had become in the course of thirty years wonderful cronies. So that was all right. The second evidence of human occupation was nearer at hand, in fact a scant half-mile distant. It was a brown little house, and it lay half hidden in the entrance to a cañon. Nothing much but the roof could be distinguished. This was the property of a man named Brainerd and, with its hundred and sixty acres, had once belonged to Del Monte. The Colonel had sold it, right from the heart of his own property, and it was the only bit of original Del Monte not still in his hands. The story is too long to tell here. But Brainerd was a gentleman, and a "lunger," and a widower, and the father of a little girl, and down on his luck, and proud enough to struggle for appearances, and intelligent, and a number of similar matters. To clinch matters he had read and could moderately quote *Moby Dick*. This seemed at the time of his coming the only available land. Indeed, with the sea on one side, the Sur mountains on the other, the rich walnut and orange farms occupying the third, and Del Monte and Las Flores on the fourth, the little town of Arguello might be said to be pretty well surrounded. To be sure, there were the sagebrush foothills of the Sur, but they were dry, desert, fit only for sheep and quail. Take it all around, a man of moderate means, ordered to live in Arguello valley if he would live at all, would be puzzled to find a little ranch unless he went far out. Then the Colonel happened along. Somehow Brainerd found himself in the little brown house.

But if the Colonel had cared to turn around he could have seen the houses of Arguello only a mile away, with the white Mission on the hill, and again the gleam of the sea, where the coast swept back almost at right angles to form the harbour.

The Colonel did not turn around, however. He stood there straight and slim in his long frock coat, with his fine, lean, kindly old face raised to the sun and the breeze, and his white hair stirring softly. The sky was very blue, and in its deeps swung buzzards in wide, stately circles. The air was warm and fragrant, and on it floated the clear liquid songs of the meadow larks and the quick buzzy notes of the quail. The sun's warmth fell softly like an essence in suspension, and the Colonel seemed to himself to be soaking it into his physical being as though it were indeed an ethereal, permeating substance. And the Colonel in his simple old heart found it good and thanked his God.

But now on a sudden he waked as though he had been called, and with an appearance of almost guilty haste he strode down the hill. The two hounds, who had been patiently awaiting his pleasure, yawned, stretched and followed after. The Colonel walked briskly around the house to the front door. To the handle of the bell-pull hung a turkey-feather duster as though left by a careless housemaid. It was there a-purpose, however, as it was there on all the bell-pulls in Southern California; and the Colonel put it to its appointed use on his boots.

He crossed the little hallway in two strides and entered the dining room.

His wife Allie sat already at table behind a silver coffee service beneath which burned an alcohol lamp. She was a small, plump, merry looking woman, with black hair in which appeared no thread of white. Her dress was of heavy fine black silk, relieved with white lace. Its cut was very plain and old-fashioned, but possessed a chic of its own that placed Allie definitely above the class of commonplace, small plump women. Her air was of brisk, amused tolerance, with a background of fine competence. Though she did not wear a bunch of keys at her girdle, one felt that it would have been symbolically appropriate for her to have done so. She raised her face for the Colonel's gallant kiss.

"You are very late this morning, Richard," she remarked.

"There was much to attend to. You remember this is a very important day."

The Colonel sat across the table, but immediately arose to set aside a cut-glass bowl of magnificent red roses that had filled the centre of the table.

"I would rather see you, dear, than the most beautiful roses in the world," he answered Allie's murmured protest.

He attacked the sliced oranges before him. A door opened noiselessly to admit the soft-footed Chinaman, bearing a laden tray. He stood waiting. The Colonel dallied with his fruit, telling Allie interestedly his morning adventure, pausing often with his spoon between plate and mouth.

"You eat fluit," broke in the Chinaman finally. "You stop talkee talkee, eat blekfus."

"Well, I declare, Sing Toy!" cried the Colonel.

But Sing Toy, secure in the righteousness of his attitude, budged not one inch from it.

"Belly late," he pointed out without excitement. "You walkee walkee, no catch blekfus, you catch headache. I know." He spoke from the profound empirical wisdom of year.. of service, in this family; and therefore he spoke in confidence. The Colonel collapsed and meekly devoured his orange. Sing Toy changed the plates and served the food. His calm eye swept the dining room masterfully.

"You change your nightgown," he told Allie, and left the room.

"I swear that Chinaman will drive me beyond bounds!" cried the Colonel.

"He merely meant the laundry boy was going to begin the week's wash to-day," chuckled Allie, placidly. "I am only thankful that he did not say it before our guests. You know perfectly well, Richard, what a faithful dear old thing he is."

"I suppose so," muttered the Colonel, "still——"

Sing Toy thrust his pig-tailed head through the door.

"Hot day," he announced. "Cunnel go catch thin coat. That one too thick. I fix um on bed. You go puttum on."

II

IN THE meantime the mounting sun was beginning to burn away the layer of high fog that had overhung the town. Each night, at this time of year, this blanket crept in from the sea and gathered out of nothing in the coolness of dawn. To one in the town it exactly resembled heavy rain clouds. Indeed, it was always difficult to persuade the tourist that his umbrella and mackintosh were unnecessary, that with absolute certainty it could be stated that those threatening, lowering clouds contained not one drop of rain. To one who had arisen early enough to have ridden up the Sur, it would have looked like a tumbled, shining silver sea through which thrust the peaks of higher hills. From either point of view it appeared a solid and permanent bit of weather that would take some time and doing to alter.

Nevertheless, about nine o'clock a weird brilliance appeared all at once to permeate the air. The heavy, inert dead clouds seemed suddenly infused with life. A glimpse of overhead blue was hinted and instantly obliterated. A phantom half-suggestion of a mountain peak in full sunshine showed for a moment through a gauze of white misty light. Then between two minutes simultaneously, all over the cup of the heavens, the dark clouds thinned to a veil. The veil was rent in two, twenty, a hundred places. It dissolved. A few shreds, drifting down a new freshness that arose from the sea, alone remained and they melted to nothing before one's eyes. Magically the blue sky was clear, and the sun was sending down its showers of golden warmth. The semi-circle of mountains rose hard and clear in the sparkling air; the sea twinkled with a thousand eyes; the surf lay white along the yellow shore. And none more foolish than the distrustful tourist compelled to convey past concealed contempts his umbrella and his mackintosh.

The town of Arguello began then, as it does now, in a wharf; a long wharf that reached a half mile to find its deep water. It ended indeterminately in open country after two miles. Its one long main street was unpaved, unimproved. All its side-walks were of wood; and there were no sidewalks except in the "centres of commerce, wealth, and fashion." The buildings in its business part were mostly one-story wooden affairs that pretended to be two-story by means of false fronts. There were, however, a number of pleasing variations, such as a four-storied brick structure with a tower and a loud-belled clock, called the Clock Building. The bank occupied part of its ground floor. All the big men had their offices upstairs; and on its upper floor was located the County Library. There were also a number of wide, deep overgrown old-fashioned gardens with square cupo-laed houses—places whose owners had refused to succumb to commercial expansion. Also remained a number of adobe structures with red-tiled roofs, houses that had been there since the earliest Spanish days. Some of these were still occupied by native Spanish California families; but most of the few still remaining on Main Street had become Chinese laundries. Near the head of Main Street, and a block apart, were two hotels. One, called the San Antonio, was three-storied, of brick, sat directly on the street, and had a wooden awning that extended over the sidewalk. The other, called the Fremont, was a huge rambling affair of wooden construction, with broad verandas. It occupied the centre of an extensive garden of palms, rubber, magnolia, and eucalyptus trees, and a great profusion of flowers of both common and rare species. Vines had covered it and shaded it and glorified it with roses, with passion flower, with wis-taria, with honeysuckle and many other sweet or brilliant blooms. A half dozen Chinamen were continuously engaged in watering and tending its lawns and gardens. Visitors from the East who had been there more than two weeks knew of a great many especial features to show the newer comers. Such as the black rose; or the LaMarque, whose stem was six inches in diameter; or the cork tree; or the camphor or bay trees, whose leaves you crushed and smelled. And of course they must eat a ripe olive off the tree:—and go around with a very puckered mouth the rest of the morning! You swept into these grounds on a curving, hospitably wide gravelled road and hitched your horse to a heavy rail made of iron pipe.

There were many of these rails, and they were always more or less occupied. Unless one happened to be a very recent and temporary tourist indeed, he never thought of walking even the shortest distances. Horses were extraordinarily cheap, either to buy or hire. All over the town horses, either under saddle or hitched to buggies, phaetons, or surries, dozed under the feathery pepper trees. If one wanted to go two blocks, he used a horse for that purpose. The length of Main Street was lined with them. Most people owned two or three and alternated them in the somnolent job of awaiting their master's pleasure. As a corollary to this state of affairs the saddler's shops were large, and fascinating with the smell of leather, the sight of carved, silver-mounted saddles, of braided rawhide bridles with long *morrales*, of inlaid spurs and horsehair work, of *riatas*, of horsehair *cinchas*, of fancy *cuartas* and the like. There were also monstrous frame stables each accommodating hundreds of animals, with corrals and horse troughs and generally a lot of lolloping dogs stretched in the sunny dust, and Mexicans who smoked brown paper cigarettes. From these each morning a long procession set forth. One man would drive a phaeton and lead a half dozen saddle horses attached to the horns of each other's saddles; another would ride and lead another half dozen. In all directions they scattered out through the town, leaving them by ones and twos here and there at the iron pipe hitching rails. When all but one had been delivered, the Mexican boy rode back to the stable, sitting his saddle loosely with the inimitable grace of the "cowboy seat." At noon it was necessary to go after the vehicles. The saddle horses, however, returned of themselves. The only requirement was to tie the reins to the horns so the animals could not stop to graze, to throw the stirrips across the saddles and to slap the beasts on the rump: they returned staidly or friskily home. At noon and toward six o'clock the streets would be full of these riderless animals. The scheme was eminently labour-saving and picturesque; but was later prohibited by law.

From the door of the bank in the Clock Building a man issued, briskly drawing on his gloves. He was followed by a bareheaded clerk who continued talking to him while he unhitched his horse and buggy. The man was rather short and slight, with a large round head, a very ruddy complexion, an old-fashioned white moustache and goatee, and rather bulging blue eyes. He was dressed carefully, though informally. His Panama hat, loose light tweeds and dark tie were eminently conservative and respectable. But in his small, cloth-topped exquisitely fitted patent leather boots one thought to catch his secret pride, his one harmless little vanity. Indeed, even as he finished his conversation with the clerk, he mechanically produced a large silk handkerchief and with it flecked imaginary dust from one foot, then the other. His name was Oliver Mills, and he was the president of the bank he was now quitting in the middle of a busy morning.

"Well, Simpson," he concluded. "You tell him that. And if he isn't satisfied, he will have to come and see me to-morrow. I wouldn't miss showing at the Colonel's jamboree for a dozen of him. In fact, to-day ought by rights to be a bank holiday, so everyone could go."

He gathered up the reins and clucked to his horse. The animal set himself in motion with a great deal of histrionic up and down and not much straightahead. It was rather a shiny and fancy horse, however, with a light tan harness and a wonderful netted fly cover that caparisoned him like a war horse of old even to his ears, and with dangling tassels that danced like jumping-jacks to his every motion. Mr. Mills, however, was apparently in no haste. He held the reins loosely in his lap, over which he had drawn a thin linen robe, and did not reach for the silver-banded whip in the socket. Up the length of Main Street he drove, bowing right and left to his numerous acquaintance, and casting an appreciative and appraising eye on signs of improvement. These would not have astonished a modern hustler, but they satisfied Mr. Mills that his town was moving on and prosperous. He liked the friendly greetings, he was glad to see a wooden sidewalk going down, he enjoyed the feel of the sun pouring on his back.

At the Fremont he turned in and drove up alongside the very wide, shady veranda, whose floor was only just above the level of the ground. A man seated in one of the capacious wooden

rocking chairs heaved himself to his feet and came forward. He
was of the build known as stocky, and was clad in a well-cut blue
serge. His large head was grown closely with a cap of very black
and rather coarse curls. His forehead was low and broad, his
eyebrows black and beetling, his eyes humorous, his moustache
black, his cheeks red and slightly veined with purple. Altogether a dashing, handsome, black and red, slightly coarse man,
with undoubtedly a fund of high spirits and obvious wit. And
his eyes and forehead showed ability.

"Good morning, Mr. Mills," he cried in a loud hearty voice.
"How are you?   Fine morning, isn't it?"

"Of course," replied the banker, a little vaguely.

The other man chuckled.

"'Of course'," he repeated. "I suppose you mean to say all
your mornings are fine, eh?"

"At this time of year; yes. How are you feeling?"

"As if the doctor who ordered me out here was a damn liar.
Never felt better in my life. If you hadn't said you would be
along I would have taken a walk over to the mountains and back
to get an appetite for lunch. Not that I need one; I'm as hungry
as a wolf."

"Would you, really," said Mills, quizzically. "Before lunch!
You are certainly no invalid, Mr. Boyd. Quite an athlete, I
should say."

"Why that's no walk," exclaimed Boyd, defensively.

"It's six miles to those mountains."

Boyd checked an exclamation and examined the other closely.

"Looks as though he meant it," he commented, as though to
himself. "Can't figure his ulterior motive. Why, you poor
chump!" he cried. "What do you take me for? If I can't walk
there and back in an hour, I'll eat a hat!"

"The air is very clear," said Mills quietly. "I should admire
to see you try. However, get your hat and your boy and we'll
be getting on."

"Well, if that's six miles it must be about a mile and a half
to the hatrack, so don't expect me back soon," was Boyd's
parting rejoinder as he started for the office door.

In a few moments he returned, accompanied by a slender lad

of about twenty. The boy was like the next step in the evolution of his father's type: taller, more lightly built, not quite so obviously curly and black and red. His hair, instead of being shiny crow black, was of a very dark brown; instead of kinking into tight ringlets, lay in loose waves. His forehead was bold and frank, as were his eyes. He walked with spring and pride, and his expression was alert and joyous and out-springing in spirit. It was obvious that the elder Boyd was extremely proud of him. Nevertheless, he made the introduction exceedingly casual, almost off hand, and at once climbed into the buggy.

"I'm very glad to meet you, Kenneth," said Mr. Mills. "There's a little seat in the back, if you can make out how it goes. That's it." He cramped the wheel carefully, and drove out of the hotel grounds. On Main Street he turned to the left, and so headed for the open country.

"I am glad to hear our climate is proving beneficial," remarked Mr. Mills, after they had made the turn successfully. "And I hope you may remain with us a long time."

"I'm all right," returned Boyd, "except that I'm beginning to be troubled a little with insomnia."

"Insomnia," repeated the banker. "You astonish me! The soporific quality of our air has been rather a matter of pride with us. I never knew of anybody who did not go to bed and sleep soundly all night long in Arguello!"

"Oh, I sleep all right nights—and afternoons," drawled Boyd, "but I'm getting a little wakeful mornings."

Mills looked doubtful for a moment, then at the sound of a snort from Kenneth in the back seat, he smiled faintly.

"Ah, that is a jest," he stated.

"Yes, it was a jest," agreed Boyd, soberly.

A very wide, squat streetcar came swaying down the uneven track in the centre of the street. It was driven by a Mexican boy in a wide hat who was perched precariously on the rail of the front platform. Hitched to it by long rope traces pattered two mules so diminutive that they looked no bigger than dogs.

"I started for the beach in that contraption yesterday," remarked Boyd, "I was the only man aboard, but there were a half dozen women. Each of those women had some shopping to

do. The car waited while they went into the stores and bought
things. I got tired after a while, and got out and walked. Can
you beat that?"

"Oh yes, that is quite the custom," was Mills's comment,
"You see, the car only makes four round trips a day."

"I see," returned Boyd, in rather a crushed voice.

They drove in silence for some moments. The open country
succeeded the last scattered houses of the town. The oak-
parked hills rolled away to right and left, unfretted by fences.
Ground squirrels scurried to their holes; little owls bobbed from
the tops of low earth mounds; a road runner flopped rangily into
the dust of the road and rocked away in challenge ahead of the
horse. Under the oak trees stood the cattle, already fed full.
The starred carpet of *alfileria* had been fitted to the hills, and in
the folds and up the slopes scarves of bright colour—lupin,
poppy, *nieve*, poor man's gold—had been flung. Quail and
meadowlark, oriole and vireo, led a chorus of birds. In tiny
pond-patches of tule and cattail, mudhens and ducks talked
busily in low voices. The yellow sunlight flooded the land like
an amber wine.

"You certainly have a wonderful country to look at, and wonderful weather. What's the matter with it?"

"Matter with it?" repeated Mills. "Nothing. What do you
mean?"

"Well, look around you. There isn't a house to be seen.
If this country was as good as it looks you ought to have a farm
house for every two hundred acres."

"Oh, I see. Well, this that you are looking at is all one big
ranch—the Corona del Monte. Belongs to Colonel Peyton,
where we are going."

"How far does he extend?"

"Up the valley? About five miles."

"What's beyond?"

"Las Flores—belongs to a Spanish family, the Cazaderos.
They owned practically the whole of the valley under the old
grant. The present ranch is not a quarter of their original
holdings."

"Sell out?"

"The usual thing with these old families. They are very generous and very extravagant, and they have no idea of the value of money. All they know is that they go to the bank and get what they need. There must come an end to it: you know that. There comes a time when the bank must foreclose, for its own protection."

"Then your land loans often require foreclosure?"

"You would be interested to look over the old tax lists. I'll take you down to the Court House sometime to see them, if you want. At first there were perhaps a dozen names, all Spanish. Then alongside each of those Spanish names came one or more American names. And the assessments against the Spanish grew smaller. You can pretty well trace the history of the county on those tax books. You ought to look them over."

"I should like to do so," asserted Boyd. "But under these conditions the bank must be in the ranching business pretty extensively."

"It is, and we don't like it; but we do as little management as we can help, and sell cheaply."

"Then," corrected Boyd, "the banks are in the real estate business."

"We are that: up to the neck. But," he pointed out, "do not forget that is about the only way we'd ever open up the back country. The native won't sell a foot of his land. The only way to get it from him is by foreclosure."

"Do these big holders, like Peyton or this Spaniard, do any farming?"

"Peyton has a walnut orchard and some fruit in the bottom-land, and of course some barley and alfalfa. All that is right near the home station. But most of it is cattle, of course; and sheep in the mountains."

"And the Spaniard?"

"They have always a little stuff for home use around the ranch houses. But none of those people ever do much but cattle."

"Land not good for much else, I suppose," suggested Boyd, with malice aforethought.

"Not good?" Mills fired up. "Let me tell you that this bottomland is the finest farming soil in the world. It will raise anything that can be raised anywhere in any climate. Why, sir, we have the finest products you ever saw in either the temperate or tropical zones. There is no use my trying to tell you about it. Drive down the valley to the south of the town and look about you."

"I should like to do so," said Boyd again.

They topped a little rise and looked ahead over the long flat across which the road led into the distance of other hills. Crawling white clouds of dust marked the progress of many other vehicles. These turned at a point about midway in the valley to enter an avenue between a double row of tall fan palms.

"The Colonel's guests are arriving," observed Mills.

The palm avenue, rustling mysteriously in the wind and flanked on either side by English walnut trees, ran straight as a string for nearly a mile to end in a slight curve around the low wide knoll on which grew the Cathedral Oaks. Just before this ascent, however, they were turned aside by a very polite Mexican into a sort of paddock enclosure where were provided an astonishing number of hitching posts and rails. Already nearly a hundred animals were there securely anchored. The rigs varied from ramshackle buggies white with dust to smart surreys or buckboards. In the centre was even a high four-seated trap. The four horses stood tied to the wheels. They were good looking animals and possessed the (then) astounding peculiarity of roached manes and banged tails.

"Who's that outfit belong to?" asked Boyd, his attention attracted by the smartness of detail of all this.

An expression of disapproval clouded the banker's prominent eyes.

"Young fellow named Corbell," he replied shortly. "Wild young fool. Owns a ranch out beyond here."

They left the paddock and made their way up the knoll and across the lawn to the ranch house.

The Colonel and Mrs. Peyton stood at the foot of the three veranda steps receiving their guests. Many of the latter were strolling about beneath the trees and on the lawn; others were wandering in groups down the slope and across the way to the picnic grove. The women looked very cool and fresh in light coloured dresses. Among those who lingered as by right on the lawns were the élite of Arguello, and they bore themselves accordingly. The men were very bluff and sententious but with a roving eye on the punchbowls. The women wore huge excrescences called bustles and little hat-bonnets on the front of their heads and they walked with elegance. To the elders all this imparted an air of great dignity and virtue; but some of the younger, fresh-faced dashing creatures managed to make of these rather awful appurtenances weapons for conquest. They flirted the bustles from one side to the other; or they looked out from under square banged hair beneath the little hats, and great was the slaughter.

III

THE stream past the Colonel and his wife swelled and slackened, but never ceased. As Boyd moved on after his conventional greeting, he heard the Colonel mention the name Corbell, and turned in curiosity to see the owner of the four-in-hand. He looked upon a rather short, dapper individual with a long, lean brown face, snapping black eyes, and a little moustache waxed to straight needle points. This man was exquisitely dressed in rough clothes of Norfolk cut—in that time and place! —a soft silk shirt and collar, a pastel necktie. He wore no jewelry but a large signet ring. His concession to the West was his hat, which was probably the widest, highest, and utmost turned out of the factory. With him seemed to be somewhat of a group of young men; of whom, however, Boyd noticed particularly only one. Indeed, that one could hardly escape notice. He stood well over six feet and bulged with enormous frame and muscles. His complexion was very blond, so that the ruddiness of his open-air skin showed in fierce and pleasing contrast to his bleached moustache and eyebrows. To make it all more emphatic he wore garments of small black and white checks. It would have been impossible to compute how many thousands of these little squares there were spread abroad over his great round chest and thick arms alone.

"Lord, there's a strong-looking chap. How'd you like to tackle him. Ken?" commented Mr. Boyd, as they drew apart.

"He's powerful big. He looks strong."

"He *is* strong," broke in a stranger who had overheard. "I saw him once crawl under a felled tree and raise it on the broad of his back."

"Who is he?"

"Rancher. Owns the next place to Corbell—that little dude there. Named Hunter, Bill Hunter. They call him Big Bill. Somebody once said he looked pneumatic."

"Why?"

"Looks sort of as if he had been blowed up with an air pump."

"That, also, is a jest," stated Boyd.

Kenneth laughed joyously.

"I wonder if he'd collapse if you stuck a pin in him?"

"I reckon *something* would collapse," agreed the stranger drily. "You from the East, I take it. Out for long?"

"Yes. I don't know. Depends on father," said Kenneth, indicating Mr. Boyd, who had by now strolled away with the banker.

"Old man sick, eh?"

"He's here for his health," admitted Kenneth.

The stranger, who was long and lank and solemn, produced a match, carefully whittled it to a point and thrust it in his mouth. He did this simple act with such a purposeful air of deliberation that Kenneth found himself watching with interest and in silence.

"My name's Paige, Jim Paige," said that individual; then: "I run the main harness shop in this place—carved leather, silver work, all that stuff."

"My name is Boyd," reciprocated Kenneth. "I don't run anything."

Paige grinned appreciatively.

"Know anybody round here?"

"Not a soul. We've only been here a week."

"A week! And don't know nobody!" Paige cast a quizzical side glance. "And you don't look extra bashful, either. Might know you were from the East."

"Have you ever been East?" countered Kenneth.

"Yes, once."

"Like it?"

"No."

"What was the matter?"

"Well, I'll tell you," drawled Paige, with an air of great privacy. "Back East when you don't do nothing, you feel guilty: but out here when you don't do nothing, you don't give a damn. But look a here: you've got to know some of the little she-devils we raise around here, a young fellow like you."

He seized Kenneth firmly above the elbow, and, before that young man knew what was up, propelled him to a group of young people giggling consumedly after the fashion of the very young.

"Hey, you, Dora. Look here; I want you to meet up with Mr. Boyd of the effete East. He's been here a week and don't know anybody and seemingly hasn't got spunk enough to get acquainted."

He surveyed the group a tolerant moment, then sauntered away, his lank figure moving loosely in his clothes, the sharpened match in the corner of his mouth, his eyes wandering lazily and humorously from group to group. Kenneth, rooted to the spot, blushing to the ears, found himself facing a laughing mischievous group of young people. He stuttered something about intrusion, his mind murderously pursuing the departing Jim Paige. There could be no doubt that these were of the town's best—and to be thrust in this way—by a harness maker——

The laughing mischievous girl addressed as Dora broke in on his agony.

"You must not mind old Jim Paige Mr. Boyd," she was saying. "He brought us all up, fairly, and taught us to ride and even to walk, I do believe. My name is Dora Stanley. We are truly glad to meet you. Look about you, if you don't believe it. Count us. Eight girls and two men——" and then, having by this chatter given him time to recover his self-possession, Miss Stanley presented him more formally to the members of the group.

In the meantime the Colonel continued to greet an unending procession of his guests. They filed before him singly, in groups, in droves There were many prominent in the life of the place who lingered importantly; there were many plainly dressed, awkward farmers and their wives, labouring men, Mexicans who uttered their greetings and hurried past, a little uncomfortable until they had lost themselves in the crowd of their own kind at the barbecue grounds. The Colonel knew them all by name, and he greeted each and every one of them with a genuine and cordial enthusiasm. With each he could exchange no more than a word; but he was really glad to see them, and they went on with little warm spots in their breasts. One can hardly catalogue over the notables of that day as they filed past, important as some of them now loom in the light of tradition and legend. Perhaps we should not omit the poet, Snowden Delmore, a tall, slender, hairless man with fine cut, pale features and exquisite long pale fingers. He took obvious moral platitude and cast them in sonnet form with Greek imagery and occasional poetic sounding words like *thalissa* that people had to look up. This was all very serious with him; and he was the centre of a group. In contrast came Doctor Wallace, the best physician, who was short and round and coarse and blunt fingered and blunt speeched. With him, just to make the contrast complete, was Judge Crosby, a tall, white, sarcastic, ultra-polite individual in a frock coat. These two were great cronies, and very canny. After paying their respects to the Colonel, they proceeded at once to the punch bowl, the contents of which they sampled cautiously.

"Belly wash," judged Doctor Wallace.

"Intended for the consumption of the ladies," agreed Judge Crosby.

"Well, Colonel Dick knows a heap better than *that*," the Doctor planted his thick square legs wide apart and looked about him. "I see Sing Toy making signals," he said. "Come on."

The Chinaman was standing at the side steps to the porch where he could keep an eye on the punch bowl.

"You come in. Miss heap muchee fun," he commanded the Doctor, who was a favourite of his.

"All right, Toy, you old rascal. How's your gizzard?"

"No hab, doctor. Gizzard velly good," replied the oriental without expression.

The doctor chuckled vastly and stumped up the steps and into the dining room.

"Will you look at this lot of hoary old highbinders!" he cried.

The little room was filled with men. The selection of the company was Sing Toy's, not the Colonel's. Therefore no one was there who had not fine raiment, respectability, an appreciable bank account and years of discretion. Your Chinaman is conventional. Hilarity there was, but not noisy hilarity. Only thin board and batten intervened between them and wives. On the table were bourbon and rye whisky.

Outside the guests had nearly all arrived. Mrs. Peyton had disappeared in the house in pursuit of some final directions or arrangements. The Colonel for the moment stood alone, looking pleasedly around the groups on his green lawn and under his green trees. His eyes lighted with especial pleasure at the sight of two latecomers, and he deserted his post to meet them as they came down the drive.

"Brainerd, my boy, I am so glad to see you here. The day would not have been complete without you. It was good of you to come after all; and to bring my Puss. How is she?"

"Hate a crowd," returned Brainerd. "Don't know why I came. Not going to stay long."

He was a long, loose-jointed man, slow moving, cool in manner, with cool gray eyes a little tired and a little sad, a ragged, chewed-looking moustache, and with long, lean brown hands. A round spot of colour burned high on his cheekbones. His expression was sardonic and his manner bristly in a slow, wearied fashion. He was dressed in loose rough tweeds that looked old but of respectable past.

The individual referred to by the Colonel as Puss, however, seemed informed with all the vitality missed in the other. She was at first glance a very large child of twelve or thirteen but a second inspection left the observer a little puzzled. Her dress was short and her long slim legs had few curves of maturity: she wore the frock of a child with a bright coloured Roman sash; her tumbled hair was tied with a ribbon. But her poise was that almost of a grown woman, and she carried with her a calm distinction difficult to define. It was perhaps an atmosphere of simplicity and freedom from the childhood conventions usually taught little girls. Or perhaps it was only the intense vitality that seemed to emanate from her. Her long slim body radiated it, each individual fine-spun hair on her tumbled head seemed to stand out from its fellows as a charged conductor, it smouldered deep below the calm of her clear gaze as she looked about her. She stood without fidget, indeed without any motion at all, completely restful; but somehow at the same time she conveyed the impression of being charged for rapid, darting motion, like a humming bird. Her cheeks were brown, with deep rich red beneath the surface, and her features were piquantly irregular. The conclusion of an observer would have been that she was at least fifteen, with an afterwonder as to why she did not dress her age.

That feature of the case scandalized Mrs. Judge Crosby. It always did scandalize her, every time she saw the child, so the novelty of the emotion was somewhat worn, though the expression of it had gained by practice. Mrs. Judge Crosby was of the type of fat woman that wears picture hats and purple, and rides in limousines with lots of glass. There were no limousines in those days, but that fact did not interfere with Mrs. Judge Crosby. She always established herself in chairs, and summoned people. Just now she was talking to Snowden Delmore.

"Just look at that child!" she cried to the attentive poet. "Did you ever see anything so utterly absurd! Great long-legged thing dressed like a kindergarten! And such an outlandish rig! She looks like a little gypsy! I tell you, Mr. Delmore, say what you will, any child needs the influence of a woman, a mother. There is an example of what happens when a child is turned over to a man. She how she stands there! You would think she was the equal in age and social standing of any one here. It is almost impertinence. You agree with me, of course?"

"Yes, yes, certainly!" hastened Delmore.

As a matter of fact the poet was thinking that the garment with its queer colour combinations had a quaint attractive distinction of its own; and that the child's clear, bold, spirited profile as she looked off into space waiting for her elders to finish their conversation was fascinating in its suggestion of the usual things lacked and the unusual gained. Snowden Delmore was deep in his soul a real poet and he could occasionally see the point though he had a pretty thick highbrow and egotistical overlay. But who was he to dispute Mrs. Judge Crosby? Only Mrs. Doctor Wallace did that.

The Colonel continued to stand with his hand affectionately on Brainerd's thin shoulder.

"You need not stay a moment longer than you wish. I am only too glad that you have come. You must wish Allie happiness on her birthday, however, before you go."

"I wouldn't fail to do that, Colonel," said Brainerd, with a softening of expression.

"That's right! that's right! And now let us get over to the Grove. Allie must be there already. How are you?"

"Me? Oh, well enough! Old Wallace says my bellows are getting fairly serviceable. I notice I can go ten hours after quail, all right enough; but I can't seem to go more than ten minutes after good honest work. Colonel, I'm beginning to believe I'm a fraud!"

"It's old Nature working her way with you, Brainerd. You mind her. She knows best. If she says hunt quail and don't build fences, you obey her. Let me tell you a secret: I found it out last time I was up in the city with Mrs. Peyton. I got all tired out going around shopping with her, and I figured afterward that I had actually walked just over two miles. Two miles, sir! and I mighty near had to go to bed when I came in. I've often ridden over to Los Quitos and back in a day, and that makes sixty-five miles. How do you account for it? Eh? It isn't what you do with your body that makes you tired: it's what you do with your mind. And so you hunt your quail and get well."

He still kept his hand on Brainerd's shoulder, which he patted gently, from time to time, emphasizing the points of this speech.

"Colonel," said the latter with a short laugh, "as an apologist for laziness you stand alone. I now feel myself the model of all the virtues."

"That's right; that's right," returned the old man, much pleased. "And how are the crops?"

"Well, the bees are laying up a lot of indifferent muddy honey. The cherry crop seems to please the birds, of which there are six to each cherry. I found a couple of young apples starting yesterday. The spring still seems to be damp. There were two coyotes on the hill last night. The mortgage is a little better than holding its own. That's about one month's history. You can repeat for next month, except that those two apples will probably get worms."

The Colonel laughed, and patted Brainerd's shoulder again.

"If I did not know you," he said, "I would say that you were getting bitter. But I know you. How does the new pony go, Puss?" he asked the girl.

She turned her direct unembarrassed gaze at him.

"He is wonderful; the best I have ridden; I love him!"

"That is something I want to speak to you about," said Brainerd. "It is good of you to keep sending Daphne ponies to ride, and I appreciate it; but I really cannot permit you to continue it. You must let me buy this pony, if it is within my means."

"The animals must be exercised. It is a favour to me to get one of them cared for and ridden."

"Nonsense, Colonel. I know better than that. And I know the value of these horses of yours. That *palomino** is fine old stock. If you will not let me pay for him, I shall certainly have to send him back. You have been more than generous in the past, and I have been weak enough to allow you to do it, but it cannot go on."

Daphne glanced up and caught the look of distress in the Colonel's face.

"Daddy, you are interfering with what does not concern you," she said calmly. "This is a matter entirely between my Fairy Godfather and me."

"Is it, really? Well upon my word!" cried Brainerd, bristling up.

But the Colonel interposed, delighted at this unexpected aid.

---

*A buckskin, but with silver mane and tail.

"Yes, yes, to be sure. How dare you interfere, Brainerd, between me and my goddaughter. That is our affair. We will settle it ourselves."

He seized Daphne's hand and the two disappeared together in the direction of the Grove, leaving Brainerd looking after them, a slight quirk relieving the bitterness of his mouth.

IV

THE Grove was a-buzz with life. The huge barbecued joints had been dug up from the pit and now lay before Benito and his assistants, who sliced them deftly with long, keen knives and laid the slices on plates. These were quickly snatched away by waiting laughing girls who took them in precarious piles to the tables. There waited the guests, cracking walnuts, eating raisins and oranges, making vast inroads on the supposedly ornamental desserts while awaiting the substantials. The volunteer waitresses darted here and there. They were girls of the country, both American and Spanish born. The former were magnificent figures cast on heroic lines; tall, full bosomed, large limbed, tawny and gold, true California products; the latter smaller, with high insteps, small bones, powdered faces, beautiful eyes. All alike were very starched and very busy. Men followed them with galvanized pails containing the celebrated sauce—composed mainly of onions, tomatoes, and chilis cunningly blended; or pans with potatoes or *tomales* or stuffed onions. One stout old California woman dressed in oldstyle *rebozo* and *mantilla*, her round face shining with heat and pleasure, carried a long platter heaped high with *tortillas* which she urged on everyone.

"Da pancak' of old time," she cried. "Eet is veray goot. Try him."

Another group were close gathered at the short table that had been erected in front of the wine kegs. Here José and a number of helpers worked busily filling tin cups that were continually thrust at their attention. At this table there seemed little need for the help of the tripping laughing young waitresses. Everyone appeared willing and able to help himself. The wine was of the country, and light in content, yet already its effects could be noticed in the loosening of tongue, the relaxing of the bucolic stiffness that had in certain quarters inaugurated the party. Young chaps besought the flitting girls to stop for but a moment's chat, or flung out an amusing impertinence that caught some damsel on the fly. There was a great deal of laughter. A Spanish orchestra back in the trees twanged away on its guitars, and even though unheeded, furnished a background to the noise.

An abatement of this noise suddenly took place. Rapid admonitions found their way to the groups and individuals who still talked or laughed on. Shortly silence reigned. The Colonel and Mrs. Peyton were leading their especial guests into the Grove.

There ensued a few moments of well-bred confusion while places were found. Then the Colonel straightened himself and faced the assembly.

"You are welcome, friends," he said. "It is pleasant to greet you here once more. This occasion is always one near my heart, and my wish is that it may continue for many years to come." He raised a wine glass to the light. "I will ask you to drink with me to the *fiesta* of her who makes this *rancho* what it is—many happy returns——" He turned and bowed low to Mrs. Peyton. The people all over the Grove struggled to their feet—no easy matter from the stationary benches. The air cried with the shouts in English and Spanish. And the spirits of the trees—which, though friendly spirits are shy—must have plucked up heart against the noise and drawn nearer to that composite glow of good feeling.

All reseated themselves, and attacked with appetite the good things offered. The food at the Colonel's tables was exactly that of the others—the juicy barbecued meat with the fiery sauce, the *tomales* and *tortillas*, the beans and soda biscuits, all brought around in pails and pans and served with dippers. But it was very good. The only difference was in the silver, the glass, the napkins and the wines. Of the latter the Colonel was proud. The white wines had been carefully chilled in the spring house: the red wines turned in the sun by the Colonel's own hand. Sing Toy and two younger replicas had charge of serving them.

At the Colonel's right sat Allie, for was she not the guest of 'honour? At his left billowed Mrs. Judge Crosby. Mrs. Doctor Wallace was across the way, and so the Colonel found himself surrounded with dignity, substantial importance, and what would have been certain stodginess had it not been for his own inexhaustible and genuine desire that everyone have a good time. He plied them with courtesy, with food, with drink, with rather elaborate old compliments, pretending to believe that remote yesterdays were but just around the corner. And every few moments he would remark with an air of discovery on the excellence of some dish, and would send for the cook thereof.

"These are real camp soda biscuits," he told Mrs. Crosby. "Just the kind you will get on *rodeo*. I wonder who made them? Who made these biscuits, Ynez?" he asked a Spanish girl who passed. "Find out, and ask the one who cooked them to stop here a moment. You won't mind, will you?" he flattered Mrs. Judge. "So you made these soda biscuits!" he said a moment later, as a lazy, awkward American cowboy stood before him twisting his broad hat. "Well. you are an artist, and I wanted Mrs. Peyton to see you and tell you so."

"Indeed, they are delicious. Better than I could do myself. And you know I am quite a cook," said Mrs. Peyton briskly.

"Yes, ma'am," said the cowboy. "You'd do a heap better always if you use a Dutch oven 'stead of a stove."

He retired hot with embarrassment, outwardly stolid, and inwardly "tickled to death."

In like manner a farmer's wife was complimented on her jelly—though in her case the Colonel gallantly hunted her up to tell her so. Indeed the Colonel was always popping up and moving about to exchange a few words with his guests at the other tables. But also some things had been contributed by those sitting at the Colonel's own table.

"Mrs. Mainwaring," the Colonel called down the line to a little middle-aged Southern woman. "Nobody north of the Mason and Dixon can make beaten biscuits. That has been proved to-day. Without your kindness we should have missed one of our most delicate gastronomic treats."

As the meat was passed he remarked loudly, so that all could hear:

"You must remember to take plenty of the sauce. The barbecue is nothing without it. None can make the pepper flavour that goes into it unless one has lived in the old days. Is it not so, Doña Paredis?"

But the great moment was when, the serving over, Benito was summoned to receive his compliment, for in the final analysis his had been the responsibility for the gastronomics of the party; and his was now the glory. It was fairly a ceremony, with courtly little speeches on both sides. Benito bore himself with dignity, and acquitted himself loftily. One would have said a knight errant acknowledging due praise from his liege.

But all was not on as high a plane. There was a good deal of noise at the Colonel's tables as well as in the Grove at large. Corbell and his half dozen boon companions had preëmpted an end of the other table, where they were having close-corporation jokes among themselves and accumulating an extraordinary number of longnecked bottles. Kenneth Boyd was still with the group of pretty girls. The other two young men proved to be rather harmless local nonentities; but the damsels were at once pretty, stylish, and lively. Kenneth possessed certain advantages, such as a New York address, a jeweled fraternity pin, a preposterously long-visored cap with tangled college insignia embroidered on the front, a small knack with a guitar, a varied repertoire of perfectly killing college songs of a humorous trend, a half dozen jingles that turned most daringly on kissing, and a tiny gold ring with enamel forget-me-nots that looked as though it might have been given him by some girl. It must not be forgotten that he was young and goodlooking and not at all shy. Of course he could not deploy all these advantages at once, nor is the above claimed to be a complete catalogue; but enough has been suggested. If the reader has even been young he—or she— can see at once that the party was here going to be a success. Indeed, soon after the cool, sliced tomatoes had been served, the whole lot of them by common consent left the tables and seated

themselves on the grass at some distance. Kenneth had borrowed a guitar from the musicians. He was surrounded by
fluffy gay nymphs of different types, but all young and charming.
Two negligible males had been supplied by Providence as wit-
nesses. He teased and was teased. He sang his little songs
dealing with naughty maidens of the bold black eye, or fishermen who sailed out of Billingsgate. He recited his little verses,
notably one that ended to the effect that "the hint with all its
sweetness her lover did discern, he flung his arms around her neck
and glued his lips to hern." This elicited shrieks and writhings.
The crass vulgarity and bad taste made a piquant contrast to
the elegance of the relations between such cultured young people.
The girls liked it, but it made them shudder—like the juice of the
sweet lemon. Kenneth had a what-cares-he-for-conventions
feeling, like the young devil he was. Dora Stanley and Myra
Welch, and Isabelle Carson played up especially well. Dora
was the vivid roguish type, Myra the languid, dark beautiful
type, and Isabelle the plump sentimental type, which was of
course why they were always together. Martin Stanley and
Winchester Carson felt a vast secret contempt, but they could
not think of a thing to do about it.

Boyd and the banker were still together, and had seated themselves near the middle of the long table. Over the Colonel's rye
and bourbon they had fallen in with a number of delightful
young-old men, and they were having rather a loud good time.
Already Boyd had agreed to go riding with them and to play
poker with them. They had a fund of dry humour, considerable native shrewdness, and a deliberate intention to have a good
time. Four of them were staying at the Fremont for the winter;
the other three owned places in the town where they had retired
after stormy northern business careers in the turbulent 'seventies.
They were after Boyd's own heart; and he after theirs.

But one other group among all the Colonel's guests requires
especial mention as having to do with the story. These were
three: an elderly Spanish gentleman and his wife, and their
daughter. They had driven up rather grandly in a victoria
with a broad-hatted coachman at the ribbons, and had greeted
the Colonel with a great deal of ceremony. Don Vincente

Cazadero was rather stout with tufted side whiskers and a clean-shaven chin. He was of course swarthy, but possessed a transparent skin and haughty eyes. His dress differed in no way from that of the Americans except that in its small details it went to a refinement, a precious meticularity that found its ultimate expression in his small, tight, exquisite varnished boots. As he was a little below the average height, and a little above the average weight he carried himself with the utmost dignity. His wife was also stout. She was placid, unruffled, a little stupid, but evidently of noble race. The daughter was pretty and amiable but rather insipid, with soft eyes and long lashes. Both women were, as was the custom of their people, over-powdered. Their gowns were of wonderful heavy China silk, and their jewels of the first water. This family paid its devoirs to the Colonel in most punctilious style, greeted sundry acquaintances, and then drew aside. Don Vincente was the owner of Las Flores rancho, which bounded Del Monte on the north.

But by now the people began rising here and there from the tables. The girls ceased to flit to and fro, and seated themselves at a side table. This was the chance for which some of the young men had waited; and they hastened to supply the damsels with food and drink. Many of the diners straggled down from the knoll in the direction of the whitewashed corrals where the *vaqueros* were already beginning the sports. Some of the younger couples were trying to dance to the music of the guitars. Couples strayed away up the cañon.

Kenneth was one of the first at the corrals. He had never seen cowboy games, and proved most eager. The idea did not at all meet with the approval of his companions. The girls had no liking to expose their fresh toilettes to the dust, nor their fresh complexions to the burning sun and heat; the two young men pretended to be bored with such things. They preferred to remain in the shade with the guitar, so they trailed along back to the lawn under the Cathedral Oaks with the rest of the Colonel's "quality" guests. The Colonel himself went to the corrals. It was part of his hospitable duty to show there, he told Mrs. Judge Crosby with apparent regret; and then he scuttled away like a dear old boy afraid that already he might have missed something. He made his way through the dense packed crowd, shaking a hand here and there, exchanging remarks and greetings.

"What has been done, Manuelo?" he asked in Spanish, when he had gained the fairway outside the ropes where a little group on foot were gathered. The audience were crowded along the lines, they perched on the top rails of all the corrals, and some of the youngest and most active had climbed to the roofs. Inside the ropes, beside the officials mentioned, lounged a number of horsemen, *vaqueros*, and cowboys awaiting their turns at the games. The Spaniards were dressed in old-time costumes exhumed for the occasion from brass-studded heirloom, chests, with the high-crowned hat heavy with silver; the short jacket and sash; the wide-legged pantaloons bound at the knee and split down the calf; the soft leather boots; the heavy silver inlaid spurs. The American cowboys were not so picturesque in their own persons; but they vied with the others in perfection of equipment. All of the heavy stock saddles were rich with carving; many of them had silver corners, or even silver pommels or cantles. They carried braided rawhide *riatas;* their horses champed with relish the copper rollers of spade bits whose broad sides were solid engraved silver; their bridles were of cunningly braided and knotted rawhide or horsehair coloured and woven in patterns. The riders sat with graceful ease far to one side, elbow on knee, smoking brown paper cigarettes.

"Nothing yet has been done." Manuelo answered the Colonel's question reproachfully. "It could not be thought of that we should begin without your presence, *señor*."

"That is good! that is good!" cried the Colonel, delighted. "Well, here I am. Let us start!"

"Will the *señor* ride Caliente and judge the games?"

"The *señor* will not," rejoined the Colonel emphatically. "You are a lazy fellow, Manuelo. I shall watch the games, and you will act as judge."

"It is good," agreed Manuelo, and swung himself into the saddle of a magnificent pinto standing near.

The Colonel retreated to the corral fence, already as full as a tree of blackbirds. However, at his approach a place magically became vacant, while all the bystanders stoutly maintained that that particular point had never had an occupant but had accidentally remained empty for the Colonel. So after some talk he mounted the fence and sat there, his heels hooked over a rail, his long legs tucked up, his black frock coat dangling, his hat on the back of his head, his fine old face alight with enthusiasm.

Kenneth Boyd was also atop the corrals, and he happened to be next the Colonel. On his other side perched a long-legged demure child dressed in a bright dress. She looked to be about twelve or thirteen years old, which was of course beneath the particular notice of a man like Kenneth. He glanced at her, thought she was rather an attractive looking kid, and gave his attention to his surroundings.

By now the sun was getting strong. Dust rose in the heated air. People were packed in close together. The sun and the crowding and the food and the red wine combined to turn faces red, to wilt collars and starched toilets; but nobody minded.

"Great fun, great fun, my boy!" cried the Colonel to Kenneth, whom of course he did not remember. "Hello, Puss!" he cried across at the child. "Why aren't you out there on the palomino?"

"I am getting much too big for such things," replied Daphne, composedly.

"So, ho!" cried the Colonel, delighted. "Getting to be a young lady, are we? Do you know," he said to Kenneth, "this very grown-up young person is one of the best riders we have. This is the first *merienda* for two years at which she has not ridden. The people will shout for you, *niña*," he told Daphne.

"They will not get me," she replied.

Kenneth, thus led by this cross conversation to observe again his neighbour, smiled upon her the smile appropriate from one of his age and station.

"I should have liked very much to see you ride," he said kindly. "Have you a pony of your own?"

But she did not reply. Kenneth looked at her sharply. He could not for a moment determine whether this chit had de-

liberately ignored him or whether her whole interest was centred
on a group of horsemen at which she seemed to be gazing.

"Now you will see the California sports as they were in the
old days," the Colonel was saying. "See, there they go now!"

The horsemen had come to life and were swooping gracefully
back and forth like swallows. It was an exhibition only. Men
"turned on a ten cent piece"; charged at full speed only to pull
to a stand in a plunge and a slide; reined their horses to the
perpendicular and half-turned in mid air; described figure eights
at full speed. It was a gay scene of animation. Then little by
little the movement died, leaving the horsemen grouped at one
end of the course.

Manuelo now rode to a middle point directing the activities
of two men with shovels. They dug a small hole and buried
something mysterious in the loosened light earth.

"Why it's a chicken!" cried Kenneth.

The fowl had been buried all but its head, which was extended
anxiously in a most comical manner. But now one of the riders
detached himself from the others and came flying down the
course at full speed. When within ten feet of the buried chicken
he seized his saddle horn with his left hand and leaned from the
saddle in a long graceful dipping swoop. The long spur slid up
to the cantle and clung there. With his right hand he reached
for the neck of the half buried fowl. But at the last instant,
as he left the saddle, his horse shied ever so slightly away from
that suspicious object on the ground. José's clutching fingers
missed by inches, and he swept grandly by and lightly up into
his saddle again empty handed.

"That looks to be quite a trick, anyhow," observed Kenneth
with respect.

"It's a knack," agreed the Colonel, "a beginner is likely to go
off on his head. Isn't he, Puss?"

"Can you do that?" Kenneth asked.

"Of course," replied Daphne blandly. "Can't you?"

Kenneth was spared the necessity of reply. Another contestant had managed to illustrate the Colonel's remark, and had
gone off on his head; a little too long a reach, a trifle too much
weight on the bent knee, the least possible hesitation in the

pendulum-like swoop. His misfortune was greeted by laughter and ironic cheers. Several mounted men shook loose their *riatas* and loped away after his horse.

But the chicken's good luck was at an end. The next contestant caught it by the neck and rode down the course swinging it triumphantly.

"That is what I do not like," said Daphne, unexpectedly. "Poor chicken."

"The shock breaks its neck," said the Colonel, "and José will have *gallina* to-night."

"I know: but I do not like it," insisted Daphne.

The next event should have pleased her better. Here horsemen armed with long and slender lances tilted at rings suspended and swaying in the light breeze. The audience, however, evinced but a languid interest in this graceful sport. It woke up for the next event, which was a race between a man afoot and a man horseback, twenty-five yards and back. This was very exciting. The man had the advantage of his quick start and quick turn; the horse of course possessed the speed. Anybody could try who wished; and there were a number of young men who confidently matched their legs or those of their horses against the other fellow. Here was a chance to bet; and the crowd took advantage of it. Then followed, of course, horse races—mere dashes of a hundred yards or so; the roping of very lively goats, that dodged fairly under the horse's legs or into the crowd which scattered laughing; and roping and tying calves against time.

"We used to have bronco riding, and bull-dogging steers," observed the Colonel regretfully, "but that is a little rough and dangerous unless you can get the people behind fences or some sort of protection. It is better at the roundup."

"What is bull-dogging?" asked Kenneth.

"The man rides up alongside the steer, seizes him by the horns and throws him."

"I don't see how he stays on——"

"His horse? He doesn't. He leaves the saddle, and lets his horse go."

"And wrestles down a full grown steer by main strength?" cried Kenneth, incredulously.

"That's it. But it is a knack very largely."

"I certainly should like to see that."

"You shall, you shall!" cried the Colonel, heartily. "We'll get up a little rough riding one of these days and invite all the people like yourself who have not seen any of it. Let me see, you are out here for the winter?"

"Yes sir, my name is Boyd. I am staying with my father at the hotel."

"I shall remember that. And now," announced the Colonel, regretfully, "I suppose I must leave. Some of our guests will be going soon, and I would displease Mrs. Peyton if I were not there to say good-bye."

He sprang down as lightly as a boy, arranged his frock coat and his hat, and made his way slowly through the crowd, a tall and commanding figure amongst even these sturdy sons and daughters of the open. Kenneth turned to say something to his companion on the other side; but she, too, had disappeared.

V

THE shadows were long and cool, and a rose light rested on the mountains. Swallows had appeared and were darting in myriads across the sky. The meadowlarks' songs seemed louder and more liquid. A thin mist of gold dust followed the wheels of the guests departing. The vivid high brilliance of the California day had sunk to a lower key; and the vivid high brilliance of men's spirits had sunk with it. From the front steps, where once more the Colonel and his wife had taken their stand, the branches of the oaks showed very black against the pale green sky. Across the flats the westerly hills stood dark before the sunset, clearly defined, with gold edges. The blue of the heavens had lost its hard surface; it had etherealized and become translucent, so that one seemed to see millions of miles into its pale green depths. And its one doubtful star, instead of being pasted against the sky, appeared to swim somewhere at an indeterminate distance in infinite space. Under the trees the shadows stole out, breathing coolness, throwing the vagueness of twilight over well known things.

Brainerd was the last of all the guests to leave. He was waiting for Daphne, who had disappeared. Caught by the spell of the slow-descending evening he stood with his host and hostess in silence, without impatience, without thought of fatigue. Then out of the dusk came Daphne, breaking the spell.

"Where in the world have you been?" demanded Brainerd, a little impatiently. "You have kept us all waiting."

"I am sorry for that," she replied, sidling up to the Colonel and taking his hand.

"Where were you?"

"Talking to my friends," she replied vaguely.

"Well, we must get back."

"Cannot I have José drive you over?" asked the Colonel.

"No, no!" disclaimed Brainerd. "The walk will do us good."

"The light on the mountains must be very fine," suggested the Colonel. "What say, mama, don't you think it would be pleasant to walk a short distance with our friends?"

"Pleasant and salutary," laughed Allie. "I feel like a stuffed turkey after these barbecues. Everything is so good. Wait until I get my shawl."

The Colonel and Daphne sauntered on ahead, while Brainerd, seating himself on the steps, lighted a pipe and waited for Mrs. Peyton.

"Had a pleasant day, Puss?" asked the Colonel, throwing one arm around the child's shoulders.

"Simply lovely, fairy godpapa," she replied, snuggling closer to him.

"That's good, that's good," said he, raising his fine old face to peer up through the interlocking branches. They were now at the edge of the Grove under a great oak whose branches, immense as the trunks of ordinary sized trees, writhed and twisted fantastically, now reaching upward toward the low hollow dome of green, now touching the ground in their wide-flung spread. The main trunk was nearly six feet in diameter but divided at so low a height that three unobtrusive cleats nailed to its side sufficed to admit even a very small climber to the great anacondalike limbs.

"Dolman's House," said Daphne. "Let's stop a minute."

She dipped slightly away from him, but continued to hold his hand. They stood side by side looking upward.

"You used to play here all your time when you were a little girl," said the Colonel. "All by yourself. I used to see you sitting there very still on the crook of that big limb; and I used to wonder what you could be doing to sit still so long."

"Godpapa, do you believe in fairies?" demanded Daphne, abruptly.

"Well, bless my soul, what a question!" cried the Colonel, looking down in mock astonishment. "Of course I don't! What sensible man does? But," he added quaintly, lowering his voice and looking about him, "there are a few near the Fern Falls."

"That is a perfect answer," Daphne told him sedately. "Well, Dolman, I believe, is a fairy: a tree fairy. He lives in this oak. That's why I named it Dolman's House."

"I often wondered," said the Colonel.

"When I was a child I used to sit on the limb and talk to Dolman."

"Did you ever see him?"

"I can't say I ever did, but I am not sure. That is something, godpapa, that I never could understand. I ought to remember clearly enough: it wasn't so very long ago."

"Not so very," agreed the Colonel.

"But it's dim, and misty, like seeing the mountains when the fog is breaking. I sometimes think I remember clearly what happened, and then it's blotted out. I can't explain exactly——"

"I think I understand," said the Colonel. "There are some things that way with my recollections of my youth."

"Only it isn't so strange with you," said Daphne seriously, "because you are so extremely old."

"Extremely," agreed the Colonel. "But tell me more about what you do remember."

"It sounds rather silly," said Daphne. "Of course, I don't believe in it now. But I used to. Somehow I always knew of Dolman. I used to play with him—I think—he used to talk with me. It is hard to remember that it was all imagination.

I remember it as real as anything. I used to sit on the limb and he would talk to me."

"What would he say?" inquired the Colonel.

"It's hard to remember. But he was kind and he did not scold." She laughed merrily. "Wasn't it silly?"

"I don't know," said the Colonel. "How long ago did you stop talking to him?"

"I can't remember that." She hesitated shyly; then went on with more haste. "It's perfectly silly, but when I come here and sit even now to read or watch the birds and get day-dreaming or half asleep I sometimes hear him as plainly as can be, only faint and far off, not near as it used to be, as if his voice were inside me, or as if it were muffled. Then I come to with an awful start!"

"That is very interesting. What does he say?"

"I never can remember. It's just a waking dream."

"You never saw Dolman, you say?"

"No; I never did. But after I had sat quite still for some time staring out through the leaves I used to see queer things. The leaves would disappear and I would see a sort of revolving disk of gold and black. It was very bright and beautiful and went around very fast. My heart used to beat so with excitement, and I would try to keep on seeing it, but I never could hold it longer than a moment or so. When I saw it my eyes seemed sort of unfocussed; and they always would come back focussed again. It was lovely, and I used to think Dolman showed it to me."

"How long since you have seen that?"

"Oh, years! But I can shut my eyes and see it sometimes yet. Memory, I suppose. It is not so bright and it moves more slowly than it used to. I can sometimes *almost* make out the pattern on it." She hesitated, and crept closer to him: "God-father, you mustn't laugh. I told you I couldn't remember anything Dolman told me. That isn't so. There is only one thing but I remember that very clearly. He said that when the disk stopped and I could make out the design on it, I would die."

The Colonel laughed. "What quaint ideas little children have, don't they, Puss?" he said in a matter-of-fact voice.

"No, but listen, godpapa: here is something I never told a soul. Promise you won't tell?"

"I promise."

"Not even Aunt Allie?"

"Not even Aunt Allie."

"Well, you remember that Miss Mathews, who visited you last spring, and how I found the watch she lost?"

"Perfectly."

"We all looked everywhere for it, and she felt so badly about it because it belonged to her mother. I was very sorry for her. While I was looking I came out here to Dolman's House. And I heard him just as plainly as when I was a child. He said: 'She dropped it when she was picking flowers'; and I found out that she had been picking flowers away up the cañon near the falls; and I went up there and found it almost first crack. How do you 'splain that?"

She was staring up at him, her face showing pale through the dusk, her eyes wide with excitement.

"I declare you do believe in Dolman!" accused the Colonel, in a light tone designed to relieve the tension, "and I'm almost inclined to myself. I would if he would tell me where I left my second-best hat."

At this moment Brainerd's voice was heard hailing them. They answered.

"Oh, there you are," he observed, slouching forward with Mrs. Peyton. "Wonder you wouldn't hide. Come, Daffy, it's very late."

Daphne made her required little speeches of thanks.

"I am going to make some marmalade to-morrow afternoon," Mrs. Peyton told her. "Better come over and make some, too. I'll show you my new recipe."

"I will, Aunt Allie. Good-night," replied Daphne. She moved away sedately for ten yards, then came flying back all swirl and legs, seized the Colonel and Mrs. Peyton, hugged and kissed them tempestuously, and was off again.

"She's a dear child," said Mrs. Peyton, rearranging her somewhat rumpled plumage. "I wish she had more young folks to play with."

"She has me," contended the Colonel.

"Oh, *you!* I didn't say an infant to care for!"

The Colonel put his arm around her and they sauntered back toward the twinkling lights of the ranch house.

"Happy day, sweetheart?" he asked.

"Do you know, Richard," she said soberly, "that we are very lucky people? We have each other, and dear friends, and live in this wonderful country, and have all the wealth we need——"

A white figure loomed before them and the Colonel withdrew his arm rather hastily.

"You catch cold," commanded Sing Toy. "You come in house light away!"

CHAPTER II

I

IN SPITE of the festivities of the day before, the Colonel was up betimes. He liked the early morning and was never late abed; but to-day he had a duty to perform, a self-imposed duty that twice a week took him to town. Without breakfast he picked up his hat, kissed the bustling Allie, and took his stately way down toward the stables. The hat he picked up was not his customary flat brimmed Stetson. It was a silk hat of some queer vintage, also flat brimmed, very straight in the crown, a typical old "stove pipe." By it everybody from dogs and children up knew that the Colonel was going to drive to town.

He entered the stable and looked around, experiencing the same warm subconscious satisfaction in his surroundings as when he looked up through his Cathedral Oaks. It was a beautiful stable, high and clean, well lighted. The woodwork was all brightly varnished. Ornamental designs in straw and grain heads were laid cunningly above the doors; fancy tufts of the same material bound with red tape ornamented the tops of the posts between stalls. The drinking troughs were of white enamel. A huge cabinet with sliding glass panels and lined with red felt contained the well oiled harnesses with polished metal. Saddles were neatly arranged on trees projecting from the walls. Over each box-stall had been screwed a brass plate showing the name of the occupant.

This occupied one wing. The high central part of the stables was the carriage room with various equipages. Its floor was covered lightly with sand on which engaging patterns had been marked with a broom. Here two Mexicans were engaged in harnessing a fine pair of chestnuts to a light wagon. The other

wing was the cow stable. Its arrangements were slightly different, but it possessed the same ornaments, the same sweet
cleanliness, and the same brass plates over the milking stalls
showing the names of the cows. The latter were in pasture
at this time of day, of course; but the bull was in a small corral
built around a tree. That was his habitual abiding place, a fine
stocky animal, with a curled front like Jove. He also had a
brass plate which was attached to the tree. It bore the name
Brigham Young, and the names over the cowstalls were those
of the Mormon prophet's favourite wives. This was the
Colonel's little joke at which Allie always pretended to be
greatly scandalized.

By now the team was hitched and ready. The Colonel lifted
the covers of two big wicker hampers in the wagon body, peered
within, then mounted the seat and drove off down the palm-
bordered road. The Mexicans wished him a *vaya con dios*. As
he passed the kitchen door Sing Toy pretended to empty ashes
in order to hurl at him an admonition. Allie waved her handkerchief. The Colonel felt particularly well and happy. It
was a fine morning without fog, which of course meant heat
later; but now the air was fresh and cool. The horses shied
playfully toward each other, pricking their ears.

At the corner where the palm drive turned into the *Camino
Real*, Daphne sat on the top rail of the fence. She was dressed
to-day in a plain wash frock of blue and a wide straw hat, but
her hair was as unruly and her legs as leggy as ever. At sight
of her the Colonel pulled up at once and set the brakes. Every
California vehicle of those days, no matter how light, had brakes.
Daphne came between the wheels and extended her hand.

"Good morning, Puss!" cried the Colonel, fumbling absent-
mindedly in his pocket to produce a peppermint lozenge.

"Now, godpapa! At this time of the morning! Without
breakfast!" she reproved him.

"I beg your pardon, my dear. And without doubt you meant
to add 'at my age'." He leaned over the back of the seat and
raised the cover of the nearest hamper. "By way of amends
permit me to offer the very first of my nosegays."

Daphne took the quaint little bouquet.

"Thank you. And now move over, for I am going in to have breakfast with you."

They drove on down the white road with the long shadows across it, and into town and the grounds of the Fremont Hotel. Here three bellboys rushed out at sight of them. One took charge of the team, while the other two carried the hampers into the hotel. Down the street the bland faced clock on the Clock Building showed at seven twenty.

The Colonel and Daphne followed the hampers across the broad high veranda, through the cool high office with the grouped easy chairs and the coco matting floors, down a long narrow hall with windows on both sides of it, and so to a pair of frosted doors flanked by hatracks. The frosted doors said *closed* most uncompromisingly, but they yielded to the Colonel's touch. They were in the dining room.

It was a long, wide, lofty, airy apartment, with many narrow, high windows looking out into foliage. A score of black-clad waitresses stood upright among the snowy tables awaiting the seven-thirty hour of official opening. By the frosted door was an elderly rather obese negro with gray wool. The latter had a full dress suit, white gloves, a ramrod down his neck and the self-contained dignity of a mud-turtle. When he moved it was as though a fanfare of trumpets had been heard. He was the headwaiter, and a very good one. In that simple age the sole requirements of a headwaiter were presence, dignity, side. The fact that a duke ushers you in with respect implies that you are several pegs above a duke, does it not?

The bellboys deposited the hampers by a centrally placed table and withdrew. The Colonel and Daphne seated themselves and attacked the first course of the breakfast that was promptly brought them. After a few moments the coloured person threw wide the portals—that is the only way to describe it. And shortly appeared the first comers to the morning meal: a prosperous but plain looking citizen and his mouse-like wife.

Instantly the Colonel was afoot. He dived into his hampers and came forth with another of the nosegays and a pair of fine oranges. With these he approached the guests.

"Good morning; good morning!" he greeted them, genially. "I trust you have slept well."

Somewhat surprised they stammered back a sort of response.

"I want you to try these oranges," the Colonel swept on. "They are of exceptionally fine stock—budded direct from the original Bahia trees. And, madam, permit me to offer you a little sample of our California flowers to greet you this morning."

And the Colonel bowed most gallantly and withdrew. A moment later the tourists might have been observed making low-toned inquiries of the waitress.

But now the guests were arriving frequently. The Colonel was very busy with his fruit and his bouquets. The latter he presented only to the ladies. To almost everybody he and his bi-weekly custom were well known. Then people came west to spend the winter, and settled down in one place. The season was now nearly over as the pleasantest time of the year approached! Colonel Peyton was among old acquaintances, and he thoroughly enjoyed himself. With each he had time for only a word or so, but he managed always to flatter the ladies!

"You are a bad old man!" said one white haired and stately dowager, "and I am half-minded to make you take back your nosegay!"

"The blossoms are blameless, at least," quoth the Colonel, "why punish them?"

At the round table in the middle of the room reserved for unattached men, a discontented looking flashily dressed new-comer expressed his surprise at the whole performance, wondering among other things why the Colonel did it or was permitted to do it.

"Well," drawled a lank Middle-Westerner with a toothpick. "He's allowed to because he owns this hotel."

"Oh, I see," sneered the first speaker. "Slick advertising, eh?"

It might have been good advertising, but any one watching the Colonel would have realized that he was enjoying it thoroughly. His face beamed, his eyes glowed, his old-fashioned manners became more elaborate, his wit and compliments more spontaneous. He sailed on a flood tide of goodfeeling. The Middle-Westerner expressed something of this.

"Lemme tell you, he don't have to advertise this hotel. Why should he? There's no competition."

"There's the San Antonio down the street."

"Colonel Peyton owns that, too."

"Then why the hell all this monkey-doodle business?"

"Because he likes it. If you can understand that!"

The tourist turned to survey the last speaker, the indignant waitress.

"Hullo, sister," he said coolly. "Who let you in this?"

About half past eight the rush slackened and the Colonel, glowing with delight, was enabled to return to the table where Daphne sat and finish his breakfast.

"I tell you, Puss," he cried, "where would they find another place in the world with a sun and sky like this! Think of it back East where they came from! Snow, ice, wind! Cannot understand why anybody should want to live there."

Truth to tell a good many of his guests were beginning vaguely to wonder about that themselves, and other hotel men's guests all over Southern California. Railroad travel across the plains was still a good deal of an adventure, nor to be lightly undertaken. People settled down for a week. They got acquainted with everybody else on the train, and visited back and forth, and even got up charades and entertainments. Every party had an elaborate hamper with tin compartments in which was great store of bread and rolls and chicken and other delicacies. Three or four times a day the train stopped out in the middle of nowhere and the passengers ran about the landscape to get the kinks out of their legs. At the end of a half hour the whistle was blown summoning them back. Buffalo were still to be seen in great numbers—indeed, not infrequently the engine had to stop to let herds of them across the tracks—and other wild animals, and wilder men. After the long, strange cold journey the tepid air, smiling landscape, and brooding mountains of California were inexpressibly grateful. The newcomer saw oranges for the first time—and was invited in to pick all he wanted to eat; and free flowers anywhere for the asking; and interestingly strange orientals. He looked out in the freshness of morning on a riot of white roses climbing over the roof below his hotel window, and across palms and pepper trees and orange groves to distant, azure, snow-capped mountains. He breathed the soft caressing air laden with perfume. His ears were filled with the buzzing of bees and humming birds, the warblings of many songsters. His eyes drank in the sunpatched world before him. He remembered that snow and ice and wind mentioned by the Colonel. And he lifted up his spirit in the sentiment expressed aloud by one tourist.

"Why *should* anybody die out here? They'll never get any nearer to heaven!"

Since the journey was long, short visits were unknown. People came in December and stayed through until June at least. By that time the country had them. They returned to their homes as insufferable nuisances. The exceeding pleasantness of Southern California was a new thing: it had not been described and over-described and advertised and made most of. The tourist had the intense proselyting zeal of one who discovers something, and has something new to tell. The term "California Liar" became current about this time. It was a misnomer. The "California Liar" was generally some Easterner or Middle-Westerner trying to translate super-enthusiasm into his native dialect.

Generally he returned the following winter and the next, until he became an habitué—provided he had the means and the leisure. If he had not these, he did one of two things: either he continued where he was and was either ignored or killed off by exasperated neighbours; or else he sold out and moved to his discovered heaven. There were a great many of the latter class; and more were coming every year. They were buying ten, twenty, forty acres and making themselves homes. Incidentally they were planting things, more or less as amusement or to keep occupied; and, astonishingly, some of them were making money. The two parent trees of Bahia navel oranges had budded thousands of old seedling stock. People were discovering irrigation. The land was stirring from its long sleep.

A small, dapper, quick-moving man entered the dining room and made his way directly to the Colonel's table. This was Watson, manager of the hotel. He carried a sheaf of papers which he deployed and on which he proceeded to comment in a rapid-fire sort of fashion. The Colonel listened, his eyes roving here and there about the dining room. Apparently he was listening with only half his mind, for he constantly threw in comments utterly irrelevant to the matters in hand.

"I wish you would step down for a moment and I will show you what I mean. The arrangements are becoming totally inadequate; and yet I hate with the present ledger showing to undertake more expense."

"I shall be delighted to do so, but not this morning," the Colonel answered him. "If the arrangements are not adequate, we must make them so. That goes without saying. Can't do things without things to do them with!"

"But, Colonel, the expense seems——"

"Pardon, it isn't a matter of expense. It's a matter of whether we've got to have them or not—don't you see? Have them installed, by all means, if you are fully of the opinion that we cannot get on without them."

"I wouldn't hesitate for a moment," worried the little manager, "if it weren't for the fact that our last statement——"

"Oh, I see!" beamed the Colonel, "why did you beat around the bush, Watson. It's ready money. Why didn't you say so? How much do you need?"

"Here is the statement," said the manager, "it is not as encouraging as I should like to have had it. If you will permit me to run over the items with you, I think I can explain——"

"I should be delighted to have you do so, Watson, and I will make it a point to drop into your office for that express purpose," said the Colonel, folding the statement and thrusting it into his inner pocket, "but not just at present. I haven't time. But I will drop in at the bank and make arrangements with Mr. Mills. Rest easy on that."

He arose from the table and held out his hand to the perplexed little manager.

"Don't worry, Watson," he said kindly. "If we have run behind a trifle lately, I can understand. There are undoubtedly a great many things to be considered."

He bowed with courtly politeness to the girl who had waited

on him, looked vaguely about him for Daphne, who had long since disappeared, and took his way out of the dining room, bowing right and left as he went. The wonderful negro held open the frosted doors—again "closed," as it was after nine o'clock. He alone of all those present managed to play up.

The pressure of the Colonel's affairs, that had prevented his giving time to Watson's explanations, seemed to lift somewhat when he had gained the wide, low, rail-less veranda. It was now well occupied. Ladies sat in deep rocking chairs; men walked up and down, or leaned over the ladies, or lounged smoking against the big square pillars. Children raced back and forth. It was approaching the hour of the daily ride. Practically all those not actually on the verge of the bedridden were preparing to sally forth on horseback. Everybody rode horseback, whether they knew how or not. It was in the air. Grandmothers who had never seen a sawhorse tried it on. The tiniest children, their legs sticking straight out across the backs of gentle beasts went forth in coveys under charge of steady old Spaniards. There were all degrees of skill, and there were all types of costume. The women rode side saddle and were encumbered with long skirts which they hooked up when afoot. The men used the stock saddle with high horns, with long stirrups hanging straight under the body, with flapping *tapaderos*—stirrup covers—that made a gay sound when they loped. Wide portable horseblocks with little flights of steps stood around for those to whom their own horses appeared like two-story buildings, however small the other fellow's horse might look. Some of the young ladies, however, were able by placing their feet in the cupped hands of their cavaliers to spring neatly into their saddles from the ground; and some of the said cavaliers loved to vault to their seats without touching stirrup at all. There was a great deal of clanking about, for all of the younger men and most of the older wore the huge loose-fitting big rowelled Spanish spurs that dragged and rattled on the floor.

The Spanish lads from the stables were continually trotting up, each leading four or five saddle horses which they tied to the iron rails. The names of the riders had been written on cards attached to the pommels. Old Patterson rode solemnly up with his string. They were noted as being the gentlest and fattest horses in town. Old Patterson hired them and himself all together in one flock, and would not hire them otherwsie. He was a solemn person with a large beard and a silver whistle. When he blew the latter the riders must instantly pull down to a walk from the very gentle lope. Patterson's horses, it is said, had never yet sweat in their long and useful lives. His convoy was naturally affected by the infants, the beginners and the ultra timid. These unfortunates were looked down upon with derision by other youngsters, who delighted in dashing madly by or through, to old Patterson's monumental indignation. Don Enrique also made his usual spectacular entry. Don Enrique was a very impressive looking elderly Spaniard, also with a large beard. He was ornamental, and therefore had been asked to lead so many parades and *fiestas* that they had ended by going to his head. He was never quite happy unless he was showing off. To this end he had spent most of his substance on a wonderful saddle and bridle. There was marvellously involved carved leather work, and about twenty pounds of silver in corners, buttons and *conchas*, and I don't know what all else. The Don had a very good horse and was an excellent horseman. He came dashing at a dead run through the gates headed at full speed toward the veranda until it seemed he would leap through the crowd, but pulled up within three feet. The horse fairly sat on its haunches and slid. A fine spray of gravel fanned out in front. Some women shrieked softly. Don Enrique, oblivious to all mundane affairs, his swarthy, handsome countenance set in a far off frown, swung from the saddle with one magnificent motion, threw the reins over his horse's head with another, and stalked clanking and unseeing across the veranda and into the office. The horse, trained to stand "tied to the ground," rolled his bit musically and stared straight ahead with a lofty air of conscious virtue.

Colonel Peyton watched this lively scene, his hands beneath his coat tails. Daphne appeared and stood beside him. After a time Kenneth Boyd came out, greeting them with a flash of his attractive smile

"I suppose you are going riding?" observed the Colonel genially.

"No sir, not this morning."

"But you do ride, I suppose?"

"I've ridden under English masters since I was seven years old," rejoined Kenneth, a little touched in his young pride that he should be even half-doubted of this manly accomplishment. Then he caught Daphne's cool level look and turned away flushing hotly. It was a perfectly respectful look, such as a gangle-legged child should give a glorious youth, but there was something in its depths Kenneth did not like. It was something too old for her! he told himself.

"You should have a horse of your own," the Colonel was saying kindly. "That is the only way to get satisfaction. The livery horses are very fair, but they are ridden by everybody, and they are ridden too much. You can buy horses here very cheap. Indeed, it is much like old days still. Then, you know, if you borrowed an outfit they did not much care whether you returned the horse or not provided you returned the saddle and bridle." He laughed contagiously at his little joke.

"How much do you suppose I could buy a horse for?" inquired Kenneth, interested.

"Twenty-five dollars," replied the Colonel, also getting interested, "and they'd take care of him for you for ten dollars a month. If you decided to get one, I might suggest something."

"Mr. Boyd would not want to ride one of our range horses," put in Daphne. Her tone was absolutely candid, but Kenneth flushed again. "They would hardly interest anybody who had taken lessons and could really ride. He ought to have something like Gipsy."

"Puss, you're an extravagant little piece," said the Colonel. "Do you realize that Gipsy is a Kentucky mare? She's a fine animal, too fine to buy and sell again in a month or two. Our range horses are very good, if you pick them right."

"I was just thinking of what Mr. Boyd said about his riding masters," said Daphne meekly.

At this moment a group loped up to the veranda and drew rein. It was led by a very dashing figure in a bottle green habit topped by a little forward-tilted chip hat. Kenneth, in relief, recognized Dora Stanley; and, with a murmured word of farewell to the Colonel, hastened to the edge of the veranda. That Brainerd kid was certainly fresh! A regular little brat, Kenneth decided resentfully.

"Well, Puss," said the Colonel. "I suppose we must be getting along, if we are to meet the boat."

"I want to see Mrs. Fortney," said Daphne. "I don't believe I'll go to the boat. Pick me up, please, on your way back."

"This is desertion!" cried the Colonel, in mock dismay.

"Take somebody else with you," suggested Daphne unmoved, "take the square jolly man: he looks like good company."

So it happened that Patrick Boyd joined the Colonel and they drove away together behind the chestnuts.

"The ship gets in this morning, and I have to be here," explained the Colonel, "—to see about the tourists and all such matters. If you just want to potter about—if you have nothing especial to do——"

They drove out of the hotel grounds, but instead of turning down the main street the Colonel tooled the chestnuts carefully on a slant across the high projecting ridges of the street car rails and so to a pepper-shaded side street. The light vehicle swayed and pitched over the metals, so that Boyd had fairly to hold on.

"I should think the town would make the company grade those things down," he growled, "they're liable to take off a wheel."

"Oh, it's a sort of makeshift affair," replied the Colonel easily. "Have you seen it?"

"Yes, I've seen it—and tried it."

"You'll appreciate the story they tell about it, then. They say a stranger saw it going down the street one day, and boarded it. 'Say', said he to the driver, 'I no *sabe* how this thing goes. Seems to slide along all by itself.' The driver looked over the dashboard. 'Hanged if those mules haven't crawled under the car again,' he said." The Colonel laughed heartily at this, one of this three favourite stories. Boyd laughed too, but could not forbear adding a word to his first criticism.

"Just the same I should think your Common Council would force them to put these tracks in some sort of shape."

"I suppose they will, some day," rejoined the Colonel, cheerfully. "We are sort of used to it."

"Where are we going over here?" asked Boyd, "I thought you said we were going to meet the ship."

"Plenty of time," replied the Colonel. "Here we are."

He drew rein beneath some wide overarching peppers before a picket fence. The sidewalks in this part of town—for that matter in any part of town off the main street—were of hard earth. Behind the picket fence was a small, white one-storied house of the commonplace box architecture of the early 'eighties. It was glorified, however, by a riot of bright flowers, growing in the lavish profusion that only Southern California can show. The Colonel fumbled in one of his hampers—which had been replaced—captured a flat basket of oranges lurking in its apparently inexhaustible depths, and pushed inside the fence. His tall figure with its "stove pipe" hat seemed to stoop in order to enter the tiny house. He did not ring or knock, but entered the sitting room, which he found empty. Thence he proceeded to explore, prowling about the premises, until at length in a little shed back of the kitchen he found a young woman in an enveloping apron, her hair covered by a mob cap, her sleeves rolled up, busy at a wash tub. She flushed a little when she saw the Colonel. The latter was quite unconscious and unembarrassed, however. He perched his long form on a work bench, thrust back his tall hat.

"So here you are," he cried, cheerfully, "looking fresh as a rose! I brought you a few oranges, my dear."

He perched, swinging one leg, for a few moments, chatting; then bade farewell and rejoined Boyd.

"Nice little couple, there," he told the latter as he took the reins. "Friends of mine. Came out from the East last year. Husband has just a touch of lungs, I think though that's just a guess. Happy as a pair of turtle doves. I like to drop in to see them. Does me good."

He turned around and headed back toward Main Street. But on the way they passed a very imposing place. It occupied a full quarter block, was planted with fine old trees, and a semicircular driveway inside the grounds swept up to and past the house. The latter was of wood and ran greatly to peaked towers and woodwork. The boards were laid in patterns around and above the window frames, the posts and rails of the veranda were lathed into graceful bulges, the roof line bristled with vertebrae of scroll fretwork like the backbone of a fossil fish. It had stained glass, and a certain proportion of iron railings and grills, and a pair of stone lions. Indeed, it might fairly be called a mansion.

"We might see if Mrs. Stanley is home," hesitated the Colonel.

"It doesn't seem just the hour for a call," said Boyd.

"Oh, we won't call," cried the Colonel. "We'll just drop in and see her. I'd like to have you meet her. She's a very fine woman."

He turned in to the drive and hitched the chestnuts to the usual rail.

"There she is now!" he cried, and started impetuously down a gravelled walk toward a distant figure. Boyd followed slowly and a little uncomfortably. It was, as he had said, no conventional hour, and Mrs. Stanley looked to be in no conventional attire nor engaged in conventional occupation. He saw a tall gaunt figure that moved widely and freely like a man. Her skirts were quite frankly pinned around her waist, exposing serviceable coloured petticoats. She wore long gauntlets and a sunbonnet from which escaped wild gray hair. Her face was large featured. In her left hand she carried an old painter's bucket into which from time to time she deposited treasure trove found under the leaves.

But she displayed no embarrassment at being thus caught.

"How do you do, Mr. Boyd," she acknowledged the introduction in a deep voice. "Newcomer, eh? Then you don't know yet what beasts snails are. They eat everything you plant."

"Medill says quick lime——" began the Colonel.

"Medill is a fool," stated Mrs. Stanley. "The only thing that does the slightest good is ducks. And I won't have the silly quacking things about the place. Do as I do: pick 'em and put them in salt."

"Very likely you are right. Of course, I have ducks on the ranch, and that may be the reason I am never bothered," said the Colonel. "You certainly have wonderful roses. I've not seen such deep colour anywhere else."

"Then it's your own fault," boomed Mrs. Stanley. "It's a matter of nails, iron filings, old cans. Bury 'em at the roots. Anybody can do it who who will take the trouble."

"That is worth knowing, isn't it, Boyd," commented the Colonel cheerfully. "But you have one rosebud whose bloom is not due to iron filings."

"Which one is that?" demanded Mrs. Stanley, casting her commanding eye about her.

"I refer to Dora," said the Colonel, gallantly. "She has grown into a beauty."

"Oh, Dora! Yes, she has a good complexion. Nothing mysterious about it. Fresh air, wholesome food, open air exercise, no late hours. Mothers are fools. They let their children go traipsing around at all hours eating messes and then wonder they look sallow and sick. Perfect nonsense!"

"I daresay you are right," was the Colonel's comment, "of course you are: the results show for themselves. Still, young people are young—seems to me when I was that age the most blissful thing in the world was to dance the whole night through. And the dance just at dawn was the best of all. We have to allow something for the young spirit."

"Young fiddlesticks!" said Mrs. Stanley, energetically. "Just a nonsensical idea. I think the way the modern child is allowed to run wild without self control or discipline is a scandal. I do my duty by my children, and I expect them to have a sense of responsibility. I furnish them with opportunity for every healthful amusement, and give them free rein; but I do not allow them to stuff or sit up all hours."

"I daresay you are right," repeated the Colonel, "of course you are. Well, we must be going. Remember me to Dora and to Winchester. You certainly have fine roses."

"Good-bye. Glad you dropped in. Glad to have made your acquaintance, Mr. Boyd. Come again and see me." She stooped her gaunt frame, raised a leaf, and pounced on what

it concealed. "Salt dissolves 'em," she remarked to the re-
treating gentlemen. Boyd had not spoken a word. He felt
somehow rather overridden. The Colonel did not seem to feel
it. On the way to the team he commented cheerily on the
various plants and trees and the cast-iron fountain of two children
under an umbrella from the tip of which spouted the water.
Only after the team was again under way did he revert to the
subject of their hostess.

"A most remarkable woman," he repeated. "Great common
sense; very firm."

"Has she a husband?" asked Boyd, with entire conviction
that Mr. Stanley must long since have passed on. This proved
to be the case.

"She has two children. Winchester is sixteen, and Dora
about eighteen," the Colonel told him. "They have been
brought up by an almost perfect regimen. They are very handsome, healthy, spirited children. Mrs. Stanley has been fully
justified—up to now."

"Up to now?"

"Boyd, don't be a humbug!" admonished the Colonel cheerily.
"You've been young, and you probably have an excellent
memory. At the ages of sixteen and eighteen, would you have
hated anything worse than being treated still as though you
were twelve? And would you have wanted a more fascinating
game to beat than that?"

"You think there's trouble coming in the Stanley family?"

"Oh, I wouldn't say trouble. Just a little shock, I hope. It
may mean trouble, of course. I think Mrs. Stanley is making a
mistake; but it is only because she doesn't realize they're grown
up. Parents rarely do until something happens. There isn't
any dividing line. They go on thinking them as they used to
be. Then something happens. I've seen it so many times.
Dora will stay out after hours at a dance; or Winchester will
take a drink—some little thing that would be rather terrible in
a child but nothing in a grown-up. Then everything will depend
on how Mrs. Stanley takes it. Dangerous time, Boyd, dangerous time!"

He chirped to his horses; and continued:

"I think it's lucky when it happens young. I've seen it go on until a boy is in his twenties before the thing happened— before they got into the new relations. That's a pity. It's more difficult. I wish Dora would throw her slipper over the moon. I really do. Unpleasant! Good Lord! But it's got to come, and it makes me nervous waiting for it."

"You are quite a philosopher, Colonel," said Boyd. He thought of Kenneth, and realized with a pang that he had really never considered the matter of their relations at all. Did he hold Ken as boy or man? It was something to think about. "How many children have you, Colonel?" he asked.

The Colonel considered a moment.

"Twenty-nine," he replied.

Boyd started. "I should not have thought it," he recovered himself. "Are they—that is—is the present Mrs. Peyton your first wife?"

The Colonel chuckled delightedly.

"Mrs. Peyton is my first and only wife, and we have neither chick nor child of our own," he explained, "but I have twenty-nine children around this place just the same. I'm not sure but it is thirty—I like the looks of that lad of yours, Boyd."

They were driving down the long length of Main Street now. The Colonel was busy responding to salutations. It was the shopping hour; and this was the era of personal shopping. Buggies, surries, phaetons with fringed canopy tops, saddle horses stood hitched to rails and posts the full length of the street. Ladies under gay parasols were conversing in the middle of the sidewalk, or selected vegetables or fruits from the displays in the open windows. Mexicans lounged in front of the saloons. Shopkeepers who for the moment did no business stood in their doorways. Down a side street Boyd looked into Chinatown—a collection of battered old frame and adobe buildings that mysteriously had been lifted sheer from squalor to splendid romance by no other means than red paper, varnished ducks, rattan baskets, calico partitions, exotic smells and a brooding, spiritual atmosphere of the orient. They passed the San Antonio hotel which the Colonel casually mentioned as his own.

"There are always a number of people no gentleman would

want to entertain in his home," he told the astonished Boyd. "I had to have some place for them."

Soon they reached the beach, a semicircle of yellow sands three miles long flanked by cliffs and rocks, with a lagoon running in from the sea, and small scattered shacks with drying nets and the odour of fish and abalone. A lazy surf dropped languidly. Sea birds wheeled and screamed or sailed in long steady processions across a tranquil sea. The smell of kelp was in the air.

It was low tide and the wet sands were exposed. On the hard, stoneless beach riding parties could be seen; and before them, when they galloped, the flash of white as of miniature snow squalls where the sanderlings wheeled in flight. The long swells rose and sucked back among the pilings of the wharf, draining and freshening the numberless barnacles, *toredos*, starfish, and sea urchins that crusted them; or lifting and letting fall their long sea tresses. The wharf was over a half mile long and ended in a platform that held many buildings, like a little city. The chestnuts trotted briskly over the hollow sounding boards.

"We're just about in time," observed the Colonel, pointing with his whip.

A cloud of black smoke was rising above the cliffs where the coast bent. After a moment the ship appeared and turned in toward the wharf. As she turned she fired a cannon. After a few seconds the report reached them; and after a long interval the echoes began faintly to return from the mountains. For Arguello had no railroad as yet. The traveller must either take a two days' stage ride, or come thus by water. The steamer was one of the most important facts in Arguello's life; and she knew it, and conducted herself accordingly with pomp and the firing of guns. Later, when the Southern Pacific completed its spur, she was content to sneak in quietly.

On the big platform at the end of the wharf quite a crowd was gathered. The long hotel busses had backed up side by side, and their runners were standing ready at their sterns. The Colonel drove alongside and stopped.

The steamer docked with the usual bustle and confusion, and the passengers streamed down the gang plank and toward the busses through a passage between two ropes. The Colonel became alert. As each passenger or group came to the runners he made a sign with his whip. The runners caught it and shunted the passenger to one or the other of the waiting busses. Thus Colonel Peyton segregated the sheep from the goats, sending the former to the Fremont and the latter to the San Antonio. At times there was a little argument from someone who had been to Arguello before and who had ideas as to where he wanted to stop. But this did him little good.

"There are no rooms left at the Fremont," said the runner of the San Antonio: a statement corroborated on appeal by the Fremont official. If the individual proved obstinate and said he would go see for himself, no objection was made. But the clerk, tipped off by the porter, who in turn had been tipped off by the runner, was very sorry, but——

All this the Colonel explained to Boyd in answer to questions while the initial stage of selection was going on.

"I look on the Fremont as a little different from the usual hotel," he explained, sincerely. "People come there to spend the whole season; and they like to get acquainted with each other and I like to get acquainted with them. So, naturally, you don't want anybody there you would not care to know."

When the busload should arrive at the Fremont, and should go to their rooms, they would find there baskets of roses with the Colonel's personal card. And when they left, whether their stay had been three months or three days, they would be presented, to refresh the journey, with a basket of fine fruit, again with Colonel Peyton's personal card. It was his custom.

II

THE Colonel drove rapidly back to the hotel.

"I am sorry to desert you so abruptly, sir," he said courteously, "but I have considerable business now to attend. I trust we shall meet often."

"It has been a most interesting morning," returned Boyd. "You may see more of me than you want. The more I see of our climate and surroundings here, the better I like them."

He watched the Colonel drive away with Daphne again by his side.

"Most extraordinary old cuss I ever saw," he remarked to one of his cronies who joined him. This was Marcus Oberman, a brewer from Milwaukee: small, white, wizened, wrinkled, not at all like a brewer, but playing a remarkably good hand at poker. "Fine old chap. He seems to have more interests here than you would think. Make this hotel pay, do you think?"

"Don't see how he can," cackled Oberman, "but he makes us comfortable and that's all that worries me."

"This is going to be a wonderful valley, Oberman, you mark my words. There's no climate like it in the world. And nowhere will you get a combination like this of mountains and the sea. Look at the flowers. It's a garden spot. The day will come when there'll be fine homes all over these foothills. The man who buys real estate and holds it is bound to make money."

"The place is as dead as pickled herring," said Oberman. "Did you ever in your born days see such streets, such lighting, such sewers, such everything? A town of this size! Disgraceful, I call it!"

"They're asleep. Just needs someone to wake them up."

"Well, I'm no alarm clock. I'm having a good time. As for making money, I know a trick worth two of that." He made a motion as though spreading a hand of cards.

"Now I can prove you wrong there, at any rate," said Boyd. "Come on, you old Dutch pirate; let's find the gang."

The Colonel drove directly to the Clock Building and pulled up.

"I'll be gone some little time," he told Daphne. "If you want, I'll hitch the team and you can play around." But Daphne preferred to sit and wait; so the Colonel entered the bank.

He made his way, bowing to the men behind the grilles, directly to the frosted door that led into Oliver Mills's office. This was customarily on the latch; but an alert and active clerk had already flitted around to slip the bolt, so the Colonel entered without delay.

"Good morning, Oliver," he greeted the banker, who half arose, "I trust I find you well."

"Quite well, Colonel, and yourself and Mrs. Peyton?"

The Colonel carefully deposited his stove-pipe hat bottom up on the desk top, spread his coat tails and sat down.

"Fine! Fine! Do you know, Oliver, you were a disgrace at my party yesterday?"

"Disgrace!" echoed Mills blankly, turning his bulging blue eyes on the Colonel.

"I had my eye on you. The way you carried on with Mrs. Stanley was a scandal. We are all much interested."

"I assure you," cried Mills earnestly, his naturally ruddy face deepening in colour, "you are quite mistaken, Colonel, quite. I esteem Mrs. Stanley and I am aware of her widowed condition and the extent of her property interests; but her possibility as an amorous vis-à-vis never has entered my head!"

The Colonel eyed him with twinkling eyes.

"You greatly relieve my mind, Oliver," he said with entire gravity. "But I must get home to dinner to-day, so I cannot go further into your domestic troubles. I just dropped in to get a little money."

Mills was eyeing him suspiciously, evidently still red and indignant, but uncertain.

"Our cashier will fix you up—how much will you want?" reaching to strike a silver call bell.

But the Colonel restrained the movement.

"No, no, Oliver, it is not a matter of currency. You misunderstand me. I want a loan."

"How much?"

"I don't know—ten or fifteen thousand, I should think."

Mills reached for an indexed desk book and consulted it.

"Collateral security, Colonel?" he asked.

"No; put it on the property."

Mills closed the book slowly. He was evidently worried and a little embarrassed.

"Is this for personal use, Colonel?" he asked.

The Colonel straightened.

"Egad, Mr. Mills," he said gently. "I cannot see the bearing of that question. Is not my credit good?"

"Perfectly, perfectly," Mills hastened, "my question was awkwardly expressed. I want to know whether this loan is for personal use, for use on the hotel properties, or on the ranchos."

"I still fail to see what bearing my use of the money has to do with the question. Egad, sir, I cannot forbear pointing out that in thirty years in this community this is the first time any difficulty has been made over the loan of so paltry a sum!"

"Now, Colonel," returned Mills, "you must not blame me for asking simple financial questions. There is no difficulty whatever making the loan. But it must be remembered that part of my duty to my stockholders and depositors is to know something about where their money goes. You are borrowing on your property, but I have no knowledge as to whether this money is to be spent inside the property for its improvement, or outside with no return."

The Colonel thought a moment.

"Possibly you are correct there, Oliver. I do not pretend to know a great deal of the banking business." The banker's brow cleared. He did not want to hurt the Colonel's feelings with the direct statement:—that the Colonel's borrowings on his property had already passed the point where general credit, is good, and was approaching the point where details would have to be looked into a little. "This loan is to fill out some trifling needs at the Fremont."

"How is the Fremont doing lately?"

"Splendidly; splendidly! We have as lovely a lot of people as you would find anywhere in the country; and all are pleased and satisfied. I fully believe all our friends intend to return next winter."

"That is good; but I mean financially."

"Watson gave me the figures this morning; I've got them somewhere. Here you are," said the Colonel, handing over the statement he had stowed away in his inside pocket.

Mills went through the foolscap sheets carefully.

"This does not seem to be as good a showing as we might expect from the very crowded season we have enjoyed," he suggested at last.

"I haven't looked over the figures," said the Colonel, "but as you know, the money end does not concern me so much. We should have a hotel here, worthy of our town, worthy of the people who come here. I cannot adopt a niggardly attitude toward my guests; that goes without saying."

"I appreciate that, Colonel; the bank appreciates it; in fact I feel safe to say the whole town appreciates it. But," he turned to his desk book, "Richard, the Fremont has run behind eight thousand dollars a month for the past year."

"God bless my soul! You don't say so!" cried the Colonel, a little dashed. "I had never figured it out. But improvements—there's the San Antonio—one must strike an average, my dear Oliver."

"The San Antonio is a little ahead, that is true. Does that suggest nothing to you?"

"What do you mean?"

"Are you satisfied that your manager is the best for the position?"

"Watson? Why, he's the best I ever saw! I defy you to find in the United States—yes, or in Europe—a better run, more comfortable hotel than the Fremont!"

"It's well run in that way; but how about this?" said Mills, laying his hand on the statement.

"I cannot afford to be niggardly with my guests," repeated the Colonel, "and I cannot afford to discredit Arguello. The money will come back many times over, later."

"Perhaps. But we are talking about now. And it's a matter of ten or fifteen thousand dollars. I hate to say so, Richard, and I would not hurt your feelings for the world, but the Fremont is carrying all the loan it can stand. In fact it is carrying far more than any other bank would advance on it."

"Oh, that is what bothers you! I see!" cried the Colonel, relieved. "I am glad to know what all the pother is about. Why, God bless your soul, put it on the rancho. You bankers are so confounded hidebound, Oliver. Just because it is to be used for the hotel! I don't care a continental red cent what I borrow it on."

Mills picked up a heavy paper knife and balanced it carefully, as though in some mysterious fashion it would add weight to his words.

"Now, Colonel, listen to me, and do not misunderstand my motives. Your credit is perfectly good, and I am not casting suspicion on it in any way. But this bank cannot loan you money for the purposes of the Fremont Hotel unless the Fremont Hotel can carry it; and the Fremont Hotel is mortgaged to the full at present. In other words this bank holds that any going business ought to take care of itself in prosperous times. If it cannot, it should retrench or change methods."

The Colonel stiffened again.

"My knowledge of banking is limited, as I said before," said he. "Do I understand this is the business policy of banks?"

Mills hesitated a little at this direct question.

"Is the Fremont Hotel a serious business with you, Colonel; or is it a toy?" he countered.

"I am of the years of discretion, sir. I do not play with toys," replied the Colonel.

"Then if it is a serious business, it should stand on its feet. Now let me tell you, Colonel, this promiscuous mortgage business is a very dangerous thing. I speak from long experience as a banker. Some day when you get time I wish you would go over to the courthouse and look over the tax lists of the outside property for years past. It would open your eyes. First lists were small and all Spanish names. Then they became larger, and alongside of each Spanish name appeared one or two American names. As time went on the lists grew longer and longer, and even the few Spanish names became fewer and the American names more numerous. Now how do you account for that?"

"The big ranchos were divided up, of course."

"Yes, but why? Not one of those old Spanish holders would sell an acre. I'll tell you how it happened in one word—mortgaged! In the case of the Cantado in the south, old Pancho borrowed twenty-five thousand dollars. The interest was high and was compounded every month. Before the matter was settled Pancho owed nearly three hundred thousand and lost the whole ranch, just on the basis of that original twenty-five thousand—that's all he ever really got for it."

"That was an exceptional case."

"It was the usual case. But take one nearer home. Take Las Flores."

"Don Vincente is not in trouble, is he?" asked the Colonel, quickly.

"Of course he is in trouble. But this is of course confidential, between us as friends. Las Flores has been mortgaged and re-mortgaged until it is like a full bucket, it will not hold a single drop more. I am afraid we shall have to foreclose on at least part of it to protect ourselves."

"Surely you would not do that!" cried the Colonel.

"No, *I* would not do that. But perhaps the bank must, and I shall have to order it because I am president. I *must* protect my stockholders against great and actual loss, no matter how reluctant I may be personally. I have let this go longer, much longer than I should even now. You must believe that."

"Of course I do; of course I do," said the Colonel, obviously much distressed. "But Don Vincente—Las Flores—how much is on it?"

"A very large amount. I am not quite at liberty to tell you. If he could begin to keep up his interest I might have been able to face the directors in his behalf with some assurance, but he is twelve thousand dollars behind on that, or will be by the first of the month."

"Well, well, I am sorry to hear that," murmured the Colonel, his brows knit. He was looking on the floor, studying hard over the situation, and only half heard the rest of the banker's remarks.

"That is why I cannot advance the sum you want for the Fremont Hotel. It should be able to carry itself. It is not so much business as friendship. I would rather see you sell something outright than borrow, no matter how well able you are to carry further loans."

"You advise me to sell something? What kind of banking advice is that? What is a bank for?"

"It is very unusual banking advice," admitted Mills frankly, "but it is offered from a friendly and not a business point of view. I would like to see you clean up there at the Fremont and make a fresh start on a new basis and with different management. If there is money anywhere in the hotel business, it ought to be here."

The Colonel thought a few moments.

"Perhaps you are right, Oliver," he concluded at last. "I will do as you say. But I must have that money now, and it will take time to sell anything without loss."

"I will tell you what I am going to do," stated Mills firmly. "I am going to loan you fifteen thousand dollars on a thirty day note; and I am going to tell you right here and now that I am not going to renew or extend it. That will give you plenty of time to make your sale. Is that satisfactory?"

"What security do you want?"

"Your word of honour to raise the money as I suggest. This is a personal transaction."

"Of course I promise, Oliver," returned the Colonel, "and may I be permitted to say this is very handsome of you."

III

TEN minutes later the Colonel emerged from the bank, his breast pocket bulging. He had taken twelve thousand dollars of the amount in currency.

"I am sorry to be so long, Puss," said he, climbing to his seat. "Hope you have not been too much bored."

They drove rapidly out of town, for these matters had consumed time, and it was now after eleven o'clock. Every few moments the Colonel chuckled aloud. For awhile Daphne made no comment on these outbursts, but finally demanded an explanation:

"What are you laughing at?"

"Nothing, Puss; nothing you would understand."

She fell silent, but after a few more repetitions she burst out indignantly.

"Godpapa," she said severely, "you are acting exactly like a bad boy who has been up to mischief."

"My dear, you must excuse me," apologized the Colonel, "I have done a very difficult thing. I've fooled Oliver Mills."

For here behold the Colonel in the rôle of gay deceiver. During all of the latter part of the interview he had been scheming. A new use for money had come into his mind. He signed the note in entire good faith, and would sell property to meet it; but this particular fifteen thousand dollars would never see the Fremont Hotel. That impecunious hostelry would have to be helped out in another way.

"Very hungry, Puss?" he asked.

"Hungry!" she scorned, "after such a breakfast! And at that hour!"

"Want to take a little drive and have fruit for lunch?"

"Where? Oh, let's! But how will we let them know at home?"

"I see Manuelo ahead. That is what gave me the notion," said the Colonel, pointing with his whip. "He can take them word."

Daphne settled back blissfully. These impromptu excursions were by no means unusual, and they were always good fun. The Colonel might drive his chestnuts directly across country to some distant spring or windmill to see how the cattle were making out. In that case there were exciting dives down the precipitous sides of *barrancas* with brakes squealing, and the jerk at the bottom as the horses took up the slack in preparation for the plunge up the other side; and tippy progressions along flower starred side hills when it seemed that they must turn over; and bump-itty-bumps across the bottom lands, with ground squirrels scurrying to the holes, and the little burrowing owls bobbing. Or he might drop in on some of his outposts, little adobe buildings whitewashed, in which case there were generally fat comfortable Mexican women and brown children, and a meal of Spanish dishes; but in any event, even when women lacked, one was sure of friendly dogs.

To-day, however, they continued straight on past the Avenue of Palms along the *Camino Real*, so Daphne knew they were going to Las Flores.

Las Flores was an old-fashioned Spanish ranch house situated atop a low wide knoll. It was one-storied and built in *patio style*, of course, with casement windows opening outward, thick walls, floors of big polished square tiles laid unevenly on the ground. The low ceilings showed huge beams hewn by hand. In the kitchen wing Daphne remembered the great smoke cowl, like a candle extinguisher, and the dark rafters, and the bright utensils glittering in the dusk. There were flowers in the *patio*, and a curious fountain; and quaint faded old brocaded furniture and fragile, inlaid glassed cabinets full of queer ancient things, and a tinkling piano with a painted scene on its cover, and many frowning, darkened portraits. It was crowded, stuffy, mysteriously ancient within; and sunny, bright, luxuriously lazy without. Daphne never went there without either discovering something inside she had never noticed before; or something lying about outside that was not there at her last visit—a saddle, or *riata*, or *matate*, or some such matter. On one or two rare occasions Don Vincente had showed her some of the things in the glassed cabinets and had explained them to her. There was, for instance, the filagreed gold smelling bottle presented to an ancestor by the Queen Isabella herself. As near as Daphne could make out the said ancestor, acting in capacity of page, had while riding in attendance on the queen been thrown off on his head. The queen on hearing the circumstances sent first aid to the injured in the form of kind inquiries and the smelling bottle. As to why the smelling bottle had not thereafter been returned to its royal owner, Don Vincente was not quite clear. But it was very interesting. Daphne, however, was a trifle uncomfortable with the rotund, side whiskered dignified little gentleman. She liked better Doña Cazadero, or Pilar, his daughter. These ladies differed only in size around and age, for Doña Cazadero and her amiable daughter were almost exact replicas inside their pretty rather silly heads and their capacious and very warm breasts. They possessed also about the same low horsepower in energy and high voltage in pride of family and race. They dwelt in wrappers and hammocks all the early part of the day, but came forth nobly every afternoon for a stately drive to town in the victoria.

Sure enough, when they descended and one of the numerous loitering Mexicans had taken charge of their team, Daphne found the ladies in their usual cool nook. The Colonel at this time of day, naturally awaited the Don in the parlour. Doña Cazadero and Pilar were this morning filled with unusual animation. Their novels were lying neglected, the chocolate box had not even been opened. Pasteboard boxes and wrapping paper lay strewn about, and over the benches that had evidently been brought up for the purpose were draped bolts of beautiful dress materials.

"It is the little one!" cried Doña Cazadero in Spanish, which Daphne had—as all children of that day—picked up after a fashion. "Just in time! You must help. See these thing₅ have but just come, and you must assist. Here are materials come straight from New York and Pilar and I must choose how they shall be made and which of us will wear them."

In five minutes Daphne was lost in the twentieth feminine heaven of ravishment. Such a profusion could nowhere else have been seen outside of a dry goods shop. There were silks heavy as canvas and light as a spider web; brocades that rivalled Chinatown's best; satins; lawns; linens patterned and plain. They were all in the piece. But also there were nearly a dozen gowns all made up, patterns of the styles, dainty ravishing creations; and slippers, and silk stockings of all colours, and many other more intimate affairs. Daphne was breathless with awe. Never before had she seen anything like it.

"It is so confusing!" cried Pilar in despair. "There are so many! For the evening gown, I cannot decide. Let us wait until the new jewels come."

"Jewels?" breathed Daphne.

"It is a nothing. But when last in San Francisco I saw a set of emeralds that was of a great beauty, a green like the new summer. Ever since they have been in my dreams. And last week papa consented. So they have been sent for, and they should come now very soon. It would be better to make an evening gown to match with them; do not you think so, niña?"

"If I had just one, just one dress like any of those," breathed Daphne, "I'd never think about emeralds. And if I had emeralds, I'd never remember a gown—like Salome before Herod."

Pilar laughed; but Doña Cazadero looked severe.

"I think you do not think what you say, *niña*," she rebuked. "It is not modest. I am not quite sure, but I think it is blasphemous as well."

In the meantime Don Vincente had come in and greeted the Colonel in his slow and dignified manner, apologizing for the delay. Fully two minutes were consumed in the leisurely exchange of beautiful compliments in the Spanish fashion; and then Don Vincente led his visitor to his own private office at the end of the east wing. This was a small, stuffy, rather dark room with a huge desk, leather chairs, sheepbound books, a large carved wood clock, an owl under a glass dome, abalone shells, some framed documents in Spanish, a leather lounge, a bridle braided of bright-dyed horsehair. It was crowded coziness. Here the gentlemen sat themselves down and lighted cigars.

"I have come on a personal matter," began the Colonel, after the preliminary conversation had been cleared away. "Between men not as intimate as ourselves, it would be an affair of some delicacy. But with us it is as one brother speaking to another within family walls. We have been neighbours and friends for thirty years."

"Proceed, Ricardo," said Don Vincente. "Nothing you could say to me would be taken amiss."

"I am informed, in confidence, that there is some difficulty in meeting a trifling obligation, and that you may lose a portion of Las Flores. Is that true?"

Don Vincente blew a cloud and shrugged his shoulders.

"True enough. It is business, I suppose. I can blame nobody; though it has seemed to me that a little patience until the season of the selling of cattle would not have been much to ask. Last season, as you know, was dry and bad. It had not seemed to me until lately that money was lacking. There has always been plenty. Some mistake, I think. Impossible to say. But Señor Mills has explained to me. I can see the justice of his remarks. He cannot be blamed. It is only a misfortune, and one must bear misfortune serenely when it comes."

The Colonel's kind old face was beaming with pleasure; and if Don Vincente had happened to be looking at him instead of staring obstinately at the stuffed owl, he might have been considerably surprised at the fact.

"What portion of the *rancho* is involved?" asked the Colonel.

"I have discussed that with the Señor Mills, and we have agreed that the *rancheria* will set things right."

"It would be a pity to lose the *rancheria*."

Don Vincente sighed.

"I shall regret the necessity; yes. In the old days it was the home of my people's Indians, before they scattered. It possesses historic and sentimental interest. But it can be the best spared."

The Colonel chuckled aloud. Don Vincente looked at him in surprise and a slight displeasure.

"See, old friend," cried the Colonel, "how fortunately these things turn out! It happens that just at this moment I have a sum of money by me that has come to me in an unexpected fashion"—Oh, sly but truth-telling old Colonel!—"just at this moment of your need! It is not as great as I would have it, perhaps it is not enough, but such as it is you are welcome to the loan of it."

Don Vincente's expression did not change, but a cloud seemed to lift in the depths of his melancholy black eyes.

"How much is it, *amigo?*" he asked, striving hard for a careless absence of haste.

"About fifteen thousand dollars."

Don Vincente's pent breath exhaled softly.

"Twelve thousand will be enough. I cannot refuse."

"Refuse! I should think not! It is what any neighbour would expect of any other. You shall pay me at your convenience—when the cattle are sold—at any time." The Colonel fumbled in his pocket and produced the roll of bills. Don Vincente received them and thrust them nonchalantly into a half open drawer.

"It shall be as you say, Ricardo; and thank you. My *vaqueros* tell me you have placed sheep on the Alisal. Is it your idea to make of that *sierra* a sheep range?"

They talked for some moments longer, and then the Colonel arose to go. The subject of the money was not again mentioned between them.

IV

"WELL, Puss," observed the Colonel cheerily, as they drove away from Las Flores. "We have had a very busy and profitable morning. If we hurry, we can get home for a late lunch after all. What say?"

"What will Sing Toy say; that's the question."

"True, true. Perhaps we'd better play hookey after all."

"I'll tell you what let's do," cried Daphne, wriggling about in her seat with the splendour of her idea. "Let's go to my house and I'll cook us both some lunch. You've never eaten my cooking. Oh, I *would* like to show you! Will you? Say yes; say yes!"

"Yes," obeyed the Colonel promptly.

"You dear!" cried Daphne, and threw her arms around him so vigorously that the chestnuts leaped and the Colonel all but lost overboard his stovepipe hat.

They turned off across country and drove down remembered shallow swales and over low flats in the hills. The air sang with insects and birds, was heavy with the odour of lupine. The bright scarves of the wild flowers lay flung across the slopes; the tiny stars of the alfileria peeped from its vivid green; under the live oaks the cattle stood as under benign, spreading arms. In the noon slept the ranges of the Sur in wonderful clarity of outline against a very blue sky, reposing until the evening when they must awaken to throw the magic of sunset changes across their ramparts. Buzzards swung in slow sleepy circles across the sky. Under the light wheels the flowers and grasses bent with a soft crushing sound; and from that crushing came a faint sweet odour different from all the rest. Nobody in the tepid sun-steeped world paid any attention to them—neither the insects, nor the birds, nor the cattle, nor the trees, nor the slumbering ranges; nobody except the sentinel ground squirrels. These scampered, and *chirked* shrilly, and sat up stiff and straight on their hind legs like so many picket pins.

After a time they came to a loose wire gate. Daphne hopped down to hold it aside, and so they drove into the tract owned by Brainerd.

The way led alongside a barbed wire fence, around the corner of a hill; and so, by a gentle grade to the bungalow. In the flat was an orchard of ten or twelve acres; up the cañon stretched a narrow strip of grain land; the sagebrush hills crowded close around; almost in the back dooryard rose the first abrupt, dark, chaparral-covered slopes of the Sur. The place did not look prosperous. Under the orchard trees the earth had been left too long uncultivated and the trees themselves were in need of pruning; deep ruts from the last rains made driving difficult; the paint on the low attractive bungalow had peeled and blistered in the sun. Nevertheless, there was none of the shiftless disorder usual in the premises of the average "sagebrusher." The few agricultural implements were under cover, there were no broken tools nor baling wire nor bottles and tin cans scattered about, the windmill had all its blades.

The Colonel hitched his team to the corral fence, and the two moved down on the bungalow.

"Daddy must be up the cañon fussing with the water," pronounced Daphne. "You go into the living room and I will have something in a jiffy. No, I don't want any help."

The Colonel walked on the wide veranda to the front of the house. The boards underfoot, slightly warped by the sun and the lack of paint, creaked under his deliberate tread. He entered the living room and sat down in a very worn leather chair, sighing with the comfort of an anticipated quarter hour's rest. His keen old eyes moved slowly from object to object in the long and narrow room. They were old and familiar to his sight, for many times in many years he had sat thus waiting, since Daphne was a little thing being put to bed.

It was a threadbare room, worn and old and never renovated; with a few pieces of much used furniture, and many shabby, faded books. A fireplace and mantel centred one side. It was a neat room withal. Even such scattered affairs as pipes, matches, magazines, and riding gear did not give an impression of things out of place.

"Here's Mugs to keep you company," said Daphne, suddenly opening the door and unceremoniously dumping down a fluffy ball that at once trundled itself in the Colonel's direction. "I won't be but a few minutes."

The tiny fat puppy came to a halt and fixed the Colonel with the blue eyes of extreme youth. The Colonel reached down and gathered him in. Immediately he snuggled down with a sleepy grunt of content.

It was nine years ago, just about this time of year. The Colonel, staring out the window across the magnificent acres of Corona del Monte, remembered every detail. Manuelo had come riding in one noon to announce that a man was camping at the mouth of Ramon Cañon. There was nothing unusual in this; but after dinner, the Colonel, having nothing better to do, rode around that way to see what the man was up to. He found a tent under the oaks, a pair of horses grazing in the bottom, and a stranger seated on the wagon pole mending harness. He was tall, gaunt, hollow-eyed, dressed in a flannel shirt and overalls. Both the latter articles were clean. High on his cheeks burned two round red spots. The Colonel knew the type—a "lunger." The man looked up from under his heavy brows, but made no move.

"Good afternoon," the Colonel greeted cheerfully.

The man merely nodded.

"You have selected a good place to camp. You will find spring water up that side about forty rods."

"I have found it," said the man grudgingly. His voice, unexpectedly, was cultivated.

"I hope you will stay just as long as you feel like doing so," pursued the Colonel, "and make yourself quite at home."

The man for the first time looked directly at him.

"I intend to do so," said he. "I have filed on this hundred and sixty."

"Filed?"

"Yes, filed—taken it up—homesteaded it."

"This is not Government land. It is part of my rancho."

"That is where you are wrong," stated the newcomer, vigorously. "Look up your titles."

"I have no need to do so, sir," rejoined the Colonel with dignity. "I have owned this rancho for twenty years."

"It doesn't matter if you have owned it for two hundred," retorted the man. "This particular corner is not yours."

The Colonel checked his reply and rode away. After all, it was beneath his dignity to quarrel with the fellow; and, besides, he looked sick. His claim was absurd, of course. Nevertheless, the Colonel next day instructed lawyer Stanley to investigate. La Corona del Monte was part of an original Spanish grant, and Spanish grants were notoriously uncertain. The grantee was given so many leagues in a given direction. He and the surveyor determined the boundaries almost by guess, and marked them by trees, small piles of rock, or even a "steer's skull." Property overlapped or left gaps. At first, when the country was pastoral, and there were no fences, this did not particularly matter; but later it resulted in a great mass of litigation. Lawyer Stanley reported that the mouth of Ramon Cañon might by a stretch of the law be considered one of these gaps and so open to entry. But it was only by a stretch of the law, and he expressed the further opinion that the claim could be easily upset. The squatter problem was at that period a great and growing nuisance. These sagebrushers, as they were called, established themselves where they pleased, if they considered themselves strong enough. Already, in the North there had been several squatter wars. Therefore the Colonel instructed Stanley to go ahead; and promptly dismissed the whole matter from his mind.

That was of a Tuesday. On Wednesday the Colonel, riding abroad, surmounted a hill to see below him on the flat a group of cattle weaving restlessly back and forth, their heads up, and all facing in the same direction. The Colonel knew well the symptoms. The half wild creatures saw something unaccustomed, and they could not make up their minds whether to rush it or to run away. The object of their curiosity might be one of the ranch dogs, or perhaps a coyote or bobcat, or—almost inconceivably—a man on foot. Almost inconceivably, because no man but knew the habits of range cattle. The latter, gentle as possible with horsemen, became fierce and dangerous when the rider dismounted. So the Colonel, more in idleness than in curiosity rode down the slope to see what was the matter. The great restless beasts gave way excitedly as he rode through them. Thus for the first time he met Daphne.

He saw a very small frightened little morsel in a Scotch plaid dress standing in the middle of the closing circle. She was bareheaded and very white, and she clasped a fat puppy—own kin to the furry ball on which the Colonel's hand instinctively tightened at the recollection. But she faced her great enemies erect and still defiant.

The Colonel knew cattle; and he realized that he had arrived on the instant. His powerful horse leaped under the spur. In true *vaquero* style, he leaned from his saddle and swept up the little maid just as the foremost cows broke into the tentative high flung trot that would precede a rush. He turned on them savagely in the relief of tension, and drove them back with shouts. They obeyed the single horseman.

After a moment the Colonel's common sense returned, and he reined down his animal. The little maid was very much rumpled, her dignity had been terribly upset, she was very frightened; but she had neither cried out nor dropped the puppy. The Colonel straightened her out and set her in front of him. His horse, a proud, docile and well trained beast, stepped softly.

"Well!" said the Colonel, "that was a close call! Who are you, and how in the world do you happen to be here?"

The child looked up at him gravely for a moment before replying.

"My name is Daphne Brainerd," she recited, with the precise directness of childhood, "'n I am six years old. I have no bumbalow. Who are you?"

"I?—I—Oh, I'm a fairy godfather, Puss," rejoined the Colonel. "But where do you live and how do you happen to be away out here all alone?"

The child looked up at him again with new interest. The idea of a fairy godfather evidently fitted accurately with rescue.

"I live with my daddy in a tent," she informed him, "and I got lost. My daddy will be very cross, 'cause he told me not to go out alone 'cause I haven't any bumbalow."

"Bumbalow?" repeated the Colonel, turning his horse toward Ramon Cañon. "What is that?"

"I don't know 'zactly," confessed Daphne. "It's something you have to have before you can go out anywhere alone. Maybe daddy will get me one when I grow older. We prob'ly can't 'ford one now. Daddy is poor and he is sick sometimes. We can't 'ford lots of things."

"Maybe he will be able to afford one later," agreed the Colonel, "though I must confess I never heard of one. What did your daddy say about it?"

"'You must not go out of sight of the tent,'" mimicked the child, "'cause you have abs'lutely no bumbalowcality.'"

"Bump of locality!" cried the Colonel with a shout of laughter.

As they neared Ramon Cañon he caught sight of something far ahead through the trees.

"I am going to put you down here," he told Daphne, "and you must stand perfectly still, and in a very few minutes your daddy will come and find you. I will vanish, as a fairy god-father should."

"Have you got any peppermint candy?" demanded the surprising child.

The Colonel, humiliated, confessed that he fell that far short of a perfect fairy godfather. But, parenthetically, from that day he never so failed again, as scores of children now grown up will testify.

He set her carefully down and withdrew. From the safe screen of chaparral he witnessed a frantic meeting. From it he rode away slowly, blowing his nose. That very afternoon he made a call on Stanley.

"I've decided not to contest that homestead in Ramon Cañon," he announced, very abruptly for the Colonel. "Drop the proceedings."

"But, Colonel, that is in the heart of——"

"It's no great use to me. Dammit, the man's sick, I tell you."

A year had passed and Brainerd had made a start. Evidently he possessed a little money, for soon materials and workmen appeared; but evidently that money no more than sufficed for permanent improvements, for after the latter were completed Brainerd rarely employed men. He tried to attend to his own cultivation, but had not the overplus energy necessary to make a success. It was not through lack of intelligence, nor ambition, nor diligence; it was plain lack of strength to carry good beginnings to good endings. The little ranch ran the classic gamut: ground squirrels took more than their share of the potatoes; the chickens and quail ruined most of the vegetables; the wildcats and foxes got in at the chickens; deer and rabbits destroyed the vines; swarms of birds took the first bearing of the fruit; gophers by thousands ruined the hardly dug irrigating ditch that was designed to bring water from the upper spring to the orange grove. These were all difficulties usual to such a situation, but to meet them successfully requires youth, strength, optimism. They superimpose themselves on the hard, physical labour required to plough, harrow, plant, cultivate, keep in repair. Brainerd did not die. The red spots in his cheeks became less vivid. But at times if it had not been for the very jackrabbits, his enemies, he might have died—of starvation. Nowadays people do not eat jackrabbit knowingly. Then they did, and blessed him as the saviour of the situation.

But Brainerd survived, and somehow made a little headway. The bungalow did not get painted; the brown grass grew in the garden; the fruit trees produced a scant crop for lack of full cultivation; there were many loose odds and ends. Still, by the time the jackrabbits learned to keep away from the immediate vicinity of the house, it was no longer necessary to depend on them for a meat supply. Brainerd worked his soil and read his books and raised his daughter after his own ideas. The books were varied and old-fashioned, *Frank Forrester's Sporting Scenes*, *Dickens* in toto, *Handley Cross*, *Moby Dick*, *The Cloister and the Hearth*, were some of them. Without discrimination he liked to read them aloud to little Daphne, who thereby acquired mixed and incomplete ideas beyond her years. He also took considerable pains with that young lady's education. The most noticeable result was a certain directness of vision resulting from an almost frantic persistence against sham and subterfuge.

"Don't pretend, Daffy, and don't dodge," he would tell her

over and over in many different ways. The result in the future would probably be admirable; but in the childish years it resulted in a rather terrible frankness.

At first he and the Colonel did not get on at all. This was not the Colonel's fault; and indeed the latter was blissfuly unaware of the fact they were not getting on. Merely he found Brainerd a trifle difficult and reserved. In his rides about the country he often swung down by the new farm; and, from the vantage of his saddle, looked about on how things were going. He saw a good many lacks, both in materials and in labour: and at first he sometimes attempted to supply them. Brainerd resented fiercely these kindly meant incursions into his affairs. To his mind they both showed humiliating knowledge of his deficiencies and scented of the big proprietor. All he wanted was to be let alone. His ill health drained down his vitality, so that after his necessary work, he had little energy to comtemplate the discouraging total of things necessarily left undone, and none at all with which to be good humoured. The Colonel's geniune neighbourliness had this effect, however, that Brainerd never quite reached the point of open rebuff, as he certainly would have done to one less sincerely desirous of being friendly. But the Colonel never succeeded in giving him an hour or a cent's worth of help.

It was Mrs. Peyton who in the end brought that about. Allie drove about the ranch and into town behind a pair of diminutive but wicked black ponies. They were not much bigger than good-sized St. Bernard dogs, and they wore long furry coats and copious manes and tails. Polished russet harness attached them to a varnished buckboard that looked several sizes too large for them. When Mrs. Peyton mounted to the seat, she looked as though she had for the fun of the thing taken over a child's equipage. Nevertheless the black ponies would go just as fast as full sized horses. Their legs fairly twinkled as they whirled the varnished buckboard down the road or across country on the *rancho;* and they could keep it up for hours, ending with the same ludicrous appearance of earnest energy with which they started out. Mrs. Peyton had to have loops in the reins by which to hold them when they felt too fresh. With

them she explored the entire countryside, displaying a fine disregard for roads.

She saw plainly enough, though the Colonel did not, Brainerd's pride, and the method he was taking to show it. One time, after Brainerd had been settled about a year, she took with her a cake. Brainerd could hardly refuse that, especially as the gift was ostensibly made to Daphne, not to him. Daphne, as may be imagined, was immensely pleased with the ponies, not to speak of comfortable, sympathetic, black-eyed Mrs. Peyton. The cake having been well digested, it was followed by a hot dish, carefully pinned in napkins.

"Once in a while Sing Toy manages to make something that is pretty good," said Allie, "and I am so pleased that I want to show off about it."

The something hot was merely half of a substantial meat pie with vegetables in it—a meal in itself. Brainerd felt uncomfortably that he was being come over; but Mrs. Peyton looked him blandly in the eye, and he decided to say nothing. Other hot dishes came at intervals; then some of the raw materials.

"Brought you over a few carrots and potatoes," she announced cheerfully. "I want you to compare them with yours. I believe that perhaps vegetables raised in the foothills have a little more flavour."

Brainerd had few fresh vegetables. At that period he was living mainly on staple groceries. Mrs. Peyton never explored about when she came over for a visit, but drove directly to the bungalow and directly away again. How much did the woman know, anyway?

"You must let me know which you think better," she was saying.

This went on for some time. Then one morning one of the Colonel's Mexicans came loping over, carrying by the bale a stoppered milk can which he left without comment. The next day he reappeared, bearing another can, and taking the old one away. Brainerd was not at home either time. He was exceedingly angry. This was going too far. It smacked of actual charity. He was simmering; and he made it a point to be at the bungalow next morning at the hour when the Mexican might be expected to appear. He did not come; but Mrs. Peyton did, with her little black ponies. She carried under her arm the stoppered milk can, which she deposited inside the door.

"Where is the empty can?" she asked Brainerd, who stood glowering by a pillar of the veranda. "Oh, that's the way it is," she stated incisively, as she looked up to see his face. "I expected as much, and that is why I am here. Come inside, my friend, I want to talk to you."

Brainerd followed her silently into the living room.

"Now, what is it?" she demanded. "Sit down, man, sit down, and don't look at me like a thunder cloud. I am not accustomed to it."

"I beg your pardon, Mrs. Peyton, I did not mean to appear discourteous. But I am seriously annoyed, and I suppose I show it."

"What are you annoyed at, pray?"

"This milk—I cannot permit——"

"You cannot permit me to do a simple neighbourly act without objecting," she interrupted him. "No, I am going to do the talking. We have sixty dairy cows. The milk is nothing; no more than if you offered me one of those daisies from your garden. Yes, I know what you're going to say. But let me say this: I am not bringing the milk on your account. I am bringing it for Daffy; and I shall continue to do so."

"My daughter is not a fit subject for charity," said Brainerd, stiffly. "I cannot agree that comparative strangers have any right to make her so."

"Your daughter will be a fit subject for a hospital if she does not get the food and care her age requires," stated Mrs. Peyton, bluntly, "and I cannot agree that you have any right to deprive her of them."

"Daphne is a perfectly healthy child," rejoined Brainerd, a shade of uncertainty creeping into his tone.

"Is she, indeed?" said Allie dryly. "How long do you think she will remain so on jackrabbits, pork and flapjacks? I do not want to seem unkind, Mr. Brainerd, nor to appear to pry into your affairs; but I do not intend that child to come to any harm through your foolishness. You can be just as fantastic and quixotic as you please in your own case; but when it is a question of Daphne, I expect and intend to use a little common sense."

She looked at him very directly. "Come now, that is a point we need not quarrel on. I have quite made up my mind." She held out her hand to him. "I will send Juan over in the morning with the milk. Where did you say the empty can was?"

"I will get it for you," said Brainerd. "And I will confess that I am very glad to get the milk for Daphne. But I insist on paying for it."

"That is handsomely said," replied Allie, "but I am not in the retail milk business, and I do not intend to be bothered with such matters. If it will relieve your mind any, Mr. Brainerd, I will say frankly that I have become very fond of your child, and that I know something of children, though I have none living. She needs certain things which you cannot supply to her in this out of the way place. I am going to give them to her. You do not interest me in the least; and I do not expect to have you interfere."

She sat very straight in her chair, like a ruffled dicky bird, and looked Brainerd uncompromisingly in the eye. The latter's shell of ill-healthy grumpiness was beginning to crack under this direct assault, and his natural sense of humour to peep forth. He surveyed her with twinkling eyes.

"Your reasoning is cogent, madam," he said gravely, "and I can see that it would be useless to resist. But it seems to me the situation should be regularized in some way. If you are to take such an interest in our destinies—Daphne's destiny—you should, to save my poor humble face, have an official position in the household," he raised his voice to call: "Daffy, oh Daffy, come here a moment!"

She toddled in from outside, her hair all towselled, her cheeks red.

"Daffy," said Brainerd gravely, addressing her with lofty courtesy, "I have called you to introduce you to a new relative, taken over without the customary benefit of clergy and ecclesiastical ceremony, but none the less real and genuine. Go and kiss your new godmother—" he hesitated a moment and rolled a humorous eye at the Colonel's wife. "——Aunt Allie," he finished boldly.

Allie gathered the mite to her arms and buried her face.

"You little darling," she choked; then she looked up, her eyes moist, "and I'm inclined to call you a big darling," said she.

"I'll get the milk can," said Brainerd, hastily.

Mrs. Peyton heroically kept away from the little ranch for a week thereafter; though she sent Manuelo to borrow Daphne one day "to see the little pigs." Then, munitioned with some foodstuff or other, she made another raid. In the course of the conversation with Brainerd she mentioned sagebrush honey.

"It has a flavour all its own—most delicious. We used to get it at San Diego, and I have always remembered it."

"I know it well," Brainerd broke in eagerly, for him. "In fact the bees I put in last year seem to prefer the sage. I can let you have some."

"Can you now, really? That would be a real treat."

Delighted to be able to reciprocate, Brainerd took the greatest pains to select the darkest and most highly flavoured of the sage honey for his gift. He was absurdly pleased at being able to do something, to offer something unique to his own small establishment. But the next time Mrs. Peyton's black ponies scrambled up the little hill, he met her with a sad shake of the head.

"You know you are an awful liar," he told her seriously.

"It can't be very serious if you call me that to my face," she smiled.

"It is serious. What do you mean by your sagebrush honey stuff?"

"What do I mean? What do *you* mean?"

"I took a Sunday off, and rode about the foothills yesterday. Why didn't you tell me the Colonel kept beehives in practically every cañon in the hills?—where there's nothing but sage?"

But Mrs. Peyton rallied instantly.

"I have no intention of being put upon," she announced, "nor of discussing my husband's affairs with you. Here are some fresh rolls for Daffy's lunch; and I have not a moment to stop. Take them!" and she drove off in full but orderly retreat.

The Colonel's experience was similar except that his victory was neither so pronounced nor so prompt. He had no luck at all with his proffers of help about the ranch. Brainerd would not listen to the loan of men, tools, or materials. He ran his own show, sometimes with scanty and inefficient help, but oftener by his own unaided and inadequate strength. For that reason the place never quite reached its proper efficiency. But Brainerd did not die, as he had been told he would, and a certain amount of produce got to the market. When the first fruit came in the Colonel offered to haul and market it with his own, charging a pro rata of expense. This seemed like a business proposition so, after some discussion, Brainerd assented. The Colonel was jubilant. He saw his chance. At the final accounting Brainerd's share proved to be pleasantly but unexpectedly heavy. On receiving it and the ingenious accounts the Colonel handed him, he said nothing. But the following season he quietly but briefly insisted that it was his turn to see to the marketing. He put it in such a way that the Colonel could not refuse.

"I don't know why, but that fellow makes me feel guilty!" he cried indignantly to Allie, "I'm ashamed to meet him——"

"You falsified accounts; you know you did," accused Allie, "and now you're going to be found out. No wonder you're ashamed to meet him."

"Well," the Colonel defended himself, "that child ought to have a few clothes and heaven knows Brainerd can't get a start in that miserable place without a little money, and——"

"I know. But now you must face the music."

The Colonel was very much disturbed. You would have thought, to judge by his furtive air whenever a fresh cloud of dust turned in to the Avenue of Palms, that he was a criminal in dread of the sheriff. He met Brainerd finally, with a false air of cheer.

"Well, my boy, fruit all sold?" he cried. "Afraid this year is not quite as good as last year. Can't expect two good years in succession, can we?"

Brainerd was eying him sardonically, and the Colonel, to his own indignation, found himself fidgeting like a school boy. Why, confound it! he was old enough to be this man's father, and he came from a proud old Blue Grass family, and he was lord of the Corona del Monte, and his name was known from end to end of the Californias. Nevertheless, he fidgeted.

"Judging by the results of our sales, you are right," said

Brainerd. "Yet our crops are as heavy as last year, and my inquiries seem to show that prices are fully as high. But our returns are a full forty per cent less. I confess that in comparison with yourself, Colonel, I am a very poor salesman. I feel greatly at fault that I have not brought you better returns."

He spoke dryly, looking the Colonel in the eye.

"Nothing to worry about. Quite expected. I had especial market for the fruit—firm gone out of business now—lucky year last year——" muttered the Colonel.

"I am relieved to hear you say so," observed Brainerd. "Of course it can never happen again."

The Colonel escaped finally, feeling like a caught small boy. He was indignant; he had done nothing to be ashamed of. But he abandoned several half-formed ideas, such as secretly guaranteeing Brainerd's grocery bills.

Nevertheless on one point he was firm, just as Alice had been. He wanted Daphne to have a pony and he gave her one, together with a miniature stock saddle and a braided rawhide bridle. So far he and Mrs. Peyton had their way. But when it came to such matters as clothes, for example, they got no farther. Daphne grew up between them into the long-legged youngster we have seen, riding her pony, raising her puppies, reading her father's books, playing in the great tree she called Dolman's House—necessarily a varied education full of hiatuses. Her life was full of hiatuses, the Colonel thought as he waited for the lunch she was preparing. The matter of dress for example— Mrs. Peyton had long since given over interference there. Brainerd had inner citadels of independence one was not wise to attack——

"Here we are, fairy godpapa!" cried Daphne, triumphantly. "Here's something Aunt Allie taught me to make last week. See how you like it. And then we must go. I just remembered I told Aunt Allie I'd help her with the preserves this afternoon."

V

COLONEL PEYTON took the next steamer to the south, debarking at San Pedro, whence he soon arrived at Los Angeles.

He carried with him a satchel full of documents. Without much difficulty he negotiated a further loan on his ranch property. He could easily have raised the amount, and more, in Arguello, but as Mills had so strongly advised against this procedure, the Colonel wished to spare the little banker's feelings. With the proceeds he paid the temporary loan, which, it will be remembered, he had passed over to Don Vincente. This left him exactly where he was before. At this juncture he recalled Mills's advice as to selling something and cleaning up the hotel indebtedness. The Colonel had nothing he particularly wanted to sell—except perhaps his stock in the First National Bank. He took this to a broker, who disposed of it inside of two days. The money more than sufficed to put the hotel in running order again. Everything was all right again; except that the Colonel became a little furtive whenever Oliver Mills hove in sight. Of course there was no reason for it. Bank stock is not a paying investment unless a man is in active business and constantly using all a bank's functions. To a ranchman like the Colonel its possession is sheer rank sentiment when another use can be found for the money. It was certainly his money to do what he pleased with. The Colonel rehearsed these and other arguments to himself, and agreed with himself on all of them. Nevertheless a vague feeling of guilt troubled him. The Colonel was always doing things that brought that vague feeling of guilt.

CHAPTER III

I

NOWADAYS the arrival of hotel guests means little or nothing to the residents of a resort town like Arguello. Then the societies of the town, the ranches, and the hotels were intermingled. A journey to California was not to be lightly undertaken. It consumed a week. The country was still wild. At this period the buffalo herds had not yet been exterminated; the blanket Indian was a commonplace, and such things as antelope, coyotes, lobo wolves, prairie dogs, and burrowing owls found their way into every letter home. The Golden State was far separated from the rest of the world, not only by space and time, but also by a zone of exotic experience. One felt oneself remote. The tourist never dreamed of undertaking the journey for less than an all-winter's stay. And since the local travel also was apt to be difficult and uncomfortable, as compared with our modern extra-fare trains, it also followed that the tourist was quite likely to settle down in one place and stay there.

Thus such a hotel as the Fremont had its regular inhabitants with whom the townspeople became intimately acquainted. The latter attended the weekly dances, and sat about the broad verandas. There was as yet no man's club in the village, and the place of it was taken by the Fremont's bar, where at one time or another could be met any of Arguello's male citizens. The Spanish-Californian element was still strong. It was the custom of certain of the young men of that race to serenade with voice and guitar such of the visiting damsels as caught their eye, whether or not they happened to be personally acquainted with said damsels. It was an entirely respectful tribute without ulterior motive, a custom of the place. Many a maiden heart has overflowed with emotion and exaltation and high romance at the plaintive, liquid sounds rising to her rosebowered window through the tepid semi-tropical night, with the moon hung like a lantern above the sea, and the mountains slumbering dark like inert beasts.

"*Adios, adios amores*——"

and the thin high thrill of frogs; and the heavy scent of orange blossoms and honeysuckle lying in the dusk like a fog—it was perhaps as well that the serenaders did take it all impersonally as a pretty custom, leaving the surcharged damsels to write reams to an utterly sceptical bosom friend in the East.

In such an intimate community the hotel register was the most consulted volume in or out of the county library. It was mounted on a revolving stand for easier reference.

Patrick Boyd and his son Kenneth received on arrival their full share of discussion. Not only were they an attractive couple personally—Boyd thick-set, blue-clad, jolly and vital; Kenneth tall, goodlooking, curly haired, laughing—but their name itself meant something to the rocking chair conference of the powers.

George Scott told them about him. Scott was a short, thick apoplectic little man who had come to California to die of various plethoric complaints, but had postponed doing so. He had never done a stroke of work in his life; but he had belonged to all the best clubs; he had travelled not only in Europe but in the Far East as well; he knew all the great names in social, political, financial, and military circles; and the latter days of his New York life had been dumpily but magnificently spent in the deep leather chairs of the Union League Club, gazing forth on the shifting Avenue. He thus possessed a wide knowledge and had acquired a biting tongue. Whether from liver or pose he was not afraid to express his full opinion, uncoated with the sugar of tact or, indeed, of common charity. If he did not like a man, he said so. He prided himself, however, in maintaining strictly the spectator's standpoint, and in never taking sides. Add a faculty of making enthusiasms look ridiculous by a mere air of detached amusement. Naturally he was much sought after and deferred to.

"Patrick Boyd," he told the other men oracularly, when the name had been reported back from the hotel register, "made his money in street railways. He is a Mick—came from Ireland in the steerage. Nevertheless he is a real person. He is nobody's fool, naturally; and those who have tried it say he is a bad man to fight. As he has no women of his class to hold him back, he has been well received—is a member of the Club. I don't need to tell Mr. Oberman what his standing is among men of wealth."

The millionaire brewer grunted. "All I got to say," he rumbled, "iss that when Pat Boyd talks pizaniss, you better pay attention."

The object of the discussion at this moment appeared in the wide doorways. His chest was thrown out, and his jolly face was twinkling with the pleasure of the fresh morning. He looked slowly about him at the mountains, the gardens, the people on the veranda. As his eye fell on the group in the rocking chairs, he strolled forward.

"How are you, Scott," he greeted the little man. "Surprised to see you here; thought you went to the Riviera, winters."

Boyd dropped easily into the group. They were all, except Scott, business men on long vacations; and they possessed all the vast leisure, boyish irresponsibility, and dry humour of their species. Boyd found them immediately congenial and proceeded to fall in step with their daily routine.

The latter was very simple. When their after-breakfast cigars were smoked out, they mounted horses and rode. In that they did not differ from all the rest of mankind. But their rides were, from the standpoint of the youngsters, intolerably pokey. Rarely, except for short distances and on the smooth roads or the beach, did they leave a walk. Nevertheless, first and last they covered a deal of country. And the amount of solemn chaffing and small practical joking that went on would have disgraced the Sixth Grade.

Occasionally, when the tide was low, they rode along the sands; and occasionally they took an excursion across the oak dotted acres of the *ranchos*. But much they preferred to clamber single file along the trails in the Sur. Then trails were not, as they are now, graded, brushed, and smoothed by Forest Services or Chambers of Commerce. They were really rough and precipitous. It took Boyd some time to become accustomed to riding on them. The park horses he knew would never have been able to keep their footing in the loose stones and on the big outcropping boulders, over which these animals clambered so blithely. These trails, too, stood disconcertingly on end, so that the horses had to scramble hard with many humping heaves to reach a foothold where they could breathe; or they bunched all their feet together and sat back to slide. It was most unhorselike. And Boyd for a long time rested his weight on the inside stirrup where the trail narrowed, and the outside stirrup hung out over blue depths where the buzzards soared below him. He leaned slightly inward and looked straight ahead and conversed rather disjointedly. It was not that he was actually afraid, but he certainly was nervous. Those gay old birds, his companions, knew perfectly for they had been there themselves. Therefore they delighted at such times in trotting their horses, leaning forward to slap Boyd's animal on the haunches with their *morales*—the braided whip-like ends of the reins. After a while Boyd came to understand that to these hillbred horses, such a terrain was as safe as a boulevard. Then he relaxed and enjoyed himself.

The trails started in the cañons with their shady oaks and sycamores, their parks of grass and flowers, their leaping sparkling streams with boulders and pools, waterfalls and fern banks; they climbed by lacets to a "hogsback"—or tributary ridge—through overarching cascara and mountain lilac; and so proceeded to upper regions. The sun against the shade and the chaparral warmed to life many odours. White of cascara, blue of lilac powdered whole mountain sides with bloom; the leaves of the mountain cherries glittered in the sun, and the satin red bark of manzanita glowed. The air was like crystal under the blue sky, and the single notes of the mountain quail rang clear as though the crystal had been struck. Cañon slopes fell away grandly. Great mathematical shadows defined the sharp ridge —and the abrupt foldings of the hills. The sky was a steady, calm watchful blue. No wonder old boys—old, but always boys—turned light hearted and played pranks that would have made their children or grandchildren ashamed—if they had known! Especially as George Scott, the amused cynic, never went riding. He spent his mornings at the beach, watching the bathers, snubbing the forward, and uttering caustic comment.

But it was when they stopped on some outlying spur and looked abroad on the scenery that the real charm of the country gripped them.

For over the panorama below them lay a misty peace, a suspended stillness as though a great Spirit had sighed in his sleep and had for a contented moment held his breath, and the moment was as the Biblical thousand years. From above, the folds of the lesser hills were soft and rounded, and on them showed the dark spots of the trees. The sea rose up from the depths below them until it met the horizon at the level of the eye. This gave it the curious effect of being the opposite wall of a cañon in the bottom of which lay Arguello and the farms and the *ranchos* and the shore. A yellow haze mellowed it. From incredible distances and with incredible clarity, rose single sounds—the stroke of a bell, the lowing of cattle. The pungent aroma of sage brush—Old Man—hung in the air.

The old boys used to stop and look on all this with great inner appreciation, but with outward indifference. At length Boyd himself broke out:

"Where on the globe," he cried, "will you find anything even approaching this? The climate is perfect; the people—look at the way that country lies! There's not another place in the world where you can ride a horse in high mountains and come home on a beach two hundred feet wide, and do it all in one afternoon! There's not another place like it in California! Why look at the size of that valley, and consider how many people, wealthy people, will flock in here when a few of them get to know it as we know it! There won't be room for them! Why, the fellow who owns real estate——"

They crowded their horses around him whooping with amusement, slapping him on the back, while even the staid old horse fidgeted.

"He's got it!" they cried. "It's bit him!" "The old cuss has a bad case; he'll come back!"

Boyd stood their banter with a grin that was at first a little shamefaced, but soon became triumphant. His was not a nature to take it lying down.

"Yes, I've got it, you poor nincompoops; and I'm bit. But I'm not coming back. Why? Because I won't have to. I'm going to stay. Just soak that up, will you? You got to go back and attend to your business. I don't have to unless I want to; and I don't want to. While you are sweating away in those pleasant eastern summers, or thawing the icicles out of the whiskers of hope before you can get away next winter, you just think of me right up here, or right down there picking oranges and flowers and filling my system up with this good air!"

"You don't mean that, do you, Boyd?" inquired Saxon, the shoe man.

"Of course I mean it."

"How about your business?"

"To hell with my business! It don't need me any more: and I don't need it."

"I don't know," rejoined Saxon doubtfully. He with the rest was sobered down from vacation irresponsibility by Boyd's decision to do what each had secretly played with as a fascinating but impractical possibility. "How about yourself? You'll get sick of this sort of a thing as a steady diet."

"I'll get me a place," said Boyd, stoutly. "I'll buy me a ranch over the mountains. There's a big future in this place. It's asleep now; sure thing. But it can be waked up. It ought to be waked up. Judging from what I've seen, that would keep a man busy for a while. Oh, I won't take root, if that's what you mean. You fellows are as blind as bats. All you see is a sleepy little backwater town that you have a good time in. It's got a great future."

"So confounded future that you won't live to see it—except of course that more and more tourists will come in. You aren't going into the resort business, are you, Boyd?" observed someone else.

"I may. Do'no yet. But you can stick a railroad up the coast, and bore a tunnel in through these mountains here for water so you can irrigate the way they've begun to do at San Bernardino, and cut up these big ranches into farms with water on them, and——"

But his companions burst out laughing.

"You're in the traction business," Saxon suggested. "How about it? After you get all these mountains knocked down and kicked out the way for your railroad, how about a new mule for the street car system?"

"I may take hold of that, too," rejoined Boyd, after the renewal of laughter.

He had not before seriously considered abandoning the East, but suddenly he could see no reason against it. Since his last merger he had practically retired from active management of the concerns that brought him his enormous income. He had no other family ties than those that bound him to his son, Kenneth. To a man of his temperament new friends quickly replaced the old. The vision, genuine though narrowly commercial, that had made him what he was, pierced the veils of apathy behind which Arguello slumbered to a sense of the rose dawn of a modern day. Now, suddenly, there on top of the mountain he came to a decision.

After lunch most of the old boys took naps as part of the complete rest they had come out here for. About three or half past, they came to life and assembled in the room back of the bar where they played hilarious poker until dinner time. Boyd did not need a nap, so he usually occupied the time before the poker game began in a stroll down the long main street.

He was of a gregarious nature and utterly democratic, and thus he became genially acquainted with about everybody who did business on Main Street, from Chipo the bootblack to Oliver Mills the banker. At first he pursued these various acquaintances idly and for the amusement and companionship they afforded him; but once he had decided to settle down in the place he began very keenly to direct his efforts. Jim Paige in his harness shop was a mine of information, and loved to gossip in his slow, drawling fashion. Boyd immensely enjoyed his humour, and at the same time gained a pretty comprehensive birds-eye-view of the valley's history and present status. Of county politics he learned from Dan Mitchell, the shirt-sleeved, tobacco chewing, fat, sleepy-eyed, cynical editor of the *Weekly Trumpet*. He even added Chinatown to his collection after a time, thrusting his head in at strange doors and shouting a cheery greeting to grave celestials with red buttoned caps. He perched for minutes at a time on the edge of Gin Gwee's counter watching the laundry boys blowing fine sprays from their mouths. On all the length of Main Street was not one shop, laundry, bank or office—on the **ground floor**—with whose interior he was not more or less familiar.

The occupant of one office eluded him for long enough to arouse his interest. It was a very small office, hardly more than a cubby hole, obviously boarded off from another and much larger establishment. Looking through the window Boyd saw a cheap golden-oak roll-top desk, one very second hand swivel chair, another chair that looked much as though its intended objective had been the kitchen. The other furnishings consisted of lithographed advertising calendars, and one or two of those framed chromos of impossibly steady steamships cutting through tossing seas in which wallowed relatively minute rival craft. The gilded letters on the window conveyed the information that this was the business abode of Ephraim Spinner who sold and rented real estate, wrote insurance of all types, did stenography and typewriting, and held the office of notary public. Boyd for some time failed to catch a glimpse of Ephraim. The desk continued closed, the door locked, and on the knob hung a neatly lettered card that read: *Back in ten minutes.* It did not state which ten minutes.

In his idleness of mind Boyd used to peer in through the window as he passed and speculate on the personality and habits of Mr. Ephraim Spinner. He made a number of deductions. The place was always neat and picked up, which, of course might argue that it was never used. But dust failed to accumulate, and the swivel chair stood at several angles. Spinner, in the final analysis, Boyd decided must be either a very young man or a rather old one, a very busy man or a very lazy one. There was no middle ground. He would not spoil this very languid interest by inquiring.

So it was with rather a pleasurable quickening that at last he perceived the door standing open.

He entered the tiny office. A tall, spare nervous individual sat at the desk. He was a young man, but his face was strongly carved. His very blond hair stuck straight up in an old fashioned brush pompadour. His eybrows and eyelashes were likewise very blond, and the skin on his face and hands a clear transparent light brown that must have been equally fair before it had been much exposed to the sun. He wore what might be described as a "smart business suit"—a sort of bob-tailed cut-away, the edges of which were bound with black braid. His manners were alert as he swung to face Boyd.

"You are Mr. Spinner?" asked the latter.

"The same," jerked back the young man. "What can I do for you?"

The air was electric, charged with energy. Spinner apparently had not a moment to waste. Nevertheless Boyd seated himself comfortably in the kitchen chair.

"Have a cigar?" he proffered, "you are very little in your office, Mr. Spinner. I suppose I have been by here a dozen times and this is the first I have found you in."

"My business is largely outside," snapped back Spinner with an air that seemed to add, "and you're keeping me from going back to it."

"My name is Boyd—Patrick Boyd," he introduced himself. "I'm staying at the Fremont. It is in my mind to stay out here for a little while, and if so I do not want to stay on at a hotel."

At Boyd's name the eyes of the young man flickered for an instant; but his manner did not change.

"Buy or rent?" he demanded.

"That depends on what I can get."

"How big? How many in family?"

"Myself and my son—grown," answered Boyd, amused.

"Would you build?"

"I might."

Spinner whirled his chair back to the desk, snatched open a drawer, flipped over a pack of green cards, another of pink cards, and a third of white cards; selected a half dozen or so of each, slammed shut the roll top desk and arose.

"Come on," he said.

"Where?"

"To look at houses, of course," rejoined Spinner impatiently.

In meekness, admiration, and considerable amusement Boyd trailed his guide around the corner to where stood a horse and buggy. Spinner ran over his cards and climbed in.

"We'll look at rent places first," he announced.

"Would you mind my looking at these cards?" asked Boyd.

"Not at all. Help yourself."

In the year eighteen hundred and eighty-odd, card filing systems were so rare as to be practically unknown. Boyd looked upon Spinner's crude beginning with respect.

"Very ingenious." he commented, "and very handy."

"Saves time," said Spinner.

As they drove about from one place to another, Spinner kept up a rattling staccato commentary on Arguello, its resources, its climate, its future. As he talked a new and different Arguello took the place of the old. The bare and vacant foothills twinkled whitely with villas looking across Italian-wise to the sea, the rutted streets smoothed under pavements echoing to horses hoofs, the rolling reaches of the cattle country became snug with irrigated farms, fountains spouted in the barren square of the city park, a boulevard skirted the sea——

"It's a comer," he repeated, "a comer! All we need is a little enterprise to grasp the chance. It will come. These people here are asleep; they're dead. It needs a new lot, people who appreciate opportunities and have the bustle and get up and git."

"You can't very well kill the inhabitants off," laughed Boyd.

"Won't need to. They'll be submerged, lost. This town will grow so fast you won't be able to find an old hard-shell with a search warrant."

"Perhaps they can be waked up," suggested Boyd.

"They're dead," repeated Spinner, "you can't wake the dead.

At least I can't. They've got no ambition. I never saw such a crowd! I've done my best, and I can't make a dent in them."

"Well, we may be able to do something," said Boyd, vaguely. He did not say so, but he could well conceive that the efforts of Patrick Boyd might get a reception that the efforts of Ephraim Spinner might lack.

In the course of investigation, which lasted over many days, they narrowed down to a quarter block lying just beyond Mrs. Stanley's place. It possessed two live oak trees; it was far enough out from the foothills to allow a view of the mountains: it caught a distant gleam of the sea; and—what Boyd foresaw would be most important—was within a few blocks of the Fremont. While the negotiations for its purchase were under way, Spinner had another suggestion.

"I've had a chance thrown my way," he said. "You're going to settle down here, you want to take an interest in the place, make a few investments, get an influence. Nothing like bank stock for that. And in a place like this bank stock is held mighty close. Formed by a few men and stock kept in the family. Now just at present I can get my hands on a good block of the First National. It's on the market, but quietly. I don't know for sure whether I'm the only agent. But it was put in my hands. It's a good buy as an investment; but it's a better buy because it's just what you need if you're going into affairs here. It's a chance you won't get every day."

"Give me the figures," said Boyd.

Thus it came about that he acquired the whole of Colonel Peyton's stock in the First National Bank, a very substantial interest that at once gave him a considerable influence in the management, should he choose to exert it.

II

Nor did Kenneth in his way make less of an initial impression than his forceful father. His handsome, laughing face and curly hair attracted attention at once; and his rather imperious manner did him no great harm. He was just past twenty, having graduated young from college; but, as is often the case with New York raised youth, gave an appearance of being older. The young life of the place absorbed him. He was good at sports, and this was essentially an out-of-door existence. His riding school instruction stood him in good stead, although he had a great deal to re-learn. At first he was inclined to be scornful of stock saddles and long straight stirrups immediately under the body, of spade bits and the loose swinging rein, simply because he had been taught on an English saddle and with curb and snaffle rigging. But after he had ridden a few trails, and especially after his first hard all-day expedition, he began to discover that these things had a logic back of them. As they were also exotic and picturesque Kenneth naturally swung to the other extreme and became intensely partisan of all western gear. He also swam well and played a decent game of tennis. But his chief asset was his eager ready zest for everything.

A party of young people rode every morning, and gathered at the Fremont as a rendezvous. Kenneth had already met them at the barbecue. It was a small group, this, and kept itself to itself. There were always a few newcomers hanging about its fringes, but they rarely lasted long enough to gain an intimacy. These youngsters had been brought up on horseback, and they were little inclined to tolerate any lack of skill or determination. Indeed one of the first things they ordinarily did to a stranger was to take him at once up a peculiarly atrocious slide rock on the Arroyo Pinto trail, named Slippery Sal. If he took that smiling, they came home down the narrow way on the full trot, plunging down the almost perpendicular mountain side in short-cuts across the angles or lacets of the trail.

There were in this group three boys and four girls, all of an age. The boys, naturally, seemed much younger, were hobble-de-hoys, with the amusing admixture of boyish diffidences or crudenesses and a pseudo-manly ease. It was very evident that they were considered as mere children, useful at times, by the young ladies, their sisters, who at eighteen were in their own opinions quite grown-up and important. Kenneth agreed with them and found them charming. There were Dora Stanley, Myra Welch, and Isabelle Carson, with brothers Martin. Stanley.

and Winchester Carson, all of whom Kenneth had met at Colonel Peyton's barbecue. Add also a small mischievous dark girl of sixteen, named Stella Maynard and a good deal of a nuisance in a gadfly fashion, and her brother John. Kenneth liked and patronized the "kids," as he looked on these fingerlings of the male sex: they made him feel old, important, a man of the world. He admired heartily the young ladies, their sisters, with their vigorous knowledge of out-of-door matters, their cool nerve, their sedate maturity flavoured with an occasional dash of tom-boy.

As was only human nature, especially at this age, he had his sentimental preference; or would have had could he have decided between two. Stella Maynard and Isabelle Carson were out of the running from the start. The former was a little brown thing with a sharp tongue and an unhappy faculty of making you feel that she was not taking you seriously at all points. The latter was too soft and slow and lazy. But between Dora Stanley and Myra Welch it was exceedingly difficult to choose. They were of quite opposite types, so their appeals could not be compared. Dora was quick, vivid in personality, exceedingly active physically, blonde, deep breasted, with a bright, high colour. She could hop on and off her sidesaddle without assistance from anybody; and she opened gates as she came to them, without masculine assistance. You could not "stump" her at anything. Once Kenneth by way of a particularly ridiculous joke said:

"I bet you don't dare ride down that rock slide."

Without a moment's hesitation she turned her horse's head toward the long, nearly perpendicular sweep of water-smoothed granite that dropped from the edge of the trail some fifty oi sixty feet to the boulder-strewn creek bed. The animal hesitated, as well he might. Dora set her teeth and raised the short heavy quirt. There seemed no doubt that she intended to force Brownie to make the plunge. But Kenneth, his face pale as paper, crowded forward past Winchester, who sat in apparent paralysis, and laid his hand on her bridle reins.

"Hold on!" he cried, "I was only fooling! Don't you know better than to try that? You'll kill yourself!"

"I won't take a dare from anybody!" she answered, looking at him defiantly.

"Shucks," confided her brother Martin to his chum Winchester a little later. "I'm on to her. She'd have done it all right—if nobody had stopped her, but she knew darn well somebody would stop her," which was fairly astute even for younger brother, in which tribe no illusions dwell.

Myra Welch was just the opposite. She was slender and very dark, with a clear colourless complexion and slumbrous eyes veiled by indecently long lashes. Sometimes she raised them and looked appealing or helpless. She never thought of trying to climb into her sidesaddle without assistance. Her foot was small and arched. She placed the instep in the hollow of Kenneth's joined hands, and at a signal sprang lightly into the saddle. The brief momentary impact of her weight, the touch of her hand on his shoulder, the swirl of her habit as she hung her knee over the horn, the fumbling of her left foot for the stirrup—in which Kenneth must assist—all these possessed a strange and fascinating thrill. Twice or thrice he caught a glimpse of her silk stocking above her short boot, perhaps an inch or so lower than the hem of a modern skirt, but this was eighteen eighty-odd, and probably Myra got her effect. Then she would thank him demurely enough, but a fraction of a second before he would turn away she would raise her long demure lashes and gaze straight at him. Nor did she open gates, but waited. She had no brothers, but did not thereby escape brotherly criticisim. The three boys had grown up with her.

"Myra makes me sick!" said Win, bitterly. "I bet she gets his frat pin away from him in a month."

But for this sporting proposition he had no takers. Myra would certainly have had the fraternity emblem—that acknowledgedly symbolic scalp of the college age—long before the month, had it not been that Kenneth was considerably intrigued by Dora's bold, vivid spirit. It was something he had not encountered in the East. Myra's type was not uncommon, though it must be confessed that she was Class A in her type.

Kenneth soon found that even the best horse he could hire at the big stables failed to do him sufficient honour. They were enduring enough. No amount of hard work could make more than a slight impression on these wiry western-bred animals, and these were certainly called upon to do their full share of the day's work. But livery horses get to be philosophers. They are ridden by so many different people that their pride of family descends to practically *nil*. They have no particular enthusiasm for scampers on the beach—who can tell how soon or for how far they will be called on again? Kenneth called his father's attention to the desirability of a private mount. Boyd saw the point.

At that time a first class California-bred horse, good in configuration, speedy, surefooted, could be had for twenty-five dollars. It was characteristic of Boyd that, from his intricate acquaintanceship on Main Street, he should know of a Kentucky mare, a chestnut, eight years old, a beautiful fine-bred animal that, nevertheless, had been raised in the back country and was as sure footed as any of the native stock. For her he paid a hundred and twenty-five dollars, an extravagant price as horse-flesh went. It was equally characteristic that he should refuse to finance Kenneth's idea as to fancy saddle and equipment.

"I'll buy you a good serviceable outfit," he proffered, "or I'll furnish half the money for any other outfit that you may want. But you will have to furnish the other half yourself."

"Where will I get the money?" returned Kenneth, doubtfully.

"You have an allowance"—Kenneth looked still more doubtful, "I know it is small, but it is sufficient if you want to deprive yourself of other things. Or you can go to work. I will find you something to do—probably in a bank. You will have no expenses, and can save all of your salary for whatever you want."

Kenneth looked out of the window toward the mountains.

"I want to work, of course," he returned, soberly, "and I suppose, since I graduated in mid-year, I ought not to wait over the summer vacation, as I should if I graduated in June. But I would like to start in the fall rather than now."

"I think myself that it would be better. I want you to have the benefit of this summer out-of-doors. It was only a suggestion."

Kenneth made arrangements for the rental of a livery outfit pending his ability to buy what he desired. He was still very much of a small boy in some respects. Jim Paige's harness shop inspired in him exactly the same longing as fills the breast of an urchin, nose pressed against the window, gazing in at an air gun or a Flobert rifle he knows to be beyond his reach. Kenneth loafed around Jim Paige's aromatic shop a great deal of the time. He half-pretended he liked to talk with Jim, whom he found to be a character, but in reality he came to gloat and yearn over certain articles he had singled out as to be his own in some impossibly remote future. It is not necessary to attempt an analysis of this feeling, nor to explain how in some mysterious manner these articles invested themselves with a compelling influence no mere physical objects ever could have. It is unnecessary because every mortal soul has experienced it.

There was, to begin with, the saddle. It was not a mere saddle, nor had it been picked out for its looks. By the time Kenneth had fully made up his mind to it, he knew a lot about saddles because there had been a great many decisions to make. The trees on which they were constructed were of different shapes—the Cheyenne, the Laramie and others—differing in the spread, the arch of the bow and the height of the cantle. Each type had its claimed advantages and its disadvantages. Each type also had its violent partisans in the persons of the cowboys who occasionally dropped across from the other side of the Sur and who roosted about Jim Paige's shop picturesquely, to the worshipful awe of the Eastern boy. His choice was decided by hearing an individual more dogmatic than the rest.

"The reason I holds with the Cheyenne is 'count of the bow," he said. "You take a centre-fire saddle and that bow and you tie to any steer on four hoofs and your outfit's going to hold."

On the strength of this Kenneth not only decided on the Cheyenne tree, but also the single cinch, or "centre-fire." Should he have the horn leather-covered or bare? Should the skirts have square corners or be cut away on a curve? Should the stirrups be of the ox-bow or California type? How about *tapaderas*, or stirrup covers? If it was decided to have them, should they be of the closed box type or the sort with long pointed flappers?

"When yo're drivin' cattle in the brush and you've got taps

with flappers on them, you can just shake a foot and scare your
stock out," stated the dogmatic cowboy.

So Kenneth decided on taps, just as he had decided on the
Cheyenne tree, as though his chief requirement was a machine
for handling heavy cattle!

The *latigos* must be of belt leather and without buckles—
effeminate devices for saving time—what if just as you had
roped a steer the buckle should tear out! For the same important reason the stirrup leathers must be quadruple, three
inches wide, of thick stock, and must be laced with thongs. To
change the length was a half hour's job, whereas a buckle will permit of their being raised or lowered in a jiffy—but consider again
that enraged and ensnared steer! He picked out a *cincha* that
was eight inches wide, woven of horsehair in a white and black
pattern, with a tassel or tuft sticking down in the centre of it.

"That's what I call a real cinch," the cowboy had cried.
"That'd hold anything!"

This new friend surveyed Kenneth's completed specifications
attentively.

"That'd make you a saddle you wouldn't need to suspicion
nohow," he pronounced.

Kenneth had already picked from the dozen beautiful made-up
saddles in the shop the carved design that pleased him most.
Of course this super-saddle must be carved! And that did not
mean any of your cheap stamped stuff, but deep rich hand carving with simple tools—an almost lost art to-day. He offered
his results to Paige and demanded a price.

"I got pretty near what you want already," said Jim, leading
the way to a saddle in the window.

But the saddle in the window differed slightly, and Kenneth
had so intently brooded over every detail that difference was
fatal. Jim Paige promised to figure on it; and then, of course,
laid the paper one side. Jim was always a very busy man.
He could work and talk at the same time, but he could not work
and figure at the same time. Every afternoon for nearly a week
Kenneth demanded the figures of the estimate; and every afternoon Jim Paige confessed that he just sort of hadn't got around
to it yet.

"Look here, young fellow," he said at last. "You sure stick to it like death to a dead nigger. Do you realize that this is getting on to harvest time? I've got my harness work to do. I couldn't make you a saddle before next month anyways."

So Kenneth mooned on into the question of bridles. There were flat leather, round leather, braided rawhide, and flat-braided horsehair; they could be made up as split-ear or regulation; they could be ornamental, with silver studs or silver *conchas*, or they could be left plain; the reins could be made California style with a lash or *morale*, or they could be made Arizona fashion, separately, so that all you had to do was to drop them and your horse was "tied to the ground." Of course he coveted a silver-mounted bit—one with wide side bars in which the silver was inlaid in blued steel and the whole heavily carved.

That much was certain, but how about the bit itself—spade, Cruces type, bronco type? It was all most fascinating. And there seemed to be a reason for each of these variations.

Of course there were also other items that had to do more with personal taste. Everybody wore big iron blunt spurs held on by broad straps. The rowels were an inch and over in diameter. There was a wide choice—anything could be had, from plain iron ones for a dollar to wonderful silver-inlaid beauties with clappers that rang against the rowels and *conchas* as big as a dollar on the carved straps. Of course one had to decide whether the shank should be straight, or should turn up, or down. Reasons having to do with hanging on by the cinch (when your horse bucked) or catching the cantle (when you left the saddle to pick things off the ground) were advanced for choosing one or the other. And there were rawhide or grass-rope *riatas*, and long hair ropes (one hopelessly expensive, incredibly soft one, of actual human hair), and *cantinas* to fit over the horn. Kenneth already possessed a broad Stetson hat, of course, with a carved leather band.

So assiduous became his devotion to the harness shop for the first ten days after the purchase of Pronto, that Boyd felt called upon to ask Jim if the young man were not a nuisance.

"Like to see him," returned Jim, carefully cutting a scoop out of a piece of leather.

"Well, you go ahead and make up that saddle he wants," said Boyd. "Don't say who it's for. I'll give it to him later for his birthday or Christmas or something. You sure he isn't a nuisance?"

"Not a bit," disclaimed Jim. "Besides, I don't believe you could keep him out with a fly screen."

III

THE first Saturday of the month Kenneth was standing on the side veranda of the Fremont awaiting the arrival of Pronto when with disconcerting suddenness a wild cavalcade dashed around the bend in the drive and pulled up before the hitching rail. They brought with them a swirl of dust and noise and rapid motion. There were five of them on horseback, and these only immediately preceded a four-horse drag that took the turn in a grand sweep. Kenneth glanced at the driver with admiration of his skill and saw a rigid, small immaculate dark man in a wide Stetson hat, a carefully tied white stock, a checked cutaway coat, and riding breeches ending in high-heeled cowboy boots. He wore brown gloves. He had glittering black eyes, glittering white teeth, and a small moustache waxed to long, stiff needle points. His handling of his four was beyond praise. He tooled them skillfully alongside the veranda and to a halt, with no more than a slight raising of his gloved hands. Then he handed the reins to a Mexican who sat beside him but at a lower elevation, and descended from his perch.

The horsemen flung themselves from the saddle and with fine disregard for rules and regulations as to hitching animals in the hotel grounds, dropped their reins over their horses' heads and left them. Then they tramped boisterously across the veranda, laughing loudly, shouting to each other, clanking the rowels of their spurs against the floor; elaborately unconscious of the spectators, and disappeared in the bar room door. The irruption and disappearance took place so quickly that Kenneth got no more than a confused impression. One had a long white beard and a rubicund face; one seemed to be a very large man. Near the hitching rail the abandoned saddle horses were tossing their heads, rolling their eyes, shifting softly to and fro. They were a wild, half-broken looking lot, curly with sweat. The leather of the equipment was dark and shiny with use, and Kenneth thrilled to observe that the necks of the horns were deeply grooved where they had taken the strain of the rope. The four harnessed horses were also restless, stamping their feet, shifting their positions, but standing, for they were evidently well trained. The vehicle to which they were attached was a wonderful creation. It consisted of two front wheels with a seat on a superstructure about eight feet immediately above it, and two rather distant hind wheels attached to the rest of it by one solid beam.

"If that ain't the darn-foolest contraption for four horses to drag!" observed a bitter voice next Kenneth's ear. He turned to meet old Patterson's bilious eye. The riding master with his tame animals was awaiting the gathering of his supertame class. "And look at them saddle hosses—one mess of sweat. Makes me sick!"

"Who are they?" asked Kenneth.

"Passel of darn fools that live on ranches over the mountains. They come in about once a month and raise hell. I don't see why people stand for them. If I was marshal I bet I'd put a stop to 'em. I'd have them up for disturbin' the peace and cruelty to animals and—there, look at that mess! Serves 'em right!"

The saddle horses had, during this colloquy, begun to quarrel and bite. The Mexican descending from the drag attempted to quiet them, whereupon the supposedly well-trained four abandoned the path of virtue and started to wheel off. They turned away from the Mexican so that in another second they would have got going, and then there would have ensued a really spectacular runaway, had not Kenneth darted out and seized the leaders' bits. The Mexican's shout evidently reached the noisy party in the bar for they piled out as rapidly as they had piled in. The little dark man with the waxed moustache strolled to the edge of the veranda. He shot a volley of Spanish at the Mexican under which the latter curled up.

"Now, darling little ones," he addressed his companions

caressingly, "since the first lovely exuberance of your spirits has spent itself, suppose you hitch that awful collection to something, as you should have done in the first place." His voice was slow and soft but carried a sarcastic edge, which it lost as his next words were addressed to Kenneth: "I have to thank you, sir, for your prompt action. My name is Herbert Corbell. You will join us, I trust."

Kenneth found himself in the dark, high cool aromatic interior of the Fremont bar, with the twinkling glasses and mirrors, and white-clad Barney eyeing him across the counter.

There were a number of round tables. Some perched on these, some dangled their legs from the bar itself. Kenneth had a confused impression of a roomful of people, which was not the reality; Corbell held him firmly by the upper arm and halted him in the middle of the room.

"Brother members of the ancient *Sociedad de los Años*," he said pleasantly; and at once the tumult died to absolute silence and all faces were turned toward him. "This young man says his name is Boyd, which I do not vouch for, of course. All I know is that he was to-day sent by Providence to take our part. He is therefore nominated Benefactor, and will be respected as such for this session only." He turned to Kenneth and gravely extended his hand. "Sir, I congratulate you," he said, ceremoniously, "on your election to the worshipful position of Benefactor."

Kenneth, much confused, blushed and shifted uneasily and wondered what he was supposed to do or say. But Corbell went smoothly on.

"Allow me to introduce in turn the members of the equally worshipful Society. The shrinking violet on the end of the bar is Bill Hunter; he is native born, free up to date—though unjustly—fairly white though inclined toward the brick red. The best he does is to swell. Hop down and swell for the Benefactor, Bill."

Bill was a compact, powerfully built thick man dressed in black and white checks that emphasized his size, with a blond, sweeping moustache, and a childlike blue eye. As Corbell's smooth voice ceased he obediently dropped from the end of the bar. Holding his arms half crooked from his sides he proceeded to expand his chest and contract all his mighty muscles. The stout cloth was instantly strained smooth around his mighty proportions.

"That's why we call him Big Bill. You should see him do it stripped," continued Corbell, blandly. "He is better at that than at headwork. Our Bill is none too bright, I am sorry to say. He has little sense of humour. That will be all, Bill."

Hunter, without appearing to mind all this in the least, grinned and heaved himself back on the end of the bar.

"The youngster over there with the long white lambrequin is Johnny Anderson. He is supposed to have died about ten years ago; but he's too contrary to obey orders. He is one of those pests known as old-timers—drove stage over the gol-ding-dest mountains and all that sort of thing. If you don't watch him very closely he'll take you one side and tell you stories of the good old days. He's a hardened old sinner who ought to know better than go around with us. The thing he does best is to drink whisky toddies, but we will not ask him to exhibit his skill. The long lank personage near Big Bill ought, of course, to be called Shorty. But he's not. His name is Frank Moore and he's chiefly noted for being the human goat. Feed a glass, Barney."

The barkeeper set out a thin edged champagne glass, empty.

"Not in that condition," objected Frank firmly.

"Obey your Potentate who watches that the lamb be not fleeced nor that the thirsty thirst. All will be made up unto you in due time," replied Corbell, cryptically.

"Oh, very well, I rely on your good faith," grumbled Moore. He picked up the empty champagne glass, bit a chunk out of it, chewed up the glass and appeared to swallow it.

"The next exhibit," proceeded Corbell without pause, and indicating a little hard muscled young Englishman in tweeds, well worn riding breeches, and old boots, "is William Maude St. Clair Ravenscroft. He claims to be British and of very high rank, but we suspect him because every one of these names is spelled just the way I pronounced it. The only mitigating circumstance is that he has named his ranch Bletherington

Towers and pronounces it Chumley Briars. So he may be all right after all. Now there are various others," he said looking severely around the room, "but I weary. All present with one exception are members in good standing." His glance rested on one after the other appraisingly, and they all stood grinning, waiting to see if he intended to continue his monologue. Kenneth's eyes followed his. To his surprise he recognized Jim Paige. The harnessmaker was never away from his bench. He saw also a round-faced, good humoured looking young chap in cowboy rig. Old George Scott was there. A vapid looking individual in tweeds and a fore-and-aft cap, wearing a monocle and a flaxen moustache—one of that very rare species, the typical stage Englishman—was looking on with an air of bewilderment illy concealed under an attempt to appear knowing. Kenneth guessed him the one exception mentioned by Corbell. In fact he proved to be a visitor addressed as Sir Edgar. He was collecting material for a book on the country, and these young men had taken him up for the pleasure of seeing that he got it. Ravenscroft was the only member who did not look pleased whenever Sir Edgar came to the front.

"Worthy Potentate," spoke up the glass eater at length. "When does the Benefactor benefact?"

"He has partly benefacted," explained Corbell, "in stopping my team. It is meet that he now complete the function of his being."

All eyes were turned on Kenneth. An expected pause ensued. He was in an agony of embarrassment, for he had not the slightest idea what to do. He caught Barney's good humoured Irish eye. Barney made the slightest gesture as though drinking.

"Will you gentleman join me?" invited Kenneth instantly.

They joined him and after the confusion of ordering, crowding about, and getting the drinks had settled Kenneth found himself, not neglected nor ignored, but simply relegated to a position of second importance. He had not money enough in his pocket to pay for the treat; but a word with Barney fixed that all right. Kenneth had a better chance to look about him and to enjoy what he saw.

The principal business of the Society seemed to be providing Sir Edgar with material for his book. All the worn old "California stories" were being trotted out for his benefit. Some of these were so steep that Kenneth could not imagine any one taking them seriously; but the nearest the Englishman came to incredulity was an anxious inquiry or so.

"I say, you're not spoofing me now?"

Kenneth watched him narrowly in suspicion that his innocence might be only apparent.

"I'm English myself," said Ravenscroft at his elbow, disgustedly, "but this is really too much of a silly ass!"

"If they believe his book in England," observed Kenneth, "the score will be more than even."

"By Jove, I believe you're right," said Ravenscroft brightening, and looking at Kenneth with a new interest. "And I'll buy an edition and distribute it."

From that moment he took more part in the stuffing of Sir Edgar. Frank Moore was explaining that the size of California products was due to the alleged fact that a galvanic current running from the North Pole to South Pole—hence the compass—in California for the first time ran across the land.

"Unfortunately the rest of its course is beneath the sea," said Frank didactically. "You have no doubt noticed, Sir Edgar, the enormous proportions of our agricultural products—it is all due to the influence on the soil of this galvanic current."

"Jolly big strawberries for breakfast," murmured Sir Edgar. "Big as tomatoes, 'pon my word."

"Not as big as our tomato, pardon me," breathed Moore with exquisite courtesy. "But strawberrries are hardly fair, for they are to a large extent non-conductors."

"Non-conductors?" echoed Sir Edgar.

"Of galvanic current. Some things are better conductors of the current than others, and naturally they get more influence from it and attain to a larger size. Take our pumpkins, for example——"

"Pumpkins?"

"A sort of squash. You know the ordinary size of squashes—well these pumpkins grow to such a size that it is quite customary to place a small pig or shoat inside. As he eats he grows, until he has attained his full size inside the pumpkin."

"I say, you are spoofing."

"Not at all—in proper localities, of course, you must understand me. The growth is necessarily very rapid. On rough ground it is sometimes necessary to place wheels or rollers beneath the pumpkins."

"What is that for?"

"To prevent their being worn out. You see the vines grow so fast that they drag the pumpkins about."

Even Sir Edgar's vacuous countenance took on an expression of derisive incredulity.

"You'll have to show me that, you know," said he.

"It is, unfortunately, the wrong time of year for pumpkins," replied Moore.

"Haw, haw!" cackled Sir Edgar triumphantly.

"Darn fool!" muttered Corbell, in reference to Frank Moore, "if he doesn't watch his step he'll spoil the whole game!" He tried to catch Frank's eye.

But that saturnine individual knew his way about.

"Well," he drawled argumentatively, "there's our asparagus. You know what asparagus is like, ordinarily. Out here, in localities where the current is strong, it grows to quite extraordinary size—quite extraordinary, I assure you. It has to be cut down with an axe and trucked to the railroad; and must be transported on flat cars."

"You'll have to show me that, you know," retorted Sir Edgar. This seemed to have been an effective bit of repartee before.

"Certainly," agreed Frank, unexpectedly. "Come along."

He slouched out to the veranda, followed curiously by all the Society and its Benefactor. Alongside the garden walk, where it had been stowed awaiting transportation to the dump heap, lay a stalk of the century plant. As most people now know this central stalk, before it branches into flower, shoots up to a height of ten to twenty feet, and almost exactly resembles a stalk of fat asparagus. But very few people knew it then. Sir Edgar gazed on this monstrosity with open mouth.

"Bah Jove, I'd never have believed it!" he gasped. "I should like to obtain a photograph!"

"If you will promise to publish it in your book," suggested

Frank, "I will get you a photograph of a bunch of it tied for market."

"Will you really?"

"Oh, rawther!" breathed the enraptured Society.

Frank evidently thought he had earned a drink by this masterly turning to account of what his quick eye had noticed on coming in. His pumpkin story was also thereby rehabilitated. But suddenly Corbell put his foot down. It was obvious that he was the leader of these wild spirits, evidently from sheer force of personality.

"We're not here to get drunk," he pronounced,—"at least not this early in the day. Programme! To the beach!" He turned politely to Kenneth, with no trace of the mock buffoonery. "Have you a horse? Yes? Suppose you ride with the others and I will take Jim Paige with me." It was assumed that Kenneth would remain with the party, and he was very glad to do so.

Corbell, the Mexican, and Jim Paige managed to squeeze themselves into the airy little seat; the others leaped into their saddles; and with shattering suddenness they burst into violent motion down the drive. Around the corner into Main Street the ponies scampered headlong. Kenneth over his shoulder saw the drag careening drunkenly after. Then he gave his attention to his riding; for, good horseman that he was, he had not yet attained that utter abandon and recklessness that comes to those brought up in pursuit of wild mountain cattle. He had rather a confused impression of people dodging out of the way, of his mare skipping nimbly over or around chuck holes or obstructions, of a whirl of dust, of more people drawing hastily aside, of considerable shouting—and he found himself at the beach. The drag stopped broadside on. The horsemen nimbly dismounted and began to strip the saddles from their mounts.

"Come over here by me," Corbell summoned him. "You don't know this game; and it is against the rules for Benefactors to take part."

They mounted bareback and at once proceeded to pull each other from their seats. It was a nice display of horsemanship and judgment. The ponies wheeled and darted, their riders clinging like Indians. They snatched at each other, attempting surprise or tactical advantage. Occasionally they came to grips and wrestled. Then it was only a question of a moment or so before one—or both—hit the sand with a thump. It was a wild, fascinating, rough, rather dangerous game. The two star performers were Bill Hunter, by reason of his enormous strength, and the Englishman Ravenscroft because of his hard wiry agility.

So interested was Kenneth that he did not observe the approach of a grave middle-aged bearded man beautifully mounted on a dapple gray. He wore a long black coat and a wide black hat. But Corbell saw him.

"Pinched again," he said disgustedly—"the sheriff!" His eye fell on Sir Edgar and lit with hope. With remarkable agility he scrambled down from his lofty perch and walked to meet the officer. For some time a whispered colloquy went on, Corbell's hand on the mane of the gray and the sheriff bending gravely forward to listen. Several times his eyes rested on Sir Edgar. At length his bearded lips parted in a reluctant smile.

"All right," he said, raising his voice so that the attentive participants in the suspended game might hear him. "This once—for the last time!"

He swung the gray's forefeet lightly and gracefully off the ground in a half circle and trotted away.

"He has no sense of humour," observed Corbell, looking sadly after him. "But we've got to behave going back. The infuriated populace is laying for us with shotguns."

They rode back to the Fremont two by two at a walk, their heads bowed, holding their hats in their right hands clasped against their breasts.

At the hotel Kenneth lost sight of them for a while, as they started off somewhere on another expedition to which they did not think to invite him. He was too shy to call himself to their attention. They reappeared for dinner at an especial table in the corner. There was wine in ice buckets and considerable noise. The rest of the decorous dining room looked indignant, amused, or scandalized. Still they were perfectly respectable, except for the noise. Sir Edgar was in evening dress

trying very hard to enter into the spirit of the occasion. He
drank considerably more wine than anybody else, to which
course he was indefatigably urged by an increasingly polite and
solicitous Frank Moore. Ravenscroft's lean, weathered face
showed a slight uneasiness. This was the night of the weekly
"hop" and many of the women had on light toilettes for the
occasion. Some of the townspeople were dining there. Corbell
caught sight of Kenneth and waved his hand, to the latter's
secret delight.

"Friends of yours?" commented Boyd. "Who are they? I
see Jim Paige and George Scott lapping it up with the best of
them, but I don't recognize the others."

"They are ranch men from over the mountains," answered
Kenneth, "and they are loads of fun." That on reflection
was all he knew about them.

After dinner the *Sociedad* adjourned directly to the bar,
whence came wild sounds. Kenneth would much have liked
to go see what fun or deviltry was up, but was not yet sufficiently
out of his boyhood openly and boldly to enter a bar-room.

The hotel "hop" began shortly after eight o'clock, which
hour then seemed entirely pleasant and appropriate. It took
place in the long hotel parlour, which had been canvased for
the purpose, and the heavier furniture of which had been moved
into a back hall. A Spanish orchestra consisting of a piano, a
violin, two mandolins, and three guitars tinkled at one end. The
guests sat in chairs lined in a row against the walls. All the
social life of the place, old and young, was there, and if to our
eyes the banged hair, the tight sleeves, the hour-glass figures,
and the bustles and flounces would seem ridiculous, nevertheless
none of these things could disguise the fresh sweet vivacious
youth, the high colour and spirits, and the feminine daintiness
whose alchemy can—temporarily—transfer the worst vagaries
of fashion into charm. They danced a hopping waltz that went
round and round and round, and the schottische and polka,
and a number of square dances. Occasionally the even tenor
of merriment would be broken by one or the other of the members of the *Sociedad de los Años* appearing in the doorway. They
were always perfectly quiet and respectable; though, it must be

admitted, a trifle flushed; and they contented themselves with standing in the doorway for a few moments looking on. Nevertheless this brief appearance always caused a flutter of uneasiness. Suppose one of them should leave the doorway and cross the floor directly at one, and ask one to dance! Horrors! What would one say? *and what would mamma say afterward!* The idea was shivery, exciting, perhaps not wholly unpleasant.

It was not until nearly ten o'clock, however, that Herbert Corbell appeared. His dark face was not in the least flushed, and his bright, quick eye was thoroughly in command. Quite coolly he ran it over the room. Then he fulfilled the secret fear-hope of the fluttered; he proceeded in the most leisurely fashion across the room straight toward the spot where sat Myra Welch. Myra from the ambush of her long sleepy lashes saw him coming, but pretended not to, and began suddenly to lavish the most unusual attention on her awkward companion. For, by chance, Myra was doing a duty dance with John Maynard; whose callow attempts bored her extremely. Therefore she had, when the music stopped, steered him over next Mrs. Stanley, who was chaperoning both Dora and herself.

Mrs. Stanley saw the approach of Corbell with a rising of the hackles. The uncompromising old lady disapproved of Corbell in every way. She did not like his waxed moustache, which she considered vaguely villainous and certainly affected; she did not like the direct, faintly quizzical concealed amusement of his glance; she did not like his silly superior accent nor his broad A's; she did not like his clothes, which she thought of as "dudish"; she thoroughly disapproved of all his actions and expected the worst. Instantly she visualized his dancing with Myra, and then walking out on the veranda or into the grounds with her, and not bringing her back until all hours, and that soft fool Myra not knowing any better than to permit it—flirtatious, soft, little fool!—and she responsible to Mrs. Welch—no use trying to drop a hint to the young people of these days; they had no idea whatever of propriety or obedience. What they needed was a good spanking—all these thoughts, and others similar, went through Mrs. Stanley's head as Corbell picked his way across the floor. They had the effect of making her look even stiffer and more formidable than ever. Mrs. Stanley had bedecked her tall spare frame with all the war harness of the ballroom, and yet one saw her still in tweeds as her best wear.

Corbell, undismayed, was bowing before her with what she mentally designated as "dancing monkey manners." He made some pleasant remark to which, after glaring at him a moment, she returned a monosyllabic reply. Then he and Myra hopped off in a waltz.

Many eyes were turned on them. Against the united suspicion of the room they did not cease dancing until the music fell; against all prediction Corbell did not suggest that they go out and look at the moon. At the end of the dance Corbell led the secretly chargrined Myra directly back to Mrs. Stanley. For several moments he stood gallantly over the two, engaging them in lofty converse. Then he bowed low in courtly fashion and left the room with the utmost dignity. Once in the big empty hall outside the ballroom, however, he dissolved into whoops of delighted laughter, bending nearly double and slapping his leg.

"Fooled the old crab!" he cried to Kenneth, who happened to be passing. "Oh, didn't I fool her!"

He seized Kenneth by the arm and propelled him to the bar. "This is too rich. Come and we'll tell the boys!"

The room was full. The members of the celebrated *Sociedad* held the centre of the floor, but the fringes and the side tables were occupied by secretly delighted old boys who sipped their drinks silently and watched the fun. Kenneth had to drink with them. Sir Edgar was still the centre of attention and, it must be conceded, Sir Edgar was pretty far along. To the most outrageous saying or doings he merely smiled vacuously and murmured protestingly:

"I say—oh, I say!"

Some of them, especially Frank Moore, were piling it on pretty thick. They were trying to get Sir Edgar to perform various difficult physical tricks, such as placing his feet thirty inches from the wall and then picking a pin out of the wall with his teeth. There were numbers of these—all familiar to you from childhood—and Frank Moore was remembering them all.

Sir Edgar was game, though it was doubtful if his evening clothes would weather the storm. Every little while Corbell pounded vigorously on the bar for silence and then made each man repeat rapidly the words: "United States twin-screw steel cruiser" on penalty of no more drinks for failure. Every little while, also, he detailed one or more to go make an appearance in the ballroom.

"We must prove individually and collectively our complete sobriety," he pronounced. "Sir Edgar is excused. His reputation is established."

After a time Colonel Peyton came in, courteous, old-fashioned, smiling. The room immediately fell silent, and those who were sitting or perching jumped to their feet.

"Good evening, boys, good evening," said the Colonel. "Having a good time? That's right! That's right! Pretty noisy—don't object to that—but——"

Corbell turned and held up his hand.

"United States twin-screw steel cruisers," a chorus answered him.

"Perfectly satisfactory, gentlemen," said the Colonel. "Your honour and the honour of the house appear to be safe as usual. Now will you honour me by drinking a little toast to the pleasure of the evening; and permit me to tell you how glad I am that you are here."

The Colonel, as beseemed a Kentucky gentleman raised in California, took a finger of bourbon in a little glass. They all insisted on clinking their glasses against his. The little ceremony consumed several minutes. Then they drank bottoms-up in silence.

"I will wish you good evening, gentlemen," then said the Colonel. "I am very glad that you are here again."

"The darn old cuss really means it," sniffled Shot Sheridan, the erstwhile silent member, suddenly becoming tearful and sentimental.

"Shot, you're drunk!" Corbell accused him severely. "Go and sit at that table. Do it!—Bill!" he said, as Sheridan showed signs of rebellion.

Bill Hunter placed his huge hand on Shot's shoulder and

propelled him like a child to the designated table.   There was
no resisting that mighty force.

"Now," continued Corbell, turning to Sir Edgar. "What are
we going to do about this thing?   I am glad to see you boys had
sense enough to crowd around and hide him.   I should have been
mortified to have the Colonel see him in this state.   It was a
narrow squeak.   While he is not a member, still we are responsible for him.   Disgracefully pickled!"

"Oh, I say!" protested Sir Edgar feebly.

But Kenneth could stay no longer to see the outcome.   He had
been for some time shifting from one foot to the other in an
agony of indecision.   Kenneth had a horrible fear that the
number of dances he was "bolting" could never be explained.
He returned to the ballroom.   When, an hour later, he looked
into the bar it was empty—save for Sir Edgar.   That peer's
swallow coat tails had been nailed to the wall.   Sir Edgar was
struggling feebly to get away.

"Chuck it, old chap, chuck it!" Kenneth understood him to
say.

IV

HOWEVER hard these joyous spirits might play, they worked
equally hard.   Only—as is always the case with such men—the
work was done far away and out of sight where it did no good to
their reputations.   On Monday morning they had disappeared,
and Kenneth learned from Barney that they would probably
not reappear until the following month.   They left behind them
the clue to one gorgeous story that kept the town chuckling for
a week, once its fragments had been pieced together.   The clue
was an inquiry by Sir Edgar, proffered so many times that at
length its repetition aroused the curiosity of the old boys around
the Fremont veranda.

"Do you know Frank Moore?" he would ask, screwing in his
monocle.   "Rum sort of chap, now, isn't he?"

"Why does he pick out Frank Moore especially from that
gang of young hoodlums?" speculated Saxon.

"I'll ask Jim Paige," said Boyd.

It seemed that there was about half way up one of the cañons

of the Sur a copious sulphur hot-spring. To it led a rough
mountain road that ended in a small hotel and facilities for
bathing. All California was full of these resorts, some of them
quite pretentious, and all of them much scroll-sawed and white
painted and fancy panelled as beseemed the Boss-Carpenter
age of decoration and architecture. Most of these structures
have fallen into complete or partial decay as men's faith in
mineral springs has waned and—it must be confessed—as other
road house facilities have increased. Frank Moore had invited
Sir Edgar to sup with him that Sunday evening at the Hot Springs
Hotel. Sir Edgar had ridden his horse toilsomely up the steep
mountain road just at dusk, and had been led by his host to a
table perfectly appointed for two. When the meal had been
served it had proved to consist entirely and solely of raw eggs
and champagne. Moore, conversing affably, with entire lack
of self consciousness, sucked the eggs, ate the shells, drank the
champagne and ate the glasses. Then the two gentlemen adjourned to the veranda overlooking the valley two thousand
feet below for a short smoke; after which they rode down the
mountain together. Sir Edgar had not emerged from his
customary stolidity during the interesting performance; nor did
he ever utter any comment beyond the one above quoted.

The old life recommenced, with its riding, bathing, and buzzing
about. Winchester Carson's prediction that Myra would get
Kenneth's fraternity pin was not fulfilled. The reason was a
damsel named Pearl Schultz. She worked in a combined bakery
and candy shop half way down Main Street; and Kenneth, by an
irony of fate, first encountered her when purchasing caramels
for Myra herself! Pearl was undoubtedly good looking, with
fresh blonde colouring, flaxen hair, large blue eyes, and a volup-
tuously redundant figure. She was very demure and ladylike,
almost prim in her manners, carried herself with a little self-
conscious stiffness, and answered Kenneth's easy young-man-
of-the-world advances with admirable and polite brevity.
Nevertheless even in that first interview some subtle attraction,
some fascination drew his interest. She was exceedingly good to
look at, after her fashion, was starchily clean in her pink wash
dress, and piqued his curiosity as to what lay behind her demure

and conventional replies to his remarks. He got intc the habit of dropping in at the Kandy Kitchen daily, on one excuse or another—purchasing candy—or even buns when his funds were low—that he hardly knew what to do with. There swiftly grew in his spirit one of those strange, purposeless, absorbing fascinations peculiar to extreme youth. It was in no sense the pursuit of a more sophisticated man. Kenneth had no clear idea of what he wanted of Pearl. He liked her looks; he felt the lure of the unexplored in her novelty. He had a rough general knowledge of how girls like Dora Stanley would look upon most things, and—within broad limits—how they would act. Pearl belonged to a different genus. What lay beneath the prim stiffness of her exceedingly proper manner? What signified the side looks she gave him with her big, staring eyes?

It took Kenneth nearly a week of brief purchasing visits and the employment of his most killing facetiousness, to break through this first reserve. At his jokes Pearl in the beginning stared coolly; but after she had learned his name and had become accustomed to his personality she would giggle and exclaim:

"Lord, Mr. Boyd, but ain't you too ridiculous!"

Then she began to answer him back; and after the delivery of her repartee she had a trick of catching her lower lip with an even row of little white teeth, and looking at him wide-eyed to see how he would take it. Kenneth found this delightful.

Nevertheless the Kandy Kitchen became a most unhandy meeting ground. People were always coming in to get waited upon in the most annoying fashion, and took the most useless time fussing over their silly purchases, serenely oblivious to a glaring young man in the background. And then, too, the counter with its glass cases was always between them. Somehow it cut off confidences, as a sort of barrier against really getting together and *talking*. Kenneth had as yet no idea nor thought of man-handling Pearl, but it would be rather pleasant not to have that old counter between them.

"What time do you get out of this hole, anyhow?" he asked her.

"We don't close until six o'clock," she told him.

That was an awkward hour for Kenneth. His absence or

tardiness at the early hotel dinner would not be objected to, of course; but it would be commented upon and would require some sort of explanation, however light.

"Can't I see you then?" he asked, nevertheless.

"Oh, I've got to go right straight home to dinner, and then to help Mama with the dishes!"

Kenneth had a bright idea.

"Well, you don't stay open on Sunday!" he pointed out. "Will you go for a walk with me on Sunday?"

She considered a moment, looking down, the wild rose on her fair cheek deepening.

"I should be very pleased to," she decided primly.

"Where do you live?" asked Kenneth.

But for some reason she did not want to tell him that.

"I will meet you at the beach near the wharf at three o'clock," she told him; nor would she consider any other arrangement.

Kenneth was on the beach fifteen minutes before the hour. A little past three she joined him. She had on a little shell-shaped hat thrust forward low over her bang, a voluminous plaited cloth skirt with bustle, and a thin knit jersey—then a new fashion—that defined frankly the upper lines of her figure. She was walking very demurely, her hands crossed in front, the muscles of her shoulders held rigid. To Kenneth's boyish hail she replied:

"I am very pleased to see you to-day, Mr. Boyd."

They turned up the hard beach and fell into step. Kenneth realized with a little start of surprise that she was a much smaller girl than he had thought—indeed, the top of her quaint forward-tilting hat was not much above his shoulder. The Kandy Kitchen surroundings had invested her with a fictitious height.

The tide was low. A hard, wide, dark-brown beach offered itself as a boulevard, shining, and with occasional puddles in depressions as though it had just been raining. A single line of surf close to shore heaved itself wearily to the height of a foot or so, and fell as though letting go all holds after the performance of a duty. The wash crept stealthily up its required distance, and retired with a faint rattling of little stones. Gulls wheeled on motionless wing. Every log mooring-buoy of the fishing boats accommodated a row of black cormorants. Surf ducks rode just outside the lazy breakers, or sprawled on the beach whence they hitched themselves awkwardly and painfully at the approach of Pearl and Kenneth. Long strings of kelp were flung in graceful festoons across the sands.

"I think the beach is elegant," said Pearl. "I just adore this salt smell."

"Salt smell!" jeered Kenneth, "rotten kelp and dead fish and things—that's what makes your 'salt sea air'!"

"I think you're just horrid!" she cried, giving him a little push.

Kenneth was full of spirits, and gambolled about like a colt. He shied pebbles at the surf ducks to see them dive; he selected flat stones and sent them skipping across the water; he found an admirable kelp skipping rope and used it with all the half-forgotten steps of his childhood. Pearl walked demurely straight ahead, duly admiring or exclaiming, but abating in no jot her air of perfect and painful propriety. It was pose that in her became a provocative quaintness. Kenneth was intrigued by it; it was outside his experience of girls. He did not know exactly what it meant. One thing, it certainly did *not* stand for awkwardness or embarrassment, for Pearl gave an impression of complete self-possession. Gradually a desire came to him to break through, to penetrate to the reality beneath it, whatever that might be. He began to tease her; to dash in, push her, and dash out again in avoidance of her retributive slap. He made a lasso out of kelp, and roped her—after many attempts. He caught sandcrabs and tried to scare her with them. With all this he managed to fluster her, succeeded in deepening the wild rose colour of her cheeks, even mussed up a bit her Sunday correctness of raiment. But though she protested in pretended anger, though she slapped at him when he pranced within reach not once did she lose her air of quaint, prim sedateness.

After a mile the beach was closed where the cliffs began. A picturesque pile called Gull Rock acted as the barrier. At high tide the surf, aroused slightly from its low-tide laziness, dashed over this barrier in clouds of spray. At low tide, however, there were left exposed about its fringes little inlets of bare sand, ledges streaming with the long green hair of the sea, clear pools beneath the surface of which lay tidy gardens like wax under glass; and the wash sucked back and forth perfunctorily as though tired. It was a famous clambering place, for it was full of cavelets and foot and hand holds, and unexpected nooks where one might sit and look seaward. A bold horseman, taking instant advantage of the waves, might dash around the foot of Gull Rock and so find himself below the cliffs on the other side. Kenneth had never done this, for the simple reason that in the other direction the beach extended almost unbroken for nearly twenty miles.

Pearl seemed to know well the possibilities of Gull Rock. Following her lead Kenneth found himself on a tiny ledge with just room comfortably for two to sit. It had a back hollowed to fit, and a place for the feet, and it looked straight out to sea with a suck of waters immediately below. But the best feature of it was that it could be reached only by the one route they had taken, which involved a scramble that would be plainly audible before the intruder could come into sight.

"Isn't this a wonder!" cried Kenneth. "Made to order! How did you happen to know of it?"

But Pearl, discreetly, did not answer this question. She disposed herself with great deliberation, spread her skirts with care and leaned back against the rocky wall.

"I always like it here," she commented. "It seems to be sort of private."

She was staring fixedly out to sea. The angle of vision of the human eyes being whatever it is, she could not—theoretically—see what Kenneth was doing. As a matter of fact Kenneth was looking her over, and she was perfectly aware of it. He was thinking that she was better looking than he thought, with her fair skin, her faint colouring, her gleaming hair, her saucy little hat pushed down over her brow, her wide, dreaming eyes. The pose she had taken, with her hands clasped back of her head, threw into relief all the fine lines of her full but firm figure, and the tight fitting "jersey" gave them all their value. Kenneth, in his attitude toward any he considered "nice" girls, was as free from actual sex impulse as any young man of his age; and Pearl was most certainly a "nice" girl; nevertheless he experienced a warm, breath-taking, generalized sort of attraction toward her that he would have repudiated indignantly as sex attraction, yet which was indubitably due neither to his aesthetic sense nor his appreciation of her sparkling conversation.

Indeed, after a dozen sentences the conversation rather lagged. They stared out to sea lulled by the ebb and flow of the water and the slow wheeling of gulls. Kenneth dropped his hand to his side and unexpectedly found it in contact with Pearl's. Her hand was a good one, soft and pink, unroughened by coarse work. Kenneth experienced a sudden, pleasurable tingling shock; Pearl appeared to be quite unconscious of this contact. She did not withdraw her hand for some moments, during which Kenneth sat almost breathless. Then she raised it quite naturally to adjust her hair, and when that operation was finished, she dropped it in her lap. Had she noticed? and was she offended? Kenneth did not know.

The affair ran its usual course. Kenneth had been through such things before with "summer girls" in the East. But what differentiated this from all the others was the girl's puzzling personality. She was so very prim and stiff and precise in her movements, the choice of her phrases; had such strange inhibitions and conventions which she insisted on, and such a disregard of other conventions which Kenneth had heretofore looked upon as essential! Her very reticence added flavour to her concessions. It was like a scarlet lining to a nun's robe. Kenneth soon found that she did not particularly object to his holding her hand, in fact would as soon hold his hand in public except that it might make people laugh. She made more fuss about his arm about her waist, but after due and decent struggle permitted him to sit so. But she became truly indignant when he tried to kiss her; and meant it.

"I'd like to know what kind of a girl you think I am!" she cried indignantly to the bewildered young man, whose simple creed saw absolutely no difference in kind between the one caress and the other. If a girl let you put your arm around her, surely she'd let you kiss her! "You must have a very low opinion of me! The idea!" and it took him some time to smooth her down.

But these bewildering inconsistencies certainly added zest

to the chase. Kenneth spent more and more of his time dangling about the Kandy Kitchen girl. He developed many of the symptoms of love; being uneasy when he was away from her, uneasy in a different way when he was with her. He had the going-going-gone feeling at the diaphragm when the appointed hour neared, and he developed extraordinary small jealousies as to the wearing of pins, rings, and knicknacks. Pearl had his fraternity pin.

"You'll have to take off that other junk if you wear my frat pin," said Kenneth, in reference to various bangles, clasps, and similar gee-gaws bestowed by other young men. Though Kenneth by virtue of his awesome social class had the inside track he was not the only one in the running.

"They were given to me by my gentlemen friends," Pearl rubbed it in, "and I certainly shall wear them. I don't know that I care for your pin."

"It isn't that I mind who gave them to you," argued Kenneth, from a high plane. "It doesn't make any difference to *me*. But you don't realize that my Fraternity is a very old Institution. It's been founded since 1826, and it's got more famous men as Brothers than any other frat in the world.. And you won't find chapters in every little jay college either. We only have eighteen chapters all told, but whenever you see a Kappa Omega Pi chapter you'll know that it is the best frat in that college. It isn't just only a silly club. It has high Ideals. I can't tell you about it, because all that is Secret, but if you knew about it you'd realize that it has the highest kind of aims and ideals. A girl ought really not to wear our frat pin at all. There used to be a rule against it, but that was modified at the Cleveland convention. Now they're permitted to wear it, but they can't wear any other frat pin at the same time. Wearing it makes you a Kap Sister, you see."

"But these others aren't frat pins," objected Pearl.

"They're practically the same thing. There isn't any college here, and these fellows haven't been to college, or they would be frat pins," returned Kenneth with convincing logic.

The upshot was that the miscellaneous hardware disappeared and was replaced by Kenneth's shining emblem.

"If you're a real Kap Sister," said Kenneth, "you ought to wear it night and day. It ought never to leave you."

"I'll pin it on my night gown," said Pearl, impressed.

Kenneth fastened the jewelled emblem with hands that trembled slightly, for he was about to make a very daring proposition.

"Of course you know," he said, trying in vain to steady his voice, "that when you become a Kap Sister I ought to teach you the secret grip."

He leaned forward suddenly and kissed her.

"You—you—what do you mean by that!" she demanded in a choking voice, her face scarlet.

"It's the grip—the Sister's grip," Kenneth hastened to explain. "If you're a Kap Sister, that's the secret grip."

"Secret grip!" she repeated scornfully.

"Yes, it is. Truly! Listen here," and Kenneth hummed to the tune of the *Last Cigar* those gay and disarming verselets written in a moment of inspiration by some questing college Lothario:

> *"And when they seek to join us*
> *The way we do is this:*
> *We put our arms around their waist*
> *And give their lips a kiss.*
> *And if they dare to murmur*
> *Or ask the reason why,*
> *We tell them 'tis the secret grip*
> *Of Kap' Omega Pi."*

Pearl pretended to be convinced.

Of course they plucked petals to the tune of *loves-me, loves-me-not;* and crossed the similar letters from their names to some sort of the amatory count.

Their meetings gained a certain fictitious element of the clandestine due to the fact that Pearl would never allow him to discover her home. She met him always either at the beach or the park. Pearl's father and mother were decidedly plain folk who sat about in shirt sleeves and dressing sacks respectively:

and while Pearl told herself that she was not ashamed of them, still there was no sense in bringing their surface drawbacks to the attention of this aristocratic young man; at least not just at the first. The element of the clandestine instilled into Kenneth's candid spirit a certain discomfort, an uneasiness, that was not shared in the slightest degree by his self-possessed companion. They sat for long hours in a rather sickly, sentimental haze, leaning against each other, occasionally exchanging a kiss. It was delicious, but the situation would hardly have been understood, Kenneth felt, by Dora Stanley, for example—or even his father, for that matter.

V

CALIFORNIA has always been hospitable. Had Patrick Boyd and his son so wished, they might have dined any and every evening in one or another of the roomy wooden dwellings that housed the "first families" of the town. As a matter of practise they did drive to such places two or three times a week, hitching their horse with the others to the commodious rails provided, dusting their shoes with the feather duster that hung by every door pull, and nodding cheerfully to the white-robed Chinaman who let them in. Only on rare occasions did these people give dinner parties. Most of the entertainments I am describing included the whole family from oldest to youngest, and also the entire families of the guests. They were clan affairs, and while they were not particularly lively for the younger people, the latter did not mind that for they did their real playing with each other during the day times and at the Fremont "hops."

One small group, however, broke with this tradition. They gave dinners, with selected guests, and a certain formality of dress and procedure. This was due to the initiative of Mrs. Gordon Carlson.

Mrs. Gordon Carlson was a willowy, bendy, uncorseted woman in her thirties, affecting very large hats, an intense manner, long earrings of jade, and a clinging, individual style in dress. She was "up" in all intellectual movements. Her husband was a poet, and one with a very genuine voice. He was also a hard rider, a tremendous climber of mountains, a redoubtable poker player, an enthusiastic hunter and fisherman, and a conscientious punisher of booze. His poems were exquisite, but he concealed the side of him that produced them as though it were a vice. The fact that he was large, burly, and redfaced helped him in this. Gordon Carlson would have resented being called a poet as he would have resented an epithet. He was sick and tired of poets, and he did everything he could think of in the way of rude, rough coarse things to prove that he did not belong to that breed. In the long run it spoiled his hand and greatly limited his output, which was a tremendous pity.

Kenneth fell under Mrs. Carlson's eye at one of the Fremont hops, and made an impression.

"The young Keats!" she murmured to Mrs. Iredell, her right bower. "We must have him with us!"

So Kenneth received his invitation and in due time presented himself, correctly attired, at the Carlson door.

He began to be awed at once. The whole place was dim. You could hardly see anything. There were queer paintings, and very dark, carved woodwork, and vases on wabbly pillars, and a faint aromatic smell as of incense. Mrs. Carlson swayed to meet him. Her black hair was parted smoothly in the middle and the braids wound around her head crown-wise—a sufficient departure from the universal choice between a square "bang" and a friz; earrings of jade almost touched her shoulder; her gown was of black and fitted closely, in defiance of the fashion. To display a plat-white skin it was cut very low, and yet the impression of Mrs. Carlson's figure was such that one felt it could have gone even lower without much damage. She addressed Kenneth in a low, deep, rich voice several tones below a contralto.

"I am so glad that you could come," she told him. She turned at once to the dim shadows. "I want you to meet the members of our little group. And to you, dear friends, I have brought the embodiment of the Spirit of Youth, the hyacinthine boy! Mrs. Iredell, may I present Mr. Boyd."

Kenneth very awkard, much embarrassed, bowed toward the fussy, fat, severe looking little woman.

"And Mr. Oliver Iredell." She turned to Kenneth in an

audible "aside." "You are of course familiar with his *Cynthia of Samothrace.*" The person designated materialized momentarily from the dimness as a tall, slim gray man crowned by a mop of back-thrust hair and wearing eyeglasses with wide black ribbons. He looked as though everybody should know all about him and *Cynthia of Samothrace* and as Kenneth had never heard of either he felt uncomfortable about it.

In like manner he met Herbert Delmore, also tall and slim, but bald as a boulder, with a white ascetic face and long white hands; and Burton Hallowell who looked like a pink cherub with a vandyke beard.

"I'm so sorry that Gordon cannot be with us to-night," Mrs. Carlson went on smoothly. "He was almost heartbroken. Some tiresome business came up." She conveyed skillfully the impression that normally Carlson would be doing the honours at the head of his board. As a fact the poet was at that moment exactly where he always was when his wife gave one of her "damn intellectual parties,"—in the room back of the Fremont bar trying to make a sceptical Jim Paige believe he held at least four kings.

One other slipped in at the last moment, just as they were about to move into dinner, a girl about Kenneth's age wearing a straight smock with a border of Greek design and squarely bobbed hair. Her skin was very white, her lips very red, her eyes were a turquoise green and held an expression of utter and somewhat disdainful weariness. Kenneth found himself beside her as they moved toward the dining room. She, as well as Mrs. Carlson, proved to possess a deep rich mahogany voice, the only difference being that Mrs. Carlson's was naturally so while Miss Wills had arrived at her depths by careful cultivation.

"You are new here," she stated to Kenneth. "You will love it. In this simple out-of-doors we meet again, after all these centuries, the spirit of shepherd Greece. Do you walk?"

"A little; I ride more."

"But you must walk. It is so much more intimate. To-day I met such a sympathetic tree."

"Huh?" ejaculated Kenneth, startled out of his politeness.

She favoured him with a long, slow stare.

"Oh, I beg pardon," she said, dropping her voice a tone or so in richness. "I thought you belonged," and she turned to him a white shoulder.

At table Kenneth, to his relief, found himself separated from this formidable young person, and placed between Mrs. Iredell and his hostess. At first the conversation was general. It had to do with poetry as an art. A bitter controversy arose between Oliver Iredell and Herbert Delmore. Delmore maintained that poetry should be the natural medium of expression, that unspoiled men would normally express themselves in poetry of one form or another, that primitive man did in essence so express himself; and in support he quoted from primitive folk-lore and literature at astonishing length. Iredell on the other hand stood stoutly for the sacredness of poetry. His thesis seemed to maintain that the art was so very holy that it was a profanation for any one below the rank of Shakespeare or Dante to touch it at all. He did not quote, but he extemporized a wonderful and eloquent argument. The sentiment of the table appeared to be with him. Miss Wills flamed into eagerness, leaning forward across the table to hurl her grenades almost breathlessly:

"Yes, yes; and remember what Matthew Arnold says,"—she could quote extensively, too.

Kenneth had nothing to contribute. It was beyond him. He could not remember a single quotation on any subject, let alone the one before the house. *The Night before Christmas* was the only visitor to his distracted brain, and he could not see how to work that in, and he had grave doubts of its reception in any case. So he looked intelligent until·he ached behind the ears, and was agonizedly embarrassed because he had no word to say. He need not have been self-conscious about that. These people needed listeners more than they needed reinforcements.

The discussion died down slowly into a victory for Iredell. Poetry, it was agreed, was a Sacred Art; and nobody below the rank of Shakespeare or Dante should fool with it. There ensued a short silence while everybody ate soup.

"Have you been doing anything lately, Oliver?" Mrs. Carlson then asked in her deep voice.

"Nothing very much, lately. It has been a barren time,"
confessed Iredell wearily. "The ideas hover but they are vague,
formless, they will not take the classical shape. Since I saw you
last, dear lady, I have done only one little sonnet."

"I should so love to hear it!" breathed Mrs. Carlson. "Didn't
you bring it with you? You know I will never forgive you, if
you did not!"

Mr. Iredell admitted that he just happened to have a copy
with him; and, on further urging, he pulled it from his pocket.
A wild wayward thought swooped across Kenneth's mind, caus-
ing him to choke in his soup. According to Iredell's own
argument poetry was too sacred for anybody but Shakespeare
and Dante; here was Iredell himself preparing to read an original
poem—*ergo?* He glanced about for sympathy in this thought,
but met only surprise and question——

It was a silly thought——

He listened to Iredell's sonnet and was tremendously impressed. Indeed, he thought it quite one of the best things he
had ever heard, and his opinion for Iredell grew to a vast respect
and admiration. Kenneth was not one of those to whom writing
of any kind comes easy, though he read much. He was young.
Iredell's poem was a good journeyman poem built according to
specifications that never fail to bring results. Its scansion and
rhymes were conventionally perfect: and Iredell could read with
effect. Its base was a commonplace platitude of morality in
Greek dress, and it contained a number of polysyllabic, unusual and exceedingly melodious words. The effect on Kenneth
was of a great piece of work.

Delmore, who had listened attentively, his head on one side,
pounced upon a detail of quantities of a transposed Greek word
offering a substitute. Everybody agreed that the meanings were
sufficiently alike, but the connotations——!! Kenneth, beyond
his depth, caught at an understandable straw: he remembered
that Longfellow had used that same word somewhere, and said
so. This remark produced a flat silence.

"Still Longfellow *has* done some good lines," said Mrs. Carlson,
after a moment.

They settled the point only by abandoning it to pursue a

subject on which they seemed to be in agreement. This was the work of Giovanni Asperoni. Kenneth gathered that this must be a poet. He had flourished in the sixteenth century and apparently had been completely forgotten by the world until Peter Younger, the publisher, had brought him out in hand-made paper, deckel-edged, with three-inch margins and Stowcroft binding. The edition had been limited to 121 copies, after which the plates had been destroyed. The present company was enthusiastically in agreement as to Asperoni. Not only in form, thought, imagery, and sheer inspiration was he the superior of all modern writers, but the best of modern poetry was modelled directly upon him. Kenneth felt himself cast into outer intellectual darkness because he had never heard of the Italian. At this point, unexpectedly, up spoke Hallowell, who had contributed little but sapient strokings of his vandyke beard. He advanced and defended the hypothesis that the Greeks had done all aesthetic things perfectly; that it is useless to attempt to improve upon perfection; therefore we should cease a vain attempt to produce art and should give all our time to study and interpretation of Greek art. This was rather a bombshell. It was necessary to one's intellectual reputation to exalt the Greek— and yet as producers of one form of modern art——

They compromised at length by excepting poetry from this sweeping relegation. Poetry was the only true art of interpretation: and it was necessary that each age interpret to itself the eternal truths that Greece had embodied as generalizations. This ingenious way out was suggested by Miss Wills.

But Delmore, who was secretly still a little sulky over Iredell's having read a poem while he had not, interposed obstinately:

"I can see how for form—in sculpture and architecture—and politics and drama we can go back to the Greeks, but how about colour, atmosphere—painting, in short?"

This plunged them into a tremendous argument. They talked Pre-Raphaelite, and Rennaissance, and Perugino, and Fra Angelico and forty-eleven old masters, with theories of light, colour, symbolism thrown in. Kenneth knew not even the common terms of painting. He took cover and stayed under, and when the party finally broke up he went back to the hotel in a curiously mixed state of mind. He felt ignorant and uncomfortable and uneducated and outclassed; yet he was elated over the chance to mingle with such superior, intelligent, and inspired people.

He found his awe shared by his usual companions.

"Good grief! Dining at the Carlson's!" cried Dora Stanley. "I'd no more dare go there than fly! They make me feel like a *worm*, a positive worm!"

Several times he came across one or the other of them and with them exchanged grave bows; but he was not again invited to dine with them, and he felt crushed and humble enough to withdraw the *Bhavaghad Gita*, a volume of Walter Pater and a random-selected title of Matthew Arnold from the public library. He might for a brief period have become a recluse and a student had not the *Sociedad de los Años* come again to town on its monthly bust.

They greeted Kenneth cordially enough, but made no move toward including him in their intimacy. Nevertheless, fascinated by the anticipation of the unexpected he tagged modestly behind them into the bar, where he withdrew to a spectator's position at one of the round tables.

Bill Hunter let out a howl that shook the gas chandeliers.

"Look who's here," he yelled, bearing down on an individual leaning against the bar talking to Barney. This was a well-built man of medium height, with a wind-reddened face, a flaxen moustache, and bright blue eyes. One would have taken him for a ranchman, or—better still—a deep-sea sailor. He began at once to speak distinctly but very rapidly.

"I warn you I go armed and I shall not hesitate to defend myself. Barney give me that mallet. If you lay a finger on me I'll break it over your iron head, you big chunk of pig-meat. Stand off, I tell you! I mean business!"

He flourished the beer mallet threateningly, his blue eyes flashing.

"Stand off!" commanded Corbell from the doorway. "He'll do it."

"Of course I'll do it! Do you think I'm going to be manhandled by a bunch of mucker hoodlums just for a little thing like mayhem or murder? Not me! That's better. Now you can approach and greet me like little gentlemen."

He dropped his mallet and they gathered about him.

"Explain yourself," said Corbell. "Where were you last month?"

"East."

"East! Poor old devil. What did you do that for?"

"Couldn't do it by mail. But it paid. Have a drink."

"Wise man that came out of the East," chirped Shotwell Sheridan, and then looked surprised when they burst into mingled laughter and applause.

"Out of the mouths of babes—he actually doesn't know he did it," remarked the stranger, dryly.

After a time, out of the press, Frank Moore emerged and sat on the edge of the table next Kenneth. He nodded in so kindly a fashion that Kenneth felt encouraged to question him.

"That?" answered Frank, surprised. "Don't you know him? That's Gordon Carlson."

"Why!" cried Kenneth startled, "I thought he was a poet."

Frank turned to him gravely, his usual air of dry raillery falling from him.

"He *is* a poet, son, make no mistake in that. Have you never read any of his stuff? No? Well, you're the only man here who hasn't. Get you a set of them. They're good *he* stuff, what a man can bite on. Lord! but he can do it. Hunt up one called *The Dogie*. That'll put hair on your chest. And if you like the pretties read *The Meadow Lark*."

Kenneth could not adjust so quickly. He looked absolutely bewildered. Moore chuckled.

"I know his wife—I dined at his house the other evening," Kenneth managed at last.

The dry quizzical look returned to Moore's face. He questioned Kenneth further; and at last lifted up his voice above the din.

"Gordy!" he called. "Gordy, come here!"

The poet disentangled himself and sauntered over, grinning pleasantly.

"I want Mr. Boyd to meet you," said Moore. "Now look

here, Gordy, this a pretty good sort of young fellow. He ain't
got any tenor voice nor such physical disabilities. He was our
last month's Benefactor, and we like him. But he's been to
dinner with the Pet Poets, and he thinks they are great people.
You've simply got to uncork a little professional jealousy."

"I'm glad to meet you, Mr. Boyd," said Carlson sincerely.
"Are you by any chance a writer or an artist?"

"The best thing he draws is his health, and the best thing he
writes is a check," interposed Frank. "But he can ride a horse
a little, and he's got a popgun he *says* will shoot—a sixteen gauge
Scott, Gordy, think of that! sixteen! I want to go out and see if
a peashooter that size will kill a quail! And he's got nice healthy
instincts; and he was being took care of good until lately. We
taught him to buy a drink or two and I understand Pearl is
giving him a little attention," continued this astonishing person
calmly, "so you see his education is in good experienced hands.
No, he don't do none of these tricks. He's just cast for the
'hyacinthine boy'—that's it, ain't it, son?"

Kenneth, overwhelmed by all this crash of preconceptions,
could only stammer something incoherent.

"Now, Gordy," pursued Moore, "just answer me a few questions honestly, to save this kid's immortal soul. What kind of a
poet is Oliver Iredell?"

"Punk!"

"Why?"

Carlson turned fully to Kenneth and addressed him solely,
in the gentlest and kindliest tones:

"You see, he is not a poet at all. He is a skillful versifier with
a good classical education. Have you seen his work?"

"I heard him read a sonnet the other evening."

"Exactly. It was probably an excellent school-room example
of a sonnet, and it probably began '*As one who*—' He takes any
moral commonplace—like be good and you'll be happy—, he
transposes them to ancient Greece, clothes them in classic imagery, and embodies them in a standard verse form. A poem
that is truly a poem *must* have either originality of thought, inspiration of sentiment, or sheer beauty of form. A great poem
has all of them."

"Professional jealousy," interposed Moore. "Time presses. We will skip the other Pets. Let's get down to cases. Puncture the high-falutin' and then we'll get back to our drinks."

"I suppose he means the type of pseudo-intellectual conversation they indulge in—sacred art of poetry, the Divine Greeks, and all the rest of it. That stuff impress you?"

Kenneth turned red but he answered valiantly.

"Yes, it did. I drew some books from the library and was trying to read up."

"Good for you!" cried Carlson, with quickened interest; but it was evident his exclamation did not refer to the books. "Did you ever read one of these big thick scientific dog books? They have so much to say about ventilation and diet and water and shelter and Lord knows what that when you get through you wonder how you ever dared keep a dog at all. Same way with art in general. When I lived East I belonged to *The Gramercy*, a club of those connected with the arts. There was always a crowd of men in the leather chairs discussing very profoundly all the fine points of writing a book. They talked of balance and proportion and relation and about two hundred things of the kind, and they got in so deep that I couldn't follow them. After I had listened to them a while I realized that I knew nothing whatever about how to write a book. And then I began to enquire around. Not a single one of those easy chair experts had ever written a book." He laughed amusedly. "I had at that time written three without knowing how; and they seemed to get by with the critics at that."

"Puncture the dear old Greeks," urged Moore.

"No, I won't puncture the dear old Greeks," returned Carlson. "The dear old Greeks were all right, and I am for them. But they didn't do all there is to be done because they didn't have either the materials nor the experience to do it with."

"I suppose they embodied perfectly the great fundamental truths," suggested Kenneth, parroting some of the talk he had heard.

"These great fundamental truths as you call them are very few in number. Their combinations and reactions vary infinitely according to the conditions of the particular time in which they are examined. Do I make myself clear?"

"I think I see what you mean," replied Kenneth, slowly.

"Well, this is no place for a discussion. Think it over. Who's the particular poet just now?"

"? ? ?"

"They generally have some obscure nonentity they quote as the greatest ever."

"Oh, yes! Giovanni Asperoni."

"Giovanni Asperoni!" repeated Carlson, with a shout of laughter. "Never heard of him!"

"Oh, haven't you?" cried Kenneth, delighted. "I'm glad. Neither had I."

"I got me a poet once and sprung him on them," said Frank, gravely. "He went fine."

"Tell Mr. Boyd about him," urged Carlson.

"I went with the Pet Poets once," grinned Moore. "It was some time ago. I wasn't no hyacinthine boy, you understand, but I was a wild free soul, I think it was. Well, they snowed me under so far I didn't even have no breath hole. That Iredell woman started in on me with the soup. Says she: 'Mr. Moore, what in your opinion was the influence of the early Egyptian mysteries on the Rosicrucians?'"

"What did you tell her?" asked Kenneth, laughing.

"I told her it wasn't a marker on the influence of the Brazilian Aztecs on modern occultism. But they had a dago poet then, too, and they shot me so full of holes with him that if I'd fell down in the gutter any peddlar would have picked me up for a colander. That Wills girl would spring one of those *as one who* lines on me and say, 'of course you remember how the rest goes,' and when I said, no ma'am, I didn't, she gave me one of those Lo, the poor insect looks, and I'd peek up at her from under the edge of my plate. She got me hostile after a while, and when I left the pen all raw and bleeding I said to myself, 'I'll *get* you, young woman'; so I did."

"How?" begged Kenneth.

"I got me a little private dago poet of my own, and sprung him on them."

"I wouldn't know where to look one up," Kenneth confessed. "Hell, I didn't look him up, I *made* him up," explained Frank. "He sure was good! I picked him a good name off three dago fishermen down at Largo's, and I wrote him a bunch of these *as one who* first lines. You know," confided Frank, "it's plumb easy to write first lines to sonnets; it's the rest of 'em that stump you. All you have to do is to get 'em sort of solemn, like *as one who died without his trousers on.* Then next time I got invited—they invited *me* twice—I waited until the right time and then pulled my dago. 'Miss Wills,' says I—you bet I can do the flossy when I want to, can't I, Gordy?—'that is indeed a beautiful thing. But I don't need to ask you if you remember the lines by John Smith'—or whatever I called him— 'beginning *as one who died et cetery!*' and by gosh she walked right in! 'I can't just quote them,' says she, 'but I remember them perfectly, of course.'"

Before he went to bed that night Kenneth had borrowed a copy of *The Ranges* and had thrilled over *The Dogie*, his eyes had filled over *The Meadow Lark*, and he had chuckled aloud at *The Ballad of Bold Bad Men.* Gordon Carlson had won him completely: and his soul was forever freed from the smothering danger of the near-culture. He saw the humour of it, and turned his light out, chuckling. Then a swift unexpected thought struck through him. What was that about Pearl?

VI

WHILE all these relations were being established California had gone on her serene way through her seasons. The carpets of flowers had come to seed and had laid them down on the warm soil to rest until another year. Over the hills the *alfileria*, the fox tail, the wild oats had turned brown and the live oak trees in contrast stood clear and rounded, cuddling each its precious shadow under the sun. And the sun drove his chariot triumphantly through blue days.

People sat out evenings in the tepid air: and the night was ecstatically alive with creatures that chirped or croaked or fluttered on painted downy wings around the dim gas jets in the

halls. At noontimes a somnolence fell, so that people over-
come by it went into cool darkened rooms, and the land slept
in a golden haze.

The next afternoon following Kenneth's illuminating talk
with Carlson and Frank Moore he rode slowly alone down Main
Street at this hour of the *siesta*. He was almost the only moving
creature to be seen. Saddle horses, heads drooping, dozed
with one hind leg comfortably out of focus; dogs spread out flat
in the shade; even the mule car, having stopped at the beach end
of the track, seemed to be staying there indefinitely. The fine
white dust of the roadway, as though animated by the life-giving
heat of the sun, stirred and rose at the lightest breath of air.
It followed Kenneth like a spirit.

Why he was out on horseback at this time of day he had no
very clear idea; nor why he had not gone riding that morning
with the other young people. He certainly was not consciously
taking stock after his illuminating experience of the evening
before; though he may have been doing so subconsciously. The
morning he had spent in his room fussing about. He had read
more of Carlson's poems, he had written a few letters, he had
oiled his shotgun, he had loaded half the brass shells. For this
was probably the first sixteen gauge shotgun ever seen on the
Pacific Coast, and ammunition for it was not to be had for purchase. People shot tens at all sorts of game; though occasionally
some small-bore crank used a twelve at quail. He would never
have thought of doing so at ducks. A sixteen was of course a
pop-gun. Kenneth had fifty brass shells which he reloaded.
After lunch he became restless.

The beach, too, was empty of human life, except for two of
Largo's men mending nets on the dry sand above high tide mark.
Kenneth drew rein for a moment, taking in the cool air that
breathed from the sea. He was in the act of turning his horse
to the left for his customary canter on the hard sands when he
heard his name called.

He turned. A girl riding a *palomino* horse followed by two
dogs had come upon him unheard through the soft sand. She
was riding astride a stock saddle, and wore a divided coat over
bloomers and boots. This was sufficiently startling at an epoch

when every woman rode side saddle and nothing more lively than a piano ever had legs. Kenneth was duly startled, and sat up and took notice. She wore the almost universal broad Stetson hat, thrust low on her head, and had gathered her hair under it. Kenneth raised his hat, puzzled. She was a very pretty girl, with a clear imperious gaze, piquantly irregular features, and a brown skin beneath which surged rich colour; and she sat her daintily stepping animal in complete nervous response to his slightest movement.

"Why are you going that way?" she asked him. "Have you never been up beyond Gull Rock, it's ever so much nicer."

"I never have," confessed Kenneth, still racking his brains, and trying to act as natural as though she were not riding astride. "I didn't know you could go beyond the next little beach. Doesn't the sea shut you off against the cliffs?"

"Come and see," she invited him.

They rode at a footpace to Gull Rock. Kenneth started much conventional small talk, to which he got little or no response. Yet she seemed neither sniffy nor unintelligent, for ever and anon she would proffer some friendly comment on what offered itself—the cormorants on the logs, the band of quicksand where the sulphur spring seeped up, a strip of kelp lying fantastically, and the like—in a manner that seemed to take for granted an identical point of view. Being at the age when a pause in conversation between members of the opposite sex is a social crime, Kenneth found this peculiarity as intriguing as the cross saddle riding.

Thus they reached Gull Rock. The tide was low, but—as has been pointed out—even at that a horseman had to make several bold dashes as the wash receded. The *palomino* made a difficulty, more in play than earnest. The girl's slim figure straightened and stiffened. Twice she brought her heavy quirt down on the *palomino's* flanks. He reared and snorted. She leaned gracefully to his motion, swung him to his feet, and seemed literally to force him by the will power in her rigid young body. He snorted and made a dash forward, the suddenness of which did not in the slightest degree disturb her seat. Pronto, more accustomed to the sea, followed soberly. They were now on a short, steep curving beach, a quarter mile in length, betw.... Gull Rock and a point where steep cliffs ran down into the sea.

"You certainly can ride!" cried Kenneth.

"That isn't riding," she replied scornfully.

"No: but I can tell by the way you sit, the way you go at it."

"Now it doesn't look as though you could possibly go another inch, does it?" she cried animatedly, dismissing Kenneth's compliment. "Come and I'll show you."

She touched heel to the *palomino*. The beach was shelving at this point and the sand soft. Her horse's hoofs flung the loose sand back by handfuls, stinging Kenneth's eyes. He had either to draw rein and fall back out of range, or race alongside in heavy laborious footing. He chose to do the former, in which his judgment coincided with that of the two dogs, who rolled their eyes comically up at him and wagged their tails. They caught up with the *palomino* dancing restlessly.

"Why didn't you come along?" she demanded.

"Pretty heavy going. That soft steep sand is mighty hard on horses."

"Good heavens! You aren't going to be one of these careful ones, are you?" she cried impatiently.

Kenneth's face flushed darkly, but he made no direct reply.

"I don't see how we go any farther," he commented.

"Follow me," she commanded.

She put her horse directly at the swirl of waters. At this point the waves broke not over twenty feet out from the cliffs, and the wash, rushing forward in a white mass, was rebuffed in whirlpools. The *palomino* snorted loudly as he was put at this, but advanced gingerly, nevertheless, feeling his way with little steps. Almost immediately the water rose above the line of his belly. The girl kicked her feet from the stirrups and raised them out of the way.

Kenneth had perforce to follow, though neither he nor Pronto favoured the move. Indeed, it required strong application of the big-rowelled blunt spurs to start him at all, although he had another horse to follow. The two dogs ran agonizedly up and down a short arc of the beach by way of formal protest, then sadly plunged in and swam in a business-like fashion. buffeted to and fro by the swirl of the tide. Then all rounded a sharp spur of the cliffs and found themselves in a far country.

On the right ran the low cliffs, unbroken as far as the eye could see, yellow and seamed and tunnelled with the rains. On the left was the sea. Between the two was the wide moist beach; and these three were the boundaries of a world beyond which the imagination refused to stray to the dry, hot dusty California mid-summer. Like islands in a river, here and there huge rocks or groups of smaller rocks outcropped from the sand; and the tide was in then, rushing and draining away. And here, out of the protection of the outflung coast, hummed a strong, sweet wind from overseas, the summer Trades, fresh and cool and bracing; and with it came a thundering, tumbling surf from which the tops were stripped and flung aloft like veils.

"Come on!" cried the girl.

Kenneth struck spurs to his horse and in a bound was alongside. He felt under his hand the momentary play against the bit, and then Pronto settled down to a rhythmical pound. The dogs, who had been idling after a roll in dry sand, came to attention and settled down to business. The brown, wet beach seemed to be flowing toward him. The pace gradually increased. Tears stood in his eyes so that he saw but dimly, and the great wind ran past him with a roar. Beneath him Pronto exulted, too, skipping pools, rocks, piles of seaweed that were gone before Kenneth had clearly sensed them; making small playful shies as the tide reached out toward him. Clumsy ducks spattered panic-stricken to the left, flocks of beach birds divided and wheeled with cries. The dogs were running at the edge of the wash, throwing the sand and the water, their tongues out. One of them rolled his eyes companionably up at Kenneth as though to say "aren't we having a good time!" Pronto, his neck stretched, felt powerful beneath him, as though he could go thus forever, like a machine.

Then he became aware that the girl was leaning back, pulling. He began to get Pronto in hand. Soon they had slowed to a hand canter, and then to a walk as they approached a wide reef of rock thrown across the beach.

Through the miniature ledges of this the animals picked a

gingerly way. Beyond it they came out upon another clear stretch. Kenneth cleared away the tears. The horses plodded soberly along. The dogs panted and grinned; and one of them, from sheer exuberance, hippity-hopped along ten paces or so on three legs. The girl settled her Stetson a little more firmly, but said nothing. She seemed to be unaware of Kenneth and to be frankly enjoying the beach. Now that her colour had been heightened by the scamper, she was most decidedly a good looking girl, one you could hardly forget, and yet Kenneth could not for the life of him remember where they had met.

The dogs discovering that their humans intended to go slowly for a time, began to range ahead, chasing up the wet sand at a great rate, or investigating painstakingly mysterious dog-interests to be found in the dry sand above high-tide mark. There was much to see. An impression of life—teeming, busy, self contained, self-sufficient, independent life—informed this remote sea land. Dozens of compact bands of tiny white sanderlings fringed the edge of the wash. They followed the receding water with a twinkle twinkle twinkle of black legs, picking busily at mysterious things they found, pursuing the spent wave fairly into the maw of its successor: and then when it seemed inevitable that they be caught and overwhelmed, twinkle twinkle twinkle back they ran, keeping always just ahead of the water no matter how fiercely it pursued. So timed and accurate and simultaneous were their evolutions that they gave the appearance of executing a preconcerted drill. Then there were also flocks of the big brown sickle-billed curlews, standing motionless, transparent like phantoms against the brown sand. They minded the dogs very little, merely lifting on wing and dropping again as these busy canines loped beneath them. But on the approach of the horsemen they arose at some distance and made long flights along the coast just above the breakers, uttering weird shrill cries. And at one place they came to a great convention of gulls and pelicans, hundreds of them, seated on the sands, that arose a few at a time, protesting, as they drew near; and at last whirled up in a cloud, and went out and sat on the water just beyond the combers, riding the waves lightly like little ships at anchor, and the wind lifted their feathers when they

turned from it. On the sands they left a tracery of fine foot-
prints, like a delicate pattern of lace.

The tide was at its lowest. Already the singing wind was
graying and ribbing the surface of the sand. A mist of fine
particles was dancing elfishly. Where lay shells or pebbles
the wind was industriously carving, so that they stood up slightly
above the surface as the caps of miniature pillars or the heads of
tiny promontories. Nevertheless, the beach itself was hard as
iron underneath and the hoofs of the horse went *k-pit k-pat*, and
the occasional popping of kelp bubbles.

From the open Pacific the breakers rolled powerfully in.
For a moment they stood erect, and one could see the green
lucence through them, and the wild sudden lift of weeds; then
they rushed forward in a roar of white, tossing, tumbling, playing wild pranks with the shore they had reached at last after so
many leagues. And alternately appeared and disappeared
spouting dripping black rocks with weeds like green hair un-
bound. And beyond was the low gray sea, lifting and falling.

Outside the breaker-lines a school of dolphins played, running up the coast as though pacing the flying horsemen. Long
lines of black "shags," or cormorants, were going somewhere;
flying close to the water, their necks stretched out. Swifter
ducks passed them or darted across their flight. Pelicans sailed
along majestically only to let go all holds and drop as though
shot, hitting the water with an awkward splash. Then the
attendant small gulls or terns bore down screaming to where
the pelican rode high on the waves like a galleon, hoping that the
great bird would drop his catch when he tossed it from his pouch
to catch it again in mid-air. A number of seals swam close in-
shore, and they raised their sleek, brown intelligent heads to
stare at these passers by. One of them held a large fish cross-
wise in his mouth. As the great waves heaved up finally before
breaking, and the green light shone through them, Kenneth
could see behind their faces, as though he looked through the
glass of an aquarium, the shadowy forms of more seals darting
agilely back and forth in the lift of the comber only to fade at the
last moment before the heavy water crashed down. They were
playing, flirting with the last moment; just as the surf ducks

were riding calmly the smaller waves, not diving until the over-whelming cataracts were upon them; just as the gulls sat on the very inner edge of possibility beyond the surf; just as the cor-morants sailed as close to the bosom of the heavy sea as they could, lifting only just far enough to let the crest of the ground swell slip beneath them and dropping smoothly into the hollow beyond; just as the sanderlings in their drilled evolutions barely escaped the pursuing wash that tugged at their twinkling little heels. The only persons out for business seemed to be the pelicans.

"They have just as much fun playing as we do," suddenly remarked the girl.

Kenneth came to with a start of surprise that his thought had been so accurately met. And for the first time he realized that he had been committing one of the worst social crimes in his young code, and it did not seem to matter: he had been rid-ing for a quarter hour absolutely silent, without one polite word to throw to the conventions. It did not seem to matter because, in a subtle way he did not understand, it came to him that up to this point they had been seeing the same things in the same way, and that speech had been unnecessary. The experience was a new one.

There seemed no end to the cliffs and the beach. Around the point of each little scallop in the coast they made their way only to find another crescent of hard sand. The smell of sea-weed was on the breeze, of fresh kelp, plucked daily by the tides. The cliffs saw to it that at each high water yesterday's lot was carried away, so that never did it become stale. Sometimes they galloped for a half mile or so, and the horses shook their heads impatient for another race, and stately herons flipped upon tilted wings gathering their legs under them, and the cries of beach birds scattered like leaves. But the greater part of the time they walked their horses side by side in a sociable silence. And the feeling persisted in Kenneth's mind that they were sharing these things completely. He did not even know her name, but it seemed that he had known her a long time.

The afternoon drew to a close. Westward the sea had thrown aside its gray and was shining in gold. The Trade was wearying

fast. Ahead of them in the distance of a broad curve, the cliffs
were proud in saffron, or tender in mauve and lilac. Alongside
the dogs pattered busily, their ears flat back, their tongues out,
fairly laughing up at their humans. The horses, still fresh, were
dancing forward with a proud half-hesitating step, begging for
another run. Kenneth came to with a start.

"We must have come an awful way!" he exclaimed. "And
look how the tide is coming in!" He reined in his horse with a
sudden dismay. "We'll never get back in time to get around
that point!" he cried.

She looked at him with tolerant amusement.

"Have you just thought of that?" she rallied him. "You
must get into terrible scrapes when you have nobody to take care
of you. See where those trees show on top? There's a trail
up a little *barranca** there. We'll take that up to the *mesa*.
It's not far from town then 'cross country. You see we've
been going on a big curve and now we can cut straight
across."

The *barranca* trail proved to be sketchy and scrambly. It led
them through stiff chaparral to an oak dotted *mesa*, like a park.
When they topped the rise they seemed to leave the fresh, damp,
cool sea world, and to return to the California summer. Tepid
air and warm faint odours enveloped them. A still peace replaced the tingling life of the beach. Across the rich, brown
meadow came liquid and sleepy the note of a belated lark.
Across the distance the great ramparts of the Sur slumbered,
wrapped in tinted veils.

They talked volubly from this time on. The girl seemed
to possess an astonishing local knowledge of things that grew or
moved out of doors. Finding that Kenneth was genuinely interested she took the delight of a child in pointing out to him
common or curious things. Kenneth, in the large way of the
foreign and uninformed, had concluded that with the passing of
the brilliant scarves laid in acres over the hills California's flower
season had passed completely. This girl showed him the in-
digo larkspur that had taken the place of the golden primroses;
the pentstemon and blue phacelias that stood where of late had

*Barranca—an eroded ravine with precipitous sides.

bloomed the shooting stars; the mimulus, scarlet among the rocks, and the silene, crimson on the slopes.

"There's no dead season here, like your winters back East," she told him, "just a ripe season, and a little season of sleep."

"That's all winter is," he told her; "a little season of sleep."

"Dead cold sleep—dead," she replied. "Here we just rest lightly for a little, and we dream in flowers."

"Why, that is a beautiful thought!" cried Kenneth. "It would make a good idea for a poem!"

She paid no attention to his compliment.

"Do you write poems?" she asked him.

"No, of course not, I couldn't," disclaimed Kenneth, with all the confusion of a healthy boy avoiding even the appearance of shame. "But I like to read good stuff. Did you ever read any of Carlson's?"

"Of course I have, what a silly question!"

"Don't you think he's bully?"

"He's California."

"Why, that's just what he is!" cried Kenneth. "You certainly put things well! You don't know what a relief it is to talk to an intelligent woman after a lot of these silly girls you meet around."

"Is it?" she smiled enigmatically.

They had crossed the *mesa* and now struck unexpectedly into the *Camino Real*. It was pastern deep in light dust at this time of the year, so they rode slowly on the brown grass alongside. To Kenneth's surprise they were only a few miles from town: in fact almost opposite the Corona del Monte ranch. They had ridden on the beach around a wide arc of a bow, and were now cutting across the chord.

"Well, good-bye," suddenly announced the girl, as they reached a willow-shaded, little-used cross roads. "I'm going to leave you here."

"Hold on!" cried Kenneth. "When do I see you again?"

But she had clapped heels to her palomino and was off in a cloud of dust followed by the dogs. Kenneth wheeled, with a half intention of following; but she disappeared on the keen run, and he knew from his late experience on the beach that Pronto was outclassed when it came to a race. While he hovered irresolute, his decision was made for him by the appearance of Dora Stanley and Myra Welch. The two girls had been horseback to call on Pilar Cazadero.

"You're a fine one!" cried Dora. "Why didn't you go with us this morning? And to go sneaking off like this in the afternoon! I declare!"

Privately Kenneth considered this harmless speech as immature and in bad taste; an opinion he would not have held two hours before. However, he might get some desired information.

"Did you see who I was riding with just now?" he asked.

"I should think you would be ashamed, cradle robber!" teased Dora.

"Who was it?" went on Kenneth, a little bewildered.

"You don't mean to say you don't remember her! What a blow!"

"Where did I ever see her before?"

"At the Peyton barbecue, for one place. That's the Brainerd kid."

"The Brainerd kid?" repeated Kenneth, still puzzled. "What do you mean?"

But Myra Welch broke in. She had been watching Kenneth from beneath her sleepy lashes.

"I truly believe he doesn't know, Dora," she drawled. "Do you think you have made another mash, Ken? You know, Dora, with her hair up under her hat that way——"

Dora went off into what Kenneth indignantly described to himself as shrieks of hyena laughter.

"You're right, Myra, you're right!" she cried. "Ken, listen. Remember that kid you watched the rough-riding with down on the corral fence?"

A great light burst on the mortified Kenneth.

"That kid!" he cried, "that gangle-legged *kid*, with her hair down her back!"

"Shouldn't speak of a young lady's leg," drawled Myra, who was daring of speech twenty years ahead of her time.

Kenneth had an engagement with Pearl that evening. He

hired one of the Spanish stable boys to take her a note of regrets. He told himself that this was because all girls certainly made him sick!

VII

LUCKILY for Ken these human tangles were all postponed, and by his own act. He did not know he was running away, but that was what it amounted to. Patrick Boyd had long contemplated a business trip to San Francisco, and Kenneth suddenly decided that it would be good for him to go along.

Boyd, as is often the case with big men of business suddenly thrown into a quiet life, was deeply involved in small affairs. He was building a house and stable and planting a garden on the new lot next Mrs. Stanley, and he was giving all his time and ability to it. It was characteristic of the man that he let no contracts, but went ahead with a master carpenter on a day labour basis. This required daily supervision and daily consultation with all sorts of artisans. Boyd gave as much ability to it as he would have bestowed on a whole traction line, and enjoyed himself hugely. He had also made the discovery that gardens grow fast in California, and had developed a tremendous interest in things of the soil. Often he donned heavy gloves and himself dug energetically for an hour or so; a great deal of the time he spent driving or pulling up stakes, or squinting along curves. In this charming occupation he was aided and abetted by Mrs. Stanley. That formidable lady strode here and there across his precious acres, delivering her opinions in the strident voice of command, bestowing much valuable information belligerently. She managed by sheer weight of authority and positiveness to lift Boyd from the first to the second stage of California gardening.

"People are all alike," she boomed. "When they first get here they are so pleased with the way things grow, and the brightness of the colours, that they slap in all the brilliant, hardy things indiscriminately."

"Well, I like bright gay flowers," urged Boyd, "and I certainly like tough ones that can take care of themselves and don't need to have you hold their hands every cold night."

"So do I," agreed Mrs. Stanley. "But let me ask you something. Do you know anything about what blooms at various
seasons? I thought not! Well, then, if you go ahead at your
own sweet will how do you know that you won't have everything
blooming at one time and not a single thing any other?"

"I thought all flowers just naturally bloomed in the spring,"
confessed Boyd.

"I thought so! Well you listen to me. Take that border
for example. What are you going to plant there?"

"Marigolds," said Boyd, boldly.

"A very good flower. What's it going to look like when the
marigolds are resting? Do you know what happens to marigolds when they aren't blooming? I thought not. Well, what
you want is some small shrubbery—say bush honeysuckle—
behind them."

Thus was the mind of Patrick Boyd illumined and his garden
laid out for him. He had his nasturtiums and red geraniums
and plumbago and other bright and common things; but he had
them where Mrs. Stanley told him to have them. The result
would be good, he had to admit, but his free and independent
masculine soul was a little irked. At times he joined battle
with Mrs. Stanley, but was always badly worsted for the reason
that he knew very little about it. One cannot fight without
ammunition. In his usual thoroughgoing manner he visited
the keeper of the local greenhouses and nursery and from him
carried back a number of choice bombshells.

"Pooh!" cried Mrs. Stanley. "You've been talking to old
MacDonald. Do you know what your garden would look like,
if he could have his way? It would be full of spindling, miserable varieties that could just make out to live because they would
be out of their natural soil and climate. MacDonald is the
worst kind of a snob."

"Snob!" echoed Boyd, recalling the surly, independent
corduroyed old Scotchman.

"Yes, plant snob. You don't believe it? Well, listen. One
day we were talking about pepper trees. 'Yes,' said he, 'it is a
beautiful tree; it's a pity it's so common.' Now what do you say
to that? *a pity it's so common*, indeed!"

They agreed amicably enough on the dividing fence between the two properties. At least, Mrs. Stanley thought a lattice affair you could grow things over would be about right; and Boyd thought so, too. But when the fence was once up and it came time to plant the "things," they locked horns. Boyd was in favour of blue moonflowers. There were some over a back fence down at the Fremont and he liked them. Also the Fremont gardener told him they grew very fast. But Mrs. Stanley was opposed.

"You don't know what you are talking about," she stated in her positive manner. "They do grow fast, to be sure; but they eat the soil, and they scatter all over the place, and they'll rot out your lattice, and a dozen other things. What you want is a banksia, or a Cecil Bruner or a Cherokee."

Boyd proved obstinate, for once. There ensued a deadlock. The space along the fence apparently remained unplanted. Then one morning Mrs. Stanley, clumping along the boundary lines in her brogans, saw some tender shoots pushing their way out of the soil. She bent incredulously to examine them. Other similar shoots were spaced along the fence. They were moon-flowers!

This was too serious for informal action. Mrs. Stanley at once clumped back to her house where she indited a note. In it she called Mr. Boyd's attention to the fact that she had equal rights in a line fence and that she unalterably opposed moonflowers. This she dispatched to the Fremont by hand. Within the half hour she had the reply:

DEAR MRS. STANLEY:

In answer to your note will state that you are in error. The fence is not a line fence but belongs entirely to me, and is situated six inches inside my property line. I had it moved one night two weeks ago. I am sorry you do not like moonflowers; but of course it is always possible to erect your own fence and grow what suits you better.

Mrs. Stanley was a staunch old warrior who could take blows as well as give them.

"Humph!" she sniffed, when she read this. "Just like a man! Well, he'll have to learn."

The subject was never brought up again. But, to anticipate for a moment, within two years Boyd found that Mrs. Stanley had been right. He pulled up the moonflowers and planted banksias, Cecil Bruners and Cherokees in one, two, three order.

Mrs. Oliver Mills, herself much of a gardener, commented on this arrangement with wonder.

"Poor man, someone ought to tell him," she said. "Of course the Cherokees will smother the others."

"It isn't how it looks but what it stands for," replied Mrs. Stanley grimly, but she would not explain what she meant.

Now at the exact point to which our history has led us, the new house had arrived at the slow finishing stage. Men were scraping and planing and fitting interminably. Boyd resolved to seize the opportunity of a visit to San Francisco for the purpose of looking over the north, and incidently to buy gas fixtures, finishing hardware, and similar matters.

At first Kenneth was inclined to stay in Arguello, but later events, as has been related, switched him so completely to a new mood that he changed his mind.

They sailed north on the *Santa Rosa*, arrived after a smooth voyage, and proceeded at once to the Occidental Hotel. From this base they made excursions in all directions, taking in the sights. Our history lies with Arguello, so we will not follow them in detail. Kenneth saw Woodward's Gardens with its record-sized grizzly bear, he slid down the slippery seats of the cable cars as they climbed fly-like up the impossible grades of California Street and Telegraph Hill, he drove to the Cliff House and watched the seals, he wandered much in the devious ways of Chinatown, he frequented the Barbary Coast and gazed upon the tall ships. When Boyd had quite completed his business they ran down to Del Monte.

There they lingered for some time. The noble gardens were already well grown, and the rambling wooden hotel—later to be burned to the ground—was most comfortable. It was then fashionable to play croquet, to try to reach the centre of the ingenious "maze" of cedar hedges. There were bowling alleys and the four huge glassed-in swimming tanks with varying depths and temperatures, and drives to the celebrated cypresses and the rock-bound coast. Monterey village was still quaint and old fashioned. People drove in basket phaetons with fringed, square tops.

The hotel society was very lively. It was the day of bonanza kings. The Floods, the O'Briens, the Stanfords, the Fairs, and many others were there. It was a very dashing life, with a good deal of champagne, a good many diamonds, high coloured complexions, startlingly blonde hair. One of the bonanza kings, a little gorilla-like Irishman, had bought him a tall, stately, glorious creature for wife. She had a regal carriage, and a proud, unhappy look in her blue eyes. She never complained, nor appeared to abate her pride, but she had evidently been tamed by her master. Lanagan was short and square and hairy and terribly strong both in physique and in will power. He wore a massive watch chain of nuggets strung together, with which his thick blunt fingers were always toying. Mrs. Lanagan was willowy and fair and stately and cold. She was always magnificently dressed and carried herself haughtily like a queen. Hers was the marble type of beauty. She spoke rarely. Never by word or faintest indication did she show annoyance or mortification at her husband's *gaucheries*. He was always calling for spittoons, or cracking bad jokes in worse taste, or eating with his knife, or performing other shuddery atrocities. And to Mrs. Lanagan his lightest word commanded an instant obedience. It seemed often as though he enjoyed testing his power; as though he commanded merely to be obeyed. Once in the crowded ball room he hailed her, passing:

"Cum here!"

She turned aside and swept to him, waiting impassively. He thrust his leg at her.

"Me foot hurts. Pull off me boot," he commanded.

And in her silks and jewels, without a word, before her partner could forestall her, she dropped on her knees and pulled off this man's boot. Ben Sansome, the old beau, veteran of social changes since the days of 'Forty-nine, cynical, surprised at nothing, often caught himself wondering what mysteries of pride, venality, contempt, will, brutality lay back of this astonishing proud acquiescence.

Lanagan had millions, as had his confrères. A few years before he had been a pick-and-shovel miner, as had many of them. But the time had struck for big, crude men, and these had answered the time. There was something elemental about them; and their vigour can be traced to the San Francisco of to-day.

With these men Boyd found himself congenial. They played a healthy game of poker. The projected week or so at Del Monte stretched to over a month. September was well advanced before the Boyds returned to Arguello.

VIII

KENNETH was by these circumstances and this excursion entirely cured of girls; but he was by no means released from uneasiness. His break with Pearl had been too abrupt to be graceful, provided Pearl knew it had taken place. That young lady was probably still living on the memory of his last kisses and expectation of his next. Some sort of explanation must be made, Kenneth fully appreciated that; and he frankly dreaded it.

Therefore it was to his great delight that he found Herbert Corbell possessed a long memory. Early in the spring he had expressed deep interest in Kenneth's sixteen gauge shotgun' and now that the quail season was about to open he put it into practical form by an invitation. Boyd did not see how he could get away at that time—the house was requiring attention—; but neither could he see any reason for Kenneth's refusing. So the latter laid in a canister of Dupont's Medium Ducking, a sack of number eight chilled shot, Eley's cardboard and felt wads, and the requisite primers. On an agreed day he climbed into a buckboard beside a saturnine looking cattleman, and so set forth to new adventures beyond the Sur.

After leaving the Camino Real five or six miles out, the road—narrow, winding, and steep—climbed rapidly the sides of the great range, taking clever advantage of the "hog's backs," diving into and out of shallow cañons on hairpin turns, wriggling in lacets where no other footholds offered. At the top they drove for a half mile in a bay-shaded cool little cañon with a singing brook, climbed a tiny dividing ridge, and so found themselves on the down grade into the back country. Kenneth had often looked abroad over this back country from the ridge, but never had he descended into it. They rattled down with a continuous shrieking and scraping of brakes. On this side of the range the various kinds of chaparral grew to a height and thickness that made of it almost a jungle. The trees, too, were larger—both the live oaks, the white oaks, and the enormous contorted sycamores along the stream beds. It was a rolling land of shallow, wide valleys with streams in them flanked by *mesas* on which trees grew parklike; and all about were very lofty, dark mountains on which the lighter coloured stratified rocks showed in patterns. The air had here a different quality—very hot, but dry, with an exhilaration in it. Everywhere, but especially along the river down the general direction of which their course lay, was a teeming bird life. The bush was full of them, hopping, perching, chirping; the ground was alive with them, scurrying and scratching; the air was traced with the slow circlings of innumerable stately buzzards or larger hawks. Brush rabbits sitting in the soft dust of the road made two hops to vanish in the bushes; jackrabbits bounded loftily away across sage flats; in every grass opening the ground squirrels scurried to their holes, or sat upright and chirked. Once Kenneth caught a glimpse of some large gray animal as it flashed away.

"What was that?" he cried, excited.

The cowboy spat over the wheel.

"Bobcat, I reckon," said he.

This cowboy was a grave and silent individual, who answered questions politely but very briefly, and volunteered nothing whatever. Yes, there were plenty of quail. Yes, there were plenty of deer. Yes, there's ducks on Pico Lake. Yes, there's trout in the river; rainbows and steelhead.

At noon they drew aside in a little grass flat where a brook ran into the river. The cowboy unhitched the team and provided it with feed. Then he rolled a paper cigarette. To Kenneth's question he replied briefly that he didn't wish for no lunch. Kenneth took his sandwiches in his hand and went down to look at the river.

He found it a tiny shallow stream, with some deep pools, making its way through a bed of boulders and small stones some hundreds of feet wide. On his return he ventured the comment that it did not seem to him much of a river. The cowman grunted.

"Low water," he vouchsafed. "Dry season. You oughta see her after the rains. She picks up them boulders and rolls 'em like marbles."

Throughout the afternoon they drove, until the sun was touching the rim of the hills, through what seemed to be a great natural park of alternate *mesa* and bottomland, with the wide oak trees spaced as though planted ornamentally. Cattle grazed or rested in large or small bands. On each of these the cowboy fixed his grave attention, staring them over deliberately as long as they remained in sight.

"That fork-ear Triangle cow has strayed over yere, I see," he remarked, "I been wonderin' where she was at."

"Do you mean to say that you can tell these animals apart, at that distance?" said Kenneth, incredulously.

"Sure."

"I suppose that you know every cow in this country by sight," observed Kenneth with sarcastic intent.

"I know most of them," replied the cowboy with a final simplicity that closed the subject.

The Corbell ranch proved to be a series of long one-storied white buildings situated on a flat below low sagebrush hills, next a deep *barranca* that contained a flowing streamlet, and beneath live oak trees that, contrary to the usual habit of that species, grew tall and overarching. Circular corrals of greasewood stakes had been built on the flat beyond; and a commodious rough board stable loomed large a short distance down stream. As the buckboard drew nearer Kenneth saw that the white buildings were adobe structures, plastered; set flat to the ground, with narrow verandas running their entire lengths.

At the sound of the wheels the door opened and Corbell appeared to greet him.

"I am glad you could come," said he, "and I'm sorry your

father could not. However, we'll have a grand shoot to-morrow. I'm going to put you in this room here at the end. Just make yourself at home. When you've washed up, come right down the veranda here to the middle door, and come in. We are all there."

The room was small and square with thick adobe walls and a floor made of square, red irregular tiles. These must have been laid directly on the hard soil for their surface was uneven. The furnishings were of the simplest. Two small windows looked out through deep embrasures across the oakdotted flat to the low, even sagebrush hills a quarter mile away. And from these hills Kenneth heard faintly through the gathering dusk the jaunty staccato notes of quail.

His toilet did not take him long. He proceeded along the narrow veranda, also tile paved, past the entrances to two rooms similar to his own, and so to a long chamber occupying the whole centre. It was lighted at this moment only by the flames of a fire leaping in a tremendous fireplace. Kenneth standing in the doorway made out a table at one end set for eating; a shelf of books; a half dozen deer heads; skins of animals tacked against the wall; pegs from which hung bridles, spurs ropes; a rack in the corner for guns; another, smaller, round table cluttered with books, magazines, pipes, tobacco jars, loose cartridges, and similar untidinesses. The floor, still of the big square uneven tiles, was partly covered by a bright rug of Indian or Mexican weave and a number of coyote skins. Overhead were heavy horizontal beams. A number of light, portable chairs, unoccupied, were scattered about. A divan and three heavy easy chairs were grouped before the fireplace, and the heads of their occupants were silhouetted against the flames. Tobacco smoke lay in strata, or eddied violently when caught by the currents of air.

Corbell came forward at once to greet his guest. The others turned their heads and waved their hands.

"Come up to the fire," invited the ranchman. "The evenings are chilly over the mountains at this time of year. You know these men. We'll have some supper shortly."

Kenneth greeted Frank Moore and Bill Hunter. A welter

of dogs raised languid heads or rapped languid tails, then sank back with sighs to toasting their brains in almost immediate contact with the fire. Shortly a lean, carven-faced brown man came in and lighted lamps; and so they moved over to the table and to a hearty supper. After that meal they moved back to the fireplace where they smoked and talked until ten o'clock. After the first twenty minutes—in which the prospects of birds and the sixteen gauge gun were the topics—Kenneth sat back and listened. It was tremendously interesting to him. These harum-scarum members of the *Sociedad* became serious men engaged in a serious business. They discussed cattle, mostly, and feed and ranges; the breed of stock; the provision that could be taken against a dry year; the relative advantages of markets. Frank Moore lost all his facetiousness as he declaimed against the tentative project of importing some Durham bulls to improve the native stock.

"I'm with you on improving the stock," said he. "There's more head than beef on these Mexican longhorns. But Durhams won't do it."

"They are a fine, beefy critter," observed Bill Hunter, "and they are hardy."

"That's it. They're hardy; but only as long as things go right. When feed gets scarce they don't rustle the way they should. They'll hang around their ranges until they just naturally starve to death. Now a Hereford is a rustler. On a dry year you'll find them 'way up on top of the mountains. They'll climb like goats for it when they have to. That's the sort of stock you want to breed to on a wild range."

"And that's the sort of stock that wanders so far they get off your range completely and you never do see them again, unless with a blanketed brand," grumbled Bill, stretching his mighty limbs.

"What is a blanketed brand?" asked Kenneth.

They explained how cattle thieves, or "rustlers," would change a brand by skillful addition of lines. But for a long time thereafter it would, of course, be easy to detect the difference between the new and the old burning. However, it had been discovered that branding through a wet blanket gave to fresh brands an appearance of age that could hardly be detected. From that point the conversation drifted to certain "rustlers" who lurked in the fastnesses of the high coast ranges back of the Sur; and what their activities were and what would eventually have to be done about it. Kenneth snuggled the bowl of his pipe, lost in delighted sense of the romantic—with the firelight playing across the game-heads and on the bright metal of the equipment, and a brace of coyotes shrieking like devils on the hill opposite.

For some time after he had turned in he lay listening to this weird ululation. A big contralto owl in the tree outside at intervals remarked *whoo! whoo! whoo!* Every once in a while, as the night cold penetrated, the old timbers of the adobe cracked loudly.

He was awakened just at dawn by the lean, carven-faced, silent man; and dressed hastily, shivering. The water in which he splashed was icy; and the air, when he emerged to the veranda, stung the lining of his nose. The day was just breaking. Eastward the hills lay in hard outline against a brightening sky. There was a stirring and rustling among the oak leaves as though of things awakening; and from the very tops of them floated softly, as thistledown floats, the infinitely remote, infinitely mournful, infinitely tender note of wild doves.

In the living room the fire was roaring and the lamps were lit. The three ranchmen dressed in stout boots, flannel shirts, and old stained canvas coats with many pockets, were piling equipment together in the middle of the floor. They were joyfully hilarious, again the members of the *Sociedad*.

"Here we are!" cried Corbell, at sight of Kenneth. "So that's the little pop-gun!" He threw it to his shoulder. "It certainly comes up nice! Here Bill, feel this."

The massive Hunter aimed the piece and grunted.

"Feel as though I were handling a toothpick! I like something I can hold steady."

"He's got it," said Frank Moore to Kenneth. "Did you ever see his cannon? Here's what he has the nerve to lug around after quail."

He handed Kenneth a huge ten bore, with thirty inch barrels, a tremendous and awe-inspiring piece of ordnance that weighed nine or ten pounds.

"It's a cylinder bore. Bill loads her with five drachms and an ounce and a half! When he turns her loose he kills everything within an angle of thirty degrees, big and little, birds, animals, insects. It's like dynamiting a pool, I say."

"You go to hell!" was all Bill's comment.

Each several times tried the feel of Kenneth's little Scott. They liked the way it handled; but they much doubted its shooting quality. It might be all right of course for very close range; but long shots now—or old birds?

Kenneth grew eloquent in defence of the sixteen. He had done considerable wing shooting in the East both at the Bob White and the ruffed grouse. They listened politely.

"You have to reload, don't you?" Corbell changed the subject. "How many shells have you?"

"Fifty."

"That is very few. I think I'll put in a little twelve I have for you."

"I ought to get all the birds I want with fifty shells," protested Kenneth. "I'm really not such a bad shot as all that."

Again they listened politely. They were all old hands at the sport, and had witnessed the downfall of much eastern pride. Corbell, as host, did his duty by letting fall a hint.

"The western *Colinus*, or quail," he stated with a burlesque of the didactic, "is as compared with the eastern *Colinus*, or quail, a swift and elusive proposition that requires especial study."

"Such being the case, suppose we go and study him," suggested Moore.

Breakfast over they picked up their guns and started forth. Full daylight had come, and the first rays of the sun were gilding the sagebrush hills on the left side of the valley. Toward these the hunters proceeded on foot.

From that moment until lunch time Kenneth acquired much valuable experience. He learned that hunting the valley quail was indeed a specialist's job. Arrived at the sagebrush slope Corbell strung his command out at such intervals as to sweep the hill. They began to move forward abreast.

Soon in the openings Kenneth began to see the quail, running busily, their heads held low, their bodies trim, darting through the sagebrush.

"Here are some, just ahead!" he shouted.

The line quickened its pace in order to flush the birds. Kenneth held his gun forward ready at any instant for a shot. But the quail kept ahead. Occasionally he caught glimpses of them still running.

"Shake it up!" cried Corbell, from near the top of the hill.

They broke into a dog trot. Kenneth felt a vexed wonder as to how any one could be expected to pick his footing, dodge sagebrush, cling to a side hill, and shoot—at this pace. Then suddenly with a whir of wings a half dozen of the birds sprang into the air about a hundred yards away. Promptly Frank Moore flung his gun to his shoulder and let drive both barrels. Kenneth's disgusted astonishment at the foolishness of firing at such an absurd range was instantly swallowed up in wonder, for as though answering the reports came a roar like a cataract, as hundreds of quail flushed in a pack. The air was blue with them, literally hundreds, perhaps thousands, Kenneth could not begin to guess. They, too, were well over a hundred yards distant. Nevertheless both Corbell and Hunter fired instantly, followed a second later by two more from Frank, who had reloaded.

"Come on! Come on!" yelled Corbell, and started after them on the run. The quail buzzed for fifty yards, set their wings and sailed for fifty yards more, then pitched down sidewise in an open space and paced away like quarter horses. The little band of sweating, stumbling hunters caught up with them— if flushing them at another hundred yards, range could be called catching up—only after a jog of nearly a quarter mile. Then once more six barrels blazed away, without of course touching a feather at such a distance. And off they set again after the vanishing pack.

To Kenneth the whole performance seemed crazy. He was accustomed to some sort of an orderly performance over dogs; he had some ideas of effective ranges and the wasting of ammunition. There was no fun in this. Twice stragglers from the main covey got out almost under his feet, but he could not even get organized for a shot; on another occasion his companions flushed individuals at good range but apparently did not see them, or at least paid them no attention.

At length after the third repetition of this silly performance Corbell called a halt, and came down the hill wiping his brow.

"I reckon we've got enough laid away," he observed. "Enough for a good shoot, anyway." He caught Kenneth's expression and laughed. "I forgot to ask you if you knew anything about this game," said he. "I see you don't. I suppose you think we're crazy."

"Well," replied Kenneth, cautiously, "I don't believe I quite understand how you expect to kill anything at that range."

"We don't," laughed Corbell. "Bless you, we aren't shooting with the expectation of killing anything. We just shoot to make a noise, raise a row."

"I see," said Kenneth blankly, but still trying desperately to be polite.

"The California quail in these big packs would run a hundred miles, if you gave them a chance," explained Corbell. "You could chase those fellows all day, and they'd always keep just about a hundred yards ahead of you. Try it and see. The only hope is to rattle them, scare them a little. Then, a few at a time, they'll scatter; and when they're scattered they'll lie close. The noise of the guns and, I suppose, the patter of spent shot, does just that. Didn't you notice that the pack was much smaller on that last rise?"

"I'm afraid I didn't notice much of anything," confessed Kenneth.

"Well, it was. There were close to seven or eight hundred birds on that first rise. I don't believe there were over three hundred the last time they got up. Where do you suppose the rest are? Why, scattered through the brush back of us, of course; where they pitched in and hid. They will lie: and that is where we are going to get our shooting. See?"

"I see."

"Well, listen."

They held quiet, and from the long brushy side hill back of

him Kenneth heard near at hand subdued clucks, whispered
calls; and from farther away, now here, now there, now half
voiced, now full strength came the jaunty clear gathering call
over and over repeated.

"*You can't shoot! You can't shoot!*"

"Now we will go back over the same ground and get our
shooting," instructed Corbell. "You will have to pick up your
own birds, and to do that you will have to mark them very
closely. This brush all looks pretty much alike. Until you
get used to it I'd advise you not to kill a second bird until you
have picked up the first. And another thing: if you fall behind
the line looking for a down bird, you don't shoot again until
you have caught up, even if you do flush something. That's
for safety. Everybody ready? All right: we're off!"

In the retracing of his steps Kenneth had many bitter truths
borne in on him. The valley quail in his full growth and
strength is one of the speediest of upland game. He is very
strong in flight, and he launches himself from the advantage of
iron-hard ground. He is like a blue bullet; and is a hard bird to
hit when flushed on level ground. But here Kenneth was midway up a steep hill. Rarely did a quail flush exactly on his
level, and rarely did it fly on the same level. It darted quarter-
ing up the hill from below, or swooped curving down the hill
from above, or deceived all calculation by rocketing up, over
and back. He shot over, he shot behind; and at his first shattering report, a bewildering, buzzing half dozen of these blue
devils darted into the air on all sides of him to confuse his second
barrel. Then he had to keep his footing and make his way
through brush. Above and below him the guns were speaking
regularly; and several times the remnants of his bewildered
attention saw the quick puff of feathers and the long slanting
fall that means a clean kill. But he became more and more
flustered and angry until at a point where the low growth of
sage came to an end, he was thoroughly rattled.

"Nice shoot: they lay nicely!" observed Corbell, as they
gathered together. He began to pull quail from the game
pockets of his canvas coat. "How did you make out, Boyd?"

"Very badly."

"Well, that's to be expected at first. How many did you get?"

"I killed two," confessed Kenneth, miserably, "but I couldn't find either of them. I don't know what's the matter with me. I'm not a crack shot by any means, but I used to be able to hit *some*thing!"

"These quail are tough customers—— Perhaps that gun——" began Bill Hunter.

"I never saw an Eastern shot, no matter how good, who could hit a flock of balloons first day out," interrupted Corbell, consolingly. "Never! It's a different game. Suppose we trade guns for a little while. I'd really like to ˌtry that little fellow."

Kenneth agreed. He found to his astonishment that of the fifty loaded brass shells only about twenty remained charged.

"I did not realize I had shot so many!" he confessed. Then more boldly. "Would you mind, Mr. Corbell, if I just trailed you for a little while? I want to see how it's done, and get some hints. I can pick up your birds for you."

"Certainly. Come along. But there isn't much to learn. It's a matter of practise."

"What do we do now? Hunt up another covey?"

"No: go right back over the same ground. We didn't get up a quarter of them. We could go back and forth there all day and still get up birds: and the oftener we went the closer they'd lie."

On this second trip Kenneth added to his humility. Corbell was a beautiful shot. And he found that, even with the preoccupation of shooting, the older man was able to mark dead birds more accurately than could Kenneth, who was giving his whole attention to it.

"You'll find him about three feet further to the left, under that brush with the dead stalk," he told Kenneth. The bird had been the first of three killed in a scattering rise from one spot, when Corbell had to turn square away for the second and third. "It's a matter of spotting some one individual bush or even spear of grass," he told Kenneth. When the shooters grouped again at the end of this drive, Corbell was enthusiastic about the little Scott.

"It kills 'em," he said, "and it kills 'em just as far as that old cannon of yours, Bill. I wouldn't have believed it! And it kills them clean. It's either a clean kill or a clean miss; and you've got to hold close. I missed several birds just because I didn't get square on and centre them. And, Lord! she does handle prettily!"

"How many did you scratch down with the thing?" inquired Hunter.

"An even dozen, with twenty shots."

"Beginner's luck," asserted Bill. "Can't repeat in a thousand years. Me, I like a gun you can depend on; not one you got to carry a rabbit's foot with."

Corbell's eyes were snapping.

"I'll tell you what I'll do," he suggested, suavely. "I'll take twenty shells to-morrow morning, after the birds are scattered, and I'll get more birds with this little popgun than you can with that old blunderbuss of yours. Only it will cost you fifty dollars to see me do it. Are you on?"

"I promised my mother I wouldn't gamble," said Bill. "But this isn't gambling: it's a sure thing. Yes, I'll take your money."

They returned to the ranch house for lunch at noon, after which saddle horses were brought and they spent the rest of the day jogging in a leisurely fashion over the ranges. Kenneth trailed along. The more he saw and the longer he listened the more impressed was he by the great complication and uncertainty of the cattle business, and the amount of specialized knowledge necessary to run it on anything but a hit-or-miss basis. As they went along Corbell told him something of what happens when two dry years come in succession; the failure, first of the feed, and then of the streams and springs; the weakening and the starvation of cattle and other stock.

"I drove a bunch of horses across country 'way over into Inyo County just to save them," he said. "You could have your pick of riding animals, if you'd promise to feed them. We shot all but the very finest stock. Some of the Spanish people drove big herds of cattle off the sea cliffs so they would not die inland and contaminate the air. They estimate that a million cattle died that time. A million's a good many!"

He shook his head as his thoughts strayed to those black years.

"Now we've got a new system. We raise hay, and bale it, and pile it up, and roof it over. Every year a crop is piled up and not used until it is in danger of spoiling. After a few years you get to have quite a lot of hay. You've seen it standing about like big buildings in all the bottom lands. When another dry year comes along, we'll feed it out."

"I should think you could raise most anything here," said Kenneth. "The soil looks fine."

But at this Corbell drew into his shell.

"It's not an agricultural country," he said shortly: and here, had he but known it, Kenneth was touching the obstinate conservatism of the cattleman, sensing dimly the quarter from which his doom was to come.

A week later Kenneth rode back alone across the mountains on a borrowed horse. He left his baggage to follow when the buckboard or the high trap next visited town; but he carried some fifty quail.

"You must come back in the pigeon season," was Corbell's parting remark. "They come down from the north in clouds. Greatest wing shooting you ever did!"

At Arguello Kenneth found himself once more in face of his problem, which had in no way diminished by being temporarily ignored. In fact it had increased by the one fact that this plunge into wholesome, manly, out-of-door pursuits had given him a positive distaste for Pearl. Nevertheless he had his code. It was his fault; not hers. He would be a dastard and a villain to go back on her now. It would be like slapping a child. He must go through with it: play his part. After balking shamefully for two days, he revolted against himself, and made an especial trip downtown for the sole purpose of stopping in at the Kandy Kitchen. Pearl was behind the counter, dressed in her usual clean pink starched things. She certainly looked neat and clean and refreshing; but somehow vapid. Kenneth had never noticed this before. He seemed to be looking at her from an outside detached viewpoint.

"Hello, Pearl," he greeted, trying for ease of mannei. "Haven't seen you for a dog's age. I've been away—up north—over the mountains, you know," he hastened to add.

"How do you do," she returned primly. "Yes, I heard you had."

A wonder crossed Kenneth's panic-stricken mind as to why it had not occurred to him to write. Actually the idea had never until this moment crossed his mind. She must be wondering the same thing!

If so, she showed no signs of it. She answered his lame sallies in her usual prim, self-possessed manner. Customers were numerous, and Kenneth made them an excuse for leaving.

"Meet me this evening?" he forced himself to ask.

"Thank you, I can't this evening."

"Well, s'm'other time," said Kenneth, making a thankful escape.

But his conscience would not let him off. It dragged him, always with increasing distaste, to the Kandy Kitchen, where were reënacted varying repetitions of the same interview. Invariably Kenneth, as in duty bound suggested a meeting, but invariably was put off by an excuse. The fourth visit discovered a black-haired young fellow leaning over the counter talking low-voiced to Pearl. Her manner was as precise as ever, but her star-eyes were downcast, and a faint pink flushed her cheeks.

"Seven o'clock near the bandstand," Kenneth heard her say.

And a great burden fell from his shoulders. For in this black-haired young man he saw again himself.

He greeted Pearl jovially, cracked some jokes, met the young man cordially, and breezed out again without suggesting further an evening or a Sunday meeting. Thereafter he liked to drop in at the Kandy Kitchen occasionally, to chaff Pearl, to join the young people at the soda fountain. Pearl was a good soul; not bad looking in her way. But never again did he see her alone.

Nor did he ever get back his jewelled fraternity pin!

CHAPTER IV

I

THE dry season stretched on beyond its wont. People began anxiously to speculate about the rain, calling upon old precedents, old signs, and portents to support their views or hopes. The brown hills turned pale silver as the grasses bleached. In the cañons lay a tangle of dead old stalks and vines. Where had been a lush thicket of ferns now the eaith lay naked and baked, displaying unexpected simplicities of contour that had before been mysteriously veiled. So hard and trodden looked this earth that it seemed incredible that any green thing had ever, or could ever again, pierce its steel-like shell. The land was stripped bare. In the trees the wind rustled drvlv. In the sky the sun shone glaringly. The morning fogs were no more. No smallest wisp of mist relieved the steel blue of the heavens. Animals and birds drowsed through the days, seeming to stir abroad only at night. Even the buzzards sat on the cross arms of the telegraph poles with their wings held half out from their bodies, as though panting. Along the roads, for many yards on either side, the earth and trees were powdered white with dust; and in the roadways lay a thick white carpet that rose to smother you at a touch. The land was as if in suspended animation, waiting, It was athirst.

All the old timers watched these things with interest, hope, or dismay, according to their temperaments. The Boyds had not been in California long enough to think of rain in terms of inches. Kenneth, if he gave it a thought, merely delighted in the unbroken sunshine; or noticed that at sunset the coloured veils over the ramparts of the Sur had deepened in tint and tenderness.

The completion of the house aroused in him a belated interest. They moved in about the first of December. Everything smelled new. It was an imposing house, two-storied, square like a box, but with its plainness relieved by a cupola. One mounted a tiny porch with pillars and passed into a narrow central hall in which arose the stairs and from which opened four doors on each side and one at the end. The two doors on the right led into the library and the dining room. The two doors on the left into the parlour and a smaller affair known as the "den"; the one at the end gave access to the kitchen by way of the pantry. All the woodwork shone with varnish. The walls were kalsomined and decorated with stencilled or "hand painted" designs. The furniture of the parlour was the last degree of spindle legged and brocaded discomfort; that of the dining room carved and massive; but the library and den, with their fireplaces and their leather upholstered chairs and sofas were, even when new, cosy and inviting. Boyd had expended considerable ingenuity on the den. It had a cellarette with spaces for all shaped bottles and glasses; a humidor like a cabinet; a card table with devices for bestowing ashes, chips, or drinks. Altogether the house was a very creditable setting for a gentleman of wealth and leisure of the early 'eighties; a woman might criticize it as too distinctly a man's house, of expensive solid comfort, but more like a furniture exhibit than an example of considered taste.

The grounds, too, were well advanced in the first stages. That is to say, they were all planted, but not yet grown. The modern practise of wealthy gentlemen of moving full grown trees at fabulous cost and great risk was then unknown. You planted things out of earthenware pots, or at most wooden tubs. An Easterner would have seen little in Boyd's new garden save a pattern and a lot of plants, all apparently alike. Not so a Californian. The latter has developed the seeing eye. Those fifty growths or so he does not see as they are, all the same size. Some to him stand as trees, some as shrubs, some as creepers or flowering plants. He sees that garden as it will be, not as it is; and so he is prepared for interested and intelligent discussion. Thus Mrs. Stanley and Boyd had an almost acrimonious argument as to whether a certain tree should be removed, the ground of argument being whether it did or did not shut off the view of the mountains. The tree was six inches tall.

Having acquired a staff, consisting of two indoor Chinamen, one garden Chinaman, and a Spanish stable boy, Boyd suggested to his son that it would be a good idea to give a party by way of house warming.

"We've been treated pretty well by all these people," said he, "and the old winter crowd is beginning to come back. Let's give a real blowout."

The plans, as they talked them over, took shape in the direction of real engraved invitations, an orchestra rather than the usual piano-mandolin-guitar combination, a caterer from San Francisco——

"Hold on!" cried Boyd, looking in dismay at the list of those to be invited, "we're getting swamped! This house will never hold that gang! The doors are too narrow for one thing. Where are you going to put the orchestra?"

But Dora Stanley had an idea. The Stanleys, as next door neighbours had been taken into full consultation; and had responded with enthusiasm, down to the Chinamen. Chinese love parties. Even Martin so far forsook his customary brotherly attitude of cynicism to admit it was a good idea.

"Have the dance in the barn!" she cried. "There's plenty of space in the carriage room. You can put sofas and things in the stalls for them to sit out. You can put refreshments in the harness room. And that leaves the house entirely free for clothes, and card tables, and supper and all the rest."

So the horses continued to board at the Fremont stables, while the barn was decorated. They used hundreds of yards of bunting and dozens of American flags until no sliver of the carriage room remained visible, and the place resembled a crazy-coloured marquee. They stretched canvas on the floor, and then laid other canvas over that in order to keep it clean. They placed locomotive lanterns for lights. They installed cartloads of furniture around the walls and in the stalls and haymow. They arranged scores of palms and other plants in tubs around the tête-à-tête corners. As an afterthought they constructed a covered way between the stable and the house. Boyd would never have thought of that, but Dora pointed out to him emphatically the perishable nature of chignons and chiffons when exposed to night breezes.

The invitations went out to every family of social pretension in the county. It was understood that a cotillion was to be danced—they called it a "German." Most people knew in a general way how you did it, but nobody was quite certain as to the details. To conduct such a thing successfully, without confusion, took knowledge and practise. Possibly Kenneth Boyd was going to "lead"; he came from New York. Then someone learned that Ben Sansome was coming down especially, from San Francisco. Ben Sansome had led San Francisco society and its dances since the pioneer days. That was all he ever did: that was his specialty. His approval made a débutante, nobody knew just why, and as a consequence he was made much of. His journeying to Arguello especially for the Boyd housewarming was quite wonderful. Boyd's stock went even higher. There was a great overhauling of feminine wardrobes. Even the men, concealing their interest under indifferent exteriors, secretly wondered whether they ought to have silk hats, and if so whether the old ones would do.

II

THIS party created considerable disturbance at Corona del Monte. Of course Colonel and Mrs. Peyton were going; it would not have been a typical party without them. But the Colonel had set his heart on taking Daphne with them; and, after a little hesitation, Allie backed him up. The proposal met with its opposition from Brainerd himself. The idea that Daphne was old enough for such an affair took him completely by surprise.

"She's nothing but a baby; look at her!" he objected.

"I'm looking at her," rejoined Allie, stoutly, "and all I see is that you don't know enough to dress her suitably for her age. She is sixteen next month, and you rig her out like a child. I was married at sixteen."

"But she *is* young," persisted Brainerd. "What does she know of dancing and ballroom conversation?"

"She's a very *good* dancer," stated Mrs. Peyton, flatly, "and as for ballroom conversation, I don't know that it is any different from any other conversation, and I certainly would not call Daffy tongue-tied."

"Where has she ever learned to dance?" demanded Brainerd.

"At dancing school, where I myself have been taking her every Thursday afternoon," stated Allie.

Brainerd flushed.

"Why did I know nothing of that?"

"I told Daffy to keep it secret—as a surprise."

"You mean you were afraid I'd put a stop to it."

Allie only smiled at this.

"My dress suit is riddled with moths," grumbled Brainerd, "and heaven knows to what hours we'd be out."

"Now we're getting down to the real reasons," said Mrs. Peyton, briskly. "Let me relieve your mind. I'm not asking you to go. We shall take charge of Daffy; and she'll sleep at the ranch. Perhaps she *is* a little young; but you must take your chances as they come. It is not every day that such a grand ball is given in a new house."

"Fine! fine!" cried the Colonel, when he heard of the capitulation. "She shall be the belle of the ball! And, Allie, I want you to get her the very grandest ball gown you can buy."

But Allie had accurately gauged Brainerd's complaisance.

"No," she vetoed. "He would not allow that. Believe me Richard, I know."

"But as a present from me—for her coming out!" pleaded the Colonel.

"No. He has made the big concession: and will be obstinate as a mule on everything else."

"She would be a beauty in a proper dress—a beauty. I know; I am a judge. But you must see that she is fitted out, someway!" cried the Colonel, much disappointed.

The situation was saved by Doña Cazadero. That amiable lady, with Pilar, came in on the discussion.

"But we have estacks and estacks of clothes, so pretty. Laid away for many years in our great chests," she drawled. "But of course among so many the *niña* will find that which will esuit her! Pilar will wear one of them, and I will wear one. They are not in the present estyle, no; but the present estyle is very ugly, no? And these are of the Spanish estyle, which is always good. Yes?"

Next day Mrs. Peyton and Daphne drove over to Las Flores behind the little ponies and spent the afternoon trying on the rich old dresses unpacked from bestudded Spanish chests. They were beautiful, and they became Daphne's piquant style. With her hair gathered hastily and held by a huge comb, with her cheeks aglow with excitement, with her slim lithe figure in the old time long corsage and flounces, Daphne was a picture. She was much pleased and a little astonished at what the mirror showed her. She even put on the silk stockings and buskins with crossed straps, and secretly rubbed her legs together to feel the silk creak. She had a keen sense of the beautiful, but was still too much of a child to have acquired an equally keen sense of the fashionable.

"It is certainly very fetching: she is really beautiful in it," commented Mrs. Peyton doubtfully, to Doña Cazadero, "but——"

"But it is not estyle. True. But always has the *niña* been esso different from all the rest. Why do you want to make her like now?" said Doña Cazadero, with unexpected insight.

"I believe you are right! But I am afraid Mr. Brainerd will never consent——"

"I know," said Doña Cazadero. She was astonishing for so apparently idle a lady. "I will myself make the call on Meester Brainerd. Daffy, you will essay nothing of the dress. But you will essay to señor, your father, that Doña Vincente Cazadero will call on heem to-morrow."

At three the following afternoon the Cazadero state coach bumped its way over the half-made road to the bungalow. Brainerd—impressed, somewhat puzzled, and a trifle suspicious over this unusual honour—helped the lady up the steps and into an armchair, where she unfolded a fan and looked about her.

"You have here the nice *ranchita*," she stated. "I have never been here."

Brainerd murmured an appropriate response. Small talk ensued. Then after suitable interval Doña Cazadero raised her voice.

"Juan!" she called.

The Cazadero footman entered bearing packages which, at a sign, he laid on the floor and began to unwrap. Brainerd watched the leisurely performance with a curiosity that changed to bewilderment as he saw what the packages contained.

"They are very pretty," observed Doña Cazadero calmly.

"They seem so," replied Brainerd, "but what——"

"Daphne she go to this ball of Señor Boyd? No? Eet is her first ball: no? Well, this gown is the present of the Cazadero for that *fiesta.*"

Brainerd stiffened.

"It is a very kind thought, Doña Cazadero, but I cannot permit——"

"Permit: what is that word?" Doña Cazadero interrupted. "But you do not understand. We are *rancheros* both; no? We are neighbours; no? It is the custom of the Espanish peoples to make the gift at thees first *fiesta* of a young girl. Always we do that. For that we keep many thing." She laughed, shaking her plump form all over. "You have no idea the many thing: in boxes, chests. It is bad luck to buy the gift. It must be of the family possession. Now theese dress," she prattled on, "eet is very old. In old time there ees a ship come in, name of *The Pilgrim,* and she bring very nice things—diamonds, dresses, combs, *mantillas,* all the thing Espanish people want. And the Espanish people send down the eskin of cow—very many—and they mak' the trade. There was no—what—you—call—wharf. You go through the wave in a boat. I remember my mother tell me how the young Yankee sailor man squeeze her little bit when he carry her through the wave to the boat!" She laughed in a jolly fashion. "So we get all the thing: and we put these away in the chest and the box."

"But this must be very valuable: priceless!" protested Brainerd.

"Oh, yes, very valuable," agreed Doña Cazadero, calmly. "You can not buy heem. They do not mak' heem now. That," she explained triumphantly, "ees why he mak' the good gift for the *fiesta !*"

She arose and offered her hand in farewell.

"But I cannot accept——" repeated Brainerd feebly.

"To riffuse the gift of the Espanish people for the first *fiesta* of the young girl, Señor Brainerd," stated the Señora courteously, but with a totally unexpected edge to her voice, "is the same thing as one who says 'I am not your frien'.' It is the custom of old time; and we are people of the old time."

"It is kind of you; most kind," said Brainerd, after a slight pause. "Daphne will be delighted. I will see that she expresses her deep appreciation."

The equipage rolled and bumped its way down the hill. It did not return at once to Las Flores, but stopped for a call at La Corona del Monte.

"Did he accept?" asked Mrs. Peyton, eagerly.

"Oh, he tak' heem," smiled Doña Cazadero, indolently. Then after a pause—"All men the same—like childs."

Daphne spent a good deal of her time now at the Peyton's. There were important, mysterious things to be done to the gown. Somewhat to his own surprise Brainerd drove over a number of times and disposed his long tweed-clad figure in an easy chair where he could watch his daughter, flushed with a repressed excitement, moving to and fro. He was looking on her with new eyes as he would look on a new specimen. Evidently he found her good, for the eyes glowed softly: evidently the thought that she had grown up disturbed him, for the weary lines of his face deepened and saddened.

"I did not know before that I was old," he told Allie. "I have been grubbing away up there with always the hope of to-morrow to console me for the shortcomings of to-day. And now I see the to-morrows are few."

"Old! Nonsense, man!" chided Mrs. Peyton briskly. "You might be the Colonel's son. And he's not old yet."

"Nor ever will be, bless him," returned Brainerd with unwonted feeling.

It was agreed that Daphne was to dine and dress at the Peytons' before the ball and spend with them what remained of the night afterward. Dinner was the least important: and was hurried over at a scandalously early hour. Then Daphne retired with Mrs. Peyton and Rosita, Manuelo's daughter. The Colonel dressed himself in his old "clawhammer" with the long tails, that somehow on him gave the impression of brass buttons, though brass buttons there were none; and tried in vain to read or smoke. He was as excited as Daphne herself, and kept jumping up to see if Manuelo understood about the team, and if they had got out the thick lap robes, and if they had remembered to put on the side curtains. The time was very long. The women, indeed, were having trouble. The difficulty was not with the gown, which fitted to a marvel, but with Daphne's hair. It simply would not lie down and be tame as the Spanish style demanded. Finally Allie abandoned the Spanish style entirely.

"This is not a masquerade: we don't have to be consistent," she mumbled through the hairpins in her mouth. "There," she pronounced, after a few moments. "You'll do. Now run down and keep the Colonel company while I slip on my dress."

"Oh, Aunt Allie!" cried Daphne, with compunction. "You've spent all the time on me! I'm so selfish!" and she would have flown at the little woman for a hug and a kiss. But Mrs. Peyton checked her.

"Hold on!" she cried sharply. "Don't you dare muss yourself, after all my pains! I have plenty of time to dress. I've done it before a thousand times or so, and I don't have to experiment. Run along!"

Daphne crept along the dim hall to the study, trying hard to avoid the numerous cracking boards. The Colonel was seated under the lamp with a book. He looked up at the bright young vision framed in the doorway.

"God bless my soul!" he exclaimed, and arose. "My dear," he said gravely, after a pause of inspection, "you will be the belle of the ball. You are exquisite." He stepped forward and raised her hand to his lips. Her colour heightened, her eyes bright, she dropped him a curtsey.

"I am glad you like it, godpapa. If you are pleased, I am very happy."

"Frightened, puss?" asked the old man.

"Not frightened, exactly: but very excited. Oh, godpapa, do you suppose I will get any dances?"

"Well, if you don't," stated the Colonel stoutly, "I'm going to have the eyesight of the young men of this town examined. Where are you going? Your aunt isn't ready yet."

"I just thought I'd go see Sing Toy," she said shyly. Why she wanted to see Sing Toy she did not exactly know. It was no mere desire to show off her grandeur before another. But Sing Toy was one of the family.

The Chinaman sat under the lamp in the middle of a spotless kitchen that looked as though it must just have been finished and furnished by a very careful person who had not yet used it. Not the smallest item was out of place. Sing Toy was in a straight backed chair. He wore loose garments of silk brocade, dark blue on the outside, with others showing edges of lilac and pink underneath. His socks were snowy white, his thick-soled shoes were stiff with embroidery. His long queque, which in daily work was coiled neatly around his head, now hung ceremonially down his back. He sat bolt upright, his hands tucked in his voluminous sleeves, staring straight ahead of him as though expecting distinguished company. This was his frequent habit, though most evenings he was with the gardeners in their quarters. Thus he sat rigid and silent the whole evening through as though receiving visitors, engaged in mysterious thoughts of his own. Perhaps he did receive visitors—who knows?

As the door opened and Daphne slipped in to the well-lighted kitchen Sing Toy turned his head and looked at her for some time without expression.

"I go to party, Sing Toy," said Daphne. "I think perhaps you like look at my new dress. Very fine silk."

"I think mebbeso you come," stated Sing Toy. "He China silk. Velly fine. Old silk. You young lady now: no litty girl. You no come want ginga snaps any more," he added, and a faint smile appeared in the depth of his eyes.

"Oh, Sing Toy! I'll put on short dresses to-morrow, if I'm to have no more of your good gingersnaps!"

Sing Toy arose and waddled deliberately to a cupboard drawer whence he produced a long shallow box of the soft yet stiff crêpe-like paper peculiar to the Chinese. It was edged with red and ornamented with the decorative Chinese words.

"Litty plesent," said Sing Toy, handing it to her.

She raised the cover and the crêpe-tissue paper beneath it to discover a silk scarf. It was a wonderful specimen of Chinese handicraft, stiff with exquisite embroidery.

"Oh, Sing Toy," she breathed, "it's wonderful."

"Yes, he velly fine," said Sing Toy, complacently, "you wear him on head."

She threw the scarf over her hair.

"It's just the thing!" she cried. "Oh, thank you so much! It's a wonderful present.

"All light. You go. I velly busy," said Sing Toy.

"Give me the box to put it in. What does this writing say?"

"Good-luck-long-life-'n-happiness," replied Sing Toy, as though it were one word. "Now you go!"

Daphne did not return to the Colonel. She slipped on the voluminous "carriage boots," threw her wrap about her shoulders and stepped out into the night. The air was very still and warm and quiet. Hardly an insect chirped. She turned down the dim tree aisles, and shortly found herself under the spreading branches of that great oak she called Dolman's House.

"Oh, Dolman," she breathed. "I'm so excited! To-night I am spreading my wings! Just like the little birds in your branches! Don't let me fall, Dolman. Make me happy!"

She looked up through the branches interlaced against the night sky; and the stars twinkled at her. As she looked they alternately grew larger and smaller. Then slowly from either side a gray mist seemed to close in. The stars grew dim, were blotted out, the twisted limbs of Dolman's House disappeared. Only the gray mist filled her eyes. And then, as slowly as it had closed in, it appeared to draw aside again. Daphne seemed to herself to be galloping up the beach, and the wind was in her hair, and the surf thundered, and the beach birds' cries were scattered before her like leaves. Close behind her she heard a horse's hoofbeats against the hard sand. They were coming nearer——

A voice called her name. There was an instant's rushing of

things as though coming into focus. Daphne was under the oaks; but so real had been the flash of her vision that almost she could taste the salt on her lips. The Colonel was calling her.

"Coming!" she cried. Then, as she turned away: "What did you mean, Dolman? Is happiness only in my old pursuits?"

But Dolman gave no further sign.

III

BALLS started early in those days. Soon after eight o'clock the first of the guests began to arrive. Arguello possessed two "glass hacks," and these were so much in demand that their owners had arranged their would-be patrons in a schedule. The first lot was instructed to be ready at eight sharp. They knew if they were not on time they would lose their chance, for the glass hack could not wait: it had its other customers to call for. All the guests went first to the house, where they deposited their wraps, and then down the covered way to the stables where they greeted their hosts and Mrs. Stanley. That competent and un-compromising lady had again donned her war harness and was assisting; all thought of boundary fences and such things forgotten. Ben Sansome, too, was in line, a jovial, plump, bald elderly gentleman, suggesting a pug dog rather than a leader of society, dressed with the most exquisite correctness, and properly though condescendingly genial. The place seemed alive with silent, unobtrusive, deft, dress-suited strangers gliding about on various errands—the caterer's men from San Francisco. One of them stood behind a small table at the door and handed to each gentleman as he entered a folded dance card from which depended a tiny pencil on a silken string. The outside of these carried an embossed monogram, which indicated that they were no mere bought-from-stock commonplaces, together with the date. The inside contained dances up to fifteen, each numbered and named, with a blank line on which to write in names. There were the Grand March, and waltzes, polkas, schottisches, lancers, and a Virginia Reel entitled the supper dance. After supper was to come the "German." Were it not for a supplementary set of dances played between each of the regular numbers

and called "extras," one's fate would thus have been cut and
dried for the entire evening. Already youths were darting here
and there inscribing names on their cards and those of their
partners-to-be. The more enterprising were not in such hurry.
They had days since bespoken certain dances: it only remained
to stroll around and see that the fair ones had properly entered
them. As each girl with any claims to popularity appeared in
the doorway she was the centre of a rush from all directions.

Sooner or later the couples strolled down to look over the
favours spread out on a big table at the end of the room. These
were satisfactorily expensive and striking. There were also
various mysterious "properties" that had to do with figures in
the German.

Only Ben Sansome knew what they were for—Ben and two
of the younger men whom he picked to assist him, and with
whom he had rehearsed solemnly the more complicated figures.
The older people were finding places in the chairs set along the
walls. The youngsters wandered into and out of the nooks and
corners, spying the lay of the land, admiring the arrangements
and the decorations. Behind some tubbed palms in one corner
the orchestra was tuning; adding to the suspended thrill of,
anticipation. Then a ball was "opened" formally; and until
it was opened there was no music, and no one shook a foot.

The entrance of the Peytons and Daphne Brainerd was hon-
oured by an instant's total silence, followed by a low buzz. The
Colonel was impressive at any time, with his erect, lean figure,
his shaven, aristocratic hawk face, and his mop of silver hair.
But as he appeared in the doorway to-night his old-fashioned
charm was only a foil to the equally old-fashioned charm of the
girl on his arm. Mrs. Peyton, with a true eye for effect, had
managed to drop a step back on excuse of greeting a friend, leaving the old man and the girl to go in alone. Doña Cazadero had
been right: the Spanish gown was not in the mode but was always in style. And Daphne's irregular features, dusky rich
colour, and mass of unruly hair added just the captivating touch
of incongruity.

Heads were together all over the room. The little receiving
line broke its routine of greetings. And Ben Sansome, who

had been standing at the end, turned and approached the group of which Boyd was the centre. They saw him bend a little stiffly from the hips acknowledging the introduction, and reach his pudgy hand for the dance card that dangled from Daphne's wrist. She passed it to him instantly, blank as it had come from the engraver's. Ben Sansome smiled at it, and looked up to meet direct, grave eyes.

"I should have said you were like that," he murmured. "It shows in all you wear so exquisitely; the look of your eyes upon all these others."

Daphne did not at all understand the speech; but she was no fool, so she smiled enigmatically. She had never been to a formal ball before, and so did not know that young ladies were accustomed to scribble random initials opposite all vacant dances in order to avoid the appearance of unpopularity. Later, of course, those initials could be erased as partners proposed themselves.

"I will put myself down for the Grand March, if I may," continued Ben Sansome. That wily and experienced warrior had not yet chosen his partners, for he did not know the society of Arguello—and no intention of contenting himself with anything second rate. He well knew that any girl present would "bolt" any engagement she might have to give him any dance he requested. It must be repeated that no one could quite have told why this was so. Ben Sansome was and had always been an idler. He had wasted every talent and opportunity he might have possessed. He looked like an obese pug dog. He drank too steadily; and, though he never disgraced himself in public, he got beastly drunk among men at the clubs. His conversation was hardly enlivening. He sold champagne for a living, inferior champagne which people bought because they were afraid he would be offended if they did not serve it when he dined with them: he always examined the labels! Other men looked upon him with good-natured contempt. Yet there is no doubt that he ruled San Francisco society. During the season three big balls were given in the name of charity, or what not. Ben Sansome attended to all the details of these balls, and of course made out the list of those who were to be invited. If you did not appear at these balls, you had no social standing. The chances of a débutante had been seriously damaged, if not destroyed, because she received no invitation to either the Charity, the Midwinter, or the Easter. Of course it was always a "mistake," an "omission," but the damage was never repaired. It was not an edifying spectacle; the social life of a great city in the hands of an old *roué* like Ben Sansome; but so it was. There is a fearful lot of drudgery, and arranging, and running of errands, and organization to a social season; and in those days of vigorous life Ben Sansome was actually the only "gentleman" of leisure. He did all the work; and he took all the reward of power. It is only fair to state that he was a very amiable gentleman, and kindly, when his little ambitions were not interfered with, and thoroughly well mannered and harmless with decent women.

But to his statement Daphne shook her head.

"Thank you, Mr. Sansome," she replied. "But I open the ball with Colonel Peyton."

This refusal was in itself enough to damn: but Ben Sansome had a very accurate eye for the advertising quality of the unusual. Once when returning from abroad he had during the whole voyage avoided a certain flashy, vulgar and boresome woman. In New York Harbour, however, it was raining, and this woman donned a scarlet rain coat. When the ship docked Sansome was leaning against the rail close to her side, engaging her in lively conversation. He knew the advertising value of that red raincoat. So to-night: there were a half dozen beautiful young girls in every way worthy of his favour, whose family and social standing he knew all about, any one of whom would have given her best ring to be selected by him; nevertheless he picked one of whom he knew nothing, not even the name; because, again, of her advertising value.

"Then you will help me lead the German," he breathed in answer.

"I am afraid you will find me a very ignorant assistant: I have never danced a German," replied Daphne.

"You will have no trouble. I will teach you," suggested Sansome, warming to the idea of annexing this vivid, striking creature to help localize his important presence. "You and I will have a dance or so together and I will have a chance to explain to you all about it. It's very simple."

"I shall be very glad," replied Daphne. She was much disappointed in the looks of the celebrated beau; but she was human and feminine and she lived on the Pacific Coast, so she was flattered.

But Kenneth, who had been hovering impatiently in the background, here broke in. Recognition had come to him in a great wave after a moment's puzzle. And with it had come a rush of other emotions, the principal one of which was a relief of spirit. Subconsciously his pride of the young man had nursed a sort of grievance over his having permitted himself to be fooled by a child. This was no child, but a young woman, glorious in her dark, glowing beauty and serene in her self-possession. That magic day on the beach was rehabilitated. He cursed his luck that had permitted him so nearly to fill out his programme; and he blessed it that his duties as host had not allowed him to crowd it full even unto the twelfth extra. Of course he was to lead the Grand March with Dora Stanley, as next door neighbour and best friend. and had engaged the cotillion with Myra.

"May I see your programme next?" he broke in, almost snatching the card from Ben Sansome's hand. "How many may I have?"

She looked at him a deliberate moment, seeming to rebuke his breathless haste; but it was the old beau who answered the question.

"My boy," he wheezed with a fat chuckle, "never ask a woman how many you may have: take what you want and marshal your forces to meet her objections."

"I believe you are right, Mr. Sansome," said Kenneth, flashing one of his charming smiles. "But if I took all I wanted, I would of course take them all," he bowed slightly toward Daphne, who returned his smile. "Since I cannot do that, I will take all I dare."

He glanced rapidly over his own programme and made sundry notes.

"The third and the seventh—and supper," he announced. As a matter of fact he had the supper dance already engaged, but his active brain had assured him of escape. He bowed again, and gave way to others who were already gathering around.

Daphne's card was soon filled. Everybody in Arguello knew her as a child. There was an alluring piquancy in this sudden emergence as a woman. By the time she and the Peytons had escaped from the swirling group near the receiving station and made their way toward the chairs along the wall, her card was full and the success of her evening assured.

All balls of those days were opened by what was known as a Grand March, a pretty and stately ceremony wherein the dancers paced in column two by two. The column turned and twisted and tied itself into knots and convolutions and extracted itself therefrom: the couples divided into other columns of single file which drew apart and performed even more complicated figures, and drew together again in such mysterious and miraculous fashion that each man found himself again with his partner after apparently hopeless separation. It took some leading, the Grand March. No hopeless amateur need apply. Ben Sansome opened all balls in San Francisco as a matter of understood social right, but here waived that privilege in favour of the son of the house. And the son of the house did it very well, without hesitation or blunder. Dan Mitchell stood by the door surveying it with approving, professional eye. Dan was dressed in his baggy blue serge suit, and he had a quid of tobacco stowed away in his cheek—which was why he stood by the door. Already he had sampled Boyd's champagne, an especial concession to his necessity of getting back to the office before the *Trumpet* was put to bed.

"I'd like to see the German," he confided to Jim Paige. "But she certainly is an eight-gauge, double-barrelled party."

He watched lazily for a few minutes more, then faded away. At the *Trumpet* office he called in his assistant.

"Cort," he ordered, "that party of Boyd's is the real thing. She's making history. Send up Miss Mullins to get all the women's dresses and decorations, and then bring the notes to

me. I'll write this story. And hold me three columns. Delay going to press"

"I held a column," said the assistant doubtfully. "and there's
just come in a peach of a Chinatown murder."

"Kill it," said the editor decisively, "and do as I tell you."
He spat at a sawdust box; then, the champagne circulating
comfortably, he vouchsafed a little of his reason. "This man
Boyd has evidently come to stay. That party, Cort, means
two things. He's rich—why he must have brought the wine
in tank cars; and he's full of energy. Man like that is always
doing something. And bye and bye he's going to want publicity.
You mark my words, Cort. And what he wants he pays for."

The assistant hopped down from his desk.

"You got a long head, chief, I'll say that for you," he conceded.

The party was swinging on its way. The violins crooned,
the rhythm beat in hot pulses, the hypnotic swing of the dancers
was like a music made visible. Cheeks were flushed, eyes sparkling or dreamy. It was as though in the flag-draped, flower-
hung enclosure, with its reflected lights, a new world had been
created out of music and dancing, wherein people dwelt as in
another element with new thoughts, new emotions informing
their souls. A magic was about them that fused their diversities,
lifted their fatigues.

After the Grand March Colonel Peyton abandoned the dancing floor, where his tall form and his old-fashioned courtly carriage had made a brave display, and took refuge with a number
of other old-timers at the card table. Thence, however, he
appeared occasionally to address a gallant word to Allie, or to
beam out on the shifting dancers.

"She is a great success," stated Mrs. Peyton, decidedly. "She
is dancing every dance, and the men are fighting for the extras.
We can be proud of her."

"She moves divinely," replied the Colonel. "I wish I were
twenty years younger!" he sighed.

"You're quite enough of a fool about women as it is," rejoined
Allie.

Daphne caught sight of them together and waved her hand.

Her dusky cheeks were flushed richly, and her eyes seemed to glow with a deep, inner fire. The first dance with Kenneth had gone. Their steps fitted, and they swung in perfect harmony with the violins. Not a dozen words were exchanged between them, yet their spirits had been in the momentary close harmony of the rhythm, and they had separated with a vague feeling of having gained in intimacy. This feeling neither experienced to the same degree with any other of their partners. Yet it was merely a question of rhythm, of catching just exactly the throb and swing of the violins.

It had a practical application, however, as the fifth extra began. Daphne, alone for a instant, saw approaching her across the crowded floor a be-spectacled, gawky youth she had suffered from at dancing school. At the same instant she caught Kenneth's eye. On the impulse, before she thought, she sent him a signal of distress. Instantly he responded, leaving abruptly the girl with whom he was talking, and making his way with eel-like dexterity through the crowded dancers.

"Come, come quick!" she breathed to him, clutching his arm.

Together they stepped behind the screen of palms and out through the barn door into the garden.

"You've saved my life!" laughed Daphne, breathless. "I don't know what I should have done if you hadn't rescued me. It's that dreadful Mitchell boy, bearing down on me like a goggle-eyed Fate. I didn't dare stay another second because I remember vaguely his saying something about some extra. And he's so persistent. Do you suppose he saw us?"

"He might have," said Kenneth, shrewdly. "I think we'd better move a little."

"Didn't you have this dance engaged?"

Kenneth hesitated.

"Yes, I did," he stated boldly, "and I don't care. It was a duty thing."

"Oh!" she cried, struck with compunction, "and you're the host!" She chuckled wickedly. "I ought to make you go back. But I don't care either. We are highly immoral."

They looked back toward the stable. It seemed to be bursting with light that leaked out of various cracks and crannies,

and poured out past the palms through the wide-opened door.
A figure silhouetted itself, an unmistakable gangling figure, and
peered short-sightedly into the darkness.

"The Mitchell boy!" breathed Daphne. "Come!" She
picked up her voluminous skirts and flew lightly down one of
the new-made paths. Only at the porch on the other side of
the house did she pause. "This is dreadful!" she cried.
"You don't suppose he will find us here? He is very persistent."

"I think we are safe here," Kenneth reassured her.

It was as though they had entered another existence. The
high-keyed, throbbing, emotional, swinging world of the rhythmical violins and the low brooding lights and the warm palpitant
air had given way to a peace of calm. The stars in contrast
seemed more than usually far away and aloof: a leisurely night
breeze, with all the time in the world to get nowhere, wandered
here and there, rustling leaves idly, or raising petals. There was
no sound, save the music that seemed now almost as distant as
the stars.

"I do love the night!" she cried.

They stood side by side for some time, and something slow and
calming seemed to come like a mist over their spirits. They
talked very little. Kenneth noted the fact with a fleeting wonder
that this silence caused no discomfort to his social nerve. He
could say nothing and still be comfortable! Indeed, he enjoyed
it. The same thing had happened that day on the beach——

"The air is so sweet and warm to-night," she said. "One lies
in it as in the warm sea. I went swimming once at night, in
midsummer. It was like lying suspended in stars. And when
I moved the water flashed—phosphorescence, you know."

"I'd like to do that," said Kenneth.

They stood again for a time without speaking. It was
almost as though they were awaiting something that would
come out of the calm night, something that interested and held
them in a suspense of expectation. Daphne was the first to
arouse herself.

"Did you notice whether they have begun another dance?"
she enquired.

Thus admitted, the music again became audible to them. But

they had not the least idea whether this was the "extra" just finishing, or another number under way. Panic-stricken they scurried back.

The night wore away. At midnight a slight lassitude overcame the dancers, but supper revived them; and the German was undertaken with zest. Ben Sansome here came into his own. This was the one thing he did superlatively well. Even Patrick Boyd acknowledged that there was something to the little fat pug-dog of a man after all, for Boyd knew executive ability when he saw it. Sansome not only taught and conducted many complicated figures, but he repressed too great exuberance and he kept order. Withal he did it with tact, so that nobody was offended. The card players came in to watch. The stray couples emerged from the cosy corners. Even the caterer's men —those who were not busy about some duties—gathered in the background; for a cotillion was not always to be seen. It was an overwhelming success.

The deep bell on the clock tower downtown had struck the half-hour after two before the German came to a triumphant conclusion. The last strains found Daphne and Kenneth together near the door. By tacit consent they stepped around the palms for a breath of air.

The brightness of the stars overhead had mysteriously dimmed. They shone wearily as though from an immense remoteness and as though invisible influences were passing between the earth and them. Elsewhere than overhead they were veiled. A slow, sweet steady air breathed from the east. The night was still, full of portent. Not a sound broke the dead, waiting silence: no cricket nor insect shrilled, no bird called, scarcely a leaf rustled in spite of the steady air from the east.

A drop of water splashed against Daphne's upturned face: another marked the brick at her feet. As though in immediate response to a signal a frog began loudly to chirp. For nine months now he had lain in patient silence, wearing down the slow time while his enemies, the dry months, passed; standing faithful sentry to announce the return of the wet months, his friends.

With an excitement that Kenneth would understand only after he had become a true Californian, Daphne ran into the ballroom. She was carried out of herself, so that she had lost all timidity or shyness before a crowd. Into the centre of the room she sped, holding up her arms for silence, a vivid, arresting figure in her old-fashioned Spanish dress. The music broke off; the dancers stopped in position, turning their heads toward her; the buzz of conversation among the onlookers died.

"It's raining! It's raining!" she cried.

They stood and sat there like so many carved images, and the silence that had been in the night outside entered the room. And as the rhythm-waves of the dance ebbed and dropped below consciousness, distinctly could be heard on the roof above a gentle, hesitant patter, as though a guest still doubtful of welcome had arrived. While they listened, it seemed to gain confidence. The pattering increased until the jolly spirit of the dance seemed to have been transferred from the silenced floor to the roof. It caught its breath for an instant, then suddenly became a deep roar. The heavens had opened in a flood; and beneath the organ tones of the storm could be heard the silvery drip of water from the eaves.

The women looked a little dismayed and abstracted as they cast over rapidly in their minds what protecting garments they had brought with them. The men were plainly delighted, and went about slapping each other on the back. On an inspiration the orchestra struck up some lively music and the leader called a Virginia reel.

A grand rush for partners took place. Everybody took part. Colonel Peyton led forth his plump little wife, in spite of her laughing protests. He was quite the feature of the dance for he combined a beautiful old-fashioned courtesy with the most delightful and killing monkey-shines as he moved through the figures. As though by common consent this dance closed the party. The guests embarked laughing. Boyd's few um-brellas were in constant use escorting people to their carriages. The women and girls tucked their skirts up around their waists, leaving their petticoats exposed. The lights shone gleaming on wet things. Raindrops flashed like jewels. And on the roofs and in the water courses sounded the steadily increasing roar of the torrential rain.

CHAPTER V

I

KENNETH allowed one day to elapse before calling for Pronto and riding out to the Bungalow. His head was full of this girl: he could think of nothing else. She haunted him as no other of his numerous flames had ever haunted him; and yet, strangely enough, the realization that he was in love with her had not entered his head. This was the more remarkable in that he had often enough been "stuck" on other girls, and had realized the fact, and been secretive or proud of it according to his age. But he did not at all consider himself "stuck" on this girl. She was just different. For one thing, you did not have to talk to her all the time; for another, she seemed to have some sense when she did talk; and she certainly was a bird of a horsewoman! Looked to Kenneth as though she would be a lot more fun than these other silly creatures who always wanted a lot of help and attention just because they were girls. So impersonal was his conscious attitude as yet that he suffered no immediate pang of disappointment when his knocking elicited finally only Brainerd in a dressing gown.

"I was riding by and I dropped in to see how Miss Brainerd survived the party," he said.

The tall man's weary eyes surveyed him detachedly. A faint glint of amusement lurked in their depths.

"Miss Brainerd"—he choked slightly over the words, but recovered himself at once and went on gravely, "was here not five minutes ago. I can't imagine what can have become of her." He examined Kenneth again and liked his looks. "I'm a little seedy to-day," he continued, in explanation both of his own presence in working hours and the costume in which he was dis-

covered. "Won't you come in and visit me a little while? I
assure you I am getting quite bored and lonely by myself."

Kenneth liked the room into which he stepped. He was still
of the chameleon age, capable instantly of taking the mental
colour of his surroundings. The worn leather armchairs, the
rows and rows of books, the wide fireplace, and the double stu-
dent-lamp on the magazine-littered table threw him instantly
into an appreciative attitude toward a quiet scholarly life by
one's fireside, far remote from the turmoil of the world, and so
forth. Corbell's ranch house had affected him in a similar manner, though in a different way. Possibly he recognized reality.

He found himself sitting in one of the armchairs at one side
the fireplace where oak logs burned quietly. The clearing wind
after the rain was singing by the eaves. On Brainerd's invitation he filled a pipe. The conversation for a few moments ran
limpingly, for Kenneth was trying, before this quiet, saturnine,
wise-seeming individual, to be very intelligent and grown up.
But Brainerd let him alone, and after a time the situation
eased.

"Yes, California is a delightful place to live in," the older
man assented, to Kenneth's remark concluding his account of
the quail hunt. "What are you going to do here?" he asked
abruptly.

"Do?"

"Yes—as your job. Every man who is worth his salt must
have a job, you know."

"I suppose he must."

"You don't want merely to suppose: you want to *know* it.
It's very simple, but people don't seem to grasp it. They seem
to think that when a man gets a certain amount of money—
enough to live on—that he can stop work if he wants to. Worst
sort of fallacy! He may change the kind of work. But the
possession of money or leisure merely means that a man has accomplished the first necessary step, and is ready to go on with
the next. I suppose merely earning a living and an economic
place in the world is made so extraordinarily difficult because
so few people go on doing things after that is accomplished. They
generally sit down and build bulgy granite houses, and buy more

horses and dogs and clothes than the next fellow, and get fat
and arrogant and short tempered or silly. Ever notice that?"

He cocked an eye over his pipe at Kenneth and stretched his
long legs toward the fire.

"I've a notion the particular Guardian Angel who was put
in charge of this planet is a hopeful sort of cuss who likes to try
it out. So every once in a while he gives a man what all the rest
of the world *has* to struggle for or die off—wealth and the leisure
that comes from relief of that pressure—in hopes that man will
go ahead and do something with it. He certainly runs against
a lot of disappointments! But I'm preaching away like a
parson!"

"No, you're not!" cried Kenneth, earnestly. "I like intellectual conversations; but you don't often find a man you can
talk to that way!"

Brainerd hastily concealed a grin that nearly surprised him.

"Well, we're getting a long way off the subject, anyway. Of
course a young man like yourself doesn't intend to settle down
and live on his father."

"Of course not. I—I thought some of going into the bank."

Brainerd was silent for so long that finally Kenneth asked him:

"What is your advice?"

"Boyd, one man can never give another advice. Advice is
a word that should be stricken from the language. The most
one can do is to call to another's attention certain *facts* in the
situation of which he may not be aware, leaving him to form his
own judgment. If you form another man's judgment for him
you have absolutely deprived him of all the value of that experience."

"How do you mean?"

"Life is a series of opportunities for making decisions. Making decisions is the only way you form character. If somebody
else makes a decision for you, he has deprived you of one chance."

"But he may be much wiser or experienced than yourself.
His decision may be a better one."

"It may be a better one as far as practical results go; yes,"
admitted Brainerd. "But no amount of practical results can
make up for a lost opportunity of growth."

"By Jove! I never thought of it that way; but you're right!" cried Kenneth.

"Now as to jobs," continued Brainerd. "They are never any good unless you get something out of them besides money. The ideal job is one that produces something either in the shape of material products or some service needed by our somewhat complicated economic system; and at the same time gets us something beside money—such as more opportunity, or interest, or satisfaction, or congenial companions or surroundings, or something like that. Also it might include chance for growth. The man who actually puts something in the world that was not there before—such as a potato—probably on the average gets more satisfaction from his job than the man who fulfills a function. The latter may be more important; but I am talking about the way the average man feels."

"Farmers are always kicking," suggested Kenneth.

"So is every other class of man on this footstool. When you discuss in the abstract you have to assume an intelligent man as your subject."

To Kenneth all this talk was fascinating. He had taken Philosophy III in college because it was considered a "snap," and the surface of his mind had taken the impress of its form long enough to get credit for the course. But never before had he happened to meet any one with a philosophic attitude toward the realities of every-day life. It was simple and understandable and yet it dealt with fundamentals; so that he had a pleasing sense of discussing deep subjects and comprehending them!

"I'd like to be a rancher," stated Kenneth, with conviction, "and keep cattle."

"Yes, that is a good business," assented Brainerd, "but it cannot be done haphazard. As at present conducted it is for California a persistence of past conditions. It will be crowded out in time by other things. Personally, if I were younger I'd rather be identified in a small way with the beginnings of future things than even in a large way with the endings of past things. Just as a matter of personal interest, you understand, not as a measuring value to the community."

"I don't quite follow you."

"I mean cattle ranching, on a big scale, and near enough centres of civilization to make life worth while, is bound to pass. Its place will be taken by agriculture and horticulture."

"Not in the South," stated Kenneth, confidently repeating statements he had heard on the quail hunt. "It's been tried, and it doesn't work except here and there on a small scale."

"Because it hasn't been tried right. Everything's been attempted on a big scale, even on a small farm. The idea has been to plant the largest number of acres possible so as to make a killing in the wet season. In dry seasons they argue they won't get anything anyhow. Result is a sort of scratch harrowing, shallow cultivation. But it's not true that in a dry season you'll get nothing, if you do proper work. And this scheme ignores the half and half years. It's shiftless. Men get used to thinking in the immense acreage of the cattle ranches and they bite off more than they can chew. Why, many don't touch the land after planting it. The crops are fouled with wild oats and mustard and such things, and so are reduced. These so-called farmers do not care for small profits. It's all or nothing with them. They are never self sustaining. They scorn to plant vegetables and such things as they need. If they'd do less but better they'd find the South would grow things all right. Why, they don't even know where their best land is."

"In the bottomlands," stated Kenneth, promptly.

"That is what they think—and you're wrong. It's rich and wet enough to grow crops without irrigation, and all that; but it's just common farming, and acre for acre it will not match that land right out there."

Kenneth stared.

"You mean that dry sagebrush, or the sand wash?" he asked, incredulously.

"Both. Properly cultivated and irrigated, they will grow more valuable crops of more valuable things than your bottomland. I have proved it on a small scale to my own satisfaction."

He went on to elucidate what was then a revolutionary idea, becoming almost animated in his interest. Kenneth listened at first sceptically; soon with growing conviction.

"You come up again," Brainerd invited him, finally, "and

I'll show you what I mean. It's all on a small scale for I have not the means nor the strength to do more. But the future of the country is in it. Some day they'll wake up. And then you'll see. If I were a young man like you, and I could command a little money, as I suppose you can, I'd certainly go in for ranching. There is no place on the globe with a better climate, with more beautiful surroundings, with more satisfying appeal. I know, for I have lived in many places. It is new, but that affords the satisfaction of being active in the building. And a small ranch intelligently conducted on new and experimental lines would have for me the intelligent interest of creating." He checked himself with a laugh. "I'm coming perilously close to offering advice after all," said he. "But to my mind there is no comparison between such a career and the 'big round suavity, the large, buttoned-up complacency of golden-bellied bankers.'"

"I'm mighty glad I found you in," said Kenneth, rising. "You've given me a lot to think about."

"Talking is one of the best things I do," observed Brainerd, "when I am sure of an understanding listener. I'm sorry Daffy isn't about. I can't imagine where she has disappeared to: her pony is in the corral."

As a matter of fact Daphne was in the next room keeping very quiet until the visitor should depart. She had no intention of being seen at this time, nor for several days yet. By the end of the period certain grown-up dresses would be finished. They were being made at the Peyton's by a little "sewing woman" who came in by the day. After the Boyd party it was as impossible that Daphne reassume her child's dresses and her pigtails as it would be for a butterfly to reënter its cocoon.

II

DAN MITCHELL had read Patrick Boyd correctly. Hardly had the echoes of the ball died away before he began to look about him for something else to do. His investigatory habit of prowling up and down Main Street stood him in good stead here. To do him entire justice it must be conceded that he started on his external affairs in Arguello actuated solely by a genuine enthusiasm for the place. His habit of mind had been formed in what was known as a live, a smart community, where men were used to big things done promptly and on a big scale. He found Arguello half asleep, accustomed to doing the simplest public affairs—if they were done at all—only after long discussions and hesitations. Things Boyd had always taken as much for granted as shoes or a hat, Arguello either lacked, or possessed inadequately, or was strongly divided in opinion as to their advisibility. To the Easterner it was nothing short of a disgrace that Main Street and its principal laterals were unpaved; that the residence part of the town was sparely lighted; that the rattletrap, one-mule car was permitted to represent city transportation; that property owners were not forced to substitute something substantial in the way of sidewalks for the beaten earth that in wet weather became slippery mud. His order-loving mind was scandalized over various easy-going tacit permissions. It was dangerous to turn saddle horses loose on the streets to find their way to the stables by themselves; it was perilous to leave building material unprotected by lights: it was unsanitary and unsightly to drop rubbish over the edge of the sidewalks into the streets; it was annoying and unnecessary to pile the sidewalks half full of merchandise and leave them so; it was unwholesome to abandon Chinatown to its unsavoury filth. And what could be said of a town that permitted its firemen to haul sand with its fire horses two miles away from the fire engine! Boyd saw all these things, and many many others typical of the easy-going time and place, through the eyes of the Eastern visitor; and, as he was by now genuinely a citizen in spirit, he suffered a real agony of mortification as to what that Eastern visitor must think of it all.

His first attempts to interest people met with little encouragement. The inert dead indifference of the opposition astounded and made him indignant. A small proportion of those he talked to agreed with him that his ideas were sound and that it would be a good thing if they could be carried out; another small proportion, with the narrow vision of the untravelled, interposed the panicky but effective opposition of men who, unless they can plainly discern the dollar spent to-day returning not later than to-morrow, clamour vehemently against all public expenditure; but by far the greatest number just plain did not care.

"Go after it if it amuses you, Boyd," said Oliver Mills, the banker. "You will find that you can get things done, to be sure; but you will spend an inordinate amount of energy. What another city would order, as you would order a pound of sugar, Arguello will talk over for two years, and squabble about, and hesitate over—and end by buying a half a pound—or else decide it's too expensive. And when it is all over, those of us who have been trying to engineer the thing are totally exhausted. We've put enough into it to have built the Washington Monument. You'll find it doesn't pay. We're getting along very comfortably: why stir things up?"

Boyd's chief comfort was the obscure, lean real estate man, Ephraim Spinner. In Spinner he uncorked a dynamic enthusiasm that warmed his heart.

"I'm glad to hear you say so!" cried Spinner. "It's what I've been hammering into these hayseeds for two years! This place should be working night and day getting itself in order for the flood of visitors that is absolutely certain to pour down upon us. Every man who goes East comes back again and brings his friends with him. The boom is bound to come someday, and when it comes!" He threw his arms out with an expressive gesture. "They'll find us asleep at the switch!" he ended gloomily. He chewed savagely at the end of the cigar Boyd handed him. "What this town ought to do is to get on to itself," he went on presently, in a calmer, wearied tone, "of course it ought to have paving and lights and all those things, just as you say, Mr. Boyd; but if it had the sense God gave a rooster it would go a lot farther than that. Look at the beach, f'rinstance. You can't get at it except afoot or horseback, and when you do get to it you find tin cans and rubbish. Yet look at that stretch from the wharf to Scott's Point! They ought to put a road in there; and they'd have no finer drive in the world than that— with the blue Pacific on one side and the lofty mountains on the other! They could advertise a drive like that all over the country, and draw tourists like a magnet. That's only one thing. And they ought to put a road along the foothills—just for a scenic attraction. Just suggest it to these old mossbacks and see what they say to you. They'd think you were crazy. Were you ever up there?"

"Yes," said Boyd.

"Can you imagine any one not seeing it? Gosh! They haven't got one single solitary blessed thing here they've done themselves to cultivate the best paying crop in the world—the tourist. What there is, old California has done by herself."

"The Fremont," suggested Boyd.

"Yes, that's a good hotel," agreed Spinner, "and it's running behind. What we need is *public* improvements. And about the first of 'em is a dozen or so first class funerals!"

With this completely altruistic interest to start from, Boyd gradually worked his way into the political life of the place. He had made his fortune through traction organization. The 'eighties did not understand political purity as we are just beginning to understand it to-day. As soon as Boyd found that he could not get things done by direct appeal, he turned naturally to manipulation. Dan Mitchell was right in his guess that the Easterner would need publicity—and would pay for it. Others received pay also for other services. It was all a sort of play for Boyd, activity undertaken at first in idleness, but later with increasing interest. Opposition aroused his combative spirit. He found it would be necessary to follow, in a modified way, Spinner's advice as to the first class funerals, only the funerals were political. It seemed desirable to replace certain sturdy, short visioned, uncompromising aldermen or supervisors. In politics, too, Boyd was past master. He had not much difficulty in electing his own council, nor in passing the ordinance to pave and curb Main Street—his first great objective. But he had to acknowledge that the resultant distrust and uneasiness among the shellbacks was going to make the next election more of a job. In short, he saw a good fight ahead; and he rejoiced; and he began quietly to build a machine that would function.

"If these mossbacks don't know what is good for them we'll make 'em take it," he observed to the exultant Spinner. "There's more than one way to skin a cat."

He bought in a slope of the sagebrush foothills back of the town, and bore much good humoured joking from his friends. His refusal to explain himself ended by fastening upon him the rumour of fantastic projects, for nobody could imagine any possible use for that waste and worthless land. As a matter of cold fact Boyd was himself a little vague on that subject. He got it very cheap, for almost nothing; he believed enthusiastically in the ultimate expansion of Arguello; certainly the view out over the valley, the town, to the wide slumbering Pacific——

But Boyd was a shrewd business man, with plenty of leisure and an enquiring and restless mind. He rode often on his horse up over the slope of his new purchase, sometimes alone, sometimes with Saxon or Marcus Oberman or others of his winter cronies. They called it his Horned Toad Ranch, not that anyone had ever seen a horned toad there, but it was considered that horned toads represented the only possibility. Boyd grinned and replied in kind. But one day he dropped into Spinner's office with an idea.

"Know those boulders up on the Tract, the ones near the little grove of live oaks at the head of the barranca?" he asked. "Well, they're an outcrop of a ledge down below; and the stuff is a real fine-grained sandstone. Makes the best building material I know of. There's a quarry of it there."

"There's mighty little demand for building stone here," said Spinner. "And the whole range is made of that sort of rock."

"Nobody's getting any of it out: and this is the nearest to town. People use quite a little for one thing and another— foundations and garden walls and such. They'd use less bricks and more stone if they could get the stone handier. There's a nice little steady business there."

Spinner looked doubtful.

"Look here, Spinner," said Boyd, suddenly. "How many miles of street are there in this town? You ought to know. Well, they're in frightful state every year with the run-off of the flood waters every time it rains. It's a disgrace. They ought to be curbed and guttered, every foot of them; and an ordinance passed providing for that would in my opinion be a very beneficial piece of legislation."

"And you would supply the stone!" cried Spinner.

"Well," and Boyd puffed slowly at his cigar, "I'd hardly consider it worth while to fuss with a little quarry business. My idea would be to use the quarry merely as a source of supply to a construction company that would be in a position to bid for the contracts."

"I take my hat off to you, Mr. Boyd," cried Spinner, as the whole splendour of the scheme came to him.

"It would make a nice little business," continued Boyd. "I would not want to appear in it personally. The thing would not look well, I suppose; though for the life of me I don't see how anybody could object. I would merely lease the quarry land to the construction company. You could head the company."

"I?" cried Spinner.

"You would have a small salary and a small share in the business. I would not expect you to attend to details. I'll look up a good managing foreman. The real estate business is not so brisk at present but that you could put a little time in on this, is it?"

Thus came into existence the Western Construction Company which for years did practically all Arguello's public improvement. It built a road, opened the quarry, purchased teams and wagons, and set to work. Gradually it acquired what it needed for a comprehensive business, not only in construction but in such things as crushed rock for roads, and grading and wall building for private grounds. It was never out of work, for whenever things got slack, the Common Council would pass an ordinance commanding the curbing and guttering of another stretch of street. The cost was an assessment against the property owners, who almost invariably uttered howls of protest. As they were very few in number as compared with those not immediately concerned, they never had much effect. Dan Mitchell had a laudatory editorial now and then on public improvement; and killed many a virulent communication. He never received any direct pay for his attitude; but he did get very high rates for a small advertisement of the Western Construc-

tion Company—whose business by its nature needed no advertisement!

In order successfully to carry on this enterprise and his contemplated scheme of improving Arguello, Boyd had to have a
Council on which he could depend. The opposition to doing
anything that cost either time or money was partly climatic,
partly habitual, partly from parsimony, partly conservative. It
was very real, and very strong; but it was not organized. Boyd
knew how to organize and he did so. His chief source of strength
was the lower wards where the most of the Mexicans lived. There
dwelt an obese, polite, suave old scoundrel who belonged to one
of the oldest Californian families and was connected by marriage
with several of the others. Don Caesar Azevedo held a great
prestige among the members of his race, because of his personality and his Falstaffian capacity for *vino*. On election days he
was given disposal of a number of surries and a sum of "expense
money." By evening he was portentously drunk, still dignified and respectable, apparently close to apoplexy, but his
two wards had voted safe. It amused Boyd to watch the other
four wards closely and to determine his action by the conditions of the moment. Sometimes it was quite sufficient to
handle his man after election. At any rate he always had his
Council.

This, it must be understood, was the development of a number of years, and carries us somewhat ahead of our story; but an
appreciation of Patrick Boyd's place and power in the community is desirable to an understanding of the history of those
who may interest us more. We should add that through his
purchase of Colonel Peyton's bank stock, and some other blocks
he picked up from time to time, he attained a position on the
directorate where soon he carried a controlling advice. He
gained thus a birds-eye-view of the affairs of the county. He
knew who borrowed and how much; who was delinquent; who
paid promptly; and he was enabled to shape policies that would
influence the future of the country he had adopted. For, though
Patrick Boyd made money in the ventures he undertook, the
making of money was not the primary incentive of his activities.
He had all the money, *per se*, he wanted. His basic desire was

to see Arguello wake up and be somebody: for he loved the valley
between the mountains and the sea as only an Easterner trans-
planted to California can love.

III

KENNETH rode again to the Bungalow: and he continued to
ride there on every opportunity. He and Brainerd had many
more talks on all subjects having to do with the philosophy of
life. The older man was an excellent influence for his forming
spirit. Only one forced to comparative failure by insuperable
obstacles could, in that age of material emphasis, have gained
to the wider views held by Brainerd. He saw· beyond the
merely utilitarian. Our moralists were prattling of Captains of
Industry, exploitation—but under a prettier name—and the
remote sacredness of being a millionaire; public office was a
matter of victory and patronage; the saving of pennies and the
spending of lives was preached as an ideal of the perfect existence. A man was morally justified in anything he did provided
he kept technically within the law. Things were ends in themselves. Brainerd had dimly seen them as in themselves only
means to something beyond. It was with him not simply a
case of get there. Kenneth was one day telling with relish of an
acquaintance who was even at college a past master at getting
others to attend to details for him.

"Yes," said Brainerd, "that quality of delegating work and
responsibility is one of the most valuable qualities of leadership.
In fact it is indispensable to leadership. But it is not always desirable to use sheer cleverness to avoid detail—only to avoid
repetition of detail. If you avoid anything in the life, you lose
the value of the experience."

"That's true, too!" cried Kenneth.

In such statements of what are now considered baldly obvious
truths did Brainerd lead Kenneth's young mind away from the
smug, old outworn conservative ideas of a passing phase, into a
contemplation of the wider outlook that was going to be possible
to a new generation. And therein he fulfilled, unknowingly, his
function in the fates of those about him.

Together the two men examined the sketchy, incomplete work that Brainerd had managed to accomplish.

"I have lacked health, and I have lacked means," said the elder, frankly, "so I have not here a prosperous money-making plant, such as I should have.   But it makes me a decent living; and, what is more, it brings me a living every year.   Dry seasons don't bother me a bit.   As to this sagebrush upland you were laughing about——"

Daphne, her wardrobe renewed, no longer concealed herself. The gangly, bare-legged child of yesterday was suddenly forgotten, as though it had never been.   Not by a flicker of the eyelash did Daphne acknowledge that such a creature had ever existed; and there was that, not in but back of her manner, that withered even a recollection of it.   Only her extraordinary vital energy, her wayward elfish fancy playing quaintly over everyday things, and her headlong zest in living she carried over with her into the new phase.   Once she had determined that Kenneth came sympathetically to the life she and her father lived at the Bungalow, she took him on wholeheartedly; and, as to a friend visiting for the first time, she was all eagerness to take him about and show him hidden lands.   Generally they went on horseback.   Daphne led, very mysterious as to their destination; very chatty in comment of the things they saw by the way.   The dogs invariably accompanied them, creating great disturbance in the colonies of ground squirrels.   The first rain had cleared promptly and no more had come.   The sun shone warmly. A timid green lay snuggled beneath the dead grasses.

"Keeping warm under a fur coat," said Daphne.

She knew intimately every nook and cranny in the hills; every grove of oaks; every secret cañon from the ranges.   To some quaint or beautiful or cozy objective she led Kenneth on each of their rides.   He learned to know when to exclaim by the small, triumphant air of expectation she assumed when they had reached their journey's end—a still dark pool beneath fragrant bay trees; a fantastic old tree twisted by long-dead gales; a flat rock looking down on the blue of deep cañons; a slope of shingle where the sun lay warm and the spicy odour of Lad's

Love wandered down to them like a gentle spirit. Never did she consciously give him any clue as to when she considered they had reached the thing that was to make the ride worth while. But when he cried out satisfactorily, she was manifestly pleased. Kenneth learned to keep his eyes and his wits about him, lest he pass by one of these favourite places unknowing. The result then was an evident disappointment and lowering of spirit. She was childishly eager to have them see with the same eyes. Then, having arrived, they liked to dismount and turn the horses loose to graze; while they lay on their backs in the grass or in the shade. They never talked much, but watched the slow circling of buzzards, or the forming and melting cloudlets, or made rainbows through their eyelashes. They could hear the horses cropping crisply, a comfortable sound. Or perhaps they crouched by the stream watching the hypnotic shift of light through branches, or the reflection on the under side of leaves. Small, busy, amusing birds complimented them with no attention as they went about their affairs. At length as the sun lowered, a chill would steal abroad. They would rouse themselves. The horses, their reins hanging, would by now be dozing with one hind leg tucked up. The dogs lay farther up the hill flat on their sides exposed to the warmest sun. Everybody seemed to stretch with yawns. But once under way the coolness of the early evening of winter seemed to fill them with a wild, playful energy. The dogs chased madly in wide circles, their quarters tucked under them, their backs humped, their hind legs spurning the soil in quick, stabbing jumps. The horses arched their necks, feeling at the bits, and made little mock shies. Daphne and Kenneth shouted foolishness at each other, and laughed a great deal.

Sometimes they went for all day. In that event they carried chops or a steak and had a picnic. Or they left the horses in the corral and tramped on foot up into the hills, or around the Peytons' ranch.

They spent a good deal of time at the Peytons' for there was a great variety of things to do and see. In the old days the ranch had been almost self-sustaining. Even now it raised many things that others were accustomed to buy in the town. The cattle work was oi course the basis, and was always interesting. They liked to ride out with one of the vaqueros on his never-ending round, spying out the distribution and condition of the stock, observing strays, helping young calves, keeping a vigilant eye for those in trouble. Daphne told of the spring round-up when the neighbouring ranches joined forces to sort and brand the stock. That was a season of hard work, but also of picturesque pleasure. But outside the cattle were many minor industries that repaid investigation—a vineyard and an olive orchard of dove-gray foliage, where dwelt a flashing smile set in the simple countenance of one Tomaso, whose duty it was to make wine and pure olive oil. Near the foothills dwelt the bee-man, a religious fanatic who wore no hat or coat and let his hair grow long, who shouted texts and Bible quotations as he strode here and there among the hives, a strange person who was nevertheless quite at home with the hot, uncertain insects and who thoroughly understood all the mysteries of honey. The vegetable garden lay in a flat below the house. It was pro-tected with wire fencing, and in its enclosure cress-grown water ditches ran in patterns, frogs croaked, and an ancient Chinaman in the wide peaked bowl of a woven hat moved like a figure on a screen. His name was Lo, and he knew little English, nor had he pride of appearance. He dwelt in a ramshackle little hut in one corner of the vegetable garden, made of old doors and lumber slung together anyhow, with a rickety stovepipe sticking out of it; not intrinsically an impressive dwelling; yet in some fashion, by means of strips of red paper with ideographs, tall-stalked bulbs growing in bowls, a queer smell or so, Lo had man-aged to make of his dwelling something exotic and picturesque. And over by the stables was the blacksmith shop; where they shod horses, and fashioned parts of agricultural machinery or wagons out of hot metal that glowed in the dusk of the shop, and hissed in water tubs like serpents. Nor must we forget the great stables for the working animals, nor the dairy stables, nor the dairy itself, with its cool, silent shelves of milk set to rise, nor its churns with its sweet smell of buttermilk, nor its rows of fragrant butter rolls, with everywhere a dampness and a clean-ness. Nor the fowl yards, seemingly endless in extent, very populous, very busy, very conversational, with wise-looking but foolish chickens, and foolish-looking but wise ducks, and apoplectic turkey gobblers scraping the stiffened ends of their wings on the ground.   An old sailor, twisted with rheumatism, had charge of the feathered creatures; and he was always eager to show the young people the latest squabs or hatchings, or to talk as long as they would listen about the remarkable examples of intelligence displayed by his charges.   The dogs, who followed them everywhere else, were here rigidly barred.   They sat outside the wire in a reproachful row conscious of being misjudged.

The half of the ranch has not been described.   It would be interesting to follow our young people to the main stables, to the cook shack and the bunk houses, to the miniature village across the ravine where dwelt all the Spanish families, retainers of the ranch.   And the hogs and the pigs, who had a self-sufficient air of competent wisdom, and liked to have their backs scratched.   On the paddocks where roamed the colts and young horses, free as deer, gentle as dogs.   But we can only enumerate them.   And in the end they always arrived at the great wide-flung oak known as Dolman's House, where they climbed into the low branches and swung their legs for a good talk.   Here, fancifully, seemed the central abiding place of the soul of the ranch, a soul born through the slow mellowing and blending of these many activities into one relationship.   The ranch had a personality of its own: it was a single thing, to be loved and remembered.   Daphne used to believe in Dolman implicitly.   Through the haze gathering across her childhood memories she thought still to discern his face, to hear his voice.   At times even yet it seemed to her that she felt a great beneficent presence that wished her well.   She joked with herself about it, and told of it to Kenneth in a playful fashion that he considered charmingly fanciful.   It would be, of course, absurd to believe such a thing literally: the imagination is a powerful agent in proper circumstances.   Yet at times something overpowering swept through Daphne's soul that left her wondering.

As their intimacy progressed they joked a good deal about Dolman, making believe, as children do, inventing legends and possibilities.   The degree to which their intimacy had unconsciously progressed may be gauged from the fact that they did not feel it necessary to act grown-up toward each other. Nobody, except perhaps United States Senators and ticket agents, of whose inner life I know nothing, is ever as grown up as he appears to his contemporaries. All he needs is a proper companion to show himself in his true kiddish colours. Kenneth did not even appreciate the fact that he was in love with Daphne. He had passed through the usual number of school and college "cases" and he thought he knew just what being in love was like. It was a tempestuous matter with a lot of violent emotion attached to it, and a number of symptoms that were pleasant or disagreeable according as you looked at it. He felt entirely differently toward Daphne. To be sure, he wanted to be with her all the time, and was totally neglectful of his old companions, but that was because she was such a good sort; you could talk foolishly with her without being silly. She was a good sport and was game for anything. She had *sense*——

Allie Peyton saw plainly enough, but she was a wise woman and said nothing. Except that she warned the Colonel against one thing.

"Don't ever call them 'children'," she said. "They are children, of course, and they act like children—I believe they're out at Sing Toy's cookey jar right now—but they'll freeze into grownups in two jiffies if you make them conscious of what they're doing."

Neither the Colonel nor Brainerd attached the slightest importance to Kenneth's constant presence. To them Daphne was still an infant. They thought it rather kind of Kenneth to spend so much time amusing the child.

IV

THE year, in spite of the encouragement of its early rain, turned out to be another dry one. The tourists were delighted. They had come out to buy climate; and climate was being delivered to them. The first rains, and a few unimportant subsequent showers, had started the green, so that the country looked well. The brilliant days followed each other, clear and sparkling.

Loud were the praises of the land as heard in such places as the
Fremont Hotel veranda.   But those who knew cast back in
mind to other dry years within their recollection, and they began to figure ahead apprehensively.

The barometers of this condition were the banks.   The men
who sat in the little varnished back offices of these modest insti-
tutions were experts in the affairs of the country.   They knew
the peculiar conditions that obtained in a land when even the
children counted the inches of rainfall for a normal February;
and they were perfectly aware of the probable sequences to any
given set of circumstances.   It was time to retrench.   It was
time to fortify for a disastrous moment when, to save the integ-
rity of the whole, it would be necessary to support wholeheartedly some of the weaker parts.   That was one of the
functions of banks; and in consequence, to one who did not understand, it would have seemed that at first they were unduly
harsh, and later unduly generous.

One of the first to feel the effects of this prescience on the part
of the bankers was Don Vincente Cazadero.   He had hung on
longer than most of his kind, partly because the situation of his
rancho was more favourable than ordinary, partly because he
was fortunate in his friends.   To the latter he was almost as
deeply indebted as to the bankers.   New ways touched him not
at all.   He lived according to the old life, which had been good
enough for his fathers, and was good enough for him.   Therefore he raised no hay against the days of adversity; he planted
no fields of alfalfa under irrigation; he made no attempts to improve the stock of his long-horned, big-headed Mexican cattle; he
maintained still the old heedless lavish manner of life.   No one
knew exactly how many human beings Las Flores directly supported; nor did anybody but Don Vincente's *major dǫmo*, who
was as hide-bound and impatient of new methods as his master,
know to whom wages were paid or how much.   There were,
as with every Spanish family, shoals of *parientes*, who might be
roughly described as relatives, though the term included all
sorts of round-about connections.   These expected, as a matter
of course, to be supported by the feudal head of the house.

Don Vincente rode over to see his neighbour as soon as he had understood that the bank had delivered an ultimatum. He deeply resented it. In his secret heart of hearts he considered it as of a piece with all the "acts of oppression" that he had chalked, rather vaguely, against the Americans' account. Nevertheless he concealed his resentment beneath his pride, and threw over it a careless scarf of nonchalance. Indeed, it was only at the end of quite a long visit, and of many casual topics, that he introduced the real subject of his call in a "by the way" manner.

"I have heard from Señor Mills," he remarked in Spanish, "who desires further payment on some matters between us. I pointed out to him that this was not the season. What *ranchero* has money at this season? It is not the time of the sale of cattle. But he has given me this and that reason. It seems to be serious with him. Is it possible, *amigo*, that you——?" he paused delicately.

Colonel Peyton's fine old face wrinkled in distress.

"I know, I know!" he cried. "It is the dry year, after last winter. I sincerely hope that it will mean no sacrifice to you, my old friend. I sincerely hope that it will amount only to an inconvenience. For I, too, have talked with Señor Mills—a serious talk, *amigo*. I have not one cent to lay my hands on. I am myself pushed to save affairs from disaster. It can be done, but——"

A chill had struck through Don Vincente's heart at the first words of his friend. For whatever secret opinion or suspicion or aristocratic contempt he might have as to others of the American usurpers of his land, he knew and trusted and loved the owner of Corona del Monte. He knew that the Colonel's refusal was final, because it must be final; and for a single instant his panic-stricken mind visaged the consequences of a failure where he had from long habit taken success for granted. But instantly he recovered command of himself, and waved his hand gracefully.

"It is a nothing," he said. "It can be arranged in other ways."

"Let me tell you my situation," urged the Colonel.

Already the little Spanish gentleman sitting opposite, ridicuious—or pitiable—in his futile and ineffective pride, owed him an immense sum of money, which, a little at a time, he had taken without interest, without notes or other formality, with hardly even spoken thanks, as one accepts a cigarette. Yet the Colonel's generous heart was eager for justification as to his reason for refusing in this further need.

"It is, nothing, nothing!" disclaimed Don Vincente. "But I am grieved to hear that you, too, are the victim of these heartless bankers. Perhaps I may in my turn be of assistance——"

"They are not dealing with their own money—I can see that," the Colonel said, in defence of his friend, "but it does not make it the easier for us, *amigo*. A bad year is coming; a serious year."

They parted with formal expressions in the ceremonious Spanish style; and went their respective ways. The Spaniard, for the first time, had had brought home to him the seriousness of a situation that had been for years preparing. Colonel Peyton for the first time had found himself without ready money.

He, too, had been summoned to the little back office in the bank, where he had passed through a series of very uncomfortable conferences. Oliver Mills had several sheets of figures, which he insisted on discussing. The figures had to do with Corona del Monte, the number of cattle it supported, the natural increase, the proportion of beef animals, the average of market prices, the average gross expenditures for some years, and a whole lot of statistics concerning dry years and compound interest and such things. It was appallingly cold blooded and accurate, and seemed to show that Corona del Monte was rapidly sinking to perdition. In vain the Colonel had pointed out that these things could not be so, for the simple reason that he had always plenty of money, and the money must have come from somewhere. Mills proceeded to show him whence it had come; and that was disconcerting, for a lot of it, it seemed, would have to go back.

"So you see, Richard," he ended, kindly, "it really is necessary to take some thought and plan to the future. You have a wonderful piece of property there, a very rich piece of property. It ought to pay you big money, instead of being a burden, which it actually is. All it needs is a retrenchment until you get it on

its feet; and then a revision of methods. The old days are over,
Richard. We old codgers have got to realize that."

"I suppose so, Oliver," acknowledged the Colonel, whose usually sunny and exuberant spirits had been depressed by the three
sheets of figures. "Have you any suggestions?"

"Yes, I have," replied Mills, briskly. "You've got to get
rid of those hotels. They're white elephants as it is now. I can
turn them over to a syndicate for you; and you will be free from
that burden, and at the same time be able to lift your most pressing needs at the ranch. You know, Richard, you are very considerably in arrears there, and while as a person I would do
anything in the world for you, as a banker I must begin to think
more of my stockholders. This is going to be a bad year. The
banks are inclined to be as liberal as possible, but they must
stop short of the safety line." The little banker was obviously
nervous and embarrassed. He saw he must speak more plainly,
and he hated to do it. The Colonel's expression was that of a
bewildered child. If the matter had depended on himself alone,
he would have managed somehow to evade it and let things drift
for a little while longer, but the board of directors had given
him some very positive instructions in this and in a number of
cases. The new director, Patrick Boyd, had made him very
uncomfortable. "We will have to do some foreclosing this year,
I am afraid," he continued; then after a pause he blurted it out:
"We want to avoid foreclosing on you."

The Colonel sat up very straight, and his eyes flashed.

"On me? On Corona del Monte?" he cried. "Exactly what
do you mean, sir?"

"Do you know just how much you owe? and how far behind
your interest payments you are? and how deeply involved your
two hotels are? and what deficit they are making?" asked the
banker, reaching for another sheet of figures.

"No, by gad, sir, I do not! At least I have not the figures
by me. But what has that to do with this extraordinary statement—foreclose on me?"

Oliver Mills was very patient and very considerate. He succeeded in convincing the Colonel that the situation was serious:
he succeeded in allaying the first indignation; he did not at all

succeed in restoring the Colonel's former engaging child-like trust that the bank was a sort of affectionate big brother.

"And if I meet your suggestion, sir, and dispose of the hotel property to this syndicate you speak of: exactly how much money would that leave me clear?" he inquired at last.

"It would pay the mortgages on the hotels, and the back interest, and the floating debts; and it would square your way for a fresh start at the ranch—that is, would catch you up on your interest, and leave you five or ten thousand."

"Five or ten thousand! For two hotels!" cried the Colonel.

He could not get over the shock of that. To all intents and purposes it seemed to him that he was selling two big modern hotels, with grounds, well furnished and in running order, both of which belonged to him personally without partnership, and all he was getting from the transaction was a miserable five or ten thousand dollars! He listened to Oliver Mills's careful explanations and understood them intellectually; he assented to the banker's conclusion that he had not really owned them for some time—a panicky thought flashed through his mind that perhaps in the same way he did not really own Corona del Monte, but he thrust it out as unthinkable—but in spite of it his instinct cried out as against a cold-blooded subversion of age-founded things. He spent the afternoon in that office; and when he left, his usual springy jauntiness was quenched. For the first time in his life he walked with his shoulders stooped. He drove back to Corona del Monte huddled over the reins trying to think it out.

He had known from the start that he would have to fall in with the banker's plans, but he hated to face it. The hotels meant so much to his large feeling of hospitality. He enjoyed every detail, from the first lordly segregating of the sheep from the goats at the weekly docking of the *Santa Rosa* to all the little personal touches of especial fruits and flowers and gallant attentions that the Colonel loved to bestow. He would miss the hotels; miss them cruelly. Instinctively he knew he would never go back as an outsider to those beloved halls where he had reigned. That one pleasant human aspect of his life would be by one stroke cut off. It was like a bereavement.

But the Colonel again experienced that swift cold pang of fear. The hotels after all were a side issue in life. Corona del Monte was life itself. He had made it; and it had made him. It was a sentient, plastic, living entity composed of its many elements of living human beings and animals, of customs grown old, of experiences joyous and tragic, of sentiments and sympathies shared. To the Colonel it had seemed as much a matter of course as the air he breathed; and as immortal. Now, apparently, that life might be in danger. Corona del Monte, as a living, breathing thing, might actually cease to exist. The possibility had never crossed the Colonel's mind before. What were the hotels in comparison to this? Nothing: less than nothing!

He turned in to the long Avenue of Palms, and the lights of the ranch house twinkled intermittently through the trees. The Colonel thrust his body upright, as though throwing off a physical weight, and carefully composed his features. To all intents and purposes it was the same old debonair Colonel who entered the low living room and strode around the centre table to kiss his wife; who, as usual, occupied her worn, old wooden "Boston" rocker. She looked up at him and smiled; but into her eyes came a trouble. It was only after supper, however, when they were once again beside the study lamp, that Allie revealed what her perceptions had told her.

"What is it, Richard?" she asked, quietly.

"What is what?" he countered, with an air of well-imitated surprise.

"That won't do. Something is on your mind. You may as well tell me first as last."

The Colonel hesitated. His first instinct was to evade; for in his simple, old-fashioned code one kept all matters of worrisome business from one's women folk. It was almost a defect of chivalry to permit the dear creatures to realize that their lightest wish could not be granted. To talk about money was nearly as indelicate as to talk about legs. Man must shelter woman from all business worries. But the Colonel was very human, and very much alone in a new and bewildering experience. It did not require much more of Allie's gentle authority to bring him to confession.

"Well, I think that might be a whole lot worse!" she cried cheerfully, when he had finished detailing the situation. "I thought when you came in to-night that your best friend had died, at least. I never did like your fussing with those two hotels. They took too much of your time and money, both of which you could have spent to much better advantage on the ranch. That, to my mind, has been the whole trouble. The ranch would have done much better for a little attention. You've simply fallen between two stools."

"I believe you're right!" cried the Colonel, brightening.

"Of course I'm right!" insisted Allie, stoutly.

The Colonel thought of some of the figures.

"We will have to economize," he said.

"Then we'll economize. That won't kill us."

The Colonel passed in rapid review the different activities of the ranch, all rendered almost sacred by long custom.

"I don't believe I know how," he said.

V

ABOUT this time Patrick Boyd suggested at supper that he would like a little talk with his son. So the two adjourned to the "den" with the leather armchairs.

"What I want to see you about is your going into some sort of business," began Boyd. "We agreed last spring that every young man worth his salt should be active in life; and we rather placed the vacation limit for the fall. It is now nearly mid-winter, and we don't seem to have made much of a start. Mind you, I'm not blaming you. And there is of course no harm done, for a man can loaf more busily in this country than any place I know. But we ought to begin to think about it."

"I have been thinking about it, Dad," replied Kenneth, unexpectedly. "Don't think I've just been sliding along. Ever since we came back from San Francisco I've been collecting ideas and making up my mind. I think I've decided."

"What."

"Ranching."

Boyd puffed for a few minutes in silence.

"Well, it's a big business; but, according to my observation, very rarely profitable nowadays. You see, I am on the board of directors at the bank, and therefore in a position to know something about it. I had rather thought some active business would have been better. There is a firm of contractors here with, I think, a big future as the town grows. It is the Western Construction Company. I happen to know that I could get you in there—with every prospect of advancement. I don't know a single big ranch that is prosperous right now——"

"Let me tell you some of the things I have learned," urged Kenneth. "Then see what you think."

"Let her go!" agreed Boyd.

The conference lasted for several hours. Kenneth did most of the talking. What he said was a compilation of the many conversations he had had with Brainerd. In brief he pointed out the effects of the old hit-or-miss, kill-or-cure, all-or-nothing methods, the ignorances of soil and climate, the possibilities back of irrigation, the advantages of special rather than common farm products, and all the rest that is so generally in practise to-day, but which was then revolutionary. Boyd's keen and practical mind was intrigued. He began his listening in tolerance; but ended it in interest.

"Your arguments sound plausible. But of course none of what you say is certain. It would have to be worked out in experiment."

"Of course! And that is just what I want to do!" cried Kenneth. "If it does work out, think what it would mean to the country! I'd feel that I'd really accomplished something worth while!"

Patrick Boyd grinned covertly. What it would mean to the country had nothing to do with it. But he saw instantly what it would mean to the owner of a large acreage could it be proved conclusively that a few acres would support a family. Sounded a little wild; but Kenneth was young, and it might do him no harm to try.

"And if it doesn't work?" he suggested.

"But it will; I'm certain of it. And you have to take **some** risks in any new thing, don't you?"

"True. But we like to make these risks as small as possible. Where did you get all this stuff, anyway?"

Kenneth mentioned his source. Boyd shouted with laughter.

"That shiftless cuss!" he cried. "Brainerd! Why, Ken, he hasn't got enough to bless himself with! He's been gophering away on that side hill of his for ten years or more, and he hasn't got two cents to bless himself with! Why, Ken, he's the worst man in the world to talk farming. He never raised anything but a pretty daughter. Oho!" concluded Boyd, struck by a sudden thought. •

Kenneth flushed, but stood by his guns.

"He hasn't made a paying business, but he made just the experiment we were talking about; and it has worked, as an experiment."

This was exactly the right tack.

"How do you mean?" asked Boyd.

Kenneth explained Brainerd's physical weakness and the handicap that came from his lack of energy. He went over in accurate detail what had been done on the little ranch, why it could not have been carried farther, and what the results were up to that time. Boyd was partly won to his son's point of view by his arguments; but was more struck by the thoroughness and intelligence with which the young man had evidently gone into the question. Those are good qualities, and Boyd felt a glow of pride at this excellent proof of them. His active mind had been working independently of his listening.

"I see," he said, when Kenneth had finished. "You may be right; and then again you may not. But you have gone into it all in a way I like. As I see the situation, however, a really conclusive experiment would take a good many years. By the time it was proved wrong, you would have put the best years of your life into it."

"I'm willing," interrupted Kenneth, eagerly.

"I don't think it necessary. According to your statement there is such an experiment pretty well along, that only needs finishing. Suppose we should make an arrangement with Mr. Brainerd to let you in partnership with him. You could supply the energy and I the capital; and we would know in short order whether or not the thing would work. If it does work, then we can think of getting a bigger ranch for a permanent proposition. What do you think of it?"

"Perfectly fine—if Mr. Brainerd will do it."

"Mind you, I don't agree to it myself, yet. I want to go out with you and look the whole thing over, and get you to explain this to me on the ground. I'm too old a bird to buy a pig in a poke!"

"All right; we'll go to-morrow," agreed Kenneth.

They went the next•day and the day after. Boyd had a long talk with Brainerd. Then, apparently, he dropped the subject; but about a week later he again called Kenneth for conference in the library.

"I have looked into this ranching matter; and I have taken considerable advice on it. I am inclined to believe you are right. Now, I have had an interview with Mr. Brainerd, and this is what I have proposed to him. He has agreed, so if you like the scheme, we can go ahead. I will furnish sufficient money to develop Mr. Brainerd's property along the lines he has laid out. You are to see that the property is developed, under Mr. Brainerd's supervision and advice. You are, however, to have charge of all details of hiring and firing men, of buying necessary supplies and all the rest of that, of attending to the details of housing and feeding your help, and all that sort of thing. My idea is not especially to make a success of this particular little ranch, but to have you learn all you can. Incidentally, of course, we get a chance to try it out—and to try you out."

"I won't fail, Dad."

"I don't think you will. But I want you to get my idea clearly. I've given considerable thought to it. I don't want you to get swamped on this little proposition. Don't try to do any of the actual work yourself, unless you have a lot of time and need exercise. Lay out the work for others: and see that it is done."

"I understand that," assured Kenneth.

"Now, next door to you is one of the biggest and finest ranches in the country—Colonel Peyton's," pursued Boyd. "You have there a fine chance to see how things are done on a big

scale. I have seen Colonel Peyton and told him what you may
be about. He will see that you have a chance to learn anything
you may want to learn. I'll leave that to you. But here is
what I propose, while our actual experiment is going——"

He paused so long that Kenneth stirred expectantly.

"Suppose, after you are in the run of things, you bring me a
weekly report in which you describe how *you* would run that big
ranch. It may be that you would do exactly as Colonel Peyton
is doing. If so, state what it is, exactly as though it were your
own method. In that way I can judge of how well you are grasp-
ing the situation."

"I see."

"If, on the other hand, you would do some things differently,
why say so; and how you would do them. It might be well that
a young man would see improvements on old methods. Put
them down, and we'll discuss them, and see how practicable they
are."

"That will be grand fun!" cried Kenneth.

"Of course," warned Boyd, "you must not make any of these
suggestions for improvement to Colonel Peyton. He would
hardly take them in good part, after doing things his own way
for forty years or so!"

"Of course not," agreed Kenneth.

"Then when we have tried it out, and if it works, we'll see
about starting you in on a ranch that is worth while."

It was agreed that Kenneth should continue to live with his
father. He would have to get up a trifle earlier in the morning;
but on the other hand the Bungalow was only a brisk twenty
minutes' ride over a beautiful country. Kenneth was delighted with the whole arrangement. His mind, excited by the
numberless possibilities of the activities he had dreamed, refused
for a long time to let him fall asleep. He reviewed the best
course of the new ditch; he determined the height and kind of a
rabbit-proof fence; and debated pro and con a gang plough.

Over and over, around and around, his thoughts milled. Yet
when at last his wearied spirit stole into the dim borderland of
sleep, its eyes saw, not the green fields and blossoming trees of
his ambition, but Daphne. He would be near her.

For some time after his son had retired Patrick Boyd sat smoking and gazing into the collapsing, glowing coals of the oakwood fire. He was well satisfied, though at the first proposal of this ranching venture he had been very much the contrary. There had seemed to him nothing in it, either of money or of opportunity for a brisk, modern young man to exercise his powers. But the week's investigation had convinced him. The money success of the thing was not certain; that would have to be determined by experiment. But there was no doubt that here was a field in which a young man could use all his intelligence and push. Even if it did not turn out, Kenneth would have acquired the experience necessary to his development; and that, in the final analysis, was all that Boyd wanted for him at first. That was all he had expected from the Western Construction Company. If, on the other hand, the experiment proved a success, Boyd had other plans. As director on the bank board he had access to the financial affairs of the whole county. It was not by-the-way that he had urged the hypothetical "reports" on Colonel Peyton's ranch. Boyd had taken pains, during the past week, to look up the Colonel's situation. He knew to a dollar the latter's troubles: and he had a shrewd guess as to why they had come about. If things went on as they were going, the Colonel must eventually find himself where he must do something. It might be possible to acquire part of the Corona del Monte; or perhaps all of it; or a partnership might be arranged. There was nothing sinister in Patrick Boyd's visioning of future possibilities—as yet. His ruthless, fighting spirit never stirred unless at the push of serious opposition.

CHAPTER VI

I

W E MUST now consider two years as passing by, and both the characters of our tale and California herself as moving toward their fates, or certain crises in their development.

Very few definite things happened that a historian would have put down with dates opposite. But many subtle forces waxed or waned, readjusting their alignments.

One of the most important, or most talked about, event was the taking over of Las Flores by the bank, and the moving of the Cazadero family bag and baggage to some obscure quarter of the town. The thing had been seen before, many times, but never with the picturesque suddenness of this instance. As far as the man in the street knew, Don Vincente was one of the few old landowners who possessed some business sense. This was proved conclusively by the fact that he was the only one who still had any land. There were, moreover, no premonitory symptoms. Las Flores did not reduce its personnel nor its scale; it did not visibly practise those small economies that are so futile in face of big basic incompetence. Simply overnight the Cazaderos packed their personal belongings and drove into town; and an agent of the bank moved into the old ranch house. It was to be presumed that the new arrangement was for the best all around; and that Cazadero received something substantial over and above his debts. At least the family managed a fairly decent establishment, including a fringe-topped surry; and they never showed outwardly the least regret. Don Vincente, indeed, would wave his small pudgy hand airily at any discreet mention of Las Flores.

"Yes, one regrets," he said, "because it is the long-time home

of the childhood. But the time change. One grows old. One
has no son——" and he shrugged his shoulders in the implication that his judgment alone had dictated this move. The
house they occupied was on a side street downtown, somewhere
among the older residences that nobody knew. A few of the older
families tried to keep track of them by means of occasional and
spasmodic visits: but, amiable as she was, Doña Cazadero had
very little to offer. Outside her traditional setting she was
nothing very much. Her apparent placid content with her
chocolate caramels and her yellow novel, her rocking chair and
her dressing sack, her slow, afternoon amble down Main Street,
robbed the situation of that sort of loyalty that springs from
pity. She seemed to be getting on all right, so why bore oneself? Don Vincente was rarely at home. He had no content
at all with his lot; though no one was permitted to know it.
His pride was wounded to the death; a bitter, smothered rage
burned in his heart against the American race and the smart
tricks by which he thought they had despoiled him. Colonel
Peyton was almost the only man he excepted from this hatred;
and Colonel Peyton he avoided sedulously for the simple reason
that his pride and his conscience were both torn over the great
sums of money he knew now he could never repay. He con-
sorted only with members of his own race, frequenting much of
the time wine halls to the west of Main Street.

The Fremont and San Antonio hotels had been transferred
to a syndicate and were being run efficiently by a professional
manager. They were good hotels. Tourists visiting them for
the first time went away loud in their praises. The staff was
excellent and polite, the food good and abundant, the rooms
clean; and the arrangements for the comfort and amusement
and information of the guests rather unusually well thought and
managed. Yet some of the old timers, like our friends Saxon
and George Scott or Marcus Oberman, would shake their heads
and regret the "good old days." They could not tell what
they missed. Indeed, cross-questioned laughingly, they had to
confess that there had been many desirable innovations. But
it was different, somehow. What they really missed was the
intimate, personal touch of Colonel Peyton's affectionate minis-

trations. The Fremont was a very perfect machine for comfortable living while away from home: it was no longer a home itself.

For the Colonel never visited the hotel any more. He felt as though he had lost a whole piece out of the close-knit structure of his life; as, indeed, he had. Nobody but Allie knew how deeply he felt his loss. Some of his old friends may have guessed, but only from the fact that he so consistently absented himself. To the world in general he presented a jovial face.

"What business has a ranchman with hotels!" he cried with a laugh. "I'm getting along toward being an old man; and why I should bother myself with a lot of business I don't need to do in the least I'm sure I don't know!"

This was the attitude he consistently maintained. The new generation of tourists knew him not, except as a fine old figure driving or walking by, with a charming old-fashioned way of bowing to every stranger who passed within ten feet of him. Occasionally he gave a picnic at the ranch to which he invited some of his old hotel friends, with a request that they bring along whom they pleased. In this fashion he was still known to a select few of the winter tourists, who loved to exclaim over his picturesqueness and the romance of his old-time ranch; to the great disgust and envy of those not favoured. These were, compared to the old barbecues, simple picnics. They had not the wide, lavish, splendid picturesqueness of the barbecue; but they were charming, and their hospitality was dispensed in memorable fashion by the Colonel and his wife. The latter was always assisted by a tall, grave-eyed dark girl of seventeen, who moved with that complete command of her body that makes grace; and a curly haired, laughing-eyed, bronzed young man in his twenties, who had many small jokes for everybody, and who kept things going in a lively fashion. The old barbecues had been discontinued completely. This was at Allie's insistence. The Colonel yielded reluctantly, for they had always been her especial festival. But they had to be one of the first economies; and Allie had set down some appalling figures as to their cost, figures in which the Colonel had no belief whatever.

In other small respects, too, the ranch gave evidence, to the

Colonel's seeing eye, that economies had been undertaken; though the casual observer would have discerned nothing wrong. But the whitewash on the outbuildings and corral fences, and the trunks of the fruit trees, to take one small example, was not scrupulously renewed twice a year, as formerly. They looked well enough, but had lost their old, dazzling, prideful freshness. The borders of the long avenue grew a jolly crop of weeds and vine tangle—as indeed did the borders of every other road in the county; but in prosperous times even such remote corners had been clean and ship-shape. In short, all the little fancy touches, the refinements of neatness, the exuberances that not only groomed the horse but polished the hooves, were all gone. For to accomplish these fancy touches a superabundance of labour is necessary, so that for each small task is a man to polish that task off with trimmings. Allie had drawn up another disconcerting list of the inhabitants of Corona del Monte. It represented a small village.

"But you can't count in old Pedro, for instance, nor Carla, and certainly not the children. We don't hire them: we only hire Pablo," protested the Colonel.

"Well, they all live on Pablo," Allie pointed out, "and Pablo gets everything he owns in life from the ranch. So the ranch is supporting them just the same, whether it is direct or indirect."

The Colonel sighed and gave it up. But when it came to cutting down that surplus population, there was more difficulty. The ones the Colonel was most willing to let go were those who had been with him the shortest time. And naturally the latter were, nine cases in ten, the most efficient.

"If you keep on this way you'll have nobody on the place but a lot of guitar playing loafers," cried Allie, with some point.

The result was a compromise, which satisfied wholly neither the demands of sentiment nor those of efficiency; but which, nevertheless, did work out better on economic lines than the old system.

Allie also stopped the old easy fashion that had always obtained of the retainers helping themselves from a community supply of vegetables and fruit.

"Just because they've always done it is no particular reason why they should always continue to do it," she answered the Colonel's protest. "There is no reason why we should pay men to make a garden when a lot of them are lying around doing nothing. I'm beginning to believe that that is most of the trouble here—too many people doing nothing."

The result was that a few acres in the flat below were set aside as a garden spot for the families living on the ranch. Those who pleased to do so could there raise vegetables. As to fruit, Allie established a rough system of credit for work done in the orchard payable in fruit. It must be confessed that this system was only partially successful. Most of the Spanish families fell back on canned goods, or a little resentfully paid Lo for vegetables from the ranch gardens. Lo sold vegetables cheap, but he drove rigid bargains. Allie's bustling, practical genius had devised a scheme by which Lo went shares. Perched atop a rattle-trap old box wagon resurrected from the ranch's scrap heap, Lo early each morning drove into Arguello with a load of fresh truck. This he peddled from door to door. From the results he paid himself and his two assistants and turned over half the net profits to Allie. This and the poultry business, which was conducted on similar lines, were the only details of this miserable and depressing economy that tickled the Colonel. He used to chuckle and ask Allie how the Oriental Trading Company was coming on.

"Just the same," the latter averred, stoutly, "we are getting our own supplies absolutely for nothing, and a very neat little sum besides. Do you know what our vegetable garden and our poultry yard were costing us before?"

"No; and I don't want to!" cried the Colonel in pretended dismay. "If you and your Chinese partners are satisfied, I am!"

But for the time being, at least, all these changes from the traditional open handed methods of the past made the Colonel miserable. He felt mean and penny pinching. It was somehow as though he were depriving all these people of something that was rightfully theirs. He felt that they must be secretly despising him as a skinflint; and so he was unable to meet them in his old hearty, open-souled fashion. Only with a few of the reliable older men, who understood the situation, like Manuelo, did he open up; and then merely in half regretful reminiscence of the old days. From all the others he thought he concealed the situation. The idea that his old retainers should think him suddenly turned skinflint actually hurt the old man less than that they should distrust the prosperity or stability of the rancho!

But old Sing Toy broke down this unhappy attitude. One evening he appeared suddenly in the doorway of the living room. Allie was, as usual, seated in her worn old wooden rocker sewing; while the Colonel, his lean, kindly old face bent over a book, was staring wide-eyed back through many years. Sing Toy was dressed up to the nines. He had on several brocaded jackets one showing below the other, the innermost of a pale lavender, and the others shading to the outermost, which was blue. His baggy trousers were also of lavender brocade, and were tied tight around the ankles with a crossed winding of white tape. Socks of snowy white disappeared into embroidered shoes with thick soles. Sing Toy wore the stiff skull cap with the red button, as was his right: and his queue hung respectfully down his back.

"Good gracious, Toy!" cried Allie, when she caught sight of this magnificence, "where's the party?"

Sing Toy bowed gravely from the waist.

"No party," said he. "I come talk to Colonel."

It was evidently a serious and ceremonial occasion. The Colonel aroused himself from his abstraction.

"Come in, Sing Toy," said he.

This, he could see was no mere contact of master and servant. With the donning of his magnificent raiment Sing Toy had put on equality. The Colonel knew his Chinamen, and realized this fact. "Sit down," he invited.

The Chinaman disposed himself deliberately, bolt upright on the edge of a chair, and folded his hands under his sleeves.

"I got tlee t'ousand dollar," he announced abruptly.

"That is very nice," observed the Colonel. "It is a large sum."

"Yes," agreed Sing Toy. "I save'm wages. I wo'k for you long-time—fifteen year."

"Is it that long?" commented the Colonel, in order to say something. He had as yet no clue to the purpose of this ceremonial vist.

"You go bloke now, mebbe," continued Sing Toy, not as asking a question but as making an assertion.

"What!" responded the Colonel, blankly.

"Yes, you go bloke. I *sabe*. I see. Every place you stop wo'k. No have party. No paint barn. Veg'table man. Cunnel velly sad. Walk alound head down. No smile. No joke. No laugh. I *sabe*. I no likeum." He smiled with the hilarious cheerfulness of the Oriental who is trying to be sympathetic. "You no ketchum money at bank any more. I *sabe*. My cousin wo'k at bank. Dat all light. He no tell Melican man."

"Well I'll be——" began the Colonel, staring with new eyes at his imperturbable servant.

"You wait," commanded Sing Toy; "I got tlee t'ousand dollar. I got no use for dat money. You take 'um. I got lots fliends, got lots money, in Chinatown. You tell me how much you want. I get 'um."

As the meaning of this speech finally reached the Colonel, he half started impulsively from his seat, then sank back, and the tears started in his eyes.

"You don't understand the situation, Sing Toy," he said. "I could offer you no security for your money—you *sabe* security? You might lose it all."

"China boy no want seculity," averred Sing Toy. "He know you pay all light."

The Colonel choked, and openly touched his eyes with his handkerchief, for recent events had keyed him tense. He told Sing Toy that the situation was not as bad as all that; but that he appreciated the offer, and would remember it if the need arose. Sing Toy listened with unmoved countenance, then arose.

"All light," said he. "Now you joke. You laugh," and he waddled out.

The Colonel watched his broad brocaded back as it disappeared through the doorway.

"By Jove, Allie, he's right!" he cried. "But isn't he a dear!
—and who in the wide world would have thought——"

That evening's visit of the cook was the turning point in the
Colonel's adjustment to the new state of things. His raw and
sore spirit had needed just that touch of personal affection and
trust. He began to take a constructive interest in the new
economies; he allowed Allie to plan openly with him, and incidentally he acquired a great respect for that person's practical
knowledge; his incipient distrust of people's attitude toward
or opinion of himself vanished, and he met everybody with a
return of his old confident friendliness; the growing sense of oppression under the burden of his debt lightened. So the end
of our two years finds the Peytons and the Rancho de la Corona
del Monte.

The experiment at the Bungalow had prospered. With
vigour and sufficient money all the obstacles that had before
proved fatal now dissipated like smoke. Proper fences well
maintained kept out the rabbits; the ground squirrels had been
diminished by use of poison at certain seasons of the year, and
the attentions of a boy and a Flobert rifle at all others. The
latter improvement was Kenneth's idea. He had been so re-
cently a small boy himself that he was able to judge; and he
canvassed gravely all the workingmen for hire; not in examina-
tion of their capacity, but as to their ownership of a small boy of
appropriate age and disposition. This individual, when found,
was installed, with his incidental wife and small daughter, as a
permanency. Kenneth next purchased a Flobert and a quantity
of .22 shorts. The youngster then took a course of training
under personal supervision for some months on accurate shooting, safe handling, and identification of fauna; after which he was
turned loose as official pest exterminator. Kenneth inaugurated
a very business-like system to which he and Timmy adhered
gravely. The cartridges Kenneth doled out a box at a time,
charging Timmy for them at wholesale rates. The latter
brought in his bag daily and was credited on the book he and
Kenneth kept between them according to a fixed schedule. He
was on honour to ask bounty only for creatures killed on the
property. The schedule was rather complicated, and was the re-

sult of many solemn confabs. Ground quirrels, gophers, moles, rabbits, bluejays and the two falcons were always on the list. Certain species, such as linnets or blackbirds, or quail, were fair game only at seasons of ripe fruit or grain. The grand prizes were, of course, coyotes and wildcats; but they were naturally somewhat in the category of unattainable ideals. The results were a straight-shooting small boy and a diminution of pests below the point of destructiveness.

There was now a sufficiency of water better used. The original spring had been greatly increased by tunneling, and the water brought down in cement conduits that obviated waste. Cultivation now was possible on a better scale. After the water had been laid on the soil, it was harrowed over and over, so that the earth was no longer allowed to bake hard. It was therefore necessary to irrigate but four or five times a year instead of twice a week. Brainerd had known well enough that all this should be done; but he had not possessed the means, financial or physical.

As a consequence of its new impetus the Bungalow was prosperous. It had changed its very appearance. The sage desert had been pushed back: and the gray Old Man brush had given place to flourishing citrus trees. The dry, powdery hard pan from which it had wrested its desiccated existence had turned into a brown, moist productive soil that justified the visionary dream that it was richer than the bottom lands. Now that every drop of the water was not needed for the crops, Daphne was permitted a garden. She went at it with enthusiasm. In the old California fashion everybody contributed plants, shrubs, or trees from their own over-flowing, older-established gardens. A little cultivation and water did the rest. Quick-growing vines, like the passion flower, the honeysuckle, the solanum, flung themselves over the low house. The dooryard was bright with strepthasolum, nasturtiums, plumbago, hybiscus and all that brilliant company. In the swift fashion of the country the trees struck vigorous root and began to grow, not by inches but by feet.

Kenneth reported to his father every week, as they had arranged. Every cent of expenditure was set down. Each month the two spent some hours tabulating; segregating the items so that in the final analysis only those having to do specifically with the commercial productiveness could be charged against the success of the experiment. And by the end of this two years it could plainly be seen that the experiment was going to be a success. The point was proved beyond a doubt.

The possibilities that opened before Patrick Boyd's vision were tremendous. If twenty acres would in the future support a family as well or better than a thousand acres had in the past, there was no limit to the country's development. And if this powdery, sagebrush upland was valuable—why, there were millions of acres like that! All that was needed was the water. A few artesian wells would supply that; or, if artesian wells did not work out, there was plenty in the mountains. That would require big handling, a utilities company to construct the necessary works on a large enough scale, to pipe it down, distribute it. Boyd's constructive mind saw the chances to sell cheap land dear.

But the best chance, and the nearest at hand, was undoubtedly Corona del Monte. It lay at the borders of the town. Its rolling, oak-dotted slopes were admirably graded for the water. In its limits it had quantities of all types of land. At the present time it was worth on an average throughout about fifteen dollars an acre. Divided into proved small farms, with the water laid down, Boyd thought it should average two or three hundred. Thousands of acres! The strip nearest town would be a veritable gold mine when people discovered, as discover they must, that here they could live in beautiful flower-smothered homes, under the fairest sky in the world—and make a living while doing it!

The only question was water. The needs of the cattle were filled by windmills and surface wells. The small amount of garden irrigation at the ranch came from similar sources. It sufficed for this purpose; but it no more than sufficed. In dry years it ran rather short. And the difficulty was that few individual twenty acres were self contained. That is to say, the ranch gardens themselves depended on wells scattered over five hundred acres or so.

There was plenty of water in the Sur to be had for the tunneling; but that would require a very considerable outlay of money and time. The artesian possibilities had never been tried. That possibility should first be proved or disproved.

Boyd shared none of these conclusions and speculations with his son. He did not even confide to the young man that in his opinion the experiment at the Bungalow had succeeded. Why, he could not have said; except this was opening out as a big thing, and his strong instinct in big things was to work close mouthed until the plan was fully formed. Therefore Kenneth was still in ignorance that his father was convinced. Boyd moved slowly and cautiously in order not to arouse any suspicions. The chance was too good to share with anybody. He had worked it out for himself, and he intended that he—and his son—should reap all the benefit. To accomplish that he would have to get hold of the land before anybody conceived the idea that it was good for anything but a cattle range. This part of it, he concluded, would not be too difficult. The country was sound asleep, and—so Boyd was convinced—would not awaken to its possibilities without considerable yawning and stretching. There was all leisure to move safely and slowly. Through his talks with Kenneth, and by virtue of his position in the bank, he was thoroughly familiar with the situation. Corona del Monte was lately managing to get along: but it skirted the ragged edge. Unless methods were to change fundamentally, these small economies and retrenchments would suffice only in calm weather. Come a time of stress, or another bad year, and the craft would founder—or could be made to founder. Boyd knew that a man like Colonel Peyton would never change methods fundamentally. It was, in his opinion, merely a question of awaiting the right moment.

For it had reached this point in Boyd's mind. The vision of the possible millions to come to the men who inaugurated the new era had aroused the wolf in him that had been sleeping since its full meal in Traction.

The immediate question, however, was whether artesian water existed below the ranch; or whether irrigation would have to come from the Sur. In the former case there was no hurry about doing anything. In the latter, however, it would be necessary quietly to acquire the necessary rights and rights-of-way before the idea became public. From the scientists he got little satis-faction. This country had never been geologically surveyed. The only point of value he learned was that if the dip was such that artesian water existed in one place, it probably would be found almost anywhere. This was satisfactory. But evidently the only thing to do was to try.

The task of inducing Colonel Peyton to drill was a delicate one. The Colonel was not looking for a chance to make new expenditures. Boyd reached him through Kenneth. It was another delicate task to keep Kenneth from knowing that he was used. Fortunately for Boyd the succession of dry years had shortened the supply in the surface wells. His secret ownership of the Western Construction Company enabled him to tip the balance of decision. They offered the Colonel ab-surdly low prices and easy terms, with a proviso that he should pay nothing if no water was found. To anybody but the Colonel this would have showed on the face of it as absurd. The Con-struction Company had to invest in well-boring machinery and some expert assistance; but Boyd did not begrudge that. As for Ephraim Spinner; if he suspected anything queer in this hap-hazard way of doing business, he gave no indication. He had hitched his wagon to an eastern star of the first magnitude, and he could see no reason for cutting the traces. A rig was erected half way down the knoll, just out of sight of the house, and the operations began.

The rest of Arguello was exactly where it had been two years before. Some of the children had grown up; some had gone away to school or college. Mrs. Carlson's highbrows continued to monkey with the sacred art of poetry. Carlson continued to drink a good deal, play rough games and frequent rough com-pany just to prove that he was not a poet. The *Sociedad* came over the mountains and went back again at irregular intervals. The mountains and the sea slumbered on, as did the inhabitants of the little village.

II

BUT for California herself these two years had meant the changing of the gray dawn to rose. She was stirring from the sleep that had fallen upon her after her hectic carouse in the days of 'Forty-nine. The reason might have been sought and found in the little bungalow farm on which Brainerd had spent so many years. The sagebrushers had ceased living on jackrabbits and wild honey. They had discovered the value of irrigation; the fact that fruit trees grew better out of the bottom lands, because in the bottom lands the water level is too variable; that values are to be found in apparent desert or gravel wash; that improvements are possible in the quality of fruit; that there are moisture-conserving possibilities in plain cultivation; in short, that the land responds to intelligent treatment. Southern California was beginning to be dotted with little settlements. The old careless, lusty, lavish days were everywhere passing. These discoveries, simple as Columbus's egg, had rarely been made by the older inhabitants. They were made by the immigrants.

These immigrants were of a class never seen before. They were mainly people with considerable or even abundant means who had come to California for a change of climate. They had invalids in the family; or they were plain sick of bad weather and saw no reason why, having retired from business or sold their farm, they should continue to live in it. These people bought places and small farms or orange groves, not primarily with the idea of making a profit out of them, but simply to have pleasant and beautiful places in which to live. They made of them bowers of blossom and vine; and incidentally they experimented in fine fruits, or especial crops of some sort, or just to see whether anything would grow in the most unlikely places. In this, the most favourable atmosphere for leisurely experiment, grew finally a great body of information and accomplishment. The thickskinned, dry, sour California oranges, and the overgrown, spongy lemons had been improved until at the New Orleans exposition they took premiums from the world. The dried fruit industry had been invented, and then proved. And so, still uncorrelated, still scattered, the elements of modern California were being worked out. Actual profits were being made here and there! Moreover, they were large profits!

The news of these things began to trickle back to the East.

Tourists came, looked, saw, returned, and boosted. Of those who listened, the many smiled and murmured something about "California Liars," but the few took a trip for themselves. The rumour thus grew rapidly. The despised "cattle country" of Southern California took on a new interest. People who were not tourists actually began to come out, not to spend the winter, but to look around. They made the astonishing discovery that the summers also were pleasant! Heretofore the tourist had fled home on the approach of spring. If the winter was warm, the summer must be intolerably hot. Nobody but bookish experts knew anything about a cooling polar current. After they had looked around, and acquired much knowledge and statistics, they returned home. And whereas the simon-pure tourist had noted and told about the birds and flowers and sunshine, this new type of visitor had bestowed most of his attention on acreage, and costs, and methods, and profits.

Thus in these two years the travel to California had wonderfully increased. The old regulars were augmented by the professional tourists who abandoned Europe for a season to see this newly talked-of land; by the wealthy business man who had heard so much of the new country that he thought he might as well combine business with pleasure and take a little jaunt to see if there was anything to be picked up; by the one-time visitor who had liked it and had gone away reluctantly in the dream of coming back if he could afford it, but who now plucked up hope of coming back to make a living; by invalids and climate seekers following the glowing stories; by hundreds of farmers who had long been sick of the uncertainties and discomforts of their lives, and were now pursuing the rumour of heaven. And also, just a trifle later, by the big capitalists and the little sharpers who followed the scent of prosperity to see what could be done about it.

Such movements come to notice suddenly, though they may have been in process and under way for some time. They resemble in this the dropping of stones into a puddle. One may drop in a great many without the slightest visible result. Then all at once they appear, and every pebble adds to the size of the pile.

By good fortune the season in which the rock pile began to show was one of early rains. Never before had the land been lovelier. From the Mexican border north the country was green and moist and warm. The orange groves were heavy with yellow fruit. The clear, sparkling streams from the mountains ran bank full. The air was like crystal, and through its unbelievable clarity one could see the ranch and farmhouses standing like toys amid the greenery of their trees and vines. There was in this air an exhilaration, an infusion of optimism. The most staid and grumpy old banker from the East would listen, with tolerant amusement to be sure, to the enthusiastic prophecies of the new species called the "booster." People drove about in fringe-topped surries, or rode abroad on horseback, and were invited in to "pick as many as you can use," in the lavish, hospitable habit of the day. They saw evidences of fertility and evidences of comfort and a pleasant life. It was only natural to inquire as to values, to talk things over, finally to figure on such matters as how many people the Los Angeles valley could support. It was a dull imagination that could not foresee the time when the demand for land would be very much greater than it was then. People gradually ceased thinking so much of what the soil could produce and began to figure what someone would be willing to pay for it next year. From that to speculative buying was a short step. The wealthy tourist, or rather the tourist with a little means, "took a flyer" for the fun of it; the man who thought himself shrewd, and was always willing to make his pleasure trips pay for themselves, looked about to see what was likely to rise. Everybody agreed that there was surely going to be a big population. The world would not be able to resist.

The average man bought town lots rather than country property because that was something he thought he could understand. Demand created supply. In orange groves and wheat fields outside the towns a crop of little white stakes began to appear. The prices were low as yet. Your winter visitor bought a few lots on spec, much as he might buy a handful of white chips. The small real estate men were happy in a small way; nothing serious, however.

But now another element of the complex situation developed and showed its strength. The transcontinental railroads began to fight each other. Within the past two or three years, as has been shown, the passenger traffic had greatly increased. The railroad heads began to see possibilities on an unhoped for scale. Naturally each wanted to hog it all. And as naturally each began to cut into his rivals by every means in his power. The word *propaganda* had not yet come into general use; but the thing itself was done to the limit. In every wayside station, almost in every country corner-store of the blizzard-ridden East hung vivid lithographs showing mammoth clusters of fruit, a dazzle of flowers to put your eyes out, and invariably a young lady of rich glowing complexion, toothful smile, and a redundant figure. Small circular inserts around the border depicted bathing in January and the ocean at the same time; showed small snapshots of the future life labelled "ranching in California"; and invariably offered a snowscape with a muffled, shivering, red nosed, belly-deep person shovelling a path to the barn. This last labelled in large type YOURSELF!, and you were urged to come to California where perpetual summer reigns. These vivid posters were backed up by tons of patent insides distributed gratis to the country newspapers. They were of course a balderdash of super-optimism. Read to-day in the light of our accurate knowledge of what is possible and what is not; what the country will do, and what it will not; what the climate is, and what it is not, these perfervid booster articles sound ridiculous enough. But it must be remembered that then California was considered so remote as almost to be outside the United States. It carried over an overload of romance from the times of the 'Forty-niners, Vigilante days, the period of the bonanza kings. People will believe anything that is far enough away. Beside which this advertising was helped by the constant publication of silly letters. Most people had in those days never been far from home. California was so different, her winter climate offered so heavenly a contrast, her beauties were so unbelievable to one accustomed only to sober landscapes that the visitor became rhapsodical. He—or she—wrote reams of silly, sloppy, sentimental stuff, mostly adjectives and adverbs. Probably he—or she—had rarely before left a pavement, and certainly had no basis on which to found the enthusiastic judgments so blithely passed out. Hundreds of these private letters were printed: as letters from the front were printed during the war. And they carried great weight because the writers were "disinterested," save the mark!

But the railroads went much further in their bid for custom than mere propaganda. Propaganda might stimulate travel, but it would not necessarily stimulate travel over your particular road. Naturally we are not considering maps where your own blood-red line darts straight as an arrow to its objective, while your rival's thin black thread goes all around Robin Hood's barn and finally snarls itself up so badly you can't tell it from a state boundary line. Everybody can have them. The road had to do something the other roads could not do. For example, sell cheaper tickets.

Thus began the great rate war of the 'eighties. It is now forgotten by the public, but at the time it attracted a lot of attention. The thought seemed to be that if you got people to going on your line, at no matter what present cost, they would forever after continue to do so, and your rival would always run dark trains. It was a nice spirited contest while it lasted. We have not space to go into details. Suffice it to say that it took six months to hammer its futility into the heads of the railroad chiefs; that fares went down to *five dollars* for a round trip from Missouri River points, and on one day only it could be had at one dollar.

They travelled by thousands, people who had never been a hundred miles from home in their lives. They packed the carpet bags, and put up cooked provisions in boxes and hied them forth. If the railroads really wanted volume of traffic, they got it. Most of these new tourists did the usual tourist things; but a certain proportion looked upon the land and found it so much better than they had known back home that they raked and they scraped and they bought. Indeed, so large was the crop of investors this year that away back in Chicago the professional "boomers" heard of it. And as the Chicago boom of that period was on the ebb, they in turn packed their grips and their methods and came west. Undoubtedly they hoped, and expected, to make a tidy little clean-up on a carefully nursed rise; they could hardly have anticipated the effect of the climate on their tender plant. It shot up like Jack's beanstalk.

III*

THE boom and boom methods were under way and in full swing before even a ripple reached Arguello. People knew vaguely that there was something doing down South; but Arguello was cut off from easy communication, so that she did not at once feel the impulse of new movements. Her inhabitants did not travel much, except in the course of business; and those who did travel were not of the type to be interested in nor to catch new methods. It remained for Ephraim Spinner, the man of quick perceptions and quicksilver imagination, to see and bring back with him an idea. This idea he hastened to share with Boyd.

"It is the waking up we've been waiting for!" cried Spinner. "And we can be in on the ground floor, if we want to be. It hasn't struck here, yet; but it is going to."

Boyd listened attentively; made no decisive comment, but took a trip south. Spinner offered to accompany him and show him the ropes, but he preferred to go alone. The morning after his arrival he breakfasted in good season, and sauntered down Spring Street to see what he could see.

He had not long to search. Down the street came a brass band dressed in gaudy gold and white uniforms, blaring stridently to the zenith. At its head strutted a drum major with tall bearskin shako, and whirling and throwing aloft a brass-headed baton that glittered in the sun. Behind it marched two men dressed as flunkeys in wine-coloured, brass-buttoned, stripe-waistcoated liveries, with white stockings. They bore an outspread banner of white bearing a legend in gold:

BANKSIA HEIGHTS SALE OF LOTS TO-DAY

FREE RIDE AND FREE LUNCH

---

*The author wishes here to repeat his indebtedness to T. S. Van Dyke's "Millionaires of a Day." The sequence of psychology could not be improved upon: indeed, the present author prefers the possibility of a cry of "imitation" to the responsibility of tampering with that sequence.

Next in line pranced a pair of milk-white horses caparisoned
:n red-lacquered harness and drawing a "low-necked hack" on
the back seat of which lolled two individuals resplendent in
shiny top hats and frock coats. After them trailed a long procession of surries and other vehicles. As these evidently represented the free ride advertised on the banner, Boyd stepped off
the curb toward one of them. Instantly it pulled up, and he
climbed aboard.

A half hour later he found himself at Banksia Heights. The
procession had wound its noisy way here and there in the downtown streets of the city, displaying its banner, dispensing im-
partially its pandemonium, collecting here and there—on the
strength of the free ride and the free lunch—occupants for the
long string of vehicles. It was a gorgeous day, bright and mild,
typical of March in Southern California. Boyd was interested
in the crowd that debarked at Banksia Heights. They were
many, and a good proportion looked prosperous, but they had
most evidently come for the lark and the picnic and the free
lunch. It did not worry them one bit that they were accepting
what amounted to hospitality from a stranger under what
equally amounted to false pretences. For not one of them had
the faintest notion of investing in Banksia Heights.

But neither did it seem to worry the two men in the shiny
silk hats. Indeed, they looked rather pleased than otherwise
as they superintended the debarking of the band from the omni-
bus that had picked it up after its processional function was
over.

"Get under that oak," they instructed the drum major, "out
of the sun; and just raise hell." Which same they certainly
did. The leaves of the oak tree shivered in their brassy blasts;
and the idly waiting crowd thrilled to the desired supernormal
simply because each and every one of them had been brought
up on country circuses, and the blatant blare of such a band
would thus ever possess the power to quicken the blood.

The land sloped away gently toward the distant sea, spread
out like a carpet. Acres of lupin, blue as the heavens; acres of
golden poppies yellower than the soft sunlight; acres more of
yellow violets or varicoloured bellflowers rolled away over the

low rises; and the squares of grove or grain, the gleaming white of houses, the lazy smokes of the city lay in the mellow sunshine. The clear liquid notes of meadowlarks made themselves heard in spite of the band. Back of all rose the Coast Range over whose nearer foothills could be discerned the wild lilac or mountain laurel, the wild pea and gooseberry among the chaparral. Stimulated and upheld by the familiar band and the prospects of the free lunch, the tourists looked about them and felt something of the spell of the country's beauty. For it is a singular fact that the average tourist never sees anything unless measures are taken. He is a good deal like a dog that way. If we are to believe what dogs tell us, there are few things they enjoy more than a good walk with plenty of smells to investigate. As such is the case, one would think dogs would go on many walks; but they rarely do, unless their master takes them. Tourists are good conscientious beasts, also. They will take infinite trouble to go anywhere any guidebook or railway folder tells them they ought to go; and they will spend any amount of money and personal discomfort to see any waterfall, or busted adobe, or view, or prehistoric ash barrel that any half-way competent authority will tell them about; and they will pay prices per hour to be driven any approved drives whereon they exclaim over whatever the driver points out, or will remain timidly silent if he does not point out anything. But they very rarely go out and find things for themselves, and they rarely see country. Between stations on the trains they read books or play cards—unless of course the railway folders tell them to observe. When the train stops they come to, and hang out the windows, and stare fascinated at the newsstand, or the station building (which needs painting), or the buildings across the street. They would never have thought of going out to Banksia Heights, or anything similar, unless lured thereto by the band and the free lunch; but once having arrived there they could not help but be influenced, each according to his receptivity, by the charm and peace and mellowness of the day.

The taller of the two men in silk hats looked on this assemblage with a satisfaction that at first was not shared by his colleague.

"There's not three people in this crowd who have come out to look at lots!" the latter confided, disgustedly. "The most of them are just out for a free picnic. They don't know one earthly thing about real estate—or California."

This was the owner of the property: that is to say, he had paid a small amount down, and was expecting to clean up at a profit before the next payment came due.

"Just exactly what we want," asserted the other, shrewdly. "That's the sort of fellow who thinks he's smarter than any other. I've handled this sort before. There's two types here: the real green ones, and the wealthy, superior ones who've just come out to see the thing work, and are too smart to come in. Like that fellow over there," said the auctioneer, indicating Patrick Boyd. "Know who he is?"

"Not a notion. But I saw Colonel Carstair—you know, the banker from St. Paul. He's an old friend of mine. I told him if he saw anything that looked good to him at the auction to bid it in and hold it for a rise. I told him he needn't pay a cent on it—just to write out a check and hand it in for appearance sake and I'd destroy it."

"What did he say?"

"Nothing much. But he's here."

"Well, they've gawped around enough. Let's get at it."

The auctioneer mounted a rostrum near the centre of the tract. Clerks took their places at tables below. He held up his hand, and the band stopped with a blat. Behind the rostrum hung a huge canvas marked as a plot. An assistant placed the tip of a long pole against one of the lots; at the same time another assistant with a flag stationed himself on the actual lot to be sold.

"Now, ladies and gentlemen," began the salesman, pushing his tall hat back in an engaging fashion. "I want to make you a little talk in general before getting down to brass tacks and the things that interest us all the most. I can make it very short, because you've got it right in front of your eyes; I refer to California and its future; and especially Los Angeles." He went on briefly, as he had said, to point out climate, soil, productivity, and future, together with a few convincing statistics. When he had finished he leaned forward and flashed his teeth in a friendly fashion. "That's off our minds. But it's true, and you know it's true. But what we are interested in is Banksia Heights, and especially in that part of it where the young man is holding the flag. It is, as you see, in the natural line of growth of what is soon to be a metropolis of the Pacific Coast. Plans are already drawn, and can be inspected in our city office, for all the usual and necessary public improvements. I don't think anybody present has ever seen a fairer outlook, felt against his cheek more salubrious breezes, planted his feet on soil better adapted to the establishment of a home. Now as to this lot. It is one of the finest on the tract. Its purchase carries with it the privilege of taking the next two at any time during the next week and at the same price. Somebody make a bid. Quick."

A lank saturnine individual, who had been openly sneering around since his arrival, promptly spoke up in a loud voice.

"Five dollars!" he cried.

The auctioneer stood on tiptoe to see the speaker. He recognized him at once as the owner of a rival tract who was trying thus at once to cast discredit on values, and also to start the bidding on so low a scale that it could never mount to desired heights.

"Thank you! Thank you, sir!" cried back the auctioneer, with every appearance of sincerity. He turned to the others as though taking them into his confidence. "Friends, you see standing here before you a poor, forlorn, broken-winded, shattered wreck from Kansas. I do not know him personally, but I can tell he comes from Kansas by his thin gaunt form, his haggard features, and his pinched nose. Half starved from living on a soil that can produce nothing better than rattlesnakes, his health broken down by blizzards, and his bank account busted by bad crops in the off years and grasshoppers in the on years, he has wandered out here to buy a home and mend his fortune. He says that he has only five dollars left, all that his folly in not coming to California in the first place has spared him of a handsome fortune. He offers it all here—all he has left in the world— for a home in Banksia Heights. Don't outbid him, friends! Don't, I beg of you, ladies and gentlemen! I declare this lot

sold, as an act of charity, to our bankrupt, broken-winded, de-
plorable friend from Kansas. John, move the flag to lot 8.
What name, please?"

But the rival had sneaked away amid the delighted laughter
of the crowd. Lot 8 was put up. After some hesitation a solid
respectable looking man with the appearance of a small-town
grocer bid a hundred and fifty dollars. Everybody looked at
him; but he bore inspection well. There were dozens like him,
all about. Nevertheless he was a hired capper. The boom
real estate man was the precursor of the movie director in his
appreciation of the value of types.

"My dear sir!" cried the auctioneer, disgustedly. "You
don't realize. I am not offering you this map. I am offering
a genuine fifty-foot lot, made out of dirt. Come now, let's have .
a real offer."

Boyd, wandering around, had unexpectedly run into three of
his old cronies, namely Saxon, Marcus Oberman, and George
Scott.

"Well, well!" he cried. "What in thunder are you three terra-
pins doing down here? I thought you never got more than ten
miles from the Fremont bar?"

"What are you doing here yourself?" countered Saxon. "The
same to you."

"Oh, I just came down on business. Saw this procession
going by, and thought I'd come along and see the fun. Great
show, isn't it?"

At the auctioneer's last appeal a voice spoke up from the out-
skirts of the crowd.

"One hundred and seventy-five," it stated with deliberate
dignity.

"Hanged if that isn't Jimmy Carstair!" cried Boyd, delightedly.

"Who's Jimmy Carstair?" asked Scott.

The others stared at him incredulously.

"Jimmy Carstair? You must know him! He's one of the
richest men in St. Paul!"

"Oh, him!" said Scott with new respect.

"I wonder what he's doing in this," speculated Boyd. "He

generally knows what is what. Let's see if he really wants this lot, or is bidding for fun. Get out of sight, fellows. One hundred and eighty!" he called.

But he had been seen and recognized by others in the crowd, lesser fry, taught by the popular periodicals of the day to look up to "Captains of Industry." These began to buzz to each other. If the big men were interested, there must be something in it.

"Two hundred," spoke up some one from the middle of the crowd. The auctioneer took a look to see that this was not one of his various cappers, and was immensely heartened to discover that it was not.

"Two hundred and ten," spoke up one of the latter on receipt of an almost imperceptible sign. It was time to feel out the temper of the crowd a little.

"This is too silly!" cried the auctioneer, with an appearance of vexation. "If some of you don't look out, this bargain is going to go off and hit you." He leaned over and appeared to consult the owner, who shook his head. "Well," he said impatiently, "there's no accounting for a man's conscience. If this property was mine, I'd call the thing off right here and now. He says he's advertised this sale as being without reserve and he's going to stick to it, if he has to give them away. I wouldn't do it, and I'll tell you that frankly."

"It is good property," said Saxon, loud enough so that several heard him. Indeed, it was good property: the only difficulty being that there were several hundred miles of exactly similar property lying all about. "I wonder if Carstair really means business," he added.

The auctioneer and the owner were anxiously wondering the same thing. His single bid had a fine moral effect, but it would be lost if the first raise were to discourage him utterly. However, Carstair was a shrewd amn. He realized that if the sale were to go well, this first lot sold would be one of the cheapest: subsequent sales would go more or less on its price as a basis. On the other hand if the sale were a failure, he would be nothing out of pocket. He accepted this certainty as one of the small perquisites of his wealth and prominence.

"Two twenty-five," he pronounced briefly.

"By Jove," said George Scott, impressed. "Carstair has never played a dead card that I've known of. He must think mighty well of this."

Nobody was aware of the fact that the mighty Carstair was only another capper. Carstair would have denied it with heat. Yet such was the case: and the principals glowed with pride and joy over the success of their ruse. The auctioneer quickly knocked down the lot to his distinguished client; and ordered the flag to another lot some distance from the first. The owner signalled him. He bent over to hear.

"Better adjourn for lunch," he was advised. "Let 'em circulate and talk."

The auctioneer nodded.

"You're right. Wait a second. Best to taper off a little for the best effect."

He straightened up and at once began to talk:

"Mothers! Fathers!" he cried. "Husbands who intend to become fathers! Look at this offer and weep for joy! The owner and founder of Banksia Heights will *give* to the first child born in Banksia one lot on the main street, just as soon as we learn the name of the said child to put it in a deed. And we don't care whether it is born in a manger or in the open air. We do know that this offer is free for all, and open to all competitors. Those who are thinking seriously of having one will do well to grasp at this offer. We will now adjourn to the viands. Eat hearty: and remember to think how fine it would be to eat all your meals under your own vine and fig tree with the mocking bird carolling outside and the soft breezes from the Pacific fanning your brow."

The lunch was a grand rush for sandwiches, coffee, cake and fruit, together with a quantity of red wine. Many of the Middle Westerners shied violently at the latter; others partook of it with an air of guilty bravado; but there is no doubt it added a pleasing exotic tinge to the occasion. People circulated freely, and talked. It became known that Carstair, who had bought the first lot, was the richest man in St. Paul; and that one of the men who had bid against him was Patrick Boyd, the traction magnate. Carstair soon recognized his fellow plutocrats and joined them. The quartette stood in a loose group, smoking their cigars, while an awe-stricken fringe—of which naturally they were unconscious—hung around, silently gathering wisdom. Carstair was an obese and rather pompous man.

"I think well of the property," he stated ponderously, in answer to a question. As a matter of fact he had not thought of the property at all until that morning, when he had come out to oblige his friend—and on the strength of free ride, free lunch, and a possibility of free profits. But it would never do to let anybody think that Carstair would take a snap for chicken feed, nor that Carstair would buy anything on impulse, nor without due and weighty deliberation. "Los Angeles," he went on, "is certain to have a great future; and this tract is situated in a particularly fortunate location."

"The soil is excellent." remarked Saxon, solely on the basis of a soft gopher-digging on which he happened to be standing. He stirred it wisely with his cane.

"Ought to grow good oranges here," said Oberman, vaguely. He knew nothing of oranges or their needs; but he did remember seeing orange trees growing out of the ground somewhere. This was also ground.

"You can't do much with one fifty-foot lot," observed Boyd.

"You forget I have the privilege of taking the next two lots at the same price," replied Carstair.

The remark was purely defensive; but a buzz took through the crowd the information that Carstair was buying the adjoining lots as well. Judging now that the conditions were right, the auctioneer again mounted the block.

The bidding started in well. Several lots were sold to outsiders at approximately the same prices. To the surprise of his companions Saxon suddenly began to bid. He procured a lot at two hundred and ten dollars.

"I'll take the rest of the block at the same price, if you'll let it go," he announced. "No use going in unless you get a piece big enough to count as an investment," he told his companions.

The auctioneer pretended to consult for some time with his principal.

"In my opinion," he stated at length, "this is too low a price for so large a piece of property. But my owner says to let it go to Mr. Charles Saxon, not because he is the celebrated New York capitalist of that name, but because he had sense enough to see the chance to make money on a sure thing. Sold to Mr. Saxon, all of Block C."

Thus encouraged the bidding became brisk. By the time the sun had reached the west fully a quarter of the property had been sold to bonafide purchasers, and only a few lots had been by circumstances forced into fake sales to cappers. The owner was already ahead of the game. The auctioneer too was pleased, for his commissions were fat. After announcing that the sale would be continued from map in the down town office, he called it a day.

On the drive back to town Scott and Oberman joked Saxon unmercifully over his purchase: telling him that he was either a hick to be stampeded by a band and oratory, or that he slavishly followed the lead of the St. Paul magnate. Saxon good humouredly defended himself.

"I've seen worse hunches than to follow Carstair," he said. "But it doesn't need a seventh son to see that that stuff is good. It's bound to go up; and I never had any objections to making my expenses on a trip."

The next morning the men came together in the lobby of the hotel. They were smoking their after breakfast cigars, and they felt leisurely and expansive. Somebody wondered what they had best do to pass the time.

"Let's go around to the Banksia office and see what it looks like there," suggested Saxon.

They laughed at him, accusing him of being anxious about his new purchase; but each had a secret urge to the same effect.

The offices of the Banksia Heights, even at this early hour, seemed very busy. There were a number of well-dressed people standing around reading the paper, or staring rather idly at the huge tract map that hung on the blank side of the wall. A half-dozen others were leaning over the counter talking earnestly to the clerks. Some of them were genuine buyers completing or adding to their purchases of the day before; while still others had never even seen the tract, but were nevertheless just picking 'em from the map. Saxon led his friends to the big chart; where, after some trouble, he identified his own property. The pieces sold were coloured red; those reserved for schools, engine houses, and other public purposes were marked in blue. After some study Saxon decided that his block was exceptionally well situated.

In the meantime Colonel Carstair had trundled in and, without looking to right or left, had steered to the counter.

"Young man," he said impressively to the youth who hurried forward. "I want to see your employer in person. Carstair is the name, James Carstair of St. Paul."

The roomful of people stopped short what they were doing, and gazed curiously and respectfully at the owner of this redoubted name. The tract owner hastened from his inner office all smiles without, and somewhat flurried within. After the first greeting the great man dropped his voice to confidential tones.

"Now about those lots I bid in yesterday," he said. Of course our understanding was that you would hold them for me on a turnover without expense."

"Yes, that's right of course, Mr. Carstair. Glad to do these little things for an old friend," replied the owner, wondering what he was driving at, and a little anxious.

"Well, I've been thinking it over. I like this town, and I believe in its future. I believe those lots are a sound investment. I will take title on them and pay up cash, if I can make the proper terms with you. Of course you understand that I bid them up pretty high yesterday to get your sale started right. Let me in on the ground floor and I'll talk business with you."

The owner's eyes gleamed and his heart leaped in triumph; though he took care to maintain an indifferent exterior.

"It wouldn't do to give you a lower price, you know," said he. "The price—well, I'll tell you. Suppose I give you a commission on the sale. You are really selling to yourself, you know."

A half minute later the interested spectators saw the magnate pull out his check book and apparently buy some more lots.

This impression was confirmed when the owner walked to the map and drew a red cross on the rest of the lots in the block containing Carstair's purchase of the day before.

"I think you ought to protect your investment with the adjoining lots," he had said to Carstair. "I'll just reserve them for a few days until you can make up your mind." But to the bystanders it looked as though the St. Paul banker had actually extended his purchase.

The effect was immediate. A buzz of conversation broke out. Several who had been hesitating made up their minds. Marcus Oberman sidled up and laid a forefinger on the block next that apparently purchased by Carstair.

"How mooch dose lots?" he asked.

Shortly he came back, breathing heavily, having purchased a half block.

"You bed your life Chimmy Carstair he knows," he said.

They drifted out eventually, chaffing each other good-naturedly. The owner, watching from his inside office, called in one of the younger men.

"See that old cuss that went out?" he asked. "Well, did you notice the gang he was with? All right. The Dutchman has half of Block E, and the little fellow with the sandy moustache has all of Block C. The Dutchman is Marcus Oberman, the brewer; and the little fellow is Charley Saxon. You look up the Judge and sick him on them. Tell him to buy back one or the other of their holdings; I don't care which. Tell him to offer four hundred per lot; but to raise 'em to five or six, if he has to. Get busy."

So it happened that Marcus Oberman sold half his lots that evening at the same price he had given for all of them. The purchaser was a very eminent looking jurist, who was a fine testimonial to the Banksia Height's owner's ability to pick types. It was the brewer's turn to crow; and he took full advantage of it in a ponderous fashion. Everybody in the dining room, the lobby and the bar heard all about it. The rumour quickly spread that "Banksia" is selling on the outside.

Just for curiosity, he told himself, Boyd drifted around to the real estate office the following morning. The place was

crowded. He pushed his way to the counter and authorita-
tively signalled the owner, who happened—just happened—to
pop out of his cubby hole as the traction man approached.

"How much are lots this morning?" he demanded.

"The very choicest ones are gone. There is a big demand.
But we are still selling all alike for two hundred and fifty
dollars."

Boyd looked at the chart. Its red patches were now labelled
prominently with the names of the purchasers. All the centre
part around the block controlled by Carstair had been sold out.

"Well, I'll take a flyer on those two lots in Block I," he said,
drawing out his check book.

His companions caught him at it, and chaffed him unmercifully.

"I'm just taking it for a little turn," he explained. "I like
to make my expenses. Can't lose much.. It's fun to play the
game. Look here: George is the only one of us not in this.
Aren't you going to sit in the game, George? Going to be the
only one out?"

They turned their batteries on George Scott. He was in the
minority. Soon he threw up his hands.

"All right, all right! I'll buy one of the damn things."
He studied the map, then made his way to the counter. "I'll
take one lot next Mr. Boyd's in I," he said. The clerk filled in
the contract of sale. Scott looked at it. "See here, young
man," he cried. "You've got this all wrong. You're charging
me four hundred dollars."

"Yes sir, that's the price," said the young man.

Scott raised an indignant protest. The owner came out of his
little office.

"The price of lots has been raised throughout," he told Scott.
"We did not intend to do so; but we find that already the cen-·
tral lots are selling like blazes outside. The market and the
demand warrants it. Ah, Mr. Boyd, you got your lots not a
moment too soon. I'll give you a hundred dollars profit on them
and take them back."

But Boyd would not sell. He had fooled George Scott to the
tune of considerable money, and he was very much pleased. He

chaffed Scott without pity, and fairly forced him to complete the bargain at the new price.

"You won't regret it, Mr. Scott," consoled the owner. "I'll predict you can sell it to-morrow at an advance, if you want to."

Boyd spent three more days in Los Angeles, then returned to Arguello, his head full of thoughts. The Banksia Heights scheme he discovered to be only one of many: and all going strong. In fact the Banksia proposition, as one of the youngest, could hardly be said to be fairly started. The suburban land was almost entirely in the hands of outsiders, who were exploiting it. The original owners had sold out gladly at what they had considered excessive prices. They had held so long that they were about ready to quit in disgust; and they could not take the money quick enough, nor get away fast enough after they had taken it, lest the "tenderfoot" change his mind. The said tenderfoot then proceeded to make a thousand or so per cent. In due time the original holder grew restless and desirous of getting in on a little of this easy money. No reason why he should be out in the cold! So he bought back—sometimes the very land he had sold—for ten, yes, twenty times what he had received for it. And was left with it when the boom broke!

But that was a later development. Now everybody was prosperous because prices were steadily going up, and cash sales were the order of the day. Therefore everybody made money, and had the gold to jingle. Farmers were abandoning their crops to live in town and gamble on real estate. Why not? It was no unusual thing to make a profit between nine o'clock and dinner time. Very little work was being done anywhere. Why work, when you could make a month's wages in an hour, if you just looked sharp? But you could not do it unless you were on the spot. New sales were attended as women go to bargain counters. One trick was to sell half an addition, and then to close the sale; reserving the balance until such time as the outside trading should have raised the public temperature. At the reopening it would be announced that the first ten lots would be sold for, say, $750, after which the flat price would be $1,000. Buy now and make $250. Long lines were formed awaiting the openings of these resales. Places near the head of

the lines often commanded a high price. Buyers hired repre-
sentatives to hold places for them: often one man would have
two or three such proxies. They had to be visited often to see
that they did not sell out to a rival. It often happened that a
place near the head would sell out to a place near the foot at a
price representing what would have been a good profit had a lot
been bought.

Twenty-five foot lots were sold. Nothing could be built on a
twenty-five foot lot: it needed at least one more of its own kind
alongside before it could be of any practical good. But some
genius discovered that the public did not think in terms of dimensions but of units; and would buy a twenty-five foot lot as
quickly and at nearly the same price as one twice as wide.

New additions adopted all sorts of methods to get hold of their
first clientele. Elephants and other menagerie animals were
used in processions. Often a mass meeting for some worthy or
patriotic cause was called, and the business seriously transacted,
merely to get the crowd for an after meeting in favour of some new
real estate scheme. Here originated the old, old story of the
funeral, when the clergyman asked if any one would like to make
a few remarks in eulogy of the deceased. As usual everybody
was bashful. After a short pause a stranger arose. "As no one
seems inclined to say anything," said he, "I'll just fill in the time
by telling you of a new addition." Or a sort of lottery idea was
used: as for example that all buyers should pay the same price,
and then should draw for their land. There were few sales that
called for complete payment, though all demanded cash down.
Contracts were given with a third paid. Unless a purchaser
were known he had to pay in hard dollars. There was no time
to cash checks, when the lot might be resold at an advance before the ink dried. For the same reason deeds were rarely re-
corded.

At first, at the time of Boyd's visit, these town lots were
staked out in the suburbs of actual towns. It was conceivable,
if not possible, that some day or another they might be occupied.
At any rate some sort of a city would always exist near there.
But very shortly such foolish conservatism was abandoned.
Two things only were necessary to a city—climate and scenery.

The little white stakes began to appear in the most unheard of places, miles from any building, absolutely isolated, deprived of any of the natural advantages necessary to human dwelling. But the climate and scenery were good. There were parcels laid aside for the Station, and the Post Office, and the City Hall, and the Court House, and the High School, and heaven knows what else, and people bought the rest in twenty-five foot lots, and the jack rabbits sat under the sagebrush and looked lonesome and wondered what were all those little white stakes.

No bit of country, within the natural habitat of· the tourist, was so unpromising, that it could not be sold. It if were a dry wash, they boosted it for its abundance of building material; if in a desert, for its healthful climate; if on a hilltop for its view; if in a swamp for its irrigable possibilities or its opportunities for a harbour. Men would start actual construction on a railroad and carry it forward for miles, knowing perfectly well that it never could pay, aware indeed that they never would finish it, merely in order to help sell land at its alleged terminal-to-be! And they sold them. Why not? The one certain thing was that the East had at last waked up to the fact that it could live in an ideal climate instead of shivering and roasting in the horrible imitation heretofore provided it. Why should any sane man live where he was uncomfortable, when he could live where he was comfortable? No reason. A tremendous shift of population was imminent.

At first some of this land had been bought by people who intended to build houses and live on it. But latterly it was all purchased for resale at a profit —to the mythical fellow who was coming after.

IV

IN SUCH lively times a space of six months may seem like the passage of years, so far as the stabilizing of conditions goes. It was so in 'Forty-nine; events moved so rapidly that in a half year they had become ancient history. So it was now. After a year of this sort of thing it took unto itself an aspect of permanence. It was the natural condition of life. People living in it came to look on it as the normal and enduring. They called it

prosperity: and it was only to be expected, for this was a prosperous country. Everybody was idle, and full of money, and
happy. The streets were full. People moved about buoyantly,
greeting each other, trading, exchanging wisdom. They stood
on the street corners and in the lobbies of the hotels, with expensive cigars in the corners of their mouths, their thumbs tucked
in the armholes of their vests. There were a good many heavy
watchchains and diamonds. New buggies were flashing about.
The streets were perpetually lively with processions of one
sort or another—decorated and placarded loads of lumber for
the new hotel, escorted by a band: visiting celebrity who has
bought property, escorted by a band; announcement of new
addition, escorted by a band, and so on. Millionaires of a day,
in Van Dyke's expressive phrase; who were yesterday living in
little outlying ranches or on windswept farms of the Middle
West.

Most of them had acquired titles of one sort or another—
Judge, Colonel, General, an occasional humble Captain, and all
had gained the respect that goes with money and position.
Their opinions were listened to and considered of value. And
the people were buying potatoes brought down from Humboldt
County, eggs imported from east of the Rockies, meat from Chicago, butter from Oregon. Their orchards and fields were growing up to mallow and mustard. Why work when you can hire
somebody else to do it for you?

These new-made magnates were firm in their optimism. Why
shouldn't they be? They were millionaires. To be sure they
had not the background of experience that comes with most
millions: they had not the habit of making considered judgments. Those who had always lived in the country knew nothing of city growths: and those who had always lived in the city
were densely ignorant of natural resources or, indeed, whether
beans grew in the ground or on trees.

"Don't it just beat hell!" they marvelled; and then loyally
answered themselves that it did beat hell, and everything else
this side of heaven, naturally, because it was California. It was
a normal development, to be expected if you stopped and looked
things squarely in the face. The only reason it seemed surprising

was that nobody had happened to look things squarely in the face. An occasional shrewd old Yankee felt it was due his traditional sagacity to inquire how long it was going to last.

"Last," they cried, astonished; "why we're just getting into our normal stride. The outside world is just beginning to realize what there is here."

"Well, it certainly is wonderful," the Yankee would hasten to say. But that was not sufficient.

"Wonderful?" they repeated. "I don't think so. Why do you call it wonderful? The only wonderful thing is that it's taken so long for the world to find us out."

Every man carried a long checkbook that stuck out of his breast pocket. One of the favourite gestures of emphasis was to flap this checkbook impressively against the leg or the palm of the hand. A large benign dignity informed the intercourse of the new millionaires.

All this had its effect on those who at first had taken the business too seriously. Owners of tracts began to go crazy and to believe in their own projects. They turned back their money into building huge hotels that could never be filled, casinos, hot springs resorts, any number of gim-cracks to catch the tourist trade. In many instances they borrowed on the money still due them. It will be remembered that most sales were made at a quarter or a third down. There was plenty of money in the banks: just as there was plenty of money—not wealth—everywhere. The oldtimers borrowed it, too, on the security of their lands; and bought town lots because they did not want these strangers to get all the bacon.

There were still some few sane ones, and some partially sane. Fortunately for California many of the former class were in the banks. The semi-sane were business men, conservatives—in the East—who had sense enough to see that this condition could not last forever, but who thought they could guess to a gnat's hair just when the top would be reached. In the meantime they were going to cash in. These wise persons did not stand on the street corners with their thumbs in their armholes: they sat about little tables in the backs of barrooms, and talked in low tones. Most of their talk was in giving reasons to one another of why the top was not coming until next year. When the time came, they intended to get out.

Very few saw the basic facts, or took the trouble to think down to them. Nine tenths of the buyers of real estate were purchasing not for use, but to sell at an advance. The same piece of property cannot go on selling and advancing forever. Since most of these purchases were made on a comparatively small payment, it follows that the moment prices should recede, even a little, most of them would have to be thrown back on the market to render possible the payment of the balances due.. There had been more town lots sold than could be settled upon in twenty years, even if every available passenger car on all the railroads were to run westward filled to capacity. But back of it all was the hard fact that they were selling climate and scenery, and there was enough of a supply of climate and scenery to break any market in the world.

CHAPTER VII

I

BOYD returned to Arguello on the *Santa Rosa* very thoughtful. He was too shrewd, too experienced, too well balanced to be swept off his feet. The situation, once he had drawn aside from the glamour, was plain enough to him. Two things he realized thoroughly. The first was that this epidemic was sure to reach Arguello sooner or later, and when it hit it would hit hard. The second was that until the boom broke, and until genuine prosperity had had a chance to struggle to its feet after being knocked flat by the explosion, his irrigated twenty-thirty acre farm scheme was as dead as Pharaoh. Few people were thinking farm.

He debarked in the early morning and drove up the long main street behind a leisurely livery horse. The high fog, also leisurely, was drawing away, permitting glimpses of the mountains. Along the street shopkeepers, or their assistants, were sweeping their sidewalks. As yet no business could be expected, although it was after nine o'clock. Near the First National Bank building stood the street car, its motive power dozing with dangled ears, the reins wound around the brake handle, the driver absent on some mysterious errand of his own. After the feverish atmosphere of Los Angeles there seemed here to dwell an ineffable peace. Even Patrick Boyd's practical spirit felt its influence; though, characteristically, he misinterpreted it and was impatient with it.

"*Mañana, mañana!*" he muttered disgustedly. "If I don't watch out, it'll get me, too. Here, driver, I won't go home. Let me out at Spinner's office."

The lank, birdlike real estate man listened with gleaming eyes to Boyd's analysis of what he had seen.

"Now we'll get it," Boyd concluded. "And we can hurry it along if we want to. We have my foothill land already. Get that laid out in some sort of shape and have a map made of it. Keep out the quarry, though; I don't want to lose that. But I don't want to start in on the foothill tract. Everybody knows that I own it. But if somebody comes in from outside, a stranger, and buys up a lot of land and has faith and enthusiasm and all the rest of it, why that will count a lot. From what I've seen, you can sell anything anywhere, once you get them started, but you got to begin with something reasonable. I own most of that abutting to the east on the foothills; and Colonel Peyton all of the north boundary. Naturally we can't sell the Pacific Ocean. I'm going to bring in a good man from below to pick up something on the south or a strip of Peyton's. That'll do to start her off."

"There are plenty of vacant lots right in town now," Spinner pointed out.

"Yes, and they're more expensive. Why pay city lot prices when you can get acreage? They'll buy lots in an addition quicker than scattered stuff inside."

Boyd also saw Dan Mitchell with whom he had a serious and confidential talk. The result was a sudden accession of items and articles on the prosperity that had struck California. There were a good many alluring statistics having to do with the number of tourists coming in, the number of land sales made, and especially the phenomenal rises in values and the fortunes that had been made therefrom. Under the impulse of these, of the reports brought by returned visitors to the south, and especially by the tourists, Arguello began to stir in her sleep. And, aware of that fact, the boomers commenced to drift in and look about and lay their plans.

Boyd was too shrewd to attempt to monopolize. He knew that up to a certain point rivals were a good thing. They made a noise: they all got in and pushed; their numbers helped work up the excitement. He contented himself by being a little more ready than they were; a little more thoroughly conversant with the local situation; with possessing the tracts—lying as they did on the foothills—that were intrinsically the most worth while.

Spinner was as busy as a cat with two tails. Boyd was giving him a fat commission and carte blanche to go as far as he liked. The only proviso was that the professional from Los Angeles should have a week's start in placing Boyd's other tract— of which his ownership was secret—on the market. Thus did the boom come to Arguello.

II

ALL Boyd's plans went well, except as respects one minor ·detail. It would have been very desirable to have been able to control a few acres north of town, simply because the natural growth of the town seemed to go in that direction. Which meant, of course, a strip off Corona del Monte. Knowing Colonel Peyton's situation financially, he thought it would be a simple matter. He wanted not more than a hundred acres or two, while Corona del Monte covered square miles. The Colonel ought to jump at the chance.

Ephraim Spinner came back from the interview his eyes standing out in astonishment.

"He's on, boss," he reported; "I didn't give him credit for so much sense."

"What do you mean?"

"Why, he wouldn't listen to me," said Spinner. "I never had a show. He was most God-awful polite, but I felt like a worm that was being laughed at and not supposed to know it. I worked up to the limit on him that you gave me."

"Probably you offered too much at the start," suggested Boyd.

"Now, boss!" pleaded Spinner, hurt to the quick. "You got to give me credit for knowing *something!*"

"I beg your pardon. I know you do. And he wouldn't sell even at a hundred an acre?"

"Wouldn't even listen. I thought he was dead asleep out there among his cows and pigs: but he must be wide awake. Nobody else in this town has a suspicion of anything coming— except this old dodo."

"You think he suspects he can get more?"

"Now I leave it to you. That kind of ranch land never sold before for more than ten or fifteen dollars. Never! And everybody knows the Colonel is hard up and needs money. And that little strip next to town don't affect his ranch one way or another, now does it? I leave it to you."

Boyd made some answer and dropped the subject. That is, in conversation. He still retained the idea. It was by no means certain that he had done a wise thing in allowing Spinner to approach the old man. The Colonel was touchy. Boyd had not much patience with that type of highfalutin' touchiness; but he had met it in his experience, and he understood it and knew how to handle it. Spinner would not know how at all; indeed, he would probably blunder blithely ahead ignorant that he was trampling down anything. Perhaps he had rubbed the Colonel the wrong way. Or it might be that Spinner was correct, that the old man was shrewd enough to foresee the boom. Boyd gravely doubted this; but it was a possibility. In that case he might have to split the profits. Anyway, he'd better see Colonel Peyton himself.

As he drove up the Avenue of Palms his eye took in the evidence that all things were not as prosperous as they had been. It was with the greatest confidence that he opened the interview. Allie and Sing Toy were performing some mysterious cleaning rites in the house, so the Colonel and his guest sat on a settee beneath the great live oak trees. Colonel Peyton listened (in silence) to Boyd's proposal to buy a strip containing approximately two hundred acres next the town limits.

"Mr. Spinner approached me with a similar proposal some days back," said he. "I told him I was not interested."

Boyd laughed.

"That was my mistake, Colonel. I sent him. I thought you might prefer to deal through an agent. Spinner is able and enthusiastic, but I can well imagine he might get off on the wrong foot. I can assure you he really meant nothing by whatever he said or did that offended you."

"But he did not offend me," cried the Colonel.

"But he says you wouldn't listen to any further proposition on his part."

"No. I told him I did not wish to sell at any price; so naturally it was useless for him to proceed."

Boyd could not quite make out the situation; though he thought he was beginning to see.

"Have a cigar, Colonel?" he proposed, to gain time to consider. "No? Mind if I smoke? Well, of course any one can see that a piece of that size and shape isn't ranch property. Arguello is going to grow; and the logical direction of growth is out this way. I suppose you naturally would expect to get more than ranch acreage prices: and on second thought I don't know why you shouldn't. I'm not going to pretend to haggle with you, Colonel. I'll give you a hundred dollars an acre flat for that piece."

"But, sir, you misapprehend——" began the Colonel; but Boyd held up his hand.

"Let me finish. I was about to add a quarter interest in the net profits on the tract." He was not about to add this: but he read refusal in the Colonel's first word, and so hastened to raise his bid.

"But, Mr. Boyd, I really have no desire to sell any portion of the ranch."

"Now listen, Colonel. This piece is not really a part of the ranch. There aren't a dozen cattle a year stray over that way. I've ridden about nearly every day and I don't believe I've seen that many in *two* years."

"It's too near town for wild cattle," explained the Colonel. "My men keep them driven back as far as possible."

"There! What did I tell you! That strip isn't any good at all to you! And it would make ideal residence sites. As acreage it isn't worth fifteen dollars, and you know that perfectly well. But I am offering you twenty thousand dollars in cash, and a quarter interest in the net profits."

"Mr. Boyd," broke in the Colonel. "I am sorry to interrupt you, but I must repeat——"

"Now, wait a minute, Colonel, let me finish before you come to any decision. That quarter interest in the net profits does not sound like much. But I am just back from the Los Angeles district, and let me tell you we are going to have a boom here that will open your eyes. I have the reputation of being a conservative business man, and I assure you that I fully expect before I have finished with that piece of land to net from a hundred and fifty to two hundred thousand dollars. I know it sounds foolish, but I am certain it is not."

"I cannot follow the figuring of you modern financiers," smiled the Colonel. "I must confess it sounds a trifle optimistic."

"I'll tell you what I'll do," urged Boyd, whose plans came nearer to half a million, all told, than to the figure he named. "I'll guarantee personally that inside of a reasonable time, say eighteen months, your share will come to forty thousand dollars —that's in addition to the purchase price. Come on: go in partnership! We'll clean up!"

"I appreciate your offer, Mr. Boyd, though I can't quite follow your figures," began the Colonel.

"You don't need to—remember I'm guaranteeing," Boyd reminded him.

"Yes, I understand that; and I'm grateful to your offer of partnership. Your reputation as a man of affairs is quite familiar to me. But I really mean what I say: I do not wish to sell any of the Rancho."

"That is a pretty liberal offer. It is really the best any business man could do. I take all the risk, you must remember; and, of course, do the actual managing of the deal. What I have offered is really the highest price the deal could justify on its merits."

"Oh, Mr. Boyd!" cried the Colonel, in a panic of deprecation. "You must not misunderstand me! I am not attempting to haggle for higher terms. Those are almost too liberal, it seems to me. But I do not care to sell."

Boyd's heavy brows came together.

"Would you mind telling me why—since it is not the price?"

At his tone the Colonel's more delicate brows went up slightly.

"I have owned the Rancho de la Corona del Monte for more than thirty years, sir," he replied politely. "It is a property that it pleases me to retain intact."

Boyd restrained a movement of exasperation, and by an effort regained control of himself.

"Where can you find anywhere a piece of land that will

bring anything approaching that return, and at the same time take so little from the ranch as a ranch?" he asked.

"Nowhere, sir. I acknowledge that," replied the Colonel. "That is not the question."

"But sooner or later you will have to find such a piece."

Colonel Peyton stiffened.

"Why did you say that, sir?"

"Come, Colonel, you know as well as I do that the time is not far distant when you must raise some money, and a good sum of money, to keep you afloat. There's no use our trying to fool each other. Here I'm offering you the chance of a lifetime to get squared away. You can't go on renewing mortgages forever, you know!"

"I find, sir, you appear too conversant with my private affairs," said Colonel Peyton, stiffly.

"I am an official in the First National Bank," Boyd pointed out, "and I am saying nothing that I do not know legitimately."

"Sir," rejoined Colonel Peyton. "I regret to seem discourteous to a guest, but I must remind you that officially, as you call it, you are concerned only with whether I pay my interest on the appointed dates. That, I believe, has been done."

"And with whether you pay the principal on the appointed dates, too," added Boyd, rising. "Don't forget that."

The Colonel bent his brows down on the shorter man.

"Am I to construe that as a threat, sir?" he demanded, coldly.

Boyd's face flushed and his neck swelled. He was not a man patiently to brook opposition at any time; but unreasonable and purposeless opposition like this was beyond all credence.

"I am not interested in constructions," he snapped. "I am stating facts it would be well to keep in mind before you turn down your chance. Look up the dates of your mortgages, I advise you, before you decide. I'll give you two days. I'll send Spinner for your answer."

"That will be quite useless, sir," replied the Colonel, icily. "You can have my answer now. I do not care to sell. And permit me to call your attention to the fact that it is the custom for bank officials to give notice of due mortgages by mail."

Boyd drove down the avenue in a glow of righteous anger.

He really felt that he had been hardly used. He had offered the old fool a chance to pull himself out of the hole, get on his feet, with no cost to himself. It had been a generous offer. Not only had this offer been refused unreasonably, but it had been refused ungraciously. That was how Boyd felt about it. His own attitude throughout the interview seemed to him eminently business-like and reasonable. By the time he had reached Ephraim Spinner's office he was boiling mad.

"I apologize to you," he informed the real estate man. "I thought you'd bungled the deal with old Peyton, but I take it back. Of all the unreasonable, short-sighted, pig-headed old fossils I ever came in contact with! Why, if I had a hound dog that couldn't size up his own situation and see the point of an open-and-shut proposition better, I'd tie a rock to him and drop him off the wharf!"

"I figured you'd tackle him yourself," grinned Spinner. "Glad of it. Now you know."

"Yes, now I know!" growled Boyd. "But he don't know— yet. He's a blight on the community, that fellow. Talk about your dog in the manger! He's holding up the development of Arguello worse than a dozen earthquakes! Has the whole north side of town blocked from further growth! Has some of the best farm land in the world, with thousands of people yelling for farms, and he sits on it like a toad! It ought not to be allowed!" He tramped up and down the little office chewing the end of a cigar that had gone out. Boyd was fully persuaded of what he was saying. No realization entered his head that the mainspring of his present anger and his future activity in this particular case was merely opposition, which always aroused his ruthless fighting spirit. He stared unseeing at a lithograph on the wall; then after a moment turned with a short laugh. "Well, nothing to be done there just now. Time's too short." He went on to give some directions as to the new additions.

III

THE boom hit Arguello; and Arguello took it just as hard as the rest of the country, once it had thoroughly awakened. It suffered all the usual symptoms, as detailed in previous pages. People bought and sold lots they had never seen, the very location of which was unknown to them. Such things as abstracts of title became totally unnecessary. Somebody soon discovered that it was equally unnecessary to bother with the pretty white stakes to mark out the lots: very few people went to look at them. It was much simpler just to have a map and mark off the lots sold.

It is not part of the purpose of this story to follow in detail the progress of the boom in Arguello. With two exceptions all the people we know were in it, some of them up to their necks. The two exceptions were Colonel Peyton and Brainerd. As a consequence they were looked upon with pity or derision or contempt as not knowing a good thing when they saw it. They were considered reactionary.

For the first time in its history Main Street was crowded. It seemed that the entire country must have poured its population in; and certainly the influx from outside made a record. The "talking point" with Arguello was her present lack of a railroad. As soon as the railroad was put through, then people would be certain to pour in, for where in the wide world could you find another such sun-kissed, ocean-washed, island-guarded, mountain-girdled paradise? There might be many mansions in another paradise, but the number of town lots was limited in this.

On Main Street one was certain to see everybody one knew. They stood on the edge of the broad walk absorbing sunshine and prosperity; they strolled the length between the Fremont and the wharf, dropping in at all the tract offices to see what was doing; they darted in and out of places, busier in appearance than any one could possibly be, each according to his temperament. The *Sociedad* moved over in a body, leaving its cattle to Mexican foremen, and gambled briskly. There was the greatest difficulty in getting the necessary work done. Men who had been digging on the sewer extension last week, now carried their checkbooks and leaned nonchalantly against the lamp posts, swapping wisdom as to the country's future. Had it not been for the Chinese, who cared nothing for booms, it is difficult to see how the necessary chores would have been done. At every trip from the north the *Santa Rosa* brought a cargo of supplies that ought to have been provided at home. Prices naturally rose; but nobody cared. Ephraim Spinner was in the twentieth plane of bliss. He believed in it literally—the millions of future population and all the rest. When he sold a lot, he sold it sincerely. His optimism and his energy seemed to know no limits.

Patrick Boyd rode the storm serenely. He was throughout one of the few who did not lose his head. From his additions he made a great sum of money; some of which he reinvested in other lots with which to gamble. But he knew he was gambling; and he estimated the chances very coolly. He recognized the immense value of Spinner's enthusiasm and energy; so he turned over to that young man the handling—but not the direction of the handling—of all his real estate ventures. Realizing that no mere commission basis would uphold any man's loyalty after the thing got going he gave Spinner an interest in the business. After that he paid no more attention to the selling end of it. Only when it came to buying did he interfere, with the insistance that Spinner should do exactly as he said. Often Spinner would tear his hair over what he stigmatized as over-caution when some tempting bait dangled in vain. But soon, of course, Spinner became a millionaire in his own right; and then, outside the partnership, he dealt at his own sweet will.

But Boyd's chief effort and influence were now otherwise directed. He was willing to gamble with his surplus, but he never lost his head. His experience showed him that the fundamental danger would not be that a certain number of people would go broke, or would not go broke, as the case might be; but in the undue expansion of credit. Sales were made, as has been explained, on the basis of a small down payment; men deep in the game would always desire to spread their money out as thin as possible; the actual cash brought in by the immigration amounted to a very large sum. There could be no doubt that the banks would have much idle money crying for investment; there was also no doubt that there would be a swarm of would-be borrowers. A bank lends on security   Much of the security would undoubtedly be land. There you have the elements of the problem in which Boyd saw danger.

He held a comparatively small block of bank stock, but from this moment he became the storm centre on the board of directors. His policy was simple, and he stuck to it through thick and thin. It was that all land loans should be based on the old valuation before the boom; not one cent more.

There were wild scenes, at times, over this. Men lost their temper in open meeting. They called him reactionary, a coward, a detriment to the county's prosperity, and some more bitter names; but he sat four-square, smiling, unmoved.

"Gentlemen," he would say, "you will do as you please. Your voting power is much in excess of mine. But, remember, it is also your responsibility. You know the value of this land in normal times. I agree that it has probably increased somewhat; but no man can say yet what that increase actually amounts to in permanent value. Until we find out, let's play safe on the old figures. A bank should play safe. In case of necessity a bank must take over the land on which it has lent money. Nothing is more unproductive than land in a bank's hands. We have too much already."

In spite of protest, within and without, this view prevailed. Nobody on the directorate, with the possible exception of Oliver Mills, believed fully with Boyd. Of course a great many of these prices were absurd, still—it must be acknowledged that the county had gone ahead—— But against Boyd's solemn warnings of responsibility they did not quite dare go. Boyd acquired thus a position of great power. He easily took the lead in banking matters: so that his opinion in all things came to prevail with almost the force of command. And since it was felt that in Boyd rested the power of local credit, he was sought after and kow-towed to and hated and cursed—behind his back —until he was thrust by the very upheaval of conflicting forces to a place of towering prominence.

A place of prominence meant more than the possession of money. Everyone had become a capitalist. A million was the unit of measurement. Why not? A man's wealth is the value of his possessions. City lots had risen to fifty and seventy-five thousand dollars apiece. As city lots did not necessarily have anything to do with a city, and as California was a large and vacant place, there was material for countless millionaires. And as if California was not big enough, they were actually slipping over into Mexico! If you own a gravel walk you can be a millionaire on pebbles at a thousand dollars each—until you try to trade them for something else.

At the height of the boom one could come pretty close to trading for something else. The man who had been willing to close out his deals and go home with his cash, would have been genuinely wealthy. A few of them did just that; probably as many as have cashed in their chips at the height of a winning streak and left the casino.

IV

As TIME went on, however, more and more people made up their minds to "clean up and get out." When they came to do so, they found that there must be a shrinkage in the paper values of their holdings. This is the normal thing. But in the present booming market, it made them indignant. They called it "sacrificing," and saw no reason for it. Or they did actually sell out, and found themselves with a good sum of actual money in the bank. They were generally back in the game within a week. Some piece of land they had been watching, or had themselves sold, had gone up, and they could not stay out. It seemed too foolish to let such chances go!

Another still craftier set secretly believed that a set-back was imminent. They talked among themselves wisely of "action and reaction." The boom was bound to burst from overloading. Then the wise guy with ready cash could take his pick of choice property at rock bottom prices; and so would be in on the ground floor when the next boom started, probably within six months. For not one of them but believed that another boom would come, almost immediately. But the collapse could not possibly over-take them before next spring at earliest. The big rush from the East always took place after the holidays. The wealthy people came then; and then our profound student would unload quickly and at magnificent prices.

The very few who not only decided to get out, but to do it now, had to be very strong-minded. Jim Paige was as little as the next inclined to be influenced by another's opinion: but he succumbed.

"Well, well, here's old Jim!" cried Bill Hunter meeting him on the street. "Hear you chucked that lot of yours in Vasquez Street for twenty thousand. It sold yesterday for thirty; and I'll bet she goes to forty. You sure have a poor eye!" and he went on chuckling over the huge joke on old Jim.

George Scott was not so easy on him.

"For God's sake, Paige!" he cried. "Don't you know any better than to spread all this talk on 'cleaning up'? Everybody's talking about it. I don't mind you throwing away your own property, but first thing you know you'll be knocking hell out of the market for the rest of us."

"The rest of you better follow my example," drawled Paige.

"The man who sells anything before spring is crazy," rejoined Scott, briefly. "Stark, staring crazy!"

A real estate man snared him as he sauntered past, and drew him aside for a low-toned coloquy.

"Say, Jim," he confided, "I've fixed it so I can buy in those two lots next your corner on Center Street for forty thousand apiece. Owner was a tourist, lunger, died. How's that for a snap? And only a quarter cash down!"

"I've sold that corner," confessed Jim.

"Sold it! *Sold* it!" cried the real estate man. "My Lord!" and holding up both hands in mock despair he darted away.

Then down the street a little farther he met Doctor Wallace with his black bag. The doctor was a millionaire, of course; but he had to keep in practise as a matter of plain humanity. Only the most pressing cases, however; as too many patients would interfere with business. He, too, drew Jim aside.

"Look here, Jim," he said. "It's only due you that some friend let you know what they're saying about you, so you can deny it. Of course I've been denying it everywhere, and so have all your other friends, but a statement from you is needed to carry the proper weight."

"What they been saying?" demanded Paige, interested.

"Why that you've been selling out," said the doctor in a hushed voice.

"I am," confessed Paige, shamefaced.

The doctor looked him over astoundedly.

"Well, I must hurry out and see Mrs. Robbins. Sudden call,'' he muttered, and disappeared.

Within three days Jim Paige was back in the game.

So it was with dozens of others to whom was vouchsafed a momentary gleam of wisdom. The trend of events was too powerful for them. The dynamic force of the combined thought of so many people swept them back in the current. During their brief absence from the market prices had gone up. An excursion arrived bringing a throng of hungry buyers. Other excursions would be running all winter. Why be content with thousands when one could just as well make a million? Chances such as this come once in a lifetime. Some people thought themselves too wise to be greedy. They were not going to try to squeeze the last dollar from the opportunity: they were going to get enough and then quit. What was enough? Last year it might have been ten thousand dollars: a princely fortune to a small farmer. What was ten thousand, a hundred thousand now? Enough was always just a little more than a man had. Of course one should get out; but next week would be time enough. And next week prices were still rising: it seemed a shame not to make just a few dollars more!

V

AND the end, when it came, stole upon them so gradually that at first they never suspected. People told each other that the market was a little dull, just for this week. They explained nonchalantly that it was always so about the holidays, that the Presidential year had its influence, that at this season the payment of taxes always more or less tied things up by taking money out of circulation, that everybody was holding tight for the rise that was sure to come with the new batches of excursionists. There were a few clear-headed men who saw the point; but they were speedily silenced by loud and wrathful outcries.

"Prices too high!" shrieked the millionaries, turning purple with rage because secretly they also feared. "Such talk as yours would bust any boom. There's no trouble at all, except that there are a lot of idiots like you around talking gloom and pessimism. The market is dull because the prices are going to be *higher*, and people have quit throwing away their property and are holding it for what it is worth!"

Nevertheless all the waverers, the people who had got out and come back in again like Jim Paige, and those who were going to get out but had postponed it until next week, now felt their wisdom stiffened. They returned to their abandoned plans, this time with conviction.

"Say, George," said Jim Paige, accidentally meeting George Scott, after looking for him for two hours. "I've decided to take that offer for my Center Street lots."

Scott changed countenance.

"Oh—I—I thought you'd refused that offer, Jim; and I've used my money elsewhere."

"I might even shade that price," pursued Jim. "I've got another buy in sight that'll make me a mint of money, but I've got to have the cash to swing it. Make me an offer."

"I don't believe I can handle it."

"You wanted it bad enough before. It's the best bargain in town, and you know it. I never knew you to refuse a trade, George."

"Don't want it."

Jim drew nearer.

"You don't think she's broke, do you?" he asked.

George Scott blew up. Of course she hadn't broke. Such talk as that. He stumped off fuming, leaving Jim Paige, very thoughtful, staring after him.

He was typical of many others. They decided to sell enough at least to pay off their debts and deferred payments. They were even willing to do so at a "sacrifice." Lots were offered at 15 per cent. off. At that moment a good many might have been got rid of for 25 per cent. off. Time was wasted finding that out. The reduction of 25 per cent. was made, but by then it was too late. The sellers were always one jump behind in their appreciation of the necessities.

Mrs. Stanley, like everyone else, was a millionaire while the boom lasted; but she was a lady of robust common sense. One morning Patrick Boyd found her gardening near the dividing fence when he came out of his house for his after-breakfast cigar. The sunbonneted, heavy-booted figure waved him imperiously.

"I want you to tell me what's going to happen in this market," she boomed at him.

He looked at her speculatively. They had enjoyed many pitched battles as antagonists; and he liked her.

"I will tell you my opinion, if you will tell me exactly where you stand in it."

"Come into the house," she invited him with instant decision.

They sat for some time in the stiff old-fashioned library examining a land book with alluring figures; a bank book; and an old probate list of securities.

"I see," observed Boyd at last. "If you were to pay up what you owe in contracts, without selling any of the land, it would just about clean out your ready assets, wouldn't it?"

"But of course I don't expect to do that. I expect to sell some land," boomed Mrs. Stanley.

"Then you'd better do so very promptly—if you can," advised Boyd.

Mrs. Stanley looked anxious.

"If I can?" she repeated. "Then you think——Oh, you must tell me all the truth without equivocation, Mr. Boyd. If I lose my income what is to become of me—of my children?" She was genuinely alarmed and distressed. For the first time this grenadier of a woman had lost her complete independence of bearing.

Boyd explained to her the situation as he saw it: and added this:

"I'll do for you what I would do for no other person I know. If you will give me power of attorney, I will see what I can do. But you must understand that all you can expect is to be relieved of the weight of your debts. The only hope of selling at all is at a price to appeal to those who believe another boom will follow this depression."

He got the power of attorney, and a week later made his report. Mrs. Stanley's one million two hundred thousand dollars worth of real estate had been sold to net her—after debts were paid—just ten thousand dollars. She was aghast. It was with the greatest difficulty that she controlled the expression of her face. Boyd smiled at her grimly.

"I know perfectly what you are thinking, Mrs. Stanley," he observed. "I may say that I anticipated it; and it is a matter of indifference to me. I want to call your attention to three things: one is that your original property is intact; the second is that you have made ten thousand dollars out of nothing; and the third is my recommendation to you to observe your friends and see how they come out."

It took Mrs. Stanley a long time to get over the shock, and still longer to come to a realization that she had not been sacrificed. Boyd's third recommendation finally swung her to the truth. Those who decided to sell, as has been said, reduced their prices too slowly to keep down with the dropping demand. They arrived this week where they might have sold last week. And of the few who, as Boyd with Mrs. Stanley's holdings, knew enough to come down to cash prices of from 25 per cent. to 35 per cent. off paper value, many were frustrated by their agents. The latter almost invariably hung on—in secret, of course—hoping to pocket the difference between the old price and the new. Thus time was wasted until it was irretrievably too late.

And now of course money tightened. Huge amounts were still going out for materials on the senseless improvements everywhere being made; greater sums were going for jewels, silks, carriages, furniture, fancy harness and luxuries, long since bought but only now being paid for; and still vaster necessary expenditures for foodstuffs that should have been raised at home. To offset this outflow of cash was one source—the money brought in from outside in the pockets of the tourists. This source suddenly choked up.

And the banks began to press for their money.

Americans are quickly adaptable, and can see the point promptly. They wasted very little time bewailing the situation. Evidently they had to get to work; so to work they got.

A few inconsolables haunted the bars—on draught beer—bewailing their fate; a few optimists continued in the real estate business and posted long lists of property with the caption *Soft Snaps*. But everybody else got to work.

And the commentary on the actual resources of the country is that it successfully absorbed the evils of this feverish time. All the elements were laid for a twenty-year set-back; but as a matter of fact even the ensuing hard times were short, and only moderately hard. The banks had kept their sanity. Not one failed. And one thing was indubitable: the population of the country had been greatly increased. Just as the gold discoveries of 'Forty-nine, disappointing in their promise of universal fortune, nevertheless were a bait that attracted to California its first flood of immigrants; so this boom, insubstantial in itself, did lure to the country tens of thousands who otherwise would not have come, and busted them, and made it necessary that they get to work. And California rewards work lavishly.

CHAPTER VIII

I

AT THE Peyton and Brainerd places things were rather prosperous, on the whole. Neither was involved in the boom. The Colonel did not understand such things, and was not interested: Brainerd's clever brain did understand them and was amused. Partly because of such economies as Allie managed to bring about, but principally because it was one of the few producing concerns in a country stricken with economic idleness, Corona del Monte was a little better than holding its head above the burden of its debt. It could not be expected to do more on mere economies and favourable times; for the fault lay deeper in the fact that its system was of the past. The Bungalow, on the other hand, was showing constantly increasing returns.

Kenneth Boyd, too, avoided being caught up by the boom. Beside the sardonic comment of Brainerd and the frank scepticism of the Colonel, the whole influence of his father was against his becoming in any way involved. Patrick Boyd saw too clearly that this must be only a flash in the pan; and he wished to avoid imbuing Kenneth with wrong habits of thought. Truth to tell little pressure was needed. Kenneth liked the life, with its open air, its open skies. He was intensely interested in what he was doing. He knew and was thoroughly in sympathy with every living creature with whom or with which he worked. In other words he fitted his environment.

The only troubling thought in his mind was the Corona del Monte. Of course he had not the faintest notion that Colonel Peyton was in any financial difficulties. As far as he knew the Rancho was bringing in its accustomed princely living. Only he saw so clearly that it might do better. The weekly "reports" suggested by his father as valuable exercises had long since ceased; but they had continued long enough for Patrick Boyd to learn what he wanted, and for Kenneth Boyd to have formulated his ideas. He saw very clearly where, to his view, the management of the Rancho could be bettered. He used to chafe openly at old extravagant methods, that seemed to him silly, useless, and so easily remedied. Daphne listened to him with both sympathy and amusement.

"I dare say you're right," was her comment, "but the old Rancho has been going along for a good many years that way. It's the Colonel's way."

"But I don't believe the Colonel knows anything about some of these things," persisted Kenneth. "It isn't that such ways give him any particular pleasure or feeling of being used to them: only his attention just hasn't been called to them. If he noticed them, he'd change them."

"Well, why don't you mention some of them to him and see what he says?" suggested Daphne.

"I don't quite feel like that—it looks rather cocky, a kid of my age giving him advice."

Daphne surveyed him amusedly.

"Since when has the fount of all wisdom begun to go dry?" she enquired.

Kenneth flushed, but turned to her eagerly.

"Oh, say! Honest Injin!" he cried. "Has it struck you that I've been too fresh about things? I suppose that I have shot off my face an awful lot. It isn't that I'm stuck on my ideas so much, really it isn't! I'm just interested and full of it. Do you think your father thinks I'm too fresh?"

In spite of his twenty-three years he looked very boyish, his sunburned forehead wrinkled in anxiety below his close cropped curls, his clear eyes appealing for her opinion. A tide of maternal, tender amusement rose in Daphne's heart. She felt, for a moment, mature and wise and yearning beyond all expression.

"What nonsense!" she reassured him, briskly. "That wasn't what I meant at all, and you know it! But I shouldn't hesitate for a moment to mention anything I saw to Colonel Peyton.

He's the dearest, most human old soul in the universe; and would be glad to hear what you have to say."

But Kenneth's clear brain had showed him something.

"It wouldn't do any good," he said. "It isn't patch work I would do, I suppose. It just strikes me that if I owned the ranch I'd run the whole thing on a different scheme."

"Tell me how you'd do it. Let's pretend. Dolman is great on making believe." They were seated on the lower limb of Dolman's House, a frequent haunt of theirs. "Now if Corona del Monte were yours, what would you do?"

Kenneth elaborated, his enthusiasm growing as he proceeded. His ideas, which might in ordinary circumstances have been haphazard and fragmentary, had been well-ordered by his former "reports" to his father. Daphne took fire. Her quick, eager, suggestive comments were caught up by Kenneth avidly. Sometimes they both talked at once. Sometimes they argued heatedly on opposite sides. Sometimes they had wonderful inspirations that were entirely new and that struck them momentarily dumb with admiration of their splendour. It was creation: as in childhood the building of cities. They finished rather breathlessly, staring at each other with brightened eyes. Then they both laughed.

"You see!" Daphne pointed out. "It's a fine scheme. And I believe it would work out, too. But it isn't the old Del Monte the least bit in the world. The Colonel wouldn't change all his life-time habits."

"I suppose that's true," conceded Kenneth, reluctantly. He grinned. "I really believe he was secretly a little relieved when the well fizzled, though he pretended nobly."

Daphne chuckled. "So you had that idea, too?"

The attempt for artesian water had failed. All that remained as souvenir was the piped hole and a little pile of borings on the side of the knoll.

"But," she went on, her imagination rekindling, "wouldn't you just *love* to have a big ranch like the Del Monte to do just as you pleased with?"

"I should like it better than anything else in the world," replied Kenneth, earnestly. "And some day I'm going to have it."

He meant that he intended some day to have such a ranch, and in this sense Daphne now understood him. But a time was to come when his speech was to return to torment her.

II

THE next fifteen months passed. Arguello was jogging along again, but not quite as before. Its spirit was no more progressive than in the old days, but the force of circumstances had raised its normal. The railroad was in at last, subject still to delay of washout or avalanche, where it crept under the cliffs or tunnelled through the mountains, but nevertheless arriving every once in a while. The receding wash of the boom had left rich spoil in the shape of settlers. The little white stakes that bounded the old corner lots still marked the graves of departed hopes, but more and more of them were being ploughed under each year. Men talked in terms not of profits, but of production. And Patrick Boyd knew that at last the time had come for him to forward his old scheme of irrigated small farms.

The idea had expanded: and curiously enough the cause of expansion was the failure of the experimental artesian well at Corona del Monte. Boyd now visioned a big water project in the Sur. During the rains water in plenty flowed back in the fastnesses of the ranges. It was possible to impound it and lead it down into the valley. Furthermore, Boyd saw a possibility of hydro-electricity, then quite a new thought. By means of suitable conduits this water could be widely distributed—over the sagebrush foothills of Boyd's original purchase, for example. To be sure most of that land belonged now in small bits to hundreds of would-be millionaires; but it could be repurchased at a song through Spinner. That young man, by the way, owned some of it: he was one of the chastened ex-millionaires. There were also other properties that would come in under such a development. But it could not be denied that the broad acres of Corona del Monte were the foundation of the scheme. Their proximity to town, their topographical character, and a dozen other considerations made them the keystone of the arch. With them the scheme was worth millions both to its originator and to the community. Without them it was still worth going into, but could not promise such rich pickings.

Boyd had long since little by little gathered the details of his project and worked them out on paper. His consulting engineers had ridden with him over all the ground. His preliminary surveys, even, had been made fairly under the noses of the Arguellans. If any of them saw the surveyors, it never occurred to them to be curious as to what it was all about. People were always running about with transits. His tables of costs were very complete, all things considered.

At the proper time a thin, gray-faced, tight-lipped silent man came to visit at the Boyd household. Nobody knew who he was, nor took more than a passing interest in him; for his personality was unobtrusive, he rarely opened his head, and he never stirred abroad except on horseback accompanied by his host. They knew him as Mr. Brown. Even Kenneth, retaining still his sleeping quarters in the house, knew—and cared—no more. But if the stranger's incognito had been guessed, what a furore there had been! For this was that mysterious, little known, powerful operator William Bates, who had never had his picture in the papers; had rarely appeared in person, and yet whose manipulations practically governed the stock market; whose constructive operations extended over two continents; whose wealth was uncounted, and whose power no man had ever been known fully to test. A lean, gray wolf-leader of the pack with which Boyd had formerly hunted.

A furore? If his presence had been guessed in Arguello the old dry bones of the defunct boom would have rattled and risen and clothed themselves with life. For William Bates did not cast for small fry: he used whales for bait. If he considered it worth the trouble personally to make a long journey for the purpose of looking at a proposition, it would be because he considered the proposition had millions in it. Part of which was true. Bates, as a matter of fact, had come only from Pasadena; but he would not even have gone downtown for a small deal.

"Your proposition is feasible," he told Boyd in the den one evening, breaking his silence with the first business comment he had permitted himself. "It needs financing, for it is a big thing, if it is anything."

"That is why I asked you to look at it," Boyd pointed out.

"Of course. Tell you what I'll do." He went on in his clipping style, mentioning names high in finance, outlining the company and defining the interests. Bates was too old a hand to try for an advantage over Boyd here; and the latter was too old a hand to suspect him of it. A usual business arrangement was outlined, to which Boyd gave his assent.

"But we can't go to these people until we have our proposition cinched," said Bates. "It's all right on paper: but it's all on paper. We've got to get our water rights, our rights of way, and our land under option. Then we can go to them and get what we need. I propose that we undertake that ourselves and reserve in compensation the promotion stock. All right?"

"Suits me," agreed Boyd.

"You should get it cheap."

"No trouble about the mountains and the rights of way. The only difficulty is in the chief tract for the farms?"

"You mean that big ranch—what do you call it?"

"Corona del Monte? Yes. It will be impossible to buy that."

"At any reasonable price, you mean?"

"At all."

"Well, that of course would block the whole scheme if there were no way out. But I imagine you did not get me down here just to tell me that. What do you propose?"

"No, of course not. It's this way: this ranch, like all those old properties, is mortgaged to the eaves. All its paper is held by the First National Bank here, and as I am a director I know all about it. The owner, an extinct old fossil of the usual kind, just manages to scrabble along. He pays the interest, but it strains him to do it."

"Yet you say he won't sell any of it?" struck in Bates keenly.

"No; not an acre. You've just got to believe that I know what I'm talking about. He's that kind of an old fool."

"All right: go ahead."

"Now this paper has been renewed at the bank as often as it

came due; and will continue to be renewed as long as the interest payments are kept up. You see the land is good security. But I have sufficient influence to induce them to sell those mortgages to us. Then we can do as we please when they come due."

"Then that means putting up the full amount of the loan instead of merely an option," interposed Bates, swiftly. "That will take a lot more money." ·

"Well," said Boyd, leaning back, "why did you suppose I let you in on this at all for, Will? Didn't you suppose I could raise enough to cover preliminary work and options myself, if that was all there was to it?"

"I was wondering. How much?"

Boyd told him.

"And how do you propose dividing?"

"Same as before," said Boyd, firmly.

"H'm! What's to prevent my taking this up by myself?"

"I am. You can't get on in this thing without me, Will, and you know it: not in this community."

Bates chewed his cigar for some time in silence.

"All right," he agreed at last. "I'll put it up. But I'd like to go see this old fellow first."

"It will do no good," said Boyd.

"It will do no harm," countered Bates.

At that moment Daphne and Kenneth were seated side by side on the great lower branch of Dolman's House. It was one of the tepid, caressing, almost tropical evenings that this season so often brings to Southern California, with a loud glad chorus of crickets and tree toads, and a deep brooding stillness back of them, and soft wandering breezes visiting flowers drowsily asleep. The house seemed small and stuffy and too much lighted. For some time they had been sitting in a happy sociable silence. Suddenly Daphne sat up with a sharp and frightened cry.

"What is it?" cried Kenneth, alarmed.

But for a few moments she was too much agitated to reply. She seized and held Kenneth's hand with both of hers. They were icy cold.

"Oh, I don't know what was the matter with me!" she cried at last. "It's too foolish! It's just one of those silly fits that once is a great while strike me all of a sudden before I know it I'm all right now."

"What was it?" asked Kenneth.

"It sounds too fantastic and silly."

"Tell me," he urged.

"Well, you know Dolman—the tree spirit I told you I used to believe in when I was little."

"Yes."

"All of a sudden he seemed to swoop down on me—terribly. Something was terribly wrong. I felt the shivers go up my back. He seemed so excited; and always Dolman has been so calm. And something was terribly wrong," she repeated. "Isn't it too absurd. Bur-r, I'm chilly. Let's go home."

III

BATES preferred to make his call alone. He was directed by Sing Toy to the east paddock, where Colonel Peyton was looking at some colts. Thus when the two withdrew to the shade, they found themselves under the wide-spreading branches of Dolman's House.

Daphne was perched aloft and invisible, and as she heard them below her, she drew herself together in a panic lest she be seen before they had moved on. Daphne was now nineteen years old; not at all an age to be discovered roosting up a tree. She thought the two men had paused for a momentary chat. When it became evident that a longer conversation was forward, her first feeling was merely of annoyance that she must remain in a cramped position for so long. But after a few sentences it came to her that she was eavesdropping on what might be extremely private business affairs, and that she should make herself known. But now a strange thing happened to her. She could not move; her surroundings became hazy to her; withdrew a vast distance from the centre of her consciousness. It seemed to her that she was physically inhibited from movement and from speech, as one is bound in a dream. The motor messages sent from her brain resulted in nothing. Only the hearing and recording faculties were clear. It was as though Dolman had laid on her his spell, that another human being might become cognizant of the danger to his realm. Or a practical psychologist might have analyzed the cumulative effects of diverse inhibitions.

"I have to apologize for bothering you, Colonel Peyton," began Bates. "My excuse is that I am vitally interested in the prosperity of this community, and I assume you are."

With this opening he approached the subject. He bore very lightly on profits to be made; but emphasized the immense value in money and settlers to the community of Arguello that must result from the opening of the land. Because of this Colonel Peyton listened to him without comment or interruption. When Bates had quite finished this part of his exposition, he said:

"I think I see your point, Mr. Brown. I think it is a perfectly legitimate and praiseworthy point. But I have given a great deal of thought to it in the past: believe me, sir, it is not new to me. I have come to the conclusion that it may not after all be so important that this little community grow and expand as you have described it. I have lived here a great many years, and the people here have always been sufficiently prosperous and happy. How can it help them in that to have more people living here?"

"Why, the wealth they'd bring in: the public improvements ——" cried Bates.

"I see you cannot understand my point of view," interposed the Colonel. "That is natural. Few people do. But this is the point: I like my property the way it is. Nothing I could do with it would make me like it better. As far as that consideration applies, I wouldn't change for the world. And I can't see it is my duty, either: for the reasons I have given you."

"You do not believe it is every man's duty to think of the growth and prosperity of his community?"

"I am not convinced that growth and prosperity, as you consider it, make happiness."

"But if everybody held those views, we'd never get anywhere."

The Colonel laughed gently, the fine lines wrinkling around his eyes.

"That used to bother me a considerable," he confessed, "and then one day it came to me that everybody doesn't hold those views. If everybody was a shoemaker, we'd have nothing but shoes." He chuckled again. "No, Mr. Brown, I've had time to think it over from all angles in the last few years. The only thing that would make me break into Corona del Monte would be because I thought I ought to. And I can't see where I ought to."

Bates considered. He had come out with a tentative idea of offering to pay off all the mortgages. Then there would be no question of their renewal or non-renewal. Also there would be no question of Patrick Boyd's retaining the whip hand in these negotiations. Of course Bates had no intention of throwing Boyd over completely—he would be of great use as being on the spot; but there was no reason why the traction man should get the lion's share. But Bates had not gained his present position by being slow at the uptake. The Colonel had said enough to afford a basis for judgment. Bates gave up his tentative plan to deal on a basis of profit or alleged duty. There remained to try the effects of a scare. His manner became icy.

"You say, Colonel Peyton, that your feeling of duty would be the only thing that would make you break up this property. I think you are mistaken. There is one other thing."

"I do not understand you, sir. What is it?"

"Necessity."

"Again I must confess that I do not understand you," a trace of formality crept into the Colonel's manner.

"I introduced myself as Brown. I am William Bates of Eleven Wall Street."

But this shot missed entirely.

"I regret. I suppose the name should be familiar; but it is not," said the Colonel.

Bates stared. Undoubtedly, incredible as it seemed, the man was sincere.

"It does not matter," continued the magnate. "I merely wanted to show that my opinion in these matters is of weight. I am acting in a friendly capacity, Colonel Peyton, however it may seem to you at the moment. I am a financier, and it is my business to know all about banking affairs. That must be my excuse for knowing so much of yours. Bluntly, I know that you are heavily mortgaged here. Has it ever occurred to you what you would do if for one reason or another these mortgages should not be renewed?"

Colonel Peyton struggled against his instinct to draw into his shell. In his opinion this sort of thing was an invasion of his private affairs; but he was broad enough to realize that from a business point of view it probably was not.

"The paper is held by our local bank, sir; and the bank is governed by my friends. · The security is certainly good, as you will admit. While the interest is of course a burden to me, I anticipate no other difficulty."

The thin, gray face before him became inscrutable. It was time to throw the scare.

"You're sure it's governed by your friends?"

"What do you mean, sir?" cried the Colonel, "——my life-long associates!"

"Colonel Peyton," pronounced the financier, "I am free to confess that I came out here to propose an arrangement in regard to your land that would be mutually profitable. I see you are in no mind to consider such a proposition. My personal interest in the matter naturally ceases. But I hate to see as fine a pro-perty in risk of being lost without compensation to you, when it would be so easy to arrange it otherwise." He leaned forward, fixing the Colonel with his small dead eyes and raising a long finger. "Let me tell you this, Colonel Peyton, there is an ele-ment in that bank that intends to take possession of this pro-perty. I refer to Patrick Boyd. He is a shrewd, forceful man. I have been with him and against him, and I know. He has the power and the knowledge. If he doesn't do it one way, he'll do it another." In his later report to Boyd, Bates referred to this casually as "I used your name to scare the old bird."

"I can hardly believe you," faltered the Colonel, impressed in spite of himself. "By what right do you slander Mr. Boyd in this way?"

"Slander!" repeated Bates, contemptuously. "It isn't slan-der to call any one a good business man. He sees here a good business opportunity. He can take advantage of it without the slightest unfairness. It's a matter of plain business. You must pardon me for saying so, sir, but if you cared enough for the sentiment of holding this ranch together, you should have gone at it with some foresight. When you get deeply into debt, you have to pay, you know."

The Colonel was so shaken and preoccupied with the main issue that he did not rear his crest at the rebuke.

"Mr. Boyd made me an offer, which I refused," said the Colonel.

"If it was a good offer, you were foolish," stated Bates. "It was decent of him to do so, for he can get the ranch without your acceptance, if he wants."

"I do not see how," argued the Colonel, but weakly. "—nor why. He is a wealthy man."

"How!" repeated Bates, contemptuously. "Colonel, it is very evident that you are no business man. I can think of half a dozen ways how. And, why! He has a son, hasn't he, in the ranching business? Don't you suppose a fine property like this would come in handy. No, Colonel, don't fool yourself." He started to move away. "I'll go now and leave you to think it over. You would better come in with me. I can save you your homestead, of course, and a good big farm around it; and a tidy sum of money to live on. Come, now, that's better than passing over the whole thing, isn't it? Like your Spanish friends who used to own Las Flores?"

He continued to move away. The Colonel stared after him, apparently benumbed.

"I'm staying at Boyd's, if you want to get hold of me," added Bates. "I'm known as Brown, remember. Travelling incog." He glanced again keenly at the Colonel's motionless figure, then strode away briskly toward his horse.

Dolman lifted his spell. Aflame with indignation and excitement Daphne scrambled down from her perch and flung herself tempestuously on the Colonel.

"Oh godpapa, godpapa!" she cried. "I couldn't help but hear! I'd no idea! Why haven't you told me? I never heard anything so atrocious!"

"Where did you come from, Puss?" asked the Colonel, wearily.

"I was up in the tree. I know I shouldn't have listened, but I couldn't help it. I'd no idea! I thought things were going on so well!"

"They're going on very ill, I'm afraid," replied the Colonel, dispiritedly.

"I don't believe him! I think he's lying!" stormed Daphne, "and the Boyds! That fat, brutal, sly old villain—and Ken!" she caught her breath in a little wail, then her wrath swept her on. "To think of his living with us, and working with us and learning with us—and spying on us—yes, *spying* on us!" she cried, vehemently, at some faint motion of dissent. "I know what I'm talking about. Spy! Spy! And we trusted and l-liked him so! Oh, godpapa!" She clung tight to the old man, her body shaken with dry sobs of excitement.

"There, there, Puss," he soothed, patting her. "Don't take it so hard. And don't let's pass hasty judgments. It isn't quite fair to condemn our young man just on the word of somebody we don't know at all—and don't like," he added.

But Daphne shook her head, her face still concealed against his shoulder.

"No, it's true," she insisted. "I know. He told me so himself."

"Told you so!" cried the Colonel, astonished.

"I didn't understand what he meant: but now I do. It's been a plot from the first. Oh! how I do hate a sneak!"

She raised her face, glowing with a new access of indignation that for the moment swept Kenneth and all his works into limbo.

"But what are you going to *do?*" she demanded. "Are you going to do what that odious man wants you to?"

"Let's sit down on the big limb and talk about it," said the Colonel. "Puss, I'd like to talk to somebody. I've had to keep it to myself; and I've thought and thought until I thought I'd go crazy."

"Oh, godpapa!" breathed Daphne, awed at this revelation of a Colonel so different from the one she, or anybody else, had ever known.

"I know that what these men advise is the sensible thing to do. Almost anybody would tell you that. I'm not a business man, Puss, but I've always got on in the old days, and made the ranch go and all the people on it. I'm afraid the old days have gone. It would be the sensible thing to deal with these men. I'd get out of debt, I'd still have the homestead and some land, and I'd have some money. They are perfectly right about it. I don't suppose anybody you'd ask could give one single reason why I shouldn't do it."

"But you won't! You can't! We must find a way!" flamed Daphne.

"Why do you say that?" asked the Colonel, turning to her with a distinct lessening of his discouraged lassitude.

"It would not be the ranch any more!" she cried, passionately—"the dear old ranch! Why it would be like cutting up, destroying a loved and living thing!"

"Ah, Puss!" the Colonel exhaled a deep sigh of relief. "You understand. I thought there could not be a person in the whole wide world who would understand."

IV

Before they separated they had talked it over more calmly. The Colonel insisted that for the time being the matter should remain between themselves.

"I would a little rather you would not tell your father of this," said the Colonel. "It would only embarrass matters. He and young Boyd are in partnership, you know."

"He wouldn't be in partnership two minutes if——" began Daphne, with spirit.

"I know," interposed the Colonel, gently. "That is just it. Such partnerships cannot be dissolved on the spur of the moment. The only way would be for your father to buy him out—and you know he can't do that. The arrangement must continue."

"I suppose so—it seems intolerable," agreed Daphne after a moment, and with reluctant distaste. "But I can't bear the thought of his—I won't be even decent to him."

"I shouldn't go to extremes, my dear," advised the Colonel.
"——for your father's sake: and a little for mine."

"For yours? What do you mean, godpapa?"

"It may be that I shall have to deal with these men yet."

"Oh!" cried Daphne, aflame at once. "I thought——"

"But I have your Aunt Allie to think of," the Colonel reminded her.

"But you won't——"

"I won't do anything because these men want me to," said the Colonel. "I won't do anything unless I have to. Come now, things may not be so bad. Of course anything *might* happen—I might step on a nail and get lockjaw. But I don't see why we shouldn't pay interest, as we have been doing for years. All we're afraid of is the mystery of these men's threats. Let's not get stampeded."

Daphne made a noble effort not to treat Kenneth as though he had not hurt the very depths of her soul—for that was what it amounted to. The result vastly mystified the young man. At first he thought her new manner a joke, and tried to reply in kind. But soon he sensed a real though concealed hostility.

"What have I done?" he beseeched her. "Whatever it was, I certainly didn't mean it. Tell me what it is, at least."

"It's nothing at all," replied Daphne, primly.

"But it *is* something," he persisted. "Why are you treating me this way?"

"I am not treating you in any especial way."

"Oh, aren't you!" he cried, ruefully. "I feel like the worm that has overslept and wasn't on hand for the early bird."

She did not condescend to smile at this.

"And you won't go riding any more——"

"I would go riding if I did not happen to be very busy just now. I haven't time."

"Busy!" repeated Kenneth. "Busy at what, I should like to know!"

But talk as long as he would, he could get no further in satisfaction. Indoors Daphne took pains never to be alone with him. In the presence of her father she sat to one side, sewing. Only when directly addressed by a question did she reply very briefly. Gone were her eager interpolations and high spirits. Brainerd glanced quizzically at her from time to time.

"What have you and Daffy been quarrelling about?" he asked Kenneth, as they rode together to the upper tunnel.

"I haven't any idea, sir," replied Kenneth. "I wish I knew. I've been trying to find out, but I can't get a thing from her but statements that she's treating me just as she always has, and that there isn't a thing the matter, and giving me the wide-eyed stare. She must think I'm an imbecile!" he ended bitterly.

Brainerd laughed softly.

"I thought it might really be something." He began to whistle *La donna e mobile.*

But to Kenneth it was no laughing matter. Against the smooth sweetly smiling opposition of her denial that things were not as usual he beat in vain.

"I'd like to shake you!" he cried one day, goaded to the limit of endurance.

For the first time her pose was dropped. She faced him straight with flashing eyes.

"I'd like to see you try!" she replied.

They stared at each other with hate.

"Well, good-bye. When you come to your senses I hope you'll let me know," rejoined Kenneth, and he turned on his heel.

For two weeks he confined his presence at the Bungalow to purely business hours, and took conspicuous pains to avoid the house itself. On the few occasions when he happened to meet Daphne, he lifted his Stetson gravely, and was bowed to gravely in return. He was very unhappy and bewildered and hurt about it. Naturally it seemed to him without all reason. But naturally, too, it brought him to a tumultuous realization of his love. Heretofore it had flowed so smoothly in the comfortable channel of their everyday joyous, open-air companionship that he had not recognized it fully. Now he suffered all the doubts and fears, the longings and despairs, to dreams and far-off hopes of his condition.

And Daphne—hurt to the soul, sick with disappointment in human nature, proud, ashamed that her confidence and trust and free companionship had been so misplaced, grieved that so fair and frank an appearance and manner should cover such falsity of heart, and unquenchingly aflame with indignation against treachery—can you not see her, one moment openly and regally scorning poor Kenneth, even as dust beneath the belly of the worm, and the next flinging herself in tears on the bed? And Kenneth spent more time than he should at the Fremont bar, and was seen dashing about in a spindly wheeled, varnished buggy with a very sporty looking damsel by his side— my dear, she had the impudence to tell me that her cheeks were such a trial to her because strangers always thought she rouged!—and these facts were told to Daphne, who said they did not interest her. And Daphne suddenly became a devotee of the Fremont hops, and was known to have danced four times in succession with that Sherwood boy from San Francisco, the one who is so dissipated, and disappeared from three more dances, but then what can you expect from any one brought up as she was: at which Kenneth laughed the approved, cynical laugh and said he didn't envy Sherwood. And each listening in all conversations to catch the other's name. Lovers separated by cruel misunderstanding: it is a situation as old as the old, old world!

CHAPTER IX

I

A DREADFUL thing happened. Allie Peyton died suddenly of heart failure. The catastrophe occurred early in the evening; but Kenneth did not hear of it until he started out the following morning. His father was away on a business trip to Los Angeles, so he rode down at once to the ranch.

Daphne opened the door to his ring. Her eyes were red and tired, but they widened in amazement and anger when she saw him. At once she stepped outside and closed the door cautiously behind her.

"You! you!" she whispered intensely. "How dare you come to this house! Are you lost to all shame, all sense of decency? Have you no feeling for that old man's grief that you should show your face here to-day? Your father, at least, had a sense of shame. Go! go at once before you are seen!"

Kenneth stared at her, his jaw dropped in amazement, his spirit struck to confusion by this fierce and unexpected onslaught. He was unable to gather his faculties. Seeing that he made no move, Daphne, still in a white heat of anger, seized his arm as though to bustle him from the veranda. At the physical touch his mind snapped into focus.

"See here," he whispered, with equal ferocity. "I don't know what's the matter with you, but I'll tell you I'm about sick of this. You've treated me like a dog lately, for no reason at all. I've come down here this morning to tell the Colonel how sorry I am this has happened and to see if there is anything I can do, and you spring out at me! I won't have it, I tell you. I was as fond of Aunt Allie——"

"Don't you dare call her that!" cried Daphne.

Kenneth, very white, stared at her a moment. Then he reached out and seized her firmly by the upper arm.

"You come with me, young woman," he commanded grimly. "You'll just explain yourself!"

She twisted trying to snatch her arm away, but his fingers bit in without mercy, and after a moment she gave up. Without easing his grip he led her down the steps, across the lawn, under the oak trees to Dolman's House. Once there he fairly flung her arm from him.

"Now, young woman!" he commanded.

She stood for a moment rubbing her arm, too angry to speak.

"You know perfectly well," she managed at last.

Kenneth faced her, his arms folded rather melodramatically across his chest. He was entirely in control of himself, very grim and determined, very cool; and seemed of a sudden to have put on an unwonted garment of cool maturity.

"We won't have any of that," he told her. "I asked you to explain your attitude, and I have the right after your treatment of me to expect you to do so."

His cold determination stiffened her own. She straightened and faced him.

"Very well, if you will have it openly," she said, and in level tones began her count. He listened without comment until she had quite finished.

"You believe all this?" he enquired then. "But that is a superfluous question: I see you do." He paced back and forth a few times considering. She watched him furtively. Strangely enough a tiny thrill of something very like hope sprang up in her heart. He was not taking it as she had expected. His face was set and gray, and his manner was of an iron repression. "I'd like to get this quite clear," he said after a moment, "so, if you don't mind, I'll restate it. Your own exposition was a little confused. As near as I can make it out, according to your story, my father has offered to buy Colonel Peyton's ranch or a portion of it." He checked the point off on his finger. "Failing in that he has entered into a plot to take the ranch away from the Colonel in spite of him, turning the old man out. The reason he wants the ranch is that he wants to turn it over to me. I am, and have been, in this plot from the beginning; and that is why I have been learning the ranch business. Incidentally I have been spying on conditions. Does that state the case?"

It did state exactly Daphne's belief and the cause of her anger. There was no reason why her sense of the rectitude of her position should weaken or her indignation abate. Yet, illogically, both of these things were happening. Somehow she actually began to feel on the defensive! That was unthinkable.

"Perfectly!" she answered, her spirit returning at the thought.

"Leaving my father out of it for the moment. Why have you thought I would be party to such a scheme—if there *was* such a scheme? Is that the opinion you have formed of me in the four or five years we have been together? Answer me, I want to know."

"N-no," hesitated Daphne. This was getting on the defensive with a vengeance.

"What was it then?"

"I heard with my own ears this Bates person tell the Colonel that that was why your father wanted it. And you told me yourself right here in this very spot that some day you would get this ranch. Don't tell me you don't remember!"

Kenneth puzzled over this statement with exasperating deliberation.

"Oh, I see," he observed at last. "I think I've got it." He looked straight at her, and the hard square lines of his face had softened and a quizzical gleam had come into his eyes. And somehow, whether it was that Kenneth's manner had an effect, that her own emotion had exhausted itself by its intensity, that the reaction from the past weeks had flung her back, or more subtly that again Dolman the wise exerted his mysterious influence; the fact remained that suddenly Daphne knew without the justification of words and arguments that it was all right.

"Daffy," said Kenneth, deliberately, "you're a goose!"

"A-am I?" she faltered.

The next instant she was shaking with sobs, tight folded in his arms, her face buried against his arm. After a few moments he raised her head and kissed her. She clung to him the harder.

"Oh, Ken! Ken!" she cried, brokenly. "It's so good to be back! So good to be back!"

"Sweetheart," he murmured.

She drew back to look at him, pushing herself away with both hands against his chest, her expression astonished and a little awed.

"Why, why Ken!" she gasped. "It is that; isn't it?"

"Of course," he soothed, drawing her back to him. "Haven't you known? I have, for weeks."

"Oh Ken," she said after a little, "we ought to be ashamed to be so happy just now. Think! Oh, we must try to be so good to the poor old Colonel!"

Thus brought back to the present problem, they sat down on the lowermost sweeping limb of Dolman's House to talk more soberly.

"Now as to my father's supposed part in all this," said Kenneth, "I don't believe it for moment. He is a business man accustomed to talking plain business, and he has been misunderstood. Probably he has some scheme of buying part of the ranch and turning it into farms, though he's never said anything to me about it. You know he's always had the small farm idea. Naturally he would suppose the Colonel would want to go in for it. But as for his plotting to do up the old man," Kenneth laughed, "why you don't know my father, that's all."

Daphne snuggled closer. There were any amount of loose ends, but they seemed unimportant. However, Kenneth proceeded to gather one of them up.

"Father's in Los Angeles," he went on. "Just as soon as he gets back I'll tell him about it." He paused, considering. "You don't suppose the Colonel would feel differently about it—now?" he suggested.

"Why should he?"

"Well—Aunt Allie—it may seem different to him now. Perhaps he'd like to get rid of the worry—— And of course we don't know all the ins and outs of the matter, do we? Certainly the situation can't change before the mortgages become due. Suppose I find out when that is: I can easily do it. Then it might be a good idea to let things alone for a little while until the Colonel gets straightened around a little and finds out just what he does want to do. We'd be very foolish to stir things all up uselessly. What do you think?"

"It might be a good idea. But, Ken, are you very sure your father——?"

"Certain sure. Let me tell you about father. He probably thinks the Colonel is either an obstructionist to progress or is trying to hold him up. In either case he'd fight; for father is a fighter. But it's only because he doesn't *understand* the Colonel. I can fix that, never fear—when the time comes."

His confidence was so absolute that she shared it.

"Are you going to let me see the Colonel now?" he asked after a moment, with a rueful smile.

"I don't see how you can; I must explain to him—you see, he thinks the same as I did."

"Oh!" cried Kenneth, distressed, "you must fix that—I can't bear that thought."

She arose slowly, holding out her fingers to his clasp.

"Come," she said, consideringly. "I'll see."

But the matter was taken out of their hands. As they turned around the low flung screen of leaves formed by the lowermost branch of Dolman's House they came face to face with the tall figure of the Colonel. His clean-cut old face looked white, and the lines of it had somehow grown finer, but no visible marks of grief blurred his countenance or dimmed the kindly clearness of his eyes. Indeed, into the latter came a faint twinkle as he surveyed them, for they had been walking hand in hand, and the surprise of the encounter had left them so. Slowly the Colonel's gaze travelled from one face to the other.

"I see it is all right," he said, "and, children, I'm very, very glad. It is as it should be."

"Oh, godpapa," breathed Daphne, with meaning, "*everything* is all right."

The Colonel fairly twinkled at her.

"No need to tell me that, Puss," he turned to Kenneth. "You have won," he said, simply, "the finest, truest woman in the world and you must be good to her. There is nothing else in life my boy, nothing!— I know," he added in a low voice.

Kenneth stammered brokenly his thanks and an attempt at the impossible translating into words of sympathy for bereavement and sense of loss.

"I know, I know," said the Colonel, hastily. He seized and pressed Kenneth's hand strongly. "That is all right, too. It must be all right. I know you loved her, children; and she loved you. She must be very happy now in your happiness."

"If there is anything at all I can do, sir——" stammered Kenneth, "anything at all——"

"I know, I know, my boy. I'll call on you," and suddenly the Colonel turned from them and walked down through the oak trees, his step firm, his shoulders squared, his tall figure erect, his head high.

Daphne cast herself sobbing on Kenneth's breast.

"Oh, I wish he weren't like that!" she cried. "He's wonderful; but he breaks my heart! If he'd only give way a little! He's too tight-strung. He sits by her with that same look in his eyes!"

II

THE funeral was the most extraordinary in the history of Arguello, some whispered. Certainly it was well attended. From all directions came people in vehicles and people on horseback. A returned traveller familiar with the old days would have said that another *fiesta* was forward at La Corona del Monte, another of Allie's birthday feasts to which came all the world and his wife. Except that on closer inspection he could not but have perceived that every form was clad in decent black, every face wore a proper expression of gravity, manners were subdued, and the tones of conversation were low. They drove into the enclosure and hitched their horses, exchanged murmurs with the old Spanish servants who were there to assist them; and so drifted up the knoll and over the lawn beneath the oaks toward the house. To many it was only too poignantly reminiscent of the old days. They saw in retrospect the Colonel and Allie at the foot of the steps waiting to greet them; and the huge punch bowls under the trees; and the gav murmur that floated from the barbecue grounds across the way. Ah, things were different then! Many of them had not been to Corona del Monte for years, not since the old *fiestas* in Allie's honour had been given up. And here they were back again to assist in her last *fiesta* of all! The place did not look the same to them. The old spirit had sickened. And in spite of themselves they could not but notice the peeling paint, the sprouting weeds, the brown patches in the lawn, all the signs that Corona del Monte was not as of yore. As they drifted slowly toward the house they recognized one another; and half nodded, as though a full salutation would in some way desecrate; and gravitated together, and whispered subdued things. Oliver Mills was there; and old Don Vincente shaking with a town-acquired palsy, and his fat, soft, sympathetic women; Jim Paige, Dr. Wallace, old Patterson the riding master. And the Arguello familes were present in force, the Stanleys, Welchs, Carsons, Maynards, and their like; George Scott had come; and the entire *Sociedad*, getting the news by a chance rider, had driven all night to be there. The ranch dependents, their numbers sadly reduced since the old days, stood one side in a subdued, sad little group. Perhaps the greatest flutter was caused by the arrival of a number of red-buttoned Chinamen.

Inside the house—and this was the extraordinary part that caused the gossips to whisper—the mourners were greeted by the Colonel. By all etiquette of the time the Colonel should not have been in evidence. But there he was, greeting them as guests of the house; grave, to be sure, but clear-eyed, cordial, unembarrassed. He had a word for each of them, and such astonishing words!

"Mrs. Peyton will feel so glad you have come," he told them in effect; and they did not know what to say, being in such matters conventional souls, but were honestly touched. Somehow they sensed that the Colonel was for the last time doing the honours in his house, for the last time greeting poor Allie's guests at this her last *fiesta* of all. Then Daphne, or Kenneth, or Brainerd took charge of them.

The little house soon filled, and overflowed on to the veranda, and then to the lawn. The windows were opened so that the service could be heard. At its close they all unhitched their horses and followed to the cemetery, a long long string of them plodding through the dust that rose like the smoke of a great fire.

Daphne and Kenneth stayed to put the house in order. They cleared away the flowers, and rearranged everything just as it was. Sing Toy helped them in silence. They fixed the centre table just as usual, with the lamp, and they laid there the Colonel's paper and book.

"How about this?" asked Kenneth uncertainly, indicating the old wooden Boston rocker in which Mrs. Peyton had always sat with her work.

Daphne considered, her brows lined.

"Put it just where it has always been," she decided at last. "There! Now we must go before he gets back. He has been wonderful; but now he will want to be alone. Sing Toy must take care of him. You got to make him eat, Sing Toy."

"You bet, I fix 'em," said Sing Toy, cheerfully.

At heart Sing Toy was desolate; and he had woven purple in his pigtail as a sign of grief. So in the gathering dusk they stole away leaving the old ranch house to its shadows of the past.

III

PATRICK BOYD wrote from Los Angeles for clothes to be sent him and departed for the East. He wrote Kenneth that a sudden and pressing call of business had summoned him. The latter easily found out that the mortgages on the ranch were not due for some time yet. So matters did not press.

The lovers lived a tip-toe. Life was all a gorgeous secret. The most commonplace affairs took on significance. Suddenly all the ordinary things in the world had entered into a conspiracy with them of some splendid sort hidden from the rest of mankind; for whom, indeed, they wore their everyday aspects as a disguise. They were very compassionate toward (a) those who were unmarried and unattached and could therefore be considered as leading a dead-alive sort of life: (b) those who were married and settled down and who consequently lived humdrum, stodgy existences; and (c) those engaged couples who did not fully apperceive the glories and possibilities of this estate and who therefore might be fairly adjudged as lost in ignorance. They did not say so; nor argue about it. They just felt it, which made George Scott want to spank them, but which merely caused everybody else to laugh in a sympathetic fashion. Not that they knew—or cared.

They were good to the Colonel, though. The innocent caller, or even passer-by, who occupied as much as five minutes of the valued leisure that they might have been devoting to each other, was often bewildered by evidences of suppressed impatience over his superfluous existence. You see, of the day, counting in sleep and occasional necessary separate tasks, but including of course all ranch work which could just as well as not be done in company, they could count on only about twelve hours a day together. As they had been closely associated only about four years, and as they could not expect to live more then fifty or sixty years more, it can readily be seen that outsiders who did not promptly get down to business and say what they had to say and then get out were a positive blight. Daphne, as of the social sex, tried to be polite in a strained sort of fashion; but Ken merely glowered.

All this did not apply to the Colonel. They followed the old man around every minute he would let them; and they were constantly popping in to see what they could do. The Colonel, to outside appearance, was the same as ever. His step had lost none of its spring, his figure none of its erectness, his kind old face none of its benevolent interest in those about him. He spoke of Allie frequently, and without the embarrassment of surface grief. People meeting him casually driving down Main Street in Arguello saw no difference in him. He was the same old Colonel.

But the ranch people knew. From the moment Allie left him the Colonel lost either his interest in or his grasp of details. Old Manuelo gave up consulting him after a while, and came to Kenneth or Brainerd to determine what to do. Details seemed to perplex, almost to irritate him. His brow cleared and his smile returned only when he had disposed of them in his usual fashion:

"I leave it to you, Manuelo. You know better than I do; and you will do for the best."

It was the same way about the place. The gardener gradually took things over and did as he pleased: Sing Toy ran the house. As a consequence the garden ran down, and the house took within itself a rigid Chinese formality of arrangement. These things distressed Daphne and Kenneth at first; but they found that any mention of them to the Colonel merely bothered him; while any attempt at direct regulation would arouse instant resentment on the part of those in charge. After all, if the Colonel did not notice these externals, why should it matter?

The Colonel walked and rode much about the ranch, to be sure; but it was in no superintending capacity. He knew its every hill and dale, almost its every bush and tree, and he went about loving them. Since his wife's death the earthly part of affection for her seemed to have transferred itself to Corona del Monte. His days took on a rough sort of routine. Except on the few occasions when he drove to town to visit Main Street, he rode or drove far afield all the morning—sometimes all day. In the afternoon he wandered about the nearer parts of the ranch, peering here and there, standing for long periods staring at the pigs, the ducks, the horses, or across the paddocks, poking into odd corners, testing hasps and well covers and bin-traps but never apparently with any purpose of suggestion or repair, greeting and chatting with the men and women and children of the ranch. Always he managed to keep up his supply of peppermint lozenges, which he distributed gravely. At evening he returned to eat his solitary dinner, after which he repaired to the sitting room where he sat down by the oil lamp and picked up his paper. Across the low table stood the old, worn wooden Boston rocker, just where it had always stood. From time to time the Colonel would glance across at it over the top of his bowed spectacles. Then he resumed his reading.

CHAPTER X

I

SHORTLY after Boyd's departure for the East Kenneth came down with a bad cold that resulted in an attack of tonsillitis. He was confined to the house for some days, and when Dr. Wallace finally permitted him to drive out to the Bungalow again, he was pretty wobbly and was afflicted with a bad cough. As may be imagined this seemingly endless separation had been a terrible thing to the lovers, and they greeted each other with the appropriate ecstasy. An apparently blind, unjust, unreasonable fate had smitten them so sorely that at times it had seemed there was no justice in the world. Seconds, minutes, hours, days even, that might have afforded each its splendid rapture, had trooped slowly—so slowly—and grayly by; and were lost irretrievably in the irrevocable past!

Townsend Brainerd remarked:

"Hullo, Ken! How's the boy? Thought you were sick: you certainly made a quick recovery."

But it developed that Ken had not made quite a recovery. He retained an annoying cough that refused to pay any attention to Dr. Wallace's concoctions. Of course he made little account of it himself; but Daphne was absurdly anxious.

"A change of air would remedy the matter," precise little Dr. Wallace told her. "A sojourn of not less than two weeks over the mountains, or anywhere away from the coast, is indicated. These bronchial affections linger persistently at this season."

Kenneth at first scouted the ideas as absurd. He was a great strong brute, and a little cough like this was nothing to bother about for a second. He couldn't get away: he had his work to do. And, besides, think of what it would mean! "Two weeks!

Perhaps you could think of it with equanimity; but it is beyond me—when one loves anybody as I do you, two weeks——"

"I know, I know!" cried Daphne. "I can't bear to think of it either. But, Ken——"

Daphne had been brought up in a household over which had hovered the menace of tuberculosis. She had acquired an instinctive horror that was even a little unreasonable. In the end it was decided that Kenneth should go. A letter from Corbell announcing the pigeons and inviting to a shoot decided the matter. The moment of parting was heartrending. It had been agreed that they were to write to one another every day, and the thought had been minutely comforting until some unkind little inner common-sense devil had pointed out that the stages only run once a week. That nearly wrecked the whole expedition. Ken was going nowhere, no matter what the consequences, where he would not hear for one whole week! They worked back slowly against this tide. Finally they arranged to write seven letters at a time, starting now; and to read one a day. Not very satisfactory, but it sufficed. Likewise they picked out a star that could be looked at—undoubtedly to its embarrassment—by both at a certain hour. Other psychically suggestive arrangements were made. Neverthless at the last moment they seemed pitifully inadequate; and if Kenneth could decently have drawn back he would have done so. But that would have been a trifle difficult, considering that he had already sent on his equipment by the stage. So he climbed his horse and rode away, with a sunken sort of feeling that it was all silly, useless; was going to be a bore, and that his main job in life was now to tackle empty days courageously.

This attitude lasted to the foot of the Pass. Then it lightened somewhat under the influence of the sun, the blue sky, the faint aromas from the warmed chaparral, and the spirit-lifting climb toward higher levels. When he topped the range and began his descent into the less familiar country, try as he would he could not keep his spirits down. He did his conscientious best. He thought of Daphne, and how long it was going to be before he saw her again, and all the rest of it, and he whipped his mind into single contemplation of this distressing situation. But the confounded thing would take surreptitious looks ahead toward the end of the day, and the big ranch room with the fire, and how much fun it was going to be to see the gang again, and as to pigeons—Ken had shot quail over here a number of times, but he had never happened to get away when the pigeons were in. They told great stories of the pigeons, how swarms of them fed across open spaces, the birds behind fluttering over those in front in order to get first pickings, and the rear rank fluttering in turn over them, until it was like a wave advancing; how they darted over the passes in the hills, on their way to water, travelling so fast that you had to hold fifteen feet ahead of them; how wary they were, so that in spite of abundance the hunter had to use all his craft; and how the falcons swooped after the killed birds, so that sometimes these swift hawks actually caught the falling pigeon before it hit the ground, leaving the hunter cursing—unless he had a second barrel for the thief! Tall story, that last! Wonder if the shooting is as hard as they make out? Corbell said five to eight shells to a bird; and Corbell was a crack shot. Ken wondered if he was going to disgrace himself. He was a pretty good quail shot now; but this overhead work! Looked as though he'd be kept pretty busy loading up those brass shells of his. And while his introspective mind raced thus like a dog new loosed, sending little thrills of enthusiasm and anticipation through his veins, his surface mind was observing and noting various matters outside. That brush rabbit thought he was hid when he crouched in that shadow; wonder if that's an eagle or a red-tailed hawk sailing yonder—by Jove, it looks a little as if it might be a condor! Those fellows are scarce! Hullo, snake track in the dust! Good deal of water in the river for this time of year—wonder how that will affect the fishing? Something made a whacking rustle in the brush— And at the same time his ordinary, physical senses were calling attention to the comfortable, warm, soaking-in feeling of the sunshine on the back of his neck, or the homely creaking of the saddle leather, or the spice smell of the sage, or the touch of the breeze on his cheek. His consciousness suddenly took command of all these things to discover that he was whistling a lilting tune and jangling his spur chains in rhythm to it! Shocked at the discovery, he was sternly and conscientiously miserable again.

But as he neared the ranch country and his way led out from the river bottoms across the rolling, oak-dotted hills of the cattle ranges, he began to see the pigeons. They slanted across the brilliance of the western sky in long, swift lines: they alighted, and fluttered, and lost balance and flapped back again on the bare branches of the white oaks; the high shrill whistling of their wings was plain to be heard. Kenneth's heart leaped and the blood coursed through his veins. He struck spurs to his dawdling mount, filled with a sudden eagerness to arrive.

And at his call there was such a heartening eruption to the long low veranda of the ranch house: Herbert Corbell, as precise as ever with his wax-pointed moustache, and yet with such a friendly gleam in his eye; and the huge form of Bill Hunter, his honest countenance glowing; and red-faced Shot Sheridan: and of course long lank Frank Moore with his wizened, quizzical humorous expression; and Ravenscroft, the Englishman; and even Carlson, the poet, who might be considered an occasional and honorary member of the *Sociedad*. Among them squirmed and wagged and bent their spines and wrinkled back their upper lips, and otherwise ingratiated themselves, all the dogs; and Mex Joe flashed his white teeth as he appeared to take Ken's horse. They all welcomed him boisterously, and dragged him in by the leaping fire. Supper was ready almost immediately. After supper a tremendous tobacco smudge was raised, and Ken's excitement was fanned by the discussion of to-day's and to-morrow's hunts.

When he remembered that star, it was already an hour later than the agreed time. He chided himself severely, and tried hard to feel miserable over his separation from Daphne; but the thought of those pigeons kept spoiling it all.

It is a pity this is not a sportsman's narrative, for it would be very interesting to tell here of the band-tailed pigeon shooting of the old days. But we are concerned with other things. Therefore it must be sufficient to say that Kenneth found his enforced absence not without its mitigations. After the first novelty had worn off he did miss Daphne cruelly, and he did look forward with increasing longing to the time when he should return. The rendezvous with the star was now faithfully kept. But that was only when he was alone: and he was alone very little. The rest of the time she lay deep in his heart, and everything he saw and did came through the medium of his love and was tinged by it to a wonderful rosiness; so that take it all in all he was getting through pretty well. The cough was certainly disappearing.

II

Now it happened that the very day after Kenneth had left Arguello, Patrick Boyd returned unexpectedly from the East. He had fully expected to be away for another month; but Bates had concluded arrangements much more quickly than he had anticipated. Boyd caught the first train. He might have telegraphed his arrival; but it hardly seemed important, and he would surprise Ken. Like most surprises, this one missed fire. From the Chinese he learned merely that the young man had gone pigeon shooting, to which Boyd mentally registered approval: Ken had earned a vacation. Then he turned his whole energies to getting action.

For Boyd had the thing sewed up in a gunnysack, as he phrased it. That is to say, Bates and his associates had found ample financial backing; the company had been incorporated under the laws of New Jersey; and Boyd himself stood in a very satisfactory relation to it all. There remained merely to go ahead with the physical details. The first of these was to acquire or tie up the most desirable irrigable property; the second to get rights of way; the third to develop the water rights Boyd had already taken up. After that would come such incidental matters as water power, electric power, municipal supply, and so forth. It looked big!

With at last something definite to which to apply his long-pent energies, Boyd went at things with a vim. The morning after his arrival he had called a special meeting of the First National's directors. He brought to their attention the Peyton loans. These mortgages had been renewed again and again; a further renewal would be asked. He then pointed out that the last interest had not been paid. This had not been pressed because of the Colonel's bereavement, and because of the Colonel's deserved personal popularity. We esteem the Colonel. But it had not been paid since. It was not likely to be paid; nor was future interest. He would show them why: and he went on to analyze exactly the affairs at the ranch, drawing on his intimate knowledge gained through Kenneth's innocent spying. It was evident that by no stretch of the imagination could it be hoped that the principal of the loans could ever be repaid from the ranch activities. In other words it was a bad loan. It was not only a bad loan, but it was too big a loan to be tied up in one piece of property. It had been bad banking, and he did not hesitate to say so. It was the type of banking that, in the financial circles of the East, would, he was free to say, call for the severest criticism, perhaps investigation. Boyd's voice became very crisp at this point. A bank's business is to use its stockholders' and depositors' money wisely and safely. That is its first duty. In opposition to this first duty, no other consideration could have weight. Its funds should at all times be so invested as to bring the highest return consistent with safety: and at the same time on such a basis that they could be liquidated at any time without loss. That was a commonplace. Had that been done here? Boyd stated with great positiveness to the contrary. Corona del Monte might be fairly considered worth more than the loans on it, to be sure; but not in a forced sale. And a forced sale was the criterion. If on foreclosure the bank could not regain its loan, and interest, from the auction price of the ranch, it would be forced to keep it. And running a ranch is about the poorest thing a bank can do.

The board listened to all this rather glumly. Nobody likes to be called a fool or scolded; and most of these men, conservatives of the old Arguello type, had no use for Boyd's dominating, enterprising schemes, anyway.

"Do I understand, Mr. Boyd, that you have called this especial meeting to advocate not renewing Colonel Peyton's mortgage?" asked Oliver Mills, dryly. "I believe those notes are not due for some months yet and consideration of them might quite well have come before a regular meeting."

"Not at all," Boyd countered, squaring his bulky form toward the speaker. "I've called this board together to do business; and I am pointing out a few basic facts to put it in mind to do business. I mean just this, if you want it plainly: You've made a damn bad deal in this Peyton business; just about as silly as the Las Flores loan."

"We got out of that in good shape," objected Squires, a director.

"By means of a miracle—the land boom," stated Boyd, caustically, "a miracle, I may add, that is not due to repeat; and will have to be paid for, in spite of what some people say." He stared sardonically at Squires, and the latter squirmed, remembering that Boyd had nipped him in the boom, and still held him. "Now when these Peyton notes come due—whether it's to-morrow or a year from to-morrow—one of two things will have to be done: either you'll have to renew the mortgage or you'll have to foreclose it. I shall resist renewal, and I shall give my reasons before the State Board of Examiners. Foreclosure will harm all concerned."

He paused so long that Oliver Mills felt constrained to say something.

"I suppose you have something to propose," he said wearily.

"Right! It is this: I will discount that paper at its full valuation."

A silence greeted this offer while the members digested the idea.

"I don't believe I quite follow Mr. Boyd," said old Mr. Donovan at last. "He has been pointing out to us the undesirability of this matter in one breath; and then in the next he offers to take it over himself. I would like to have that discrepancy explained."

"Now, that is good, clear common sense," said Boyd, heartily, "and I am glad to explain in two words. My son is interested in the ranch business, and I am certain he can develop this property and put it on a paying basis."

"Have you talked with Colonel Peyton on this matter?" someone asked.

"I have made the Colonel substantial offers—more than he

can get by foreclosure; but I regret to say that he does not see them. I may add that I stand ready to repeat those offers at any time—nothing could be fairer than that."

"I don't like it," mumbled Squiers, doubtfully.

Boyd turned on him swiftly.

"Good Lord, neither do I!" he cried. "But what has that to do with it? It's a plain business transaction. The man has borrowed more than he can pay. The matter, gentlemen, is not in your discretion. You are not acting as individuals, but as trustees for others. I tell you here and plainly that one of two things is going to happen: either you sell me these notes now, in which case I will personally take care of the Colonel; or you will most certainly be required to foreclose, in which case the exact legal steps of the law will be taken, and not one step more!"

"And what if we do neither?" demanded Donovan, half rising.

Boyd hit the table with his clenched fist.

"I'm here to see that you do," he thundered. "I've been through this mill before, gentlemen; and, believe me, I mean business!" He glanced down the director's table. "There are others beside Colonel Peyton who are skating on thin ice," he added significantly.

"Is that to be understood as a threat?" asked Donovan, pugnaciously.

"You bet your sweet life that's a threat!" rejoined Boyd with unexpected candour. "And if you don't believe I can make good on it, just try it and see! Mind you," he added, "I'm not pretending to dictate *what* you shall do; but you've got to do something legal in this matter, and do it now." He glanced again down the board table. Two of the directors were glaring back at him belligerently. The rest were staring at the polished surface of the table. "Your course of action is as follows: you can sell to me; you can sell to somebody else—and I wish you joy in finding another human being who would give you three cents for the proposition as it stands; you can foreclose. In the first case, all right. In the second place, all right, and God bless you, *if* you can find a purchaser. In the third case you're going against bank examiners and plenty of publicity, I can promise you that."

Boyd sat down. Donovan and the other belligerent member jumped into the ring excitedly; but the others remained troubled, looking down. Three of them were absolutely in Boyd's hands, financially, since the collapse of the boom. The others recognized his power as a fighting man, as a financial magnate, as an experienced manipulator; they understood the weakness of their own position insofar as it had been based on sentiment rather than sound business considerations. After a time Oliver Mills interrupted the acrimonious flow.

"Gentlemen, in my opinion Mr. Boyd is right, much as some of us may deplore that fact. We are here to function as bankers. Colonel Peyton's case has been many times paralleled in the history of California. He is one of my dearest friends. I would much rather this would happen to me than to him," the little president was speaking with real emotion. "Owing to that fact perhaps we have let things run beyond discretion. Left to ourselves," his voice took on an edge, "possibly we might have continued to do so."

Twenty minutes later the matter was settled. It was voted to sell the notes and the mortgage underlying them to Patrick Boyd. Oliver Mills, with a heavy heart, agreed himself to tell Colonel Peyton and to explain the necessity. It was promised that the papers would be ready and the transaction finished the first day of the following month. Boyd himself stipulated for this delay. He was in haste to get the sale voted upon and entered in the minutes; but was reluctant to hand over funds until he had the other elements of his scheme a little more in hand. He had no fear that another purchaser of the notes could be found. It was too soon after the boom: you couldn't have sold a corner lot in the New Jerusalem for seventy-five cents.

The meeting broke up sadly. The board members talked low-voiced among themselves, pointedly ignoring Boyd's exit. Much he cared! The opinion for or against of these country bumpkins, these sentimental old maids, these spineless weaklings that could not stand up in a fair fight for even one round, was not worth having. Boyd knew by experience that success is the thing. In two years everybody would have forgotten all about everything; except possibly a few of the closest friends of this obstructive old fool. And to the new population, the dwellers on the prosperous, smiling irrigated farms; the thousands who must flock to this garden spot of the world, Patrick Boyd would be what he was—leading citizen, public benefactor, bringer of prosperity, the man with vision who had seen and brought in a new era. Outside the bank building he paused to light a cigar. He was well satisfied.

"I'm sorry; you don't know how sorry I am," Oliver Mills was saying to his confrères, who were too dejected to disperse. "But it has been a long time coming. I don't see how it could be helped."

"There isn't one thing anybody can do, as I can see," agreed someone.

"It's happened to about all the big Spanish grants," said another, "but, gosh! I do wish it hadn't happened to this one."

"Well, there's nothing to be done about it," repeated the first speaker.

III

THE Chinese factotum of the bank, who had all this time been deliberately washing the tall windows at the end of the room, now folded up his step ladder, picked up his pail and mop, and padded out on his felt-soled shoes. His name was Sing Gee, and he was very high among the Sings. In business hours he washed floors and windows and cuspidors and ink wells and things for the bank. Out of business hours he occupied an airless back room behind a store that sold highly varnished ducks. Where repaired to him many oriental magnificos and bravos who from him took orders. He was in addition a graduate of Harvard and spoke English almost without an accent; an accomplishment that, for some mysterious reason of his own, he hid under an inscrutable demeanour and almost inunderstandable "pidgin."

Depositing the utensils of his bondage in a closet he approached the cashier.

"I go now," he stated.

"Go now?" repeated the cashier. "What for you go? Him 'leven o'clock. You no go now."

"Yes. I go now. My second-uncle he sick."

The cashier was an old Californian, and instantly conceded the point, contenting himself with asking if Sing Gee expected to return or whether his second-uncle's illness was to result in a permanent withdrawal.

"I come back wo'k tomollah," stated Sing Gee, and departed.

From the little room behind the varnished ducks he sharply despatched a youth, who sped so well that within two hours he returned driving with old Sing Toy behind the ancient furry animal that drew Corona del Monte's Chinese vegetable wagon. Sing Toy bowed profoundly from the waist and stood with his hands folded across his stomach, his beady black eyes fixed on Sing Gee's face while the latter apparently indulged in a long cantata. Then Sing Toy clucked twice, bowed again from the waist, and withdrew. The rest of the afternoon he devoted to what might have been a house to house canvass of Chinatown, holding long animated confabulations with many red-button Celestials. At the close of each of these interviews he wrote several characters on a tablet he produced from his sleeve. When he had finished all his visits he seated himself before a teakwood abacus, or counting frame, and referring to the marks on his tablet he rapidly flipped the polished buttons back and forth on their wires. He contemplated the result with a slight frown; sighed; and returned to the back room. Sing Gee listened to what he had to say, nodded, spoke low-toned to an attendant, and went on puffing at his long-stemmed pipe. The attendant disappeared for a moment, but returned carrying a revolver. It was a wicked looking weapon, a Colts 45, but with the barrel sawed off within two inches of the frame. He handed this to Sing Toy, who glanced at the cylinders, tucked it in his sleeve, bowed again, and departed.

Next he drove the vegetable wagon around to Patrick Boyd's residence where he carried on a long conversation with the Chinaman—also a Sing—employed in that household. Thence he returned to the ranch, which he reached about sunset.

"Well, Sing Toy," observed the Colonel, as he drove up, "I began to think I wasn't going to get any dinner."

Sing Toy's beady eyes rested on him, and their inscrutable surface clouded and something very like compassion arose from their unsuspected depths.

"My second-uncle, he got sick," said Sing Toy.

IV

THE rumour went abroad with astonishing rapidity that Cor ona del Monte was to pass from its present owner. There were a very few to say I-told-you-so; but the sincere regret was almost universal. The Colonel was not only popular: he represented the good old days that had gone forever. This was the last of the original Ranchos to stand intact on the tax books of the county. All the others had been divided and divided again, new names constantly edging in, until the old names were lost, swamped. Everybody remembered the old lavish *fiestas;* nobody but at one time or another, whether at occasion of rejoicing or distress, but had received from the overflowing bounty of Corona del Monte, whether it was substantial help in dire need, or merely a bouquet of flowers, a basket of fruit, or a visit instinct with genuine kindly feeling. People gathered on the corners and talked of it, with shakes of the head. It was considered remarkable, of course, that it had not happened long ago. The passing of all grandeurs was in the course of nature. Nothing could be done about it. Certainly no one was to blame. But there was a genuine sorrow over it for a day or two.

This rumour did not reach to the Bungalow until it was two days old; and to the Colonel not at all. Oliver Mills had put off informing his old friend of the contemplated change, partly from cowardice, partly because he wanted to spare pain as long as possible. The situation would in no way be altered by the first of the month. As to Townsend Brainerd and Daphne, the story came to them in such diluted form that it did not arouse any immediate alarm.

"There are always these fool rumours of foreclosure," said Brainerd contemptuously, and dismissed it from his mind.

Daphne, as more on the inside, realized that Boyd's return probably meant the beginning of what they had feared. But by now she shared Kenneth's confidence that he would be able to clear the matter. Kenneth would be returning the next week. As none of the mortgages came due for some months yet, there seemed to her no pressing emergency. However, she wrote Kenneth that his father had returned, and that rumour was busy with his intentions as to Corona del Monte; and sent the letter by the stage, which happened to go next day.

This letter, which was a fat one, was brought in to Corbell's ranch by a rider who had met the stage for that purpose at a point some miles distant. It was accompanied by various other letters and papers for all members of the party. The others drew up around the lamp to read their share at leisure; but Kenneth seized his prize and withdrew to the privacy of his room.

For a time there was silence, except for the crackling of the fire and the sucking sound of pipes. Then Corbell uttered a profane exclamation that caused them all to look up.

"Look here, what Jim Paige writes!" he cried, and began to read:

"There's been a story floating around for a couple of days about the bank's foreclosing on Colonel Peyton. It got so strong that I called in Chan Squiers and tackled him about it. Seems I struck it right there, for Chan was pretty mad about it. They had a meeting the other day at the bank and voted to sell the Colonel's mortgage to Patrick Boyd. He announced flatly that it was his intention to put the Colonel out and put his precious son in. What do you think of that after said precious son has been 'learning the business' right at the Colonel's for the last three or four years? Pretty neat, I call it. I asked Chan why the devil they ever sold the notes, and he said Boyd just bull-dozed them into it, there was no way out. I guess myself that he had it on them someway, but that wasn't the important point. It was pretty serious, so I took pains to inquire carefully. I sort of liked young Boyd, and I felt pretty sorry about it. But it's so, all right. I'm no financier, but it looks like a damn dirty deal. But I suppose there's nothing to be done."

A flat silence succeeded this reading.

"I—I don't quite get it," said Bill Hunter at last.

"It's sufficiently surprising; but it's plain enough," said Corbell, icily. "This pair of sharps is trying to do the Colonel out of his property, and I don't doubt they'll succeed."

Bill whistled slowly.

"But I don't believe Ken had a thing to do with it," he blurted, "I like that kid."

"Jim Paige doesn't shoot his mouth off at random," Corbell pointed out, "especially a thing like this. He was pretty friendly with young Boyd, too."

"I must say I like his cheek, chumming about with us all this fashion—and with the Colonel, too, for that matter," observed Ravenscroft.

"In all probability he sees nothing out of the way in it," replied Corbell, bitterly. "It's just business with that sort. Probably he'd be surprised to know that anybody could see anything to object to!"

"Well, he's going to know pretty plain that *I* see something to object to!" stated Frank Moore, with great positiveness.

"Here he comes now," said Big Bill.

Kenneth appeared in the doorway. The letter had been very satisfactory, and therefore he was feeling, and looking, particularly cheerful.

"Well, where you decided to shoot to-morrow?" he called, as he entered the room.

There was no response. Kenneth looked about in surprise. The men were sitting in constraint, and were looking at him.

"What's up?" demanded Kenneth with a slight laugh. "You look solemn."

"Boyd," began Corbell, crisply, "I have known you off and on for some time in rather a casual fashion, and have always liked you. But neither I nor my friends have ever had occasion to inquire into your standards. We have assumed them to be the same as ours. We have received you as one of us on that basis."

Kenneth looked from one to the other puzzled. The smile had faded from his lips, but lingered in the corners of his mouth, ready to come back if it only proved to be another of the typical elaborate hoaxes.

"But there are some things that, according to our standards, no decent man would do."

"May I ask what you are driving at?" asked Kenneth, defensively.

Corbell handed him the letter. Kenneth read it through, slowly, the colour ebbing from his face. When he had finished he threw his head back.

"Do you believe this of me?" he asked simply.

"Jim Paige is not a man to make rash statements," said Corbell.

"I am not referring to what the *facts* may or may not be. I am referring to your inferences as to motives. This," Kenneth struck the letter violently with his fingers, but immediately regained control of himself, "states that there have been certain negotiations as to Colonel Peyton's ranch between my father and the bank. It goes on to impute base motives both to my father and myself. I am not asking you about my father— you don't know him. I am asking you about myself; you do know me. Do you believe this of me?"

"If the facts are as stated, what else are we to believe?" asked Frank Moore bluntly.

Kenneth turned on him almost savagely.

"Facts or no facts, do you think I am the sort to do a dirty trick to a man like Colonel Peyton; that's what I want to know?"

"No, by God, I don't!" roared big Bill Hunter.

"Thank you, Bill," said Kenneth gently, but he continued to look at the others.

It was Carlson, the poet, who took the situation out of the emotional and brought it to a basis of sense.

"Now see here, Kenneth," he said. "You know you can't, in the circumstances, expect to put *us* on the defensive. I don't think anybody suspects that you would deliberately do anything you would think wrong. What we are trying to find out is what *do* you think wrong, when it comes to a matter of business? We think this thing needs explanation; and, personally, I believe we have a right to an explanation."

"I haven't been asked for an explanation, I've been condemned," stated Kenneth curtly.

"Beg your pardon, Boyd," said Corbell, **stiffly.** "My fault."

"Now, Kenneth," said Carlson, not unkindly. "Tell us all you know of this, if you feel like doing so."

Kenneth hesitated, half in anger and half in embarrassment as to how to begin.

"Come on, kid," rumbled Big Bill.

"I don't understand all of this, myself," he said. "It's largely rumour with me. My father has never talked to me about it, nor even mentioned the subject. I do know he made an offer to the Colonel of some kind, but that the Colonel refused. I do know, too, that the Colonel is in serious difficulties. But as to this talk about my father's putting the Colonel off and getting the ranch for me, that is just *rot.* There has been nothing of that sort in view. I wouldn't be party to any such arrangement: and you know I wouldn't, fellows." He looked about with almost boyish appeal; but, meeting only grave attention, except in the direction of Bill Hunter, he regathered himself and went on. "Nor would my father, of that I am sure, if he understood the whole situation. He is an Eastern business man trained in business methods. He wouldn't do the Colonel a harm for the world; but I do not doubt he sees the situation from the business point of view only. Fellows, I'm positively certain that when I get a chance to talk to him I can make him see how much the old ranch means to the Colonel. He's never thought of that side of it. To him the ranch is just a piece of property; and he's thinking of it as property all the time. He knows that the Colonel has involved it deeply, and that as a business proposition it is in bad shape, and the natural thing for him to do as a business man is to figure on how the business situation can be bettered——" He broke off in apparent despair of adequate expression of this point of view. "I can't make you see it: but, fellows, please don't make up your minds until I get a chance to talk to him! I *know* I can fix it all right!"

The men were glancing doubtfully toward one another. No one spoke. Carlson again took charge of the situation.

"Would you mind letting us talk over this situation alone?" he suggested. He smiled. "Looks a little like a jury out for a verdict, doesn't it? But it isn't that, Kenneth. We value your friendship too much not to wish to retain it. On the other hand we are old-timers here, you know. Won't you think of us as friends anxious to find a way out of a very difficult situation? Come back in half an hour and we'll talk our plan over."

Kenneth made no sign, except that his gaze rested on one after the other.

"Come on, kid," rumbled Big Bill again.

The young man apparently found what he wanted in the eyes of the other men, for he turned and, without a word, went out.

"The boy is square," said Carlson decidedly, the moment he disappeared.

"You bet you!" chimed in Bill Hunter.

"I'm not so absolutely certain," doubted Frank Moore.

"I am," reasserted Carlson. "I watched him closely. He's just trying to be loyal to his father. I am convinced he knows no more about this than we do, and that he's nearly as much surprised."

"I agree with you," put in Ravenscroft.

"How about the old man, then?" asked Frank, abandoning the other point for the moment.

"He!" cried Carlson. "He's a wolf! I saw something of his methods in the boom; and I know his type in the East. He is what they're calling a captain of industry. He thinks he is perfectly honest and fair, and that makes him more dangerous. His honesty is keeping inside a hair line of legality. His fairness is an idea that the other fellow ought to be able to take care of himself. I'll believe anything of *him*—except perhaps that he'd ever go back on his word once it was clearly given."

"You talk like you'd burnt your fingers at that fire," drawled Frank Moore.

"I know what I'm talking about," shot back Carlson.

"Ken thinks it will be all right once he gets a chance to explain the situation," suggested Corbell.

Carlson hesitated. "I have no faith in it," he said at last. "That's just as I read human nature, though, and the type. Once any of these so-called big men get their course laid you can talk a thousand years and not swerve them a hair's breadth. He won't pay any attention to Ken's argument: he will simply look on it as idealistic talk of a boy who doesn't understand the situation. Those fellows have a huge conceit for their point of view."

"Then your opinion is that Ken won't be able to do anything?" asked Corbell.

"Not because of any *reasons* he may give. I don't know whether, if he presses it strongly enough, Boyd will give way to him on grounds of affection or not. I believe he is very fond of Kenneth. Personally I think he will not. What do you think, Bert.?"

"I agree with you," said Corbell.

"Gosh! It's kind of tough on Ken!" cried Bill Hunter.

"Tough on Ken!" repeated Frank Moore, disgustedly. "You fellows make me sick! I'm not worried about Ken; I'm thinking about the old Colonel. Ken's young. He's got a tough time coming out of this—sure! But he'll get over it. That's his business. Got to take that sort of thing as it comes. But the Colonel won't get over it. You take Corona del Monte away from him now, and he's going to *die*, that's all! Quit your thinking about this kid and his poor feelings and get down to brass tacks."

"You're right, Frank," agreed Corbell to this outburst. "I think we ought to give Ken a chance to see what he can do, but I think we ought to assume for purposes of discussion that he will fail."

"You bet your life he'll fail," growled Moore.

Then ensued a short silence. Nobody, apparently, could think of anything.

"The Colonel," said Corbell hesitatingly, after a moment, "probably did more kind things to me personally when I first came out here to go into the ranching business than any of you know. I'd do anything I could for him, and I'd take up his notes myself like a shot if I could afford it."

"The Colonel's done a lot for every man jack of us," struck in Carlson, "but if he hadn't done one damn thing for me I'd be there with the bells on to my limit. Fellows, it's a bad thing for the human race to see a man live his life as kindly, as affectionately, as nobly, as broadly and unselfishly as Colonel Peyton has in this community, and then at the last seem to fail.

Talk about public improvements! He's worth more in making Arguello stand out than a thousand public improvements!"

"Hear, hear!" said Frank Moore, ironically. "But where are we getting? What we going to do about it? I don't know how deep this trouble is, but I can raise exactly five thousand dollars on my old shack and surrounding landscape: they told me so at the bank last week. Wish it was more, but the sons of guns have no hearts." •

They drew together and compared notes. The total did not look very satisfactory. To be sure the aggregate represented what was to them a very large sum; but they were all practical ranchmen, they knew the value of Corona del Monte, and they realized that the liabilities must be heavy seriously to threaten it. They stared at each other a little hopelessly.

"I know what I'd do," stated Big Bill at length, "I'd just naturally shanghai the son of a gun after he'd bought that mortgage and sort of induce him to sign it over to us, or renew it, or something."

"Of course he'd do it!" said Frank, sarcastically.

"He would by the time I'd got through with him."

"You'd have to kill him first," said Corbell, impatiently.

"I'd just as leave kill him," replied Big Bill; and meant it.

They savoured this idea for a moment.

"No good," Corbell decided, with a sigh, "a signature obtained under threat is not legal."

"Well, who's going to know how we got the signature," urged Bill. "Let him tell his yarn: we'll just deny it."

"He'd get you into court and put you under oath. You'd *have* to tell the truth; or perjure yourself."

"Well, I'd perjure myself," agreed Bill, equably.

"What?" gasped Ravenscroft.

"In a holy minute!" insisted Bill, stoutly. "And so would you. All we got to do is to agree, and stay with it. I'd do worse than that for a man like Colonel Peyton against a man like this Boyd."

This idea, too, fascinated them to the point of silence for a moment. It was broken by Carlson. Again the poet proved himself practical.

"Leaving all those questions of ethics aside," he said. "It wouldn't work. You might actually kill the man, but you'd never get his signature. Nobody could ever force him to do anything. He's a fighter. I know the type."

And such was the respect of these ranchmen for the intuitive knowledge of mankind in this their one creative artist, that they accepted his dictum as a fact, and instantly abandoned Bill Hunter's gorgeous wild-west idea.

For ten minutes longer they discussed possibilities but arrived nowhere. Then Carlson went out to find Ken.

"I think I can fix things up better with him alone than having him in here before us all as though he were getting a verdict," he said. "You know, after all, the situation *is* rather hard on him."

They were only too glad to agree; for, like all men, they hated the idea of a possible open display of sentiment or emotion.

VI

EARLY the following morning the party took horse to a man and moved back to Arguello. Kenneth's renewed expressions of confidence in his ability to arrange matters were received without open scepticism. Nevertheless, it was felt desirable that Colonel Peyton's friends should be on hand to receive an immediate report. That was the way they put it. Kenneth agreed to interview his father at once, and then to meet the *Sociedad* no matter what the hour, in the little room back of the Fremont bar. Accordingly he rode on into town and directly to his home. He cast a longing eye on the cross roads leading up to the Bungalow. It would not take very long to gallop up there, greet Daphne and hurry on. He desired to do so with a great desire, but put the thought from him.

It was not until after the evening meal, however, that Patrick Boyd would touch on business.

"I know; I've got something to tell you, too," he informed Kenneth; "but let's talk it over in the den. I want to hear about you, since I've been gone."

Once settled in a big easy chair and his cigar alight, Boyd said:

"Well, what you got on your mind?"

Kenneth found it unexpectedly difficult to begin.

"Why, it's this business of Colonel Peyton's ranch," he blurted at last.

Boyd's heavy face lit with pleasure.

"Why, that's funny; that's just what I wanted to talk to *you* about. Ken, that's one of the biggest propositions I've seen on this coast, as it stacks up at present. I can't conceive of a better opening for a young fellow in a big operation than there is right there now. That's what I've been East to see about. And I fixed it! Why, my boy, I've got the biggest names in New York back of me! I didn't want to tell you much about it before it was a settled matter, because I didn't want to disappoint you if it fell through; but, son, it's riveted tight now!"

He beamed and slapped his thick leg resoundingly.

"But, father——" Kenneth began.

"Hold on! My innings! You can talk later. I've been holding in long enough. Listen here——" he leaned forward in his easy chair. "I've got Bates into this thing, and Van Steyn of the Old National, and Saltonstall, the Wall Street man. We're incorporated in New Jersey for a million. All I've got to do is to gather up the loose ends, and we can start right in with our heavy construction."

"Heavy construction?" repeated Kenneth. He was puzzled. This did not sound like anything to do with Colonel Peyton.

Boyd laughed.

"I forgot you didn't know. Well, the scheme is this: I've got water rights in the Sur staked out and tied down. All that is necessary, my engineers say, is to do certain tunnel work and build certain dams. I've got, or got options upon, rights of way for pipe lines or ditches. We can bring water enough down to irrigate an immense area of land. In addition when Arguello outgrows her present water supply—as anybody but these mossbacks here could see is bound to happen—we'll be in shape to step in. Also we're figuring on some scheme to generate electricity—possibly by a series of reservoirs at different levels so as not to waste the irrigation water. It's a big proposition!"

"It certainly is!" cried Kenneth, fired with the enthusiasm of the vision, and greatly relieved that this scheme seemed to be the basis of his father's activities. But the next speech dashed him.

"The big money, though, at the start is from this Peyton property," pursued Boyd. He laughed like a delighted boy. "That's where you come in, Ken: that's your part of it. You've earned the chance. Without you the scheme wouldn't have been considered."

"What do you mean?" demanded Kenneth.

"Your work at Brainerd's—that gave me the idea. Don't you see, if you hadn't showed there what could actually be done on a small scale—demonstrated it—, that nobody'd have the nerve to tackle it on a big scale? With that example right next door, you can satisfy anybody that, with the water we can supply them, they can make a living off ten acres and a darn good thing off twenty! Now you take that Peyton property. It can be taken over at the present time for what amounts to an average of ten dollars an acre. And that's every cent it's worth," he added, noting a change in Kenneth's expression. "Don't forget that final value is what is put into raw material. And any land around here is nothing but raw material. Now that same land, divided, will sell at the start-off for three hundred an acre; and later some of it will go as high as a thousand. That's where the really big profits of the water scheme will come in."

He leaned back, smiling triumphantly at his son.

"But, father, it would kill Colonel Peyton to lose his ranch."

"He's lost it already," Boyd waved this aside. "Of course, we'll take care of the old man. He'll be a lot better off than he would be otherwise."

"The ranch is part of his very existence, father. Wouldn't some other property do?"

"Of course a great deal of property will come under irrigation when the water is developed," answered Boyd, patiently, "but there is nothing as centrally located, as directly in line of the water, that lays as well for irrigation, or that offers near the chance. And I don't believe we could find anything anywhere else as cheap."

Kenneth was silent for some moments. He did not know how to begin.

"Father," he said at last, "you say this land part of it is mine. I'm willing to take less profits. Consider something else beside the Peyton ranch."

Boyd opened his eyes wide.

"What's the idea?" he demanded.

"I like the Colonel. I don't want to see him in trouble."

"What's that got to do with it? He's in trouble already."

"Yes, I know. But he could go on as he is, if you did not act. You know that, father. Let's leave the old man in peace. He's lived on that place for a long time."

"Ken, I do wish you would grow up and be a man," said Boyd impatiently, but not unkindly. "You must get over this sentimentalizing and look at plain facts."

Kenneth threw himself heart and soul into his plea. It must be confessed that he was not too coherent: his feelings were too deeply involved. Boyd listened at first with incredulity, then with impatience, ending in an attitude of combined amusement and toleration. His thought could have been read by a disinterested bystander. Kenneth was younger than he had imagined. Also he was disappointed. Where he had anticipated sympathy and understanding, he encountered opposite. Well, he had generally played a lone hand.

"You don't quite know what you are talking about, Ken," he said. "When you are older you will see things in a more practical way; and you will thank me for not doing as you wish now. I know you mean it, but it's moonshine; it's not practical."

Kenneth experienced at once a sinking of dismay and a flush of anger. No one likes to be relegated cavalierly to the infant class.

"Then you're going right ahead in this—this scheme?" he stammered.

"Why, of course, my boy."

"But if I understand it, you are doing this mostly for me. I don't want it. I'll gladly give up any interest I may have."

"I wouldn't let you," said Boyd, decidedly.

"But——"

"See here, Ken, I don't want to treat you as anything but as a grown-up man: but you must act like one. Good Lord! How

In the world can you expect to succeed in business if you act like this every time you step on any one's toes!"

"Well, then, I don't want to succeed in business!" cried Kenneth.

This was too childish. Boyd looked at his son coldly.

"Well, I do," he stated. "I've put a lot of time and thought into this scheme. I am very much disappointed that it does not meet with your approval, but it will of course go on without it. Do you realize that I am involved in this thing, that I have given my word and pledged my honour to associates in the East? Even if I were inclined to drop this matter on account of your attitude toward it—which I am not——, it would be impossible. It has gone too far. How would I look trying to draw back from my agreements because my son felt sorry for someone? You can see yourself that it is nonsense."

He had kept his hard direct gaze fixed on his son's face during the delivery of this speech. Kenneth's head had dropped as the unexpected realization was forced on him that his father would be as impervious to influence as a diving suit to water. Boyd thought this attitude of sadness betokened resignation.

"You'll feel differently about it," he said more kindly. "Think it over. And don't worry about old Peyton. We'll take care of him in good shape. You can pretty near fix him up to suit yourself, if you want to. Better turn in. I'm going to read awhile before I go over for the mail."

Kenneth hesitated. His spirit was like lead. It fluttered its bruised wings, but could not stir from the depths. There was nothing he could add to his impassioned appeal: there was no other angle from which the steel fortress of Boyd's ideas, training, and ethical code could be approached.

"Good night, Father," he said miserably, and went out.

VII

THE four blocks' walk to the Fremont was a bitter one. Kenneth's confidence had been so great that all that would be necessary would be to make his father understand the situation, that he would rather have died than face his friends with a confession of failure. And worse than this he would have to acknowledge before them that his father—his own father—was capable of actions that he himself could not approve. Ken's feeling of family loyalty fought hard. Was he to turn against his own father? Should he not stick to him, right or wrong? His affectional instincts tore at his decision. Slower and slower became his steps, as he pondered.

At the square devoted to the beginnings of a city park he turned in one of the paths and sat down on a bench beneath a pepper tree; and there fought the matter out with himself. So absorbed was he that for twenty minutes his attitude did not change by so much as a hair's breadth. At last he arose, his mind made up. The immediate, the insistent thing was to serve justice. If he could do anything to help Colonel Peyton, he must do it. He must be personally loyal to his father, and must make that evident to the others.

He found the situation unexpectedly easy. The members of the *Sociedad* glanced at his face, nodded gravely to his constrained statement that his father seemed too deeply involved with Eastern men to abandon the scheme, and dismissed that aspect of the subject.

"We've been getting a few details while you were away," Corbell told him. "We know the amount of the notes and how much in arrears the interest is. Also we know that the mortgage is to be made over to Mr. Boyd the first of the month. That gives us four days. Now it remains to see if we can do anything."

"I've been thinking," suggested Kenneth, "that if I only had time to make the arrangements, I could get hold of my own property. That might help in some way."

"Own property?"—"how much?"—"what do you mean?" cried Corbell, Carlson, and Frank Moore in a breath.

"I have an inheritance—from my mother," said Kenneth. "It would take care of about half of this thing, if I could realize on it. Perhaps we could fix up the other half somehow."

"You mean you'd use this?" asked Corbell.

"Why, of course."

"On what basis?"

"What do you mean?"

"I mean how would you invest it here? How would you expect it to be secured at the ranch?"

"Oh, I don't know. I don't care much. That could be fixed in any way, just so the Colonel was all right."

"Well, what's the use of talking? You haven't got it," grumbled Frank Moore.

"I know it!" cried Ken. "If we only had more time! I suppose it would take ten days, anyway, even if we wired."

"You could realize in ten days? Your property is in securities?" struck in Corbell keenly.

"Yes," replied Kenneth to both questions.

"And you'd do it?"

"Of course I would. But we haven't got but four days."

Corbell turned to big Bill Hunter.

"Here's where you have your innings, old hippopotamus," he said. "No, listen," he commanded, as the others started to speak. "I think we can pull this off. Ken will send for his money: that makes half. We'll get busy at the banks and raise what we can. That leaves only about thirty thousand dollars shy. Hell! We'll either raise that, somehow, or leave it."

"But we've only got four days," objected Frank Moore.

"We've got until Patrick Boyd goes down to complete the transaction."

"Well, he'll be there on the minute——" began Bill Hunter; but the quicker-witted practical joker in Frank Moore caught the point.

"Kipnap him!" he cried. "Great! That's where you come in, Bill."

"And hold him nice and safe and peaceful and mad until we've completed the deal and got the thing tied down," added Corbell.

"The bank has voted to sell to Boyd," interposed Ravenscroft, with one of his common-sense flashes. "Suppose it will not sell to us?"

"It will to Kenneth, if he works it right. They can be gently led to believe he's acting for his father."

"Will you do that, old man?" asked Ravenscroft.

"I suppose so," said Kenneth, miserably. "If it's the only way."

"You're all right, kid," rumbled Big Bill.

Ravenscroft, who was near him, patted him on the shoulder. Such a demonstration from the usually self-contained Englishman caused a lump to form in Kenneth's throat.

"We'll make it as easy as we know how," said Frank Moore, and at this amend Ken had to wink hard. The strain had been relieved; and the old atmosphere of trust and good-fellowship reëstablished. A little warmth of comfort crept into Kenneth's heart. He could not but feel himself a traitor in some way, and the whole situation a disaster. He was going through with his duty, but dully; and after it was performed he could not see how the future was to help him.

Corbell briskly brought the conference back to practical considerations.

"The agreement with the bank was that these notes were to be bought in four days, as I understand it. Suppose they stick tight on that, and refuse to extend the time? We've got to think of everything, you know."

But Frank Moore could see no difficulty here.

"Ken will go ahead at the proper day," said he, "and then he can insist on an abstract, and search title, and fiddle around. Get a lawyer; that's what they are for."

"I guess you're right. All right. Now let's get this straight. Ken is to wire for his money at once. We are to raise ours right away."

"How about the remaining thirty thousand?" "On what basis is this money to be put in?" asked Carlson and Frank in a breath.

"We've got ten days to figure all those details," Corbell reminded them. His black eyes were dancing, and the sharp, waxed points of his moustache seemed to stick out as though quivering with eagerness. "I'm laying out present activities. Kenneth goes into the bank Monday and fixes it up, in his name. In the meantime we see that Mr. Boyd has a good pigeon shoot over the mountains. That all clear?"

"Oh, I feel like a traitor!" burst out Kenneth. "My own father!"

"You mustn't feel that way, Ken," said the poet, gently. "We all know that your father is honestly acting according to his lights. But there isn't time to convince him. It's a matter of education. We have to adopt measures to fit an immediate need. You must keep in mind all the time through this that we know you are doing what is right against all your natural instincts and affections, and that we honour and admire you for it from the bottom of our hearts."

"Hear! hear!" applauded Ravenscroft.

"And that we understand how your father looks at it, and we understand that it is not himself nor his business we disapprove of, but only the fact that those methods cannot fit this case. And we realize that this case is so different from your father's experience that he simply cannot understand it as we do, who have been brought up here. We esteem your father as much as you do, really."

"The hell we do!" growled Frank Moore, but he said it under his breath; and he received a kick in the shin from Corbell for his pains.

Kenneth looked measurably relieved at this speech. He was in the frame of mind when a little comfort goes a long way.

"Now perhaps you'd better get down town to the telegraph office," Corbell suggested to Ken. "Nothing like the present!"

The moment the young man had departed, Corbell drew the group closer together.

"Now to get hold of Boyd," said he. "We can't precisely storm his house, and we can't precisely abduct him off the streets in broad daylight."

"Ask him to go somewhere with us, and then nail him," suggested Moore, carelessly.

Corbell thought for some moments.

"I've got it. Get some letter paper, someone. I'll tell him we want his opinion as a banker on the value of that old hog wallow Frank bought in the boom, and ask him to drive out there in the morning."

But Frank, who had gone out for the paper, came hurrying back.

"He's out there in the office now!" he cried. "Barney says he comes over every evening about this time after his mail."

"He probably goes straight home from here," surmised the quick-witted Corbell. "He wouldn't carry a lot of mail around with him otherwise."

"The park is a nice dark place," observed Bill Hunter. "He must pass that."

Corbell leaped delightedly on the big man and rumpled up his hair.

"Bill, at times you are without price!" he cried. "Quick— Frank, you run around and get the buckboard and drive to the southeast corner of the park and wait there. Go on; get! You want to hurry! Come on, Bill, get up your muscle: we'll need you!"

They all trooped out through the bar and disappeared into the night. At about the same instant another individual, to whom Boyd's habits had become accurately known, descended at the edge of town from a ramshackle vegetable wagon and took his leisurely way toward the park. He held his arms folded placidly across his stomach, and in one of his flowing sleeves he carried a 45 Colt's revolver with the barrel sawed off short.

VIII

ARRIVED at the park, the men sat down to await Patrick Boyd's arrival. There was no reason to conceal themselves; Boyd would have no suspicion; so they merely sat on one of the benches so placed as to give them a view of the corner with the street lamp. After five minutes a dark figure came into view. It was obviously not Boyd, so the *Sociedad* sat tight. The newcomer, instead of passing, looked up and down the street, and then slipped into the shadow of a cassia, where he waited. This was interesting. The *Sociedad* sat up and took notice.

"Looks like a hold-up," breathed Corbell to Shot Sheridan.

Big Bill Hunter was stooped over busily unlacing his shoes. He leaned toward his companions.

"Watch me get him," he whispered; and started across the soft grass.

They watched him, fascinated. Here was where Big Bill excelled. An inch at a time he stole forward, without abrupt motions. His huge body seemed to melt from one shadow to another. The shrill chorus of the tree-toads overlaid any slight noises that his movements might have caused. If those sitting on the bench had not seen him start, and had not followed closely his progress, they would not have been able to guess his whereabouts; nor, indeed, to suspect that he existed at all. Certainly the watcher under the cassia bush, his back to his danger, his attention riveted on the street, had no faintest warning. A great black bulk arose silently behind him. There was a muffled cry, as though a rat had squeaked; a brief upheaval; and then the black bulk, considerably augmented, turned toward them openly across the grass.

"Wonderful work, Bill!" they congratulated him. "What you got?"

"Chink," grunted Bill, who was carrying his captive bodily, "hatchet man, I guess. Anyway, he's got a gun. Layin' for some other highbinder, I reckon. Seems to be a popular hold-up ground here."

"Set him down and lets take a look at him," said Corbell.

Shot lighted a match and held it up.

"Sing Toy!" cried someone out of a stupified silence.

"Here comes Boyd," warned Carlson.

They turned down the slanting walk in a close group holding Sing Toy among them. Just outside the light from the street lamp they stopped and allowed the financier to approach. Boyd peered at the group, trying to make them out.

"Ah, gentlemen, good evening;" he recognized them at last. As they occupied the whole of the sidewalk and did not give way he perforce came to a halt.

"We have been waiting for you, Mr. Boyd," said Corbell. "We are driving back to the ranch to-night, and we want you to go with us. There are plenty of pigeons just now."

"Why, that's very kind of you, gentlemen," laughed Boyd, "but you see I am not prepared. I could hardly go at such short notice." He thought them perhaps a little drunk, and so to be humoured.

"We can supply you with all the necessities," continued Corbell, "we must really insist on your accompanying us."

"Well, come over to the house and have a drink, and we'll talk it over," said Boyd. There is no bigger nuisance than an insistent, drunken man.

"You do not understand. You must go with us now."

Boyd looked up in surprise at the tone of Corbell's voice. Big Bill Hunter had edged around behind him, Shot Sheridan and Ravenscroft stood at either elbow; all three big, strong men. Carlson was in the background holding Sing Toy above the elbow: but to Boyd they looked like two more available combatants. He suddenly became deadly serious.

"May I ask you gentlemen what this joke means?" he enquired.

"We will have all the time in the world for explanations later," replied Corbell, "at the present you are to go with us over the mountains. You can go voluntarily and comfortably; or you can refuse and simply be taken. You are a man of common-sense and you realize you will be taken if we choose to take you."

Boyd was silent for several moments.

"I have no idea what this is all about," he snarled at last, "but I warn you, I see no humour in it at all; and I warn you that I shall take steps to see that you regret it. If it's a joke, it is a poor one; if it is intimidation for some purpose I can't even guess at, you've got the wrong man, for I can't be forced; if it is blackmail——"

But at this point Corbell interrupted.

"Come, Mr. Boyd, there is no use in all that. The point is, *you are going with us*. The rest can wait. But let me, in turn, tell you this; as long as you go peaceably and quietly, you will go comfortably, as you are; but the moment you attempt to struggle or cry out Mr. Hunter will take charge. You say you are not to be frightened by threats; but that is one you would do well to attend."

Without further parley the group moved compactly along the diagonal walk that led across the park. At the farther corner waited Frank Moore with the buckboard and José, Corbell's horse wrangler. He peered at them interestedly as they approached, but said nothing.

"Now, here's the plan," said Corbell. "José will drive you back

to the ranch. Bill, you and Shot will occupy the back seat with
Mr. Boyd between you. I don't need to tell you what to do.
The rest of us will be over by to-morrow evening or next day
sometime. We've got to get things moving at this end. I suppose you got a fresh team, José, and some grub?"

"Sure," replied the Mexican.

"All right, you're off. See you later."

No one spoke. Boyd at a signal mounted to the back seat
in the buckboard, which presently drove off.

"If you're going to abduct, nothing like having a sensible man
to abduct," observed Corbell.

"No trouble, eh?" asked Frank.

"Not a bit. At first he thought we were drunk. Then, when
he saw we were in earnest he came along like a lamb."

"Yellow, you think?"

"Not a little bit. Just cool and sensible. I'll bet he's doing
a lot of wondering. Well, let's get back to the hotel and see what
wires Ken has sent."

"Hold on," interposed Carlson, "what am I to do with this?"

"Hullo, who you got there?" cried Frank.

"Sing Toy; the Colonel's chink; sneaking around with a gun.
Oh Lord! I forgot all about him! And he saw it all! We've got
to keep him quiet. Bring him along."

IX

THEY returned to their old gathering place, the little room
back of the Fremont bar, Sing Toy paddling contentedly alongside. He seated himself on the edge of a chair, tucked his feet
demurely underneath it, and proceeded at once to cross-question
his captors.

"What you do with dat man?" he demanded.

"What you do with that gun?" countered Corbell.

"Dat allee light," Sing Toy brushed this minor detail aside.
"I wan' know what you do with dat man?"

"Look here, Sing Toy," said Corbell, earnestly. "We no hurt
him. We take him across the mountain, keep him one week, two
week, bring him back."

"What for?" demanded Sing Toy.

"That our pidgin,"* replied Corbell. "You good friend to us; you say nothing at all to anybody."

"What for you take him?" said Sing Toy.

He looked from one to the other with his beady eyes, but without moving his head.

"Good Lord!" ejaculated Corbell in despair. He knew the Chinese—everyone knew the Chinese in those days—and he recognized the bland persistency that would be neither swerved nor balked. "Look here, Sing Toy," he explained, with an elaborate appearance of patience. "You live long time with the Colonel, good many years."

"Fo'teen year, tlee month," supplied Sing Toy.

"All right. You like Colonel very much?"

Sing Toy nodded, unblinking.

"Well, this man not good friend to Colonel. So we take him over mountains because he do bad pidgin for the Colonel and we want to stop it."

"Aren't you giving this show away too much? He'll get us into trouble if he blabs," interposed Frank swiftly.

"He can get us into just as much trouble with what he saw to-night—if he wants to," Corbell pointed out. "Better let me run this."

Sing Toy waited until this by-play was finished, quite as though he had not understood a word of it.

"We want you to say nothing," continued Corbell. "We no hurt him."

"You kill him, you want to," stated Sing Toy astonishingly. "I no care. I kill him myself, but you go stop me."

They stared at him in blank astonishment.

"Well, I'll be damned!" ejaculated Corbell. "So you were laying for Boyd with that baby cannon of yours, were you? What for you want kill him?"

"Same t'ing. He make bad pidgin for Cunnel."

"What do you know about it."

"Know all 'bout it. My second-uncle he wo'k in bank."

Suddenly Sing Toy became voluble. His monosyllabic style

---

*Pidgin—business.

of discourse gave way to a flood of apparently uncorrelated syllables. It did not sound exactly like Chinese. As a matter of fact it was Sing Toy's kind of English produced under excitement. Ravenscroft stared rather wildly. But the others smoked in placid calm. They knew the Chinese, and they were waiting for Sing Toy to run down. When this at length happened, Corbell resumed his catechism. Patiently, by question, he elicited sentence by sentence what the oration had been about. Sing Toy's second uncle seemed to have been possessed of astonishingly particularized information. Sing Toy knew more about the Colonel's affairs, the amount and kind of his paper, and especially all the details of the directors' meeting, including its discussions and the nature of its agreements and resolutions than any man present. The four white men listened with a growing respect.

"So you sorted out your gun and went after him. What you think you make by that?" commented Carlson, when he had finished.

"Eve'ybody say they solly, velly solly. Nobody do nothing at all. Nobody," stated Sing Toy. "I try get money. All China-man know Cunnel. They know he good man, that he pay some time. They jus' soon lend Cunnel money. No can get enough. So I go kill him."

"Sing Toy, you're all right!" cried Carlson warmly.

"What for you take him? What you do with dat man?" Sing Toy returned inexorably to his first question.

Corbell rolled a comical eye at his friends and began painstakingly to explain in words of one syllable. He was cut short.

"I savvy," said Sing Toy. "You got 'nuff money?"

"Well—no—not quite," confessed Corbell, "but we'll fix that somehow."

"How much you need?"

"Oh, quite a lot."

"How much?"

"Better tell him first as last," laughed Carlson. "He'll never let up on you."

"Thirty thousand dollars," said Corbell.

"All light," agreed Sing Toy, placidly. "I ketch 'um."

"You'll get it? Thirty thousand dollars? Where can you raise that sum?" cried Corbell, with scornful incredulity.

"Chinatown, I ketch 'um."

"But, Sing Toy, you can't take any such sum from your friends on this sort of a thing. The security is not very good."

"You tell me some day he pay him back?" asked Sing Toy.

"Yes, if we can. But we can't be sure—it's very uncertain——"

"All light," interrupted Sing Toy, comfortably. "Cunnel my fliend, you my fliend, all fliends of Chinaman in Chinatown. You say pay him some day. Dat all light. I ketch 'um."

At that moment Kenneth's voice was heard in the barroom enquiring of Barney.

"He's all right," said Corbell, hurriedly. "He's good boy. He's not in this."

"I know. He all light," said Sing Toy; and the men looking on his kind, carved old face confessed to respectful wonder. In him seemed to be embodied all the mysterious knowledge and wisdom of the Orient.

X

THE night drive over the mountains was without especial incident. Boyd disgustedly thought his captors drunk and informed with one of the wild ideas for which they were famous. Another prank for which they would be sorry and very apologetic in the morning. And he would see that they were good and sorry, he thought savagely. It was about time that someone showed this gang of hoodlums that they couldn't break laws and annoy peaceful citizens for their own amusement. There had been too much leniency, too much good-natured tolerance. These were men; not irresponsible boys. It was time they grew up.

With these and similar thoughts did Boyd pass the long, slow journey and keep himself warm in the cool night air of the valley. Nobody uttered a syllable the whole distance. The silence was unbroken except for the creak and rattle of the buckboard, the scrape of the brakes, the strain of the harness, the soft, occasional snorting or blowing of the horses. On either side of Boyd the bulky forms of Bill Hunter and Sheridan were wedged in so tightly that movement was all but impossible. They did not act drunk.

The arrival at Corbell's ranch house was at a little after daybreak, that time just before the sun comes over the hill, when the air is shivery, the light gray, and the rose-coloured east is paling rapidly to the clarities of yellow and green. In the half light the men's faces looked gray and fatigued. The flame of Boyd's anger had sunk with his vitality. He had become viciously sullen.

Sheridan and Hunter got out stiffly either side the buckboard.

"We stop here," said Sheridan, briefly.

They went into the central part of the ranch house, and after a moment's hesitation Boyd followed them. Hunter was rapidly constructing a fire in the big fireplace, while Sheridan was fussing with an alcohol coffee machine that stood ready on the side table. Presently the flames were leaping up the chimney. Hunter then went out; and a moment later his huge voice could be heard arousing the Chinese cook.

"We'll have breakfast in a few minutes," he observed, returning. "Better thaw out, Mr. Boyd."

Boyd drew near the grateful warmth. These men were cold sober. The prank, if it was a prank, was not the freak product of whim; it was being carried out deliberately. For what earthly purpose? A bet? That might well be; but in the last analysis this did not seem a convincing solution. These men were wild enough and careless enough of opinion: but they were gentlemen and good sportsmen and not likely to bet in cold blood on a feat that would bring so great a degree of discomfort and inconvenience to an outsider. Nor would it be a funny bet, as it might be were they to kidnap old Major Gaylord, or somebody of like dignity. It seemed more serious, more planned than a joke.

If not a joke, then what the motive? Self-interest. What self-interest, and how was it to be served? Boyd's logical mind attacked these problems one at a time. Leaving for later consideration what the self-interest might be, how could kidnapping him in this fashion further it? Either they would try to intimidate him into some course of action: or they were getting him out of the way for a certain length of time for some purpose. What, then, was the self interest? Boyd had certain definite interests in Arguello County and he ran them over mentally to determine possible points of contact. The real estate transactions were dead and buried; the water rights and works were entirely out of their ken:—it was undoubtedly the matter of the Peyton ranch. The notes were to be handed over in four days——

This lead opened many possibilities—too many to canvass. They might think that by keeping him beyond the appointed time, the deal would fall through; they might have some arrangement to take it over themselves when Boyd failed to complete the transaction; they might hope to force him by threat to some course of action—— Boyd was too tired after his all-night drive to think the thing out to its conclusion. But he felt he was on the right track. Therefore he drew up to the breakfast with a more cheerful countenance. He resented being made the victim of a silly joke. But this!—here was a fight worthy of him. Intimidation? He'd show them that a man who had faced the wolf pack had no fear of them! A more subtle scheme? He had used his wit before. What could these inexperienced back country ranchmen concoct that would be proof against his experience! He eyed Big Bill and Shot with sardonic amusement. Thick-headed watchdogs, these. No use wasting time on them. He had heard Corbell tell them to expect him that evening. There was his real antagonist.

"Well, gentlemen," he remarked, as he drew up his chair. "I assure you I do not know what this is all about, unless you will enlighten me."

"Better wait for Bert—Corbell," mumbled Bill.

"I thought so. But perhaps you can tell me what are my privileges. I *am* a prisoner?"

"Do anything you please," answered Sheridan. "We'll show you a room, and I'll get you some plunder to make you comfortable. There's plenty of smokes and drinks. You probably want some sleep. You're welcome to move around all you want."

"Around, but not away," suggested Boyd.

"Oh, you're not going to get away," replied Shotwell, grimly.
"We're responsible for your appearance this evening; and you're
going to appear! It's some few miles to the nearest house—
except some of our ranch houses; the country is open; and there
will be men on watch. Try to get away, if you think it will
amuse you: you have my permission."

"Thanks," returned Boyd dryly, "but I'm too heavy for all
that foot work. Besides, I'd rather like to be here this evening.
I may have a word to say myself."

"That'll be all right," Shot yawned prodigiously. "Suit yourself. I'm going to turn in for a snooze. Want me to show you
where you bunk?"

Corbell's trap drew in about four o'clock, followed shortly by
two horsemen. Boyd who had awakened refreshed and was
taking a cigar under the big cottonwood trees up the creek, saw
them dismount and disappear in the ranch house. He smiled
sardonically. The time for a show down had come. They
would find with whom they had to deal. He was in no hurry:
let them come to him.

But they did not come to him. He finished his cigar; then,
making up his mind, he started off briskly down the road. He
could make the stage station in about three hours, he figured,
provided he was not prevented. Boyd did not really expect
to accomplish an escape, but he was grimly amused to determine
how much rope he was to be allowed. About a mile down the
road he turned off into the sagebrush and across country in the
general direction of the stage station. He came to a bare knoll
wooded on top. Struck with an idea, he circled this, climbed
rapidly on the far side to the summit, and there advanced cautiously through the low growth until he could look back. The
rolling countryside lay spread before him, bathed in the yellow
light of late afternoon. The scattered oaks and patches of
sagebrush stood out with stereoscopic clearness. Boyd scanned
very foot carefully. Nothing moved, save strings of cattle
sauntering placidly in the direction of water. For ten minutes
Boyd lay there waiting for something to appear. Nothing did.
Then he arose and walked on briskly. It was incredible, but it
actually seemed as though his abandoning of the road had set

him free of surveillance: or perhaps the watcher had nodded. At any rate it was too good a chance to lose. And at every moment the chance grew better, for the sun was touching the mountains.

At the end of an hour he came over the edge of a grass hill square upon Bill Hunter seated in the buckboard smoking his pipe.

"Nice day for a walk," said Bill. "Fellow gets farther than he thinks. Thought you might like a lift back. It's getting close to supper time."

Boyd stared. How had the man contrived to intercept him in this uncanny fashion? Never mind that for the present. His eye had noticed the spirited, restless team and an idea had struck him.

"I'm through with your foolishness; and you drive on out of the way. I'm not going with you."

"Oh, yes you are."

"How will you make me?"

Bill surveyed him lazily.

"If this was the wild west," said he. "I'd pull a gun on you and tell you to climb in."

"A lot of attention I'd pay to your gun!" returned Boyd, contemptuously. "I'm not fool enough to think that you mean murder. I'd call your bluff. You wouldn't shoot."

"Oh, I wouldn't mind," said Bill, his voice hardening for a moment. "But we needn't argue that: it ain't necessary. I can handle two of you, and I'll just lift you in like a baby. Want me to show you?"

Boyd grinned triumphantly, and stooped to pick up a handful of the hard *adobe*.

"The first little move you make toward leaving your seat I'll bombard your horses. I think you'd have your hands full then. Now you drive right on peacefully ahead of me until we get to the stage station. I know something about horses, and I know a few handfuls of this will give you something to manage, even if you were as big as a house."

"Ingenious cuss, ain't you?" observed Bill. "But I was aiming to let Chino hold the horses."

He waved his hand. Boyd whirled to find behind him a stolid carvenfaced dark man.

"Chino is quite an Injin," said Bill, cheerfully. "Say, how did you suppose I happened to meet you here, anyway? You must think I'm a good guesser!" He spoke a few words in Spanish and received a reply. "I was just asking him which way you'd come," he volunteered to Boyd. "That hill is a good place to spy from, all right. You had the right idea there. But you're too green at this sort of thing. You were just watching your back track to see if you were followed, and you saw nothing. Good reason: there was nothing there. Chino was away off your flank all the time." He laughed his great guffaw. "Come on; hop in: it's getting on to sunset."

Boyd climbed aboard without another word, and they drove back to the ranch.

There he was greeted politely, as though nothing had happened. He ate supper in almost complete silence, answering direct questions in monosyllables. After supper he sat four-square and smoked his cigar. He made up his mind to force them to make the first move. That was good strategy. Only they did not make it. All sorts of topics were discussed, as though Boyd were not present at all. At nine o'clock Corbell arose.

"Let's hit the hay," he suggested. "We must all be tired."

And before he knew it, Boyd found himself in his bedroom; as much at sea as ever concerning what it was all about.

Nor did he obtain any more satisfaction when, wearying of the waiting game, he took the offensive. Everybody listened to him; and no one said anything in reply. He warned them that he was not a man tamely to submit to outrage, and they would do well to remember that he intended to carry this matter away through: they inclined their ears sympathetically. He lost his temper and told him what he thought of them; they inclined their ears sympathetically. He argued with them as reasonable beings that his time was valuable, that this joke had gone far enough: they inclined their ears sympathetically. He even accused them boldly of conspiracy in regard to the Peyton ranch, and warned them that they were butting their heads against a stone wall;

they inclined their ears sympathetically; but by not one syllable did they indicate whether a single pellet of all his broadsides had reached the mark. And when he had finished, they went right on with everyday matters as though he had not opened his mouth. It was maddening.

They invited him to participate in everything they did— pigeon shooting, riding the ranch, poker parties, and the like. They expressed regret when he declined curtly, but did not press the matter. Apparently he was as free as air, yet several little things happened to show him that he was well and constantly watched. For example, one day Boyd saw from his room window a stranger driving in with one of the white-topped, spring buggies used for light travelling. This seemed an opportunity to place the fact of his captivity duly on record. Boyd threw open the door, only to find himself confronted by the burly forms of Chino and another.

"You go back now," they told him.

At last he fell into a fiercely sullen fit, like a resentful, impotent, teased bear. The very pressure of his ignorance began to make him uneasy. Try as he would he had gained no inkling of what it was all about, nor how long his detention was to last. His mind had swung to the Peyton deal as the pivot of all this; but for the life of him he could not see how he was there vulnerable. Item by item he went over the whole plan. It was copper-riveted! Nevertheless the cumulative effect of the long hours brought him finally to an instinctive, though non-reasoning, un-easiness in regard to it all. Everything was all right, of course; but he wished he could be there and find out. The only possible way these men could put a spoke in his wheel was by purchasing the notes themselves—if the bank would sell to them! Small chance! Boyd knew both their circumstances and their con-nections; and he was positive they could raise no such amount. How about raising it elsewhere? Remotely, very remotely possible: but it would have to be from some source unknown to Boyd: and his knowledge of their affiliations was pretty com-plete. Undoubtedly they were doing this melodramatic kid-napping to give themselves time to try to raise the money. If he had to remain captive until that result was achieved, he reflected with grim amusement, he was due for a long visit. But if they did manage to accomplish the miracle of commanding that much credit, it would get them nowhere. Boyd's confidence, after all, rested on the bank. He knew positively his power there. He knew positively that the officials would dare sell to nobody but himself. Let them try it!

Nevertheless, he wished he could call at the bank for five minutes!

XI

ABOUT six o'clock one evening at the end of the eighth day, Boyd, pacing up and down the veranda smoking a solitary cigar, saw a horseman draw rein under the big cottonwood at the edge of the road. A moment later Chino stepped from some mysterious concealment. The horseman conversed with him a moment, handed him a letter, and rode off the way he had come, without giving Boyd an opportunity to see who he was. That evening Corbell casually informed him that they would be returning to Arguello the following morning.

They drove back together in Corbell's high trap. Evidently it was no longer considered worth while to guard him. The other members of the *Sociedad* had vanished; they did not even appear at breakfast. Boyd did not enquire of them; nor did Corbell volunteer any information. As a matter of fact they were already well on toward Arguello, having started on horseback across the short cut trail long before daylight.

The long drive was made almost in silence. Corbell seemed entirely interested and occupied in the tooling of his fine team around the curves and narrow places of the pass; while Boyd remained wrapped in his thoughts. As they struck out on the level road below the grade on the Arguello side, he said:

"I wish to say again, Mr. Corbell, that I consider this whole performance an inexcusable outrage. And I wish to warn you that I shall determine what legal steps are possible and shall pursue them with the ultmost vigour."

"As to that you must suit yourself, Mr. Boyd," rejoined Corbell, gravely. "I can speak for my associates as well as myself in saying that we accept fu'l responsibility before any jury that can be got together in Arguello County." His tone was perfectly polite, but a faint shadow of a smile touched his lips beneath his neat moustache. Confound the fellow, thought Boyd, he knows only too well what to expect of these jay juries! And the thought caused a new surge of anger within him.

No further word was spoken until they approached the edge of town.

"Where can I put you down?" asked Corbell, courteously.

Boyd glanced at his watch. It was after four. The higher officials would have gone home, in accordance with the leisurely custom of the day; but the subordinates would still be at work.

"Leave me at the First National," he said, curtly.

The curtains were drawn, but his rattle of the door brought him speedy admittance. Crosby, the assistant cashier, sat at the big flat desk in the front office.

"How do, Mr. Boyd," he greeted, cheerfully. "Been off on quite a trip!"

"Yes," rejoined Boyd shortly. "Just back. Delayed. Now about that Peyton deal. Sorry not to have been here on the appointed day. Papers all ready?"

"Oh, that's all finished up——"

"Finished up?" repeated Boyd. "What do y'mean!"

"We handed over the papers and got our money yesterday."

Boyd's heavy brows shot together menacingly, and his neck swelled. But Crosby, unconscious of an impending outburst, went on.

"We would have liked your written authorization, naturally," he remarked, with a delicate shade of reproof in his tone, "but of course it was all right. Both Mr. Mills and myself remembered you said that the property was for Kenneth; but we could not recall, nor did the minutes show, whether you wanted the transfer made in his name or in yours. But you can fix it with him of course in any way you please. We told him your absence did not matter: that we could wait until your return, but he seemed anxious to finish it up, so we did so."

"Would you mind telling me what you are talking about?" growled Boyd.

"Why our finishing the transaction with Kenneth instead of with you direct," said Crosby, looking up in surprise at the tone, "wasn't that all right?"

Boyd made an effort and about-faced. The surprise was almost too much.

"Perfectly," he managed to say, "but I haven't been home yet. I didn't know he had considered it necessary. You say he has the notes and the transfer of mortgage? Did he pay for them? In full?"

Ten minutes later Boyd left the bank with his chest out and his head up. All the details were not yet clear—as, for example, where Kenneth had raised such a sum of money. But they were only details. Undoubtedly he had used Boyd's credit with Los Angeles banks; or hypothecated securities in the East—it did not matter. The big thing was that Ken had gone to the bat. He had seen the crisis and had acted. That was the kind of a boy to have! Took considerable business judgment to appreciate the importance of action; and a lot of business initiative to carry the thing through! Think they could do up the Boyd clan, did they? Well, they could think again.

At this moment his eye chanced on Herbert Corbell leaning against a lamp post on the corner. So high ran his fierce exultation that Boyd, contrary to his usual instinct, could not forbear triumphing over him. Those eight days of savage repression must be remembered.

"Well, young man," he sneered. "I hope you know by this time that your little scheme has failed."

"I don't know what you mean by that," replied Corbell, looking at him steadily.

"Oh, don't you? Well. I'm sick of all this mystery bluff; and I'm going to tell you to your face. I'm sick of acting the fool; and I'm sick of letting you think you've fooled me at any stage of the game. You got me out of the way so you and your associates could step in and buy the Peyton mortgage. Do you deny that?"

"No, I don't deny that," agreed Corbell, equably.

"Aha, I thought not! Well, you forgot I had a son, didn't you? And a son with a damned good head on his shoulders.

I'll bet you had your turn at feeling sick when you found out what he'd done!"

Corbell stared at him a moment; then reached into his inside pocket to produce a thin sheaf of papers.

"Are these," he enquired, blandly, "by any chance what you are talking about?"

CHAPTER XI

I

ABOUT eight o'clock that evening Daphne raised her head at the sound of footsteps; listened a moment; and then, with a look of concern on her face, laid aside her sewing and glided out through the door. She met Kenneth at the foot of the veranda steps, and without a word took his arm and led him out of the path of the lamplight to the head of the lower terrace. There she forced him to sit beside her. She gathered his head to her breast, and held him close, saying nothing. At first every fibre of his body was tense, but after a while his muscles began slowly to relax. He drew a long, shuddering breath and sat up.

"Daffy," he demanded, intensely, "will you marry me?"

"You know I will, sweetheart," she replied.

"I mean right away—now."

"This very night, if you want me to."

He sighed again, and in his turn drew her to him. She snuggled into the hollow of his arm.

"I feel better," he told her. "Daffy, you're such a comfort. You do know what to do. Oh, sweetheart, let's not wait for anything: let's get married, and get away from it, just us together!"

"At any time you say, dear."

"Daffy," he said solemnly, sitting up straight in order to give greater effect to his words. "I had no idea!—it was terrible to me! I can't tell you! Some day I will, but not now. I could not think that my own father—Daffy, I'm not going back there. He accused me—I couldn't believe it——"

"Never mind, dear. Don't try to talk about it. You did the right thing: noturing can change that. Come, let's walk down to Dolman's House and look up at the stars through the branches."

353

"He ordered me out of the house," said Kenneth, in a strangled voice.

For a moment Daphne's form stiffened. Then resolutely she put all thought from her but the one of comfort.

"Don't think of any of it now. Leave it until to-morrow. Come let's walk."

They strolled down the gentle slope and across the field. Daphne took his arm in both hers, pressing close to him. It was the dark of the moon, but the starlight filled the cup of heaven-like mist. From near at hand and far away came the singing of frogs, exultant and joyous, falling instantly silent or breaking instantly out full strength, as though some supreme and omni-present frog-leader had waved a baton. In the abrupt swift silences an owl spoke solemnly. Things not of the night, the simple beautiful peaceful night, such as the strivings and pas-sions of men, seemed to settle to earth, as a veil that is cast flut-ters and sinks slowly and lies dead. In spite of himself Kenneth's high-leaping thoughts little by little lost their throb. The fever ebbed from his brain. His mind cleared as the sky clears of clouds. From the surface of his soul, stilled after the tempest, again reflected the stars.

Daphne seemed to have been waiting for and to sense this moment.

"You must keep one thought before you always, Ken dear," she said, "and that is that you have done right. And you must remember that your father has not consciously done wrong, because he really cannot see it is wrong. Now let's talk of our plans. The hard part is over now; remember that. But we must make it a success yet. It won't do to let the whole thing fail just for a little scheming at the last minute."

"Why, what do you mean?" asked Kenneth, his attention caught.

"Practical details: that's what I mean. I don't know any-thing about your business arrangements: I suppose you've made them. I'm interested. Don't you want to tell me about them?"

"What arrangements do you mean?"

"Why, as I understand it, you've put in a lot of money, and

those dear ridiculous men have put in some, and nice old Sing Toy and his friends the rest. And you've bought the mortgage."

"Yes; that's it."

"Well, what are you going to do with it?"

"Why, just let it run, I suppose."

"And how about repayment?"

"I don't know. We'll have to fix that up. It will have to wait. I'll see that they are paid back some day."

"And the Colonel?" suggested Daphne.

"What about him?"

"How are you going to explain to him?"

"Why do we have to explain to him at all?"

"Well, naturally, he is going to know that the mortgage has changed hands; and when he finds it is in your name—why, don't you see?"

"Good Lord! Of course! I *am* a dumbhead! He'll think this is part of the same old scheme! What can we do about it?"

"I don't know," confessed Daphne, "but it must be thought about."

"I should think so! I wish it hadn't been done in my name—but no, then it couldn't have been done at all. What shall we do, Daffy? Can't you do something? Yes, that's it. You can fix it. See him and reassure him. Tell him anything you want. Will you?"

"I'll think it over," agreed Daphne, slowly. "It will be difficult."

When they returned to the Bungalow it was very late. Townsend Brainerd was still reading by the student lamp. He had it in mind to utter an impatient reproof at young people's remaining out until this hour, but at Daphne's warning gesture and a look at Kenneth's face he closed his book and rose.

"You can lend Ken some night things, can't you, Dad? It's so late I tell him he had better stay with us to-night. He can sleep in the Cubby Hole: it's all made up."

"Surely; I'll get them," said Brainerd, moving his lank form with unwonted alacrity. He was in the current of events, and made a shrewd guess as to the nature of the trouble that had so evidently ravaged Kenneth.

The moment he had disappeared Kenneth turned eagerly to Daphne.

"Won't you promise to fix it up with the Colonel?" he pleaded. "You are the only one who can do it. Please promise!"

She looked at him considering, her head on one side.

"Will you let me arrange it entirely my own way?" she asked.

"Lord, yes."

"Well, I will. But not until after we are married."

"I think we ought to be married right away, then," stated Kenneth.

"I think so, too," she agreed, half mischievously, but with a hint of tenderness that caused Kenneth to seize her hungrily in his arms.

At this moment Brainerd returned from the back part of the house.

"Ahem!" he exclaimed from the doorway. "Can't you young people do enough spooning elsewhere? Consider my age and dignity and spare my blushes."

They turned to face him, Kenneth a trifle embarrassed, but Daphne laughing.

"Father," she said, "we are going **to drive into** town to-morrow, get a license, and be married."

"Just like that!" said Brainerd. "Let me sit down and get this clear. To-morrow, you said. I hope not before nine o'clock: I hate to get up too early." He looked them over. "Are you in on these arrangements?" he asked Kenneth, politely, "or are they the sole idea of my daughter?" But his scrutiny had inhibited any objections or adverse comment he may have intended to make. Brainerd had lived long and acquired wisdom in the process: and he knew a crisis when he saw it.

"That is Kenneth's business, not yours, sir," rejoined Daphne.

"I stand corrected. Then, I gather, no choir, no bridesmaids, no brass bands, no wedding dress?"

"Nothing but you, Dad, to give me away."

"And of course no presents. Well that relieves my mind, anyway. At what time do you want me to show up, and where? I've got some manure to put on the apricots to-morrow, and I don't want to waste any more time than I have to."

"Then you don't object?"

"Object? Why should I? That's yours and Kenneth's business, not mine," paraphrased Brainerd.

"You are a dear! a gem of a father! You always *do* understand!" cried Daphne, casting herself upon him.

"She used to do this when she was a child," Brainerd explained to Kenneth over her shoulder, "and she doesn't know that she has grown. She hits you with all the lightsome abandon of a three-ton steam roller. And I'm hanged if I understand! But what matters that? Do I gather this is what you might call a secret, a clandestine wedding? Nobody to know? Not even the Colonel? It will break the Colonel's heart not to be at your wedding, Daffy."

"Oh, particularly not the Colonel!" cried Daphne. "That is part of it!"

"I see," returned Brainerd, gratefully. "Thank you for your explanation. It makes everything perfectly clear. But there's one thing I wish you'd done."

"What is that?"

"Why in blazes, if there's all this secrecy, didn't you elope? Then I'd have been able to manure my apricots."

II

DAPHNE's husband and father, by her insistence, dropped her at the Avenue of Palms and drove on to the Bungalow. She looked after them a moment, and then walked slowly and thoughtfully up the long rise that led to Corona del Monte. She found the Colonel seated on the top step of the veranda, his hat beside him, looking up rather vaguely into the tops of his great oaks. At sight of her he arose with his customary old-fashioned courtesy.

"Well, Puss!" he cried, "but this is a pleasure!"

She settled herself on the top step and pulled him down beside her.

"Listen, godpapa, I am very serious," she said. "I have come to tell you something very important. I have been worrying about you a great deal, godpapa, and the ranch. No; listen! Don't interrupt! What you need here is a partner."

"A partner!" echoed the Colonel.

"Yes, a partner," went on Daphne rapidly, before he had a chance to say more. "A man who would bring enough capital to help the ranch out of debt: a man who knows the ranching business so he could take an active part in running it—you know very well there's more than you can do."

"Daffy, I don't think I could stand another man managing things after I've done it so long."

"He'd be a junior partner, of course. You would control just as you do now."

The Colonel shook his head doubtfully.

"You wouldn't find anybody nowadays who would work with my ideas. I am an old fogey."

"But if you could find some one; don't you think it's a good idea?"

"It's a good idea, Puss," acknowledged the Colonel, reluctantly. "I've thought of it a good many times myself. Perhaps I might find an active partner. But I am afraid of how it would work out. I'm getting a little old and tired, and I dislike the thought of fighting another man's ideas. Still, it would be a sensible way out, I suppose. But, Daffy dear, I am an old man; and lately all my hopes have been centred on two things. As long as I lived I wanted to keep the old ranch together just as it has always been, as your Aunt Allie and I lived in it and loved it in the old days. I feel that I want to keep the place for Aunt Allie as long as she needs it."

Daphne, puzzled at this speech, looked at him. But he continued placidly:

"I suppose that could be done with the right kind of a partner—if such a partner exists."

"I know just the man," said Daphne. "He would put in the money, and he would work under you as I said."

"Who is he?" inquired the Colonel.

"I'll tell you pretty soon. But tell me first, would you consider selling an interest in the ranch to the right person on the right understanding? I mean as an idea?"

"I would if you wish it, Daffy," agreed the Colonel a little sadly.

"I!" cried Daphne. "Oh no, godpapa! I don't come in it at all! You make me feel so responsible! You shouldn't put it on me that way!"

"I don't mean it that way," said the Colonel, smiling at her panic. "It is very simple. It is only this: besides keeping the ranch for Allie as long as I lived, I had hoped to leave it to you when I died. And if somebody else owned a share of it, it complicated it so for you."

"I?" repeated Daphne. "I? Corona del Monte?"

"Who else, dear child: who else in all the world?" asked the Colonel gently. "I have no flesh and blood: and ever since that spring day when I came on you alone among the wildflowers so bravely facing the cattle, you have grown into my heart until you are more than flesh and blood could ever be. Why, dearie, I can't take the old ranch with me when I go, and to whom should it go but to the one I love best now in the world?"

Daphne clung to him, weeping a little. There were tears in the Colonel's eyes too, open and unashamed.

"So you see, dear, why I am such a cranky old codger; and why I have been so reluctant to do what I know is the sensible thing. And why I wish there were some other way. But I suppose there isn't," he sighed.

Daphne drew away from him. Her eyes were wet, but she did not dry them.

"Listen, godpapa!" she said solemnly. "We have joked half seriously many times about Dolman, and how I used to believe in him when I was a little girl. Last night I was down at Dolman's House with—with Ken; and something said to me—no it didn't say to me, it just welled up inside of me—anyway *I was told* to do what I did and what I am doing now. I could not see how it would work: I did not believe it would work. But I obeyed the telling. And what you have just said made it all

clear. It was as if Dolman had really spoken; as I used to think
he did when I was a little girl." She grasped his arm. "Godpapa, do you believe it could really be?"

The old man merely smiled and put his arm around her.
Daphne knit her brows for a moment, then went on.

"The partner I meant is Kenneth. He has enough money
from his mother's estate; and he wants to put it in the ranch,
but he is afraid you might misunderstand."

At the mention of the name the Colonel stirred uneasily.
His confidence in Kenneth personally was absolute; but who
could tell what was in the background? He voiced his thought:
a little apologetically.

"I knew you must feel that way," said Daphne; "so did Kenneth. That is why I was so doubtful of what was *told* me last
night. But what you have just told me makes it so plain. Ken
loves Corona del Monte almost as much as you and I do; he
would not for worlds do a thing of which you did not approve.
And as for your second objection, that you want it to come to
me as a whole—why, Ken and I were married this morning!"

She sprang to her feet in an uncontrollable burst of released
excitement, pirouetted across the lawn in an abandon of joyous
motion, and ended with a low curtsey before the astounded
Colonel, skirts outheld in the tips of her fingers.

"Hurrah for Dolman! Good old Dolman!" she cried; and
cast herself in her impetuous steam-roller fashion on the Colonel. "Oh, isn't it wonderful!"

But the Colonel had recovered from his first astonishment.

"Stop it! Sit up here and explain yourself!" he cried in mock
vexation. "What do you mean?"

"Ken and I got married this morning," said Daphne from his
shoulder, "and I didn't know why I did it that way; and now
I know; and I *do* believe in Dolman; and he's a darling; and so
are you, and aren't we all going to be happy now forever and
ever, amen!"

The Colonel gave her a shake.

"Explain yourself!" he repeated, severely. "What do you
mean getting married in that hasty fashion? Why did you do
it? How *could* you, without letting me know?"

"It was so father could manure his apricots," chanted Daphne "and Dolman told me to do it that way and——"

"Heaven has cursed me with an imbecile godchild!" lamented the Colonel.

They talked it out, while the sun descended to gild the edge of the mountains; and Kenneth chafed and waited; and Brainerd, who was now fully in the current of events, wisely restrained him from going after Daphne and bodily ravishing her away.

"She is as eager to get back as you are to have her," warned Brainerd. "This is the crucial time. The whole success of the scheme depends on it." At last at about half past five he departed. He had himself arranged a trip to Los Angeles, and he must go to catch the train. There seemed to him considerable humour in the situation: he was marrying off his daughter, and then himself going on the wedding trip! Well, they were needed at home; and he was not; and they ought to have the Bungalow to themselves.

"What I advise you to do," he told Kenneth, "is to get busy and show how much of a cook you are," with which parting advice he drove away, leaving the young man to follow his suggestion.

Down at Corona del Monte the Colonel and Daphne came to an understanding of all the details on both sides. The old man seemed to have straightened and thrown off the burden of years. He became almost buoyant in talking of the future. Ken and I will do this: Ken and I will do that, was the burden of his song. The old vanished engaging enthusiasm that had been hi' returned to him. At one point he checked himself:

"There is one thing I want understood—no, I want it pr' ised," he said earnestly. "As long as I am with you we wi' to keep the old ranch as it is. But when I am gone: wh' completely yours and Ken's, I don't want any pious se about it. I want it divided and sold, or developed ir that seems best. Don't think I am such an old fool I know we're old fogeys, the ranch and I. You r this!"

After a time it became dusk: and the Colonel r an exclamation.

"Your husband will never forgive me!" he cried; and Daphne felt an odd thrill at the word. "You must run along. Come in and I'll give you some little gift to take him, just so the day will not pass unmarked by me. To-morrow I shall call upon you in state."

They turned in through the little hall to the sitting room where burned the student lamp. Daphne stopped short in the doorway with a startled gasp. She turned pale and seized convulsively the Colonel's arm.

"What is it, my dear?" he asked.

Daphne swallowed twice, and laughed a little uncertainly.

"Nothing; nothing," she disclaimed, but her eyes were still turned staring past the student lamp.

"But it must have been something," insisted the Colonel. He was smiling down on her; and somehow there seemed to be in his smile an understanding.

"Godpapa," Daphne was impelled to confess, "it sounds foolish and queer. But as I came into the doorway I looked across the table and there in the old Boston rocker, just for a second, I thought I saw Aunt Allie sitting as she used to. And she was so real! so very real!"

"You must not mind that, my dear," said the Colonel, gently. "Why, I've seen her there always."

CHAPTER XII

IT IS later by twenty years. All things have changed. Arguello is famed throughout the world. It has de luxe trains running to it; and two huge hotels; and a sublimated boarding house where by dint of waitresses in fancy costume, decorations of orange-yellow and black, and a haughty manner they can charge you three prices; and its former sagebrush heights are crowned with the humble cottages of the sniffy rich, and the gardens, and garages, and servants' quarters thereunto appertaining. You would never know Main Street, with its paving and its fancy concrete street lights, and its glittering exclusive shops ready equally to awe you or flatter you as long as they get to your pocketbook. Motors flash by on their way to country places that would have been prohibitively remote in the old days.

And certain things have gone. You will rarely now see an old-fashioned Mexican saddle; nor, indeed, many saddle horses. Yes, some people ride, to be sure. You will see them very correctly turned out, rising to the trot on the beach or along one of the back roads, generally with a groom pounding along behind. They are taking horse exercise. They know nothing about the old trails that lead, or used to lead, up into the fastnesses of the Sur; nor the trickle of water nor the smell of bay and the pearl blue deeps where the buzzards swing. Those things are too far away, they take too much time; nobody sees you and your clothes and your flat-country horse rig. Such an expedition takes an afternoon. There are too many things to do; too many people to see. Everybody entertains everybody else at the aforementioned humble cottages or at the Country Club; and afterward there must be bridge. Life has folded its wings. It struts about and preens; but it knows no more the wide spaces. Not one in a hundred of these people

who now call themselves Arguellans have ever been to the ridge
of the Sur and looked abroad; nor have they ever even heard
that this experience, so near at hand that one can reach and
touch it in a day, is one of those great rarities capable of lifting
the soul. All the things nowhere else available, but here in this
smiling land offered abundantly, they know nothing of; but
bring with them the mode of existence they learned elsewhere,
and have not the imagination to transcend. And the age-
old ramparts of the Sur look down curiously; and their gods
wonder whether this strange new people running after little
stupid pleasures, building about them their smothery accustomed
environment in apparent fear of touching the new, feeding,
gambling, posing, dressing, performing not one useful function
in their idleness, and looking up from their absorption only in
self-gratulation, whether these also are of a provisional race
that must in its turn give way.

For answer in the year of 1910, of which we are speaking, you
would have to go below the surface appearance. To the winter
visitor, to the shopkeepers along Main Street, and indeed to
rumour in the world outside, these fashionable, pleasant, comfortable, unimaginative futile people meant modern Arguello.
They and their activites filled the eye; and as they were thoroughly satisfied with themselves, and thoroughly oblivious to all
but themselves, that was natural. But to the life of the nation
the significant Arguellans were those who dwelt in the neat little
flower-covered bungalows scattered through what was apparently one endless orchard. Miles and miles it stretched,
without distinguishable boundaries. Hardsurfaced roads tra-
versed it, on which were to be seen small busy motor cars, or
convoys of a hundred Orientals on bicycles shifting their field
of work. For this immense orchard, belonging to the many
inhabitants of the bungalows, was nevertheless handled as a
unit, as far as such things as pruning, irrigation, cultivation and
picking were concerned. In the slack seasons the employees
worked at the borders of the roadways, so that in time they were
edged with gardens; and the inhabitants of the "cottages" on
the hills and the rubber-neck tourists loved to drive there.
Down where the railroad tracks left town was a new packing

house. That, too, was run on a coöperative basis: and the product was marketed through an Association. It was all very simple. Each owner of a bungalow did as much or as little work as he pleased. He was credited with what he did and was charged with what he got; and his fruit was sold for what it was worth. And let us hasten to disclaim the idea that this system was in any way unique to Arguello: it is the usual thing in the fruit belts of California.

If the ghost of old Colonel Peyton should return and seek for the Corona del Monte of former days, he would be somewhat puzzled until in his wanderings down what he would never recognize as the Camino Real he came to the entrance of the Avenue of Palms. Then he would find himself at home. Nothing thenceforth he would find changed—unless he chose to turn right or left through the screen of shrubbery; in which case he would discover that here, too, the grazing had given way to trees and cultivation. But straight the old avenue led to the knoll and the Cathedral Oaks, and the little, homey, vine-covered, board-and-batten ranch house. And down the slope he would glimpse the whitewash of the great stables, the gleam of the duck waters inside the wire fence; he would even find the earthen *olla* full of cool water hanging under a tree. Should he ring the bell—if ghosts can ring bells—he would find it answered by Sing Toy, now old and wrinkled, but as white and starched as ever, a refreshment to the eye. Certain little things he might miss, like the feather duster that used to hang by the door; and certain new things he might not recognize, such as a tennis court down near Dolman's House, and indeed, a brand new wing to the ranch house itself! But Corona del Monte it still was.

This and the packing house were about the only things that induced a pause when the modern Arguellans drove, or more rarely rode, on this side of town. . . . The ranch was so quaint and old-fashioned, my dear, you ought to have come here as I did in the Old Times before Colonel Peyton died; he was the most picturesque old creature! He used to ride in the flower shows— pity they don't have them any more—on a magnificent horse and the most wonderful silver mounted saddle. Of course everybody knows the Boyds; they're quite nice, but peculiar

They don't play bridge nor dance, so of course they rarely go out. Their children are away at school somewhere. Now I ask you—with all their money—it's millions, my dear—can you imagine living in a shack like that! And think what they could build on that lovely knoll! Of course they would not exactly be in the desirable neighbourhood. But still—— Let's go in and get her to give us a cup of tea. You'll see what I mean. . . .

So they would go in and have their cup of tea, and go away disordered in mind. They could recognize reality as opposed to their as yet undeveloped sense of values, but were not yet far enough along in social evolution to analyze it. You cannot very well patronize the possessor of so much wealth: and yet normally any one outside the round of feeds, and cards and dances is a fit subject for patronage. It was very disturbing. The conventional mind resents anything queer that it cannot eject; and unlike the oyster cannot render it valuable.

"Oh, you see we are farmers, like our neighbours," Daphne would explain with a smile. "We might enjoy going out; but you know yourself that if you start, you soon have to go all the time. And we haven't the time."

In spite of a firm refusal to enter wholly into the new social life, the old ranch saw much social activity. The Boyds were not recluse. They attended many of the larger parties where they could refresh acquaintance *en bloc*, or small dinners where they could meet distinguished visitors. Truth to tell, the latter seemed always to find their way to Corona del Monte. They found this type of modern farming interesting; they discovered in Kenneth a keen intellect with a broad grasp of this especial subject; they confessed in Daphne an individual charm that the fashion of the day had hardened over in most of their hostesses; they were intrigued by the flavour of old days. In addition the spare rooms were often occupied by old friends. Over the mountains the cattle business—modified by barbed wire and barley and alfalfa fields—still flourished; and from over the mountains often whizzed the members of the *Sociedad*. All but Herbert Corbell. He never whizzed; but continued as of old to drive satiny spirited horses caparisoned in russet harness and attached to strange vehicles. The "cottage" people thought it quaint. These men always stopped at Corona del Monte. They were in middle age now, of course, but they had lost very little of the high spirits of their youth. Perhaps they were a trifle more inclined to reminisce than to inaugurate anything new, but the reminiscence was lively enough. Corona del Monte was sure of a high old time when the *Sociedad* came aboard.

They went out in society, every one of them, and freebooted it terrifyingly. It was easier to consider them quaint than to try to account for them: so quaint they were. That solved everything. They were in some mysterious way not only acceptable, but even much sought for, and yet they never quite belonged. And they in their turn came back to the ranch and gave imitations or made characterizations that sent Daphne into shrieks of laughter. Which of course was not right after you have accepted hospitality. No one could understand how they, with their education, their wealth, and what should have been their tastes could bear to live 'way over the mountains year in and year out!

For they also had wealth. Some of it was from the cattle business, but most of it was from Corona del Monte. When the time for arrangement came, they tried to make Kenneth see that a return of the amounts they had advanced, with interest, was all they should have. But Kenneth insisted that they—and Sing Toy's contributors—should have shares with them proportionate to what they had put in. So in the long run they were all paid back many times over.

Thus it may be surmised that Sing Toy was very well off, and was in reality under no necessity of remaining in the kitchen. But he was "an old-fashioned Chinaman," so there he was.

There remains only to account for a rather bulky figure sitting smoking under one of the big trees across the lawn.

The reconciliation between Patrick Boyd and his son waited long. Boyd felt that his honour had been engaged with his Eastern associates and that his own son had made it impossible for him to fulfill his pledged engagement. That thought struck deeper than any loss of potential gains, or even that his son had cut in under him. This fidelity to what 'he considered his business honour was one of the strongest of Boyd's traits; and would probably go far to redeem many other qualities. He was hurt and sore and angry: and the natural combativeness of his nature made him a little vindictive. Nevertheless he grieved much, in his still and secretive fashion. At length two incidents brought about the change.

The first of these was a visit of inspection by William Bates.

In spite of the failure to acquire the Peyton property, the development of the water had gone forward. Boyd had announced briefly to his associates that he had failed to acquire Corona del Monte, and had let it go at that. He in his turn had received no comment, but Bates had called him East, and had gone over with him in detail the projected scheme.

"Go ahead," he decided at last, "and buy in that next piece of property, Las Flores."

"Too far out," said Boyd.

"Too far now," corrected Bates. "By the time we're ready there will be better roads and faster transportation."

Boyd asked him what he meant by the latter, but he was not quite sure: perhaps a trolley line from their power; he had seen a horseless carriage a man named King was playing with in Detroit——

He laughed with Boyd at his mentioning the latter; but he stuck to his main point, and Las Flores was bought in cheap from the bank. And concrete roads and the automobile in the long run justified his imaginative instinct.

But that was in the future. At the time of his visit the system was but just finished. He looked it all over without comment. Their way led them past the beginnings of new farms on Corona del Monte. Bates suddenly cackled.

"Pretty shrewd boy, that of yours," he observed. "Put one over on you, didn't he! Oh, I know all about it. Did you think I was greenhorn enough not to have found out all about that transaction? At first I thought you were double-crossing me. He certainly caught you napping! He's got to have our water; but on the other hand we've got to sell it to him—he's our first and obvious market. Also he's our biggest ad. If his farms fail we'll never sell an acre of Las Flores. And he knows it; the sly rascal!'"

This expert opinion as to the ethics of business rascality greatly heartened Boyd. To be sure as respects this transaction he cut a sorry figure in the eyes of the financier: but that was better than being considered to have gone back on his business word. And, after all, it took his own son to catch him!

Then one day Brainerd driving down Main Street saw him on the sidewalk and drove up alongside. This was sufficiently unusual, as the men had never more than nodded stiffly.

"Hullo, grandpa," cried Brainerd, jovially. "How's it feel?"

Boyd looked his inquiry.

"Came off last night. Everything flourishing. And it's a boy, too."

Boyd repressed a pang. He had not known. And to him it was significant of the community's attitude that nobody had hinted to him that this important event was to occur.

The reconciliation followed, and grew at equal pace with the grandson. At first matters were a trifle awkward; but Kenneth Second arranged all that. Patrick Boyd became as doting a grandfather as Brainerd; and as much about the place. All was well.

Once or twice he attempted to utter a veiled, mild joke as to how skillfully Kenneth had managed things, but with an implication that he entertained no resentment: and he was met with so bewildering an outburst that he never reopened the subject. But to the end of his days he was to retain deep in his heart the idea that his son had overreached him very cleverly; and to cherish a mingled feeling of hurt and admiration at the feat.

THE END